NATHAN STARK, ARMY SCOUT

NATHAN STARK, ARMY SCOUT

WILLIAM W. JOHNSTONE
with J. A. Johnstone

PINNACLE BOOKS
Kensington Publishing Corp.
www.kensingtonbooks.com

PINNACLE BOOKS are published by

Kensington Publishing Corp.
119 West 40th Street
New York, NY 10018

PUBLISHER'S NOTE
Following the death of William W. Johnstone, the Johnstone family is working with a carefully selected writer to organize and complete Mr. Johnstone's outlines and many unfinished manuscripts to create additional novels in all of his series like The Last Gunfighter, Mountain Man, and Eagles, among others. This novel was inspired by Mr. Johnstone's superb storytelling.

ISBN-13: 978-0-7860-4785-7
ISBN-10: 0-7860-4785-2

First Pinnacle paperback printing: March 2018

10 9 8 7 6 5 4 3 2

Printed in the United States of America

Electronic edition:

ISBN-13: 978-0-7860-4727-8 (e-book)
ISBN-10: 0-7860-4727-0 (e-book)

CHAPTER 1

If there was anything Nathan Stark hated, it was an Indian. God knew he'd killed his share of them—whenever and wherever he could—and this fine July morning would be no exception.

From where he and his fellow scout and friend, Cullen Jefferson, hunkered down in the brush along the face of the embankment at their backs, Nathan eased the trigger of the Winchester repeater back gently, taking up the slack in it. The rifle was an old friend, carried through thick and thin for many a mile. He'd been tempted to buy a newer model, the '73, but in the end, he'd held on to the 1866 model he'd had for the past eight years. He wasn't sorry. The repeater had stood him in good stead, and he trusted it.

Cullen crouched beside him, their positioning as familiar as the breath they drew. Neither looked at the other. There was no need. Nearly ten years of traveling and working together more often than not in their assignments with the U.S. Army had brought them as close-knit as brothers.

Closer, in fact, than the kinship Nathan felt with his

own flesh-and-blood brothers he'd been raised with. Though Cullen had a good fifteen years on Nathan, they'd seen one another out of plenty of scrapes so far—the present one being nothing out of the ordinary.

"Hear somethin'?" Cullen whispered, his own finger ready on the trigger of his .52 caliber Spencer carbine. He was bigger, shaggier, grayer than the lean, dark-haired, wolfish Nathan Stark.

"Not yet. But they're out there."

Coming up through the eastern part of Indian Territory on their way to their latest assignment at Fort Randall in the Dakota Territory, they'd detoured to Fort Smith. It was the nearest town of any size, and they'd needed to pick up much-needed supplies to see them through the rest of their journey north.

Nathan had been sent from their last post at Fort Sill. Cullen was to cool his heels with nothing to do. The Apaches and Comanches in that area had been installed on reservation lands, the hostilities having calmed considerably in the eighteen months since the two scouts had been assigned to the Fort Sill command post. The flare-ups that occurred were nothing that couldn't be handled without them so Cullen had saddled up and ridden north with Nathan when his friend received orders to leave Fort Sill and head to Fort Randall. Cullen had told Colonel Bixby, "Guess my orders were delayed. Nate and me are pardners. Command oughta know that by now."

Nathan squinted, waiting for the Creek—at least, he thought that was what they were—to make their appearance again. They'd be along shortly. He and Cullen hadn't had much of a lead on them.

They'd spotted at least three of them, and there

was no doubt in Nathan's mind that when he and
Cullen rode out of the canyon nestled in the San Bois
Mountains of east central Indian Territory, there'd be
at least three less Indians in the world—no matter
what tribe they hailed from.

"Come on . . . I know you red devils is out there,"
Cullen muttered under his breath.

"Only three, you think?"

"More, somethin' tells me."

The two didn't look at one another, keeping their
eyes on the place they knew the Indians would appear.
It was the path of least resistance—a wide clearing in
the trees and brush that surrounded them.

Just then, the first Creek rode into view, and Nathan
pulled the rifle up a notch, taking aim. No need to
worry about windage today . . . not with the air as still
as the depths of a murky pond. Not a breeze stirred,
and the small sounds of the land itself had disappeared around them from the time they'd dismounted,
hidden their horses behind an outcropping near the
mountainous wall of stone behind them, and taken
their position where they could dispense swift and
sure justice to the redskins.

There were three, just as Nathan had thought—but
that didn't mean Cullen wasn't right about more.
They might have separated—being cautious. Could
be testing the waters to see where Cullen and Nathan
were—or quite possibly, they had no idea that the two
scouts traveled ahead of them. Somehow, Nathan
didn't think that was the case.

Catching the first man in his sights, Nathan pulled
back farther on the trigger. The Winchester cracked
wickedly. The sound came as the bullet found its mark,

and the man's side instantly turned red with blood. Pain filled the Indian's eyes, and he let out a shriek of surprised agony as he fell from his pony.

The other two Indians looked at one another, then at their fallen comrade. They seemed to be at a loss as to whether to try to help him or light a shuck out of there. They spoke rapidly between themselves and then Nathan knew they were Creek. Through his travels he'd picked up a smattering of so many dialects he couldn't keep track. Though not fluent in any one language, he knew a few words and phrases in all of them. One word he recognized immediately—*father*, one of them had said.

From beside him, Cullen took careful aim, squeezing the trigger of his Spencer. The one who had seemed reluctant to ride away, who'd wanted to offer help, fell from his horse's back, nearly landing atop Nathan's kill.

"Two down . . . one to go . . ." Nathan muttered, taking aim again as Cullen watched for the others he felt were "out there" following.

The third Indian had dismounted. Overcome by anger and anguish at the deaths of his two friends, he ran straight toward where Nathan and Cullen knelt behind the scrub brush.

Nathan watched as the savage ran screaming right at him. He took aim and pulled back on the trigger, only to hear the sickening click of an empty chamber . . . or a misfire, his mind corrected. He'd been carrying a fully-loaded weapon, fifteen rounds.

Maybe he should have given more thought to buying that '73 model at Johannsen's General Store in Fort Smith.

With a curse, Cullen brought his rifle up, but not to aim at the enraged Indian who was almost on them. He whirled toward something behind them.

With one part of his brain, Nathan heard the deadly hiss of rattles, a sound dreaded by anyone who spent much time on the frontier. Almost at the same instant, the roar of Cullen's Spencer reverberated through the still, hot air, accompanied by the Creek's bloodcurdling cry of vengeance as he drew his tomahawk from his waistband with a practiced hand.

Nathan threw the rifle aside and drew his Colt, but the lanky young brave had already let his tomahawk fly. Nathan flung himself to the left, and by no more than inches, the weapon barely missed splitting his skull open.

A wild curse burst from him in a breath of mingled anger and surprise as he hit the ground, hard and off balance. He rolled and came up on his elbows, still gripping the Army Colt, but the Creek leaped at that moment and landed on him heavily, just as he rolled again onto his back.

The Indian knocked the pistol from his hand and smashed his fist into Nathan's nose as he snarled like a mad dog and spoke in a steady stream of Muscogee-Creek.

Between his lack of knowledge of the language and his preoccupation with trying to stay alive, Nathan could make out little of it. He lunged upward, unseating the Creek, and both men scrambled to their feet. They circled warily, hands flexing, ready to go at one another as soon as either of them recognized an advantage.

The Indian was young—young and reckless. The

heat of his anger made him careless. He couldn't wait and threw himself at Nathan again, the impact carrying both of them to the rough ground.

Where in the hell was Cullen? Nathan had a fleeting thought that maybe the rattlesnake had gotten him before he got his shot off.

Nathan and the Indian rolled and tumbled, kicked and gouged, fists slamming at one another as their blood mixed and dotted the dirt and rocks beneath them.

From somewhere nearby, a rifle boomed again. Cullen's. But again, not giving Nathan any relief from the crazed Indian pitted against him.

Must mean Cullen had been right. There were more of the varmints . . .

The late-morning sun was merciless, and in the July-hot air of the foothills of the San Bois, Nathan could smell the odor of blood, sweat . . . and rage. The madness that gripped him and the savage in their hand-to-hand battle was palpable. One of them was going to die and be left for the buzzards to feast on.

The brave was stronger than Nathan had anticipated, and younger. More boy than man . . . but all killer.

Nathan was surprised at his opponent's tenacious strength that didn't seem to flag in the least, no matter how long they battled. He fought with the ruthless intensity of a madman. His relative inexperience, stacked up to Nathan's years of battles, was offset by the false strength that filled him in the rush of shock and anger over the deaths of his companions.

A rifle sounded from several yards away . . . one of the others this time.

How many were there? Nathan couldn't spare a glance to see how Cullen fared.

The brave suddenly flipped Nathan beneath him, his hands encircling Nathan's throat, fingers taking on a crushing life of their own as they closed around Nathan's neck. The black eyes glaring down at him burned with murderous rage.

Nathan didn't fear his own death. He'd left that feeling behind years ago. Fifteen years past, to be exact. The day everything had been taken from him. He had prayed for his own end, as well, that day. When it hadn't happened, he'd rediscovered his purpose.

Vengeance.

He had not figured on meeting his death in eastern Indian Territory, however. The bright sunlight began to dim as he tried to dislodge the Indian, to no avail. Joyous murder was in the Creek's eyes, but Nathan had determined he wasn't going to be killed today. He would not allow it.

With every ounce of his strength, he threw the Creek off him, rolled, and lunged to his feet. He glanced around for the Colt, but it was too far away to make a grab for it. He pulled his knife instead, a wicked Bowie that he'd taken from his father's hand when he'd found him that day—fifteen years past—when Nathan hadn't been much older than the Indian he fought.

CHAPTER 2

The Creek's eyes widened briefly. A grim smile of satisfaction touched Nathan's bloodied mouth. He hadn't felt fear in fifteen years, not through the years of fighting in the war, nor through his dangerous service to the Army in the decade since—but the Indian sure as hell did, and he'd made the mistake of showing it. No matter how fleeting that look had been, Nathan recognized it for what it was.

The Indian pulled his own knife, a weapon made of bone, sharpened to a fine point, and nearly as long as the Bowie Nathan brandished.

The two men circled each other once more. Nathan still panted, trying to catch his breath. The lingering feel of the Indian's hands at his neck made his skin crawl. He would have hated to meet his end by being choked to death, but somehow, it wouldn't have been nearly so distasteful had it been a white man who killed him. To die at the hands of a red savage—well, nothing could be worse than that.

As they circled one another warily, he watched the

Indian's eyes. When the Creek made his move, Nathan was ready.

The brave rushed toward Nathan, seemingly unable to wait another instant to come at him. Nathan easily deflected the Indian's knife hand and gave a quick upward jab with his own blade. The Indian moved lightly on his feet, turning away in anticipation of the strike, and Nathan stabbed air instead of flesh and bone.

The Creek tried to dodge away, but Nathan grabbed the Indian's blade hand with a lightning-quick move and held it immobile.

Nathan had hunted Indians long enough to know one thing about them—you could never be sure of anything when it came to what a red man might do or think or how he might act or react. He also knew he needed to end the fight soon.

He cursed his own failure. He should've been able to shoot the savage before he had the chance to distract him with the tomahawk and come running at him.

A part of him grudgingly recognized the courage of those actions, even as he wondered if Cullen was all right, yet knowing he couldn't let his attention wander to check.

A swipe of the bone knife as the Creek fought free brought blood flowing down Nathan's left arm, crimson soaking the blue shirt he wore. He barreled into the Indian and they both went to the ground again, with Nathan on top in a clearly advantageous position. The Creek had had the wind knocked out of him, but he fought to push Nathan off of him, even so.

Hearing the distinctive sound of Cullen's old long-barreled .44 Remington revolver exploding nearby, Nathan hoped it meant an end to all the Creek warriors . . . all but the one he was fighting.

He struck the Indian's knife hand on the hard ground again and again, until the knife fell free, then he brought the tip of the Bowie up to the man's face and deliberately cut him across his cheek.

The Creek made a grunt of pain, but his eyes glittered with hatred, not pain. "I will kill you," the Indian said from between clenched teeth. In English.

Nathan's eyes narrowed. *This one has brass.*

At that point there wasn't much chance he could manage to kill Nathan, but the certainty in his tone couldn't be denied.

"You haven't managed to do it yet," Nathan said, pushing himself away from the warrior. "And I've killed a heap of men braver than you."

"The day is young." The Indian's blood streaked across his skin, staining his black hair. He'd lost none of the challenge in his voice or his demeanor.

Nathan stood up, breathing hard. "How many others are out there?"

The Indian glared up at him in silence. Nathan tossed the Bowie end over end and deftly caught it by the handle. "I don't mind cutting your tongue out— either for silence or a lie. Think before you answer."

The Creek scowled and started up from the ground. Nathan kicked him back to the earth.

"How many?"

"Only four," the Indian answered sullenly.

"You better be telling the truth." Nathan gave a sharp, short whistle, and Buck headed toward them from behind the outcropping of rock.

When the horse came to stand beside him, Nathan

quickly searched for the short length of rope he needed and roughly rolled the Indian over onto his stomach. "Put your hands behind your back."

When the Indian was slow to comply, Nathan gave him a swift kick in the ribs. The Creek cried out in surprise and pain, and put his hands behind his back as Nathan had ordered. Quickly, Nathan bent, putting one knee in the Creek's back, and tied the wrists together with the length of rope. Standing, he glanced up to see Cullen coming toward him, blood staining the side of his buckskin shirt.

"Cullen—"

"Just a cut," he replied. "Let him get a little too close. Last thing he ever did." He looked down at the crimson stain. "I'm gettin' too old for this—gettin' too slow."

The brave at Nathan's feet cried out in frustration and anger at Cullen's words.

"Don't move," Nathan said quietly. He walked to where his pistol lay at the foot of a scraggly redbud tree and put it in his holster, then retrieved his rifle and the Indian's tomahawk. He put the rifle into his saddle scabbard with a last, disgusted look at it, and then secured the tomahawk in one of his saddlebags.

The Indian had inched his way over to where the bone knife lay on the ground. Nathan wasn't sure how the Indian intended to make use of the weapon with his hands tied behind him, but he wasn't about to find out.

"Thought I said *don't move*, Injun." The pistol was in his hand, hammer cocked with a sinister click.

The other man lay still at the warning.

Nathan walked over and picked up the knife, wiping

his own blood off of the blade on the Indian's pant leg. Then he put the knife in the saddlebag alongside the tomahawk.

He reached up and unknotted the bandana he wore, taking it from his neck and wrapping it around the gash the savage had given him on his forearm. He pulled the ends tight around the wound, cut shirt and all, with his right hand and his teeth. He'd gotten good at makeshift bandaging over the years.

"Let's have a look, Cullen," Nathan said, turning toward his friend. "From the looks of it, he got you pretty good."

"This? Huh. I been gilled by a catfish worse 'n this little ol' cut. This ain't nothin'."

"Still, can't have you bleedin' all over everything while we're traveling. Let's take care of it."

At Nathan's no-nonsense tone, Cullen whistled for his own horse, and gave Nathan a disgusted look. "You ain't my nursemaid, Nate."

"How well I know it—and glad of it," Nathan answered, a quick smile taking the sting out of his words. "Just easier on both of us if someone has the good sense to patch up your side and keep a little blood inside you, right?"

"It ain't that bad," Cullen grumbled, turning his side away from the Creek's view. "And one of us had the good sense to shoot that there rattler dead before he got his chance at you. You sure weren't payin' attention."

"Had my hands full, Cul. In case you didn't notice," Nathan answered gruffly. "But thanks for savin' my hide. Hard choice—death by snakebite or tomahawk."

Cullen gave a short laugh. "You sure enough had yourself in a jam, come to think of it."

As Nathan applied a makeshift bandage from a strip of one of Cullen's spare shirts, Cullen gave him a sharp look than nodded toward the brave. "What about him?" he asked in a low voice.

Nathan glanced at the Creek. The warrior stoically waited for Nathan to kill him. He didn't beg for mercy. In fact, he made no sound at all.

"Never known you to leave one of them red devils alive before."

"Nope. Never have." Nathan hadn't realized until Cullen mentioned it that he had planned to leave the brave alive.

Nathan tied off the bandage tightly. "That'll have to do till we get farther on up the trail. We need to move on out of here."

"You gonna just leave this one behind, then?" Cullen persisted.

"Want me to check the bodies for valuables or did you already do that?" Nathan didn't look at Cullen.

"I did it. Got it all. Got the weapons. Got ever'thing but the scalps."

Nathan nodded, ignoring the edge in Cullen's voice. "We don't need 'em."

Cullen's head shot up, his gray eyes narrowing. "Never thought I'd see the day when Nathan Stark would pass up takin' a redskin scalp."

Nathan finally met Cullen's steady stare. "Count yourself lucky. You lived to see it. Do you need the money so bad you're willing to carry those bloody hanks of hair up to Fort Randall with you or detour back over to Fort Smith? Two nearest places to collect on those scalps, you know."

Cullen pulled his hat off and wiped his forehead. "This heat must've got to your head, Nate. This ain't like you at all."

"Maybe not," Nate agreed. "Like I said—if you want to take those scalps and collect on 'em, I'll head on up north to Fort Randall and let 'em know you'll be along shortly—"

"No need." Cullen gave him a look that said he still believed Nathan was a bit touched in the head.

Nathan gave him an easy grin. "Let's get the hell out of here, pard. We've got us five ponies to sell. That beats scalps, any day."

"Kill me!"

Nathan and Cullen turned to look at the brave who was still on his stomach, trying to look over his shoulder at them.

Nathan gave a short bark of laughter. "Why?" He strode to where the Indian lay and turned him over with a boot.

Black eyes glared up at him. Blood dried across the young warrior's cheek from the cut Nathan had given him. More crimson was smeared across his mouth from the punch Nathan had landed squarely on his nose, breaking it. If an Indian could sport a black eye, this one did, and it was swelling shut.

"Why should I kill you because you ask it?"

"I could not avenge my brother and father . . . and the others. I am—"

"So . . . you feel humiliated? Good."

You beg for death as my Camilla begged for her life—for the lives of herself and our child—

"Kill me!"

Nathan knelt over the Creek. "Remember my name every time you think of this day. I'm Nathan Stark." He leaned closer and said distinctly, "Nathan. Robert. Stark. Indian killer. You're the only one in fifteen years that's lived to tell the tale. I *let* you live. You by God didn't earn it! I could have killed you any time, you Muscogee scum!"

"Then do it!" The Indian rose up on his elbows as far as he could, glaring. Only inches separated them.

Nathan's fists clenched. He cursed the fact that the damn repeater had misfired and the inconceivable chain of events that unforeseen action had set in motion. Why had he not been a split second sooner? Gotten that fatal shot off with the Colt? He should have ended the fight and been on his way.

Indians, of any kind, weren't worth wasting time, energy, or breath on. They weren't real people. No one who claimed to be a human being could wreak the vengeful chaos and destruction as they did—with smiles on their faces and joy in their hearts.

No one could kill an innocent young woman . . . a pregnant woman . . . and ride away joyfully having done something so heinous.

No human being could steal children . . . his little sister, Rena . . . three years old. Was she even still alive?

He shook his head, clearing away the cobwebs of memories—memories that kept him going, kept him seeking vengeance for all of them from fifteen years past . . . his parents, his little sister, his wife . . . their unborn baby . . . and the other friends and neighbors who had lost family during the Pawnee raid.

"Kill me, then, Nathan Robert Stark. I will come

after you. Black Sun will kill you." He leaned forward, straining toward Nathan that last impossible half-inch. "This, I promise you." He spat in Nathan's face. *"I swear it!"*

Nathan wiped the spittle away with his shirt sleeve, then stood slowly. He understood. The warrior Black Sun was not so different from what he had been fifteen years ago . . . before the raid, the deaths, the kidnappings. Before the war . . . before his time in the army revealed his true calling. Scout. And Indian killer.

Black Sun was of an age that Nathan had been when it had all started. He wouldn't kill the Creek. Let him suffer as Nathan had. Let him plot his own vengeance for what had been taken from him. Let the young man face the coming days, wondering if there had been something—anything—he might have done to change the outcome of this day—the deaths of his brother and father.

Let the Creek live.

CHAPTER 3

Nathan and Cullen mounted up after stringing the Indian ponies together and tying them to Cullen's horse. They wound their way deeper through the San Bois.

It was slow going with the five ponies, but they'd bring a good price, and neither man was one to leave an animal to suffer.

Black Sun had been a wily one, and stronger than Nathan had anticipated with the anger born of his shock. Something else Nathan understood completely. After Camilla's murder at the hands of those red devils, Nathan had felt as if he needed no food, no sleep, nothing but the need for revenge that raged through his soul.

Black Sun would follow him. It had been a mistake to let the Indian live. Why had he? He refused to accept the kinship he'd felt when he looked into the savage's face. They were nothing alike. *Nothing.* Except . . . Nathan knew, without a doubt, that Black Sun would follow him as soon as he managed to free himself from where he'd been left, trussed hand and foot.

Black Sun's heart burned with revenge. Though he'd been spared, he knew he would be shunned by his people. He'd seen his father and brother murdered before his eyes, but had not been able to avenge them. He had not even been able to die fighting the men who had slain them.

Instead, he'd been captured and tied up, left to watch as the man they called the greatest Indian killer alive rifled the bodies of Kikikwawason and Hasse Ola, who lay fallen in the prairie grass. Black Sun managed to crawl near the bodies where he found a rock with a sharp edge.

He tried not to look at his father and his brother. Nathan Stark and the other man had been accurate and deadly with their rifles. Mercifully, his father and brother hadn't suffered, nor had the others . . . but Nathan Stark wouldn't be so lucky when he met his death. He was going to die very, very slowly. As would the man called Cullen.

Black Sun was completely humiliated as the tears began. Hasse Ola—Rising Sun, named for the time of his birth—had been his best friend as well as his only brother. They shared similar names, because on the day of *his* birth, the spirits had obscured the sun, sliding blackness across it until only a ring of light remained for a short time, before the fiery orb returned from hiding. The brothers had always believed that a bond of destiny as well as blood existed between them.

That bond had been abruptly and cruelly severed

by the Indian Killer. Black Sun's father and brother had been taken in an ambush. They'd had no chance to defend themselves, to fight and die like warriors.

But he, Black Sun, would see that Nathan Stark and this Cullen met their end—and it didn't matter how long it took.

By the time Black Sun had painstakingly sawed through the rope binding his wrists, they were chafed and bloodied. He barely noticed, he was so triumphant in his success at getting his hands free. With fumbling fingers, he finally got the rope untied at his ankles.

After a quick appraisal of his father's and brother's bodies, he saw that Nathan Stark had taken everything of any value, any usefulness, with him. He checked the bodies of Lamochattee and Chekilli, the two warriors killed by the white man called Cullen. Black Sun had no weapons. Stark and Cullen had gathered them all. He had no pony—again, the white demons had taken all. And on those ponies were the skins containing their water.

Black Sun didn't bother trying to wipe the dried blood from his face. He would wear it. The stickiness had gone from it, making it feel like war paint—and that was what it was to him.

He had no way to collect the bodies of his father and brother, or the others. He had to save himself. He had to go back the way they'd come riding earlier . . . back toward the Creek encampment.

His ribs groaned with every painful step. He hadn't gone far when it came to him that his brother and father must be left for the coyotes and the wolves; to have their eyes pecked out by buzzards . . . to not have the warriors' burial they were so richly entitled to.

He drew in a mighty breath and a keening wail rose up from deep inside him, echoing through the flat prairie behind him, the nearby mountains, and the small hills in the distance, far away. He didn't care who heard it. He'd fought a worthy enemy, and he was still alive.

Bloodied, battered, bruised . . . and shamed.

But alive.

He would remove the shame. He would find Nathan Stark and Cullen, and he would kill them both. If it took to the end of his days, he would do it. To have to leave Hasse Ola and Kikikwawason behind was the worst of all.

Nathan Stark had forced him to this path.

Killing him would be a pleasure.

Nathan and Cullen had ridden several hours, stopping only to clean the cut on Nathan's arm, check Cullen's wound, and let the horses get a cool drink of water in one of the clear streams. The horses drank, and Nathan backed them off after a few moments, not wanting them to get too much water too quickly.

The Indian ponies were surefooted and hardy, and it was easy to see they had been well-cared for. Nathan checked them over quickly while they were resting. They'd bring some extra supplies or go toward a new rifle, if a good deal could be found at the next trading post of any size on up the trail. What had happened during the fight had tempered his affection for the Winchester '66.

As he let the ponies have one last drink, he let

Cullen rest while he filled their canteens and the ones on the other animals, just in case. They could make it to the next settlement, Statler's Mill, by late tonight, if they pushed on, but the temptation to stop and make camp for the night in a couple hours was strong in Nathan.

Maybe he'd lost more blood than he thought. He cut a glance at Cullen, who seemed to be holding his own. That gash in his side had to be painful. The thought of another night of eating jerky and most likely having a cold camp was enough to push them both over the edge. He'd see how he felt when they had made a few more miles, and then he'd have a word with Cullen. Cullen was tough, but he was right—they were both getting older.

At least there were four Indians who wouldn't be on their tail tonight . . . but that fifth one?

Nathan shook his head. He should have killed Black Sun. Big mistake. He had made it this far in life by following one simple rule.

Never leave an enemy alive behind you.

Statler's Mill never closed. The settlement and the trading post were open for business—of all kinds—twenty-four hours a day, seven days a week.

Nathan had traveled that way a few times in the past. It was always the same—a defiant, lawless settlement in the Cherokee Nation that seemed to mock God by surviving and thriving. Anything could be bought and sold—from animal pelts to fresh fish; from a good, hearty meal to a fine wine; from a rifle to a woman—whichever a man might find himself in need of.

But as late as it was, Nathan wanted nothing more than to see to Cullen and the horses, then grab some grub. Then he'd find a real mattress somewhere in a relatively clean hotel.

Female company was the last thing on Nathan Stark's mind. Once they got the horses stabled for what was left of the night, they could find a room at the Lucky Strike Hotel and stow their gear. It was a familiar place, and one of the cleanest and most reputable lodgings in town.

At the late hour, no meals would be served in the hotel. They'd have to find a saloon that would rustle them up some kind of supper, whatever might be available or left over. Neither of them would be particular about the food, but both were hungry for something other than jerky.

Though they'd seen rabbits and squirrels along the ride toward Statler's Mill, they hadn't wanted to risk the sound of gunfire while they were riding through the borderlands of the Choctaws, passing through the tip of the Muscogee Creek domain, and then into the Cherokees' land. Statler's Mill was still in the Cherokee Nation, but close to where the Miami lands bordered.

Nathan shook his head at his own thoughts as he dismounted in the darkness in front of Anderson's Livery. How much of his caution had been in not wanting to alert any nearby Indians . . . and how much had been not wanting to let the one who followed know where he was? He gave a disgusted sigh.

Should've killed him . . .

Getting soft, Nathan?

He scowled at his thoughts and looked up as the hostler on duty came toward him and Cullen, wiping his bleary eyes. Cullen dismounted gingerly with a grimace of pain. His hand went to his side, and then his eyes met Nathan's.

"You okay?"

"Like I said, I'm gettin' too old for this."

"Hep ya?" the hostler asked in a tone that said he'd like nothing more than to go back to his bed.

"Need these horses fed, watered, and given a good rubdown," Nathan directed.

The man scratched his tousled head, cocking it to one side. "These *Injun* ponies?"

Nathan's gaze sharpened. "What of it?"

The man shrugged. "Just askin', is all, Mister . . . ?"

"Stark. Nathan Stark." He put his hand out and the man shook. "This is Cullen Jefferson."

"John Donaldson," the man said with a glance of acknowledgment at Cullen. "You lookin' to sell these animals?"

Nathan gave a quick nod. "These five, yeah." He pointed at the Creek ponies. "But I want them well taken care of. They can't help who owned 'em," he added pointedly.

Donaldson nodded his understanding. "True. I'll see to 'em myself. Make sure they all get some good grain and a rubdown. Finish it off with a cool drink of water and a clean stall. Almost as good as a room over to the hotel."

Nathan handed Buck's reins to Donaldson, and Cullen handed his over, as well.

"Don't bother untying them." Donaldson nodded toward the string of ponies as he took both leather leads. "I'll take care of things." He headed for the door.

"I'll take off for the hotel, Nate," Cullen said. "Lucky Strike all right with you?"

Nathan nodded. "Sure. Go on. I'll finish up here and see you in a bit."

Nathan followed Donaldson into the livery, helping him separate the horses and putting them in clean vacant stalls. Despite what Donaldson had said about taking care of everything, Nathan wanted to see for himself that Buck was tended to properly, along with Cullen's horse.

He removed his saddlebags from Buck and slung them over his shoulder, then took the Winchester in hand. Giving the buckskin a weary pat, he started for the door and then stopped. "Got any idea where we might get a decent meal at this time of night?"

Donaldson efficiently stripped the second pony of its colorful blanket, laying it over the partition between the stalls. The sparse gear, consisting of only a skin of water and a worn saddle scabbard with an old rifle, he placed on the ground at the end of the stall. He moved to the third pony and removed the blanket from the horse's back before he spoke. "Lenny's cookin's purty good. Over at the Silver Moon. It's a purty good place. Open all the time. Lenny cooks at night, Jack cooks days."

"Which way?" Nathan turned to look at him, not caring who cooked when.

"Right next to the hotel. Down at the end of Main." The hostler pointed in the general direction.

"Okay. How much do I owe you, John?" Nathan started to dig in his pocket for money, but the stocky livery man held up a hand.

"Just settle up in the mornin', Mr. Stark. My brother-in-law owns this here business. He might be interested in takin' these horses off your hands for the right price. Shame you didn't collect the scalps of the savages you took 'em from while you were at it. Ed Leonard's payin' five dollars for each head o' hair brought in. You'd 've been twenty-five bucks to the good right there!"

Nathan nodded and turned away. *Twenty bucks. Only twenty.*

CHAPTER 4

By the time Nathan made his way up to the hotel room, Cullen was already sacked out on his side of the bed.

"Hungry, Cul?" Nathan murmured.

Cullen didn't answer.

"Suit yourself, pard. I'm starving." Nathan headed back out and made for the Silver Moon, anxious for a filling meal even if it was after midnight.

It had been some years since he'd come through there, and if it weren't for his very specific orders from Colonel Ledbetter at Fort Randall, Dakota Territory, asking for him particularly, he might have been content to stay in the Indian Territory and Arizona Territory areas for the rest of his "career"—if you could call it that—and scout for the Army. But things had come to a lull in those areas, and they needed him farther north, now that the Sioux were spoiling for all out war.

It wasn't as if it was anything sudden. The first big clash with the Sioux had happened more than twenty

years earlier, in 1854, when nineteen good men—
U.S. soldiers—had been killed at Fort Laramie.

The next year, in retaliation, the army had killed
over a hundred Sioux in Nebraska and imprisoned
their chief.

There had been other battles and deaths on both
sides until 1866 when the next major showdown had
occurred with Red Cloud's War. That had ended with
the U.S. signing a treaty with the Sioux Nation, grant-
ing them the Black Hills area "in perpetuity"—which
had lasted a grand total of maybe five years . . . when
the first gold miners had found their way to the
region.

Now there were more problems in that territory
than a man could shake a stick at. Nathan had held
out for as long as possible, not wanting to make the
journey so far from his usual stomping grounds.

But in the end, Colonel Bixby, his commanding officer at Fort Sill, had convinced him to go where he
was needed . . . and where his other obsession might
be found.

Since the day his little sister, along with four other
children, had been stolen by the Cheyenne, Nathan
had vowed to find them—find them and bring them
back to their own people—dead or alive. That had
been fifteen years ago. He'd often been discouraged
and on the verge of giving up the search, reconciling
himself to the idea that he might never locate any of
them. They seemed to have vanished with the winds
that had whipped the burning Kansas settlement of
Badger Creek into a blazing inferno that hellish day.

He'd spent the better part of two years searching
for his little golden-haired sister, with no help from

anyone. With their parents murdered in the raid, and his own wife and unborn child killed as well, Nathan had no one to turn to for help—not even his own older brother Reid, who had joined the army and not even been there when the Pawnee came howling and killing.

But that was then. Time had passed. Nathan had gone to war to fight for the Confederacy. The raid, followed by the war that had found the surviving Stark brothers fighting on opposite sides, had ripped their family apart. Nathan hadn't seen Reid in years and didn't care to. Cullen Jefferson was more of a brother to him than stiff-necked Reid ever could be again.

Nathan and Cullen had met during the war, hit it off well working as scouts for the cavalry unit to which they'd been assigned, and when the long, bitter struggle finally came to its even more bitter end, the two men had drifted aimlessly for a while. They had no real talents other than riding, scouting, and fighting. While the idea of working for the bluebelly army didn't sit well with either man, it gradually sunk in on them that signing up as scouts would allow them to use their unique skills again. Besides, they would be civilians and wouldn't have to wear the hated uniform.

Since the army's main chore following the war was to make the frontier safe for expansion by pushing the Indians onto reservations—or eradicating them—throwing in with the bluecoats gave Nathan a chance to do the only thing that gave him any pleasure.

Even though it was unlikely anything would come of it, if Colonel Bixby had an idea that Nathan's sister Rena might be in Sioux Territory after all this time, that was exactly where Nathan would go. And if it didn't work out, more than likely he'd get to kill some more of the red bastards.

Nathan pushed open the doors to the Silver Moon saloon and walked in, taking a quick look around, then let his gaze linger on the occupants of the room.

The place was lively, even at the late hour. Most times, the men who were so inclined would have already gone upstairs with the soiled doves who were available, and the other men—those who had jobs—had already gone home for the night.

Nathan walked to the end of the bar closest to the door, put his back to the glass window that faced out on Main Street, and propped a foot on the rail.

The bartender, who was drawing beers for some other customers, nodded to Nathan to indicate that he would be there shortly. Nathan inclined his head in acknowledgment, then continued to survey the room.

The piano player pounded away as if his life depended on it. Two garishly dressed women with heavily painted faces stood talking near the other end of the bar, and Nathan sighed as their short conversation ended and the bosomy blonde headed in his direction, swaying her hips in what was supposed to be a sensuous manner. It didn't quite succeed.

"Hello, cowboy," she said with a smile as she came up to Nathan. "Looking for some company tonight?"

He forced a smile. "No, I'm afraid not. Just a meal and a bed."

The woman's grin widened invitingly. "I can arrange both . . . along with a bit of . . . entertainment . . ."

Nathan's patience was slipping. "No. No, thank you, ma'am."

She leaned toward him. "Think you're too good, Mr. High and Mighty?"

"No. Just want to eat and sleep."

Just then, the bartender walked up, giving the blonde a dismissive glance. She turned and huffed away, throwing Nathan a pouting look over her bare shoulder.

"Sorry, mister. Nita doesn't have her timing down yet." The bartender smiled. "Always best to wait until the customer has had a chance to wet his whistle and think of something besides being so gosh-darned thirsty he could drink the river dry."

"In my case, it's hunger I need to put an end to," Nathan said. "Any chance of getting a decent meal at this hour? I'm not picky, just tired of living off jerky."

The barkeep nodded. "Come up through the Territory, did you? I wouldn't want to risk hunting, either—*you* might end up being the *hunted* if they hear you, eh?" He laughed at his own joke. "Well, let's see . . . let me see what Lenny might have. I'll let you know before I tell him to dish it up." He moved away, heading for a door that, Nathan figured, had to lead to the kitchen.

In a moment, he reappeared and made a beeline for Nathan, ignoring one of his customers' calls for *"More beer!"*

"Lenny's got some leftover biscuits from earlier this evening and some mashed taters. Said he can cook you a couple pork chops right quicklike and make some gravy."

Nathan nodded. "Sounds good. But tell him not too quicklike on the chops. I like mine well done."

The bartender nodded. "Will do, mister. And what can I bring you to drink?"

"Beer's fine, long as it's cold."

"It is. There's an empty table right yonder if you want to grab it and take a load off. I'll let Lenny know and I'll get your beer out to you in a jiffy."

"Thanks, uh—what did you say your name was?"

"Oh, Homer. Homer Mason."

"Thanks, Homer. Much obliged." Nathan turned away and headed for the table.

Just as he reached to pull out his chair, a soft hand fell across his. Nathan looked up quickly, his eyes meeting the brilliant blue of the other soiled dove who'd been speaking with Blondie earlier when he'd come in.

"We don't let handsome men eat alone in the Silver Moon, Mister . . . ?" She smiled, waiting for him to supply his name. When he didn't, she removed her hand in the awkward silence, but her stare wouldn't release his as easily. "Would I be welcome to keep you company while you eat, sir?" Her voice carried a hint of a tremble, and she took a deep breath.

In that instant, Nathan saw how much she hated the life she was living . . . and he realized she was younger than he'd first believed. What would it hurt to show her some kindness? Or was he too far beyond even that bit of humanity anymore?

Well, he'd damn sure been *kind* yesterday, hadn't he? He'd let that Creek keep his scalp—and keep on breathing. He'd put himself and Cullen in a world of danger if that savage decided to make good on his promise.

"If you'll sit here, ma'am." He pulled the other chair out for her, the one that faced the wall.

She smiled at him—a smile more of relief than of want or desire—and that eased his mind. She sat down and then Nathan took his own chair, his back to the wall so there'd be no surprises.

"You don't really want company," the brunette blurted. "I see it in your eyes."

Nathan shook his head and leaned back, shifting in the chair to work out the pain in his saddle-weary muscles. "Nope. I don't. But if you want to sit here with me, that's fine."

She was already shaking her head. "No. I don't want to bother you—"

"I just said sit here. That's no bother. I'll buy you a drink, but that's it. Unless you want to eat something, too."

"No, no. I'm not hungry and I—" She broke off, lowering her gaze.

"What's your name?"

"Leah. Leah's my real name. But here, they make me call myself something more exotic for my . . . my saloon name. They call me Arianna."

In spite of his determination not to get involved, Nathan couldn't help but have a little pity for the lady. She clearly was out of her element. He wondered how she'd ended up in the Silver Moon.

He smiled. "That's a mouthful. I like Leah better."

She smiled back, and Nathan swore she couldn't be more than twenty. Pretty, too. He'd like to scrub all that paint off her face.

"How'd you come to be here, Miss Leah?" He

leaned forward, but kept his voice as low as possible in the din around them.

"I . . . I . . . well, I was adopted by a preacher and his wife. Turned out he wasn't as godly as he liked to believe. I told his wife when he tried—" She looked down, a blush staining her cheeks.

"Go on. I'm an army man, Miss Leah. I've heard everything."

"She believed *him*. Said the red devils had ruined me, and—"

"What?" Nathan's tone sharpened. "Start at the beginning. You said you were adopted by—"

But Leah's features were shuttered, and she looked away. "I'm sorry, mister. I shouldn't have told that. It's a lie. It's the lie I have to tell to get sympathy. Wasn't no call to speak it to you, since you got no desire for me, anyhow."

But was it a lie? She'd seemed so sincere . . . so honest . . . maybe . . .

"My name is Nathan. Nathan Stark." He said it slowly, deliberately, watching her expression for even the smallest sign of recognition. He knew he was grasping at straws. But something made him believe she had told the truth in that one instant of letting her guard down.

"How old are you, Le—uh, Arianna?" His food and drink had just arrived, and he didn't want to do anything that might place her in danger. He had noticed the armed guards who negligently stood their watch at the two doors to the outside.

"Homer says sorry the beer's just getting here along with the food," the older man said, setting the plate down in front of Nathan along with the cold beer. "He said you wanted a cold one, and we had to send the boy down to the crick to fetch a new keg. We keep 'em there short term to get 'em good an' cold."

"Thank you," Nathan responded.

"If ya need anything else, send Arianna to fetch it for ya. My old leg's about to give out on me." With that, he turned and limped away.

"That's Lenny," Leah said.

Nathan started to eat, watching as Leah sat quietly staring off into the distance. "Do they force you to stay here?" he asked conversationally.

Leah's gaze snapped to his, fear evident in her features. "Please don't speak of it, Mr. Stark."

"Call me Nathan. What I want to know about is this lie you're forced to repeat for sympathy."

She laughed nervously and shrugged. "A fabrication, for sure."

"Well?"

"What?"

"Let's hear it."

"Oh, no—I mean—it's not true. No need to tell it if I don't have to."

"But you do."

She gave him a defiant look, green eyes glittering with anger.

"If you don't, I'm going to ask Homer over there to tell me your sad story. Where you came from. How you ended up here, of all places."

"Why? Why are you doing this?" Tears welled in her eyes, and Nathan tamped down the sympathy that rose inside him. But he was determined to learn what she knew. It was a long shot. In the past years, there had been countless raids and abductions all across the country by the red demons. Tribe, faction, clan—none of that mattered. They were all enemies of the white man.

But . . . could it be that Leah had been among the children kidnapped from Badger Creek? Righteous determination gripped his guts. He would hear her story, one way or the other.

"I need to know . . . where you are from. In the beginning—not after you were adopted." He pushed his plate of food aside in a frustrated motion.

"Why?" Panic twisted her face, filled her voice.

"Keep it down!"

She blinked and sat back away from him as if he'd struck her.

He let his breath out in a rush and looked away. "Fifteen years ago, my family was torn apart in an Indian raid. My little sister was stolen. It was just over the line in Kansas, not all that far from this place . . . but tribes exchange hostages . . . I was told there could be a possibility some of those hostages wound up with the Sioux. I'm headed to my next assignment at Fort Randall in the Dakota Territory and I . . . she's my blood, Leah. I'm not ever going to give up looking for her."

Leah's eyes grew cold as frosted emeralds. "And what if you do find her, Nathan Stark? What if you discover this precious sister of yours? By now, she won't speak English anymore. She'll be fluent in Sioux . . . or Comanche . . . or Apache."

Leah pushed her chair back slowly and stood. "And she'll have changed hands many times, been with many men . . . against her will . . . maybe be married . . . have children—" Her voice broke and she fought back tears.

"Maybe she'll even be dead! What will you do then, Nathan Stark? Will you hate her for what has been done to her against her will? Maybe . . . maybe her death would be best for everyone . . . *including her*!"

"Leah—"

"That's as much of me as you're getting tonight, Army man. I tell my story when I wish—to who I wish. My story is just that—*mine*. Something you won't know unless I choose to tell it!" She walked away from him, head held high. The entire room of bar patrons watched as she made her regal exit, going up the stairs alone.

Nathan stood and fished in his pocket for the money for his meal, which sat untouched since his appetite was gone. Casually, he laid the coin on the table and turned for the door. He caught Homer's eye and moved toward the bar as the piano player began his pounding once more and the general noise swelled along with the notes of the piano.

Nathan leaned close to Homer. "I have something to give to, uh, Arianna."

Homer nodded. "I'll see she gets it."

Nathan handed him a double eagle, and Homer's eyes widened. "You didn't go upstairs—"

Nathan shook his head. "I didn't mean to upset her, Homer. Tell her this is from me—as a friend. I just want her to have it. Tell her I'm sorry."

Homer nodded and put the coin in his pocket. "I'll give it to her, Mr. Stark, my word on that. But later, when she might be more willing to accept it."

CHAPTER 5

As tired as Nathan was, it was impossible to sleep after the conversation he'd had with Leah. He lay on the bed, trying to relax. The feather-stuffed mattress was like heaven to the bruised flesh and sore muscles he sported from the fight with Black Sun and the days in the saddle.

Cullen lay close to the far edge, breathing deeply, having been asleep for hours.

In the morning, Nathan planned to get a bath, haircut, and the decent meal he hadn't had tonight. A new shirt was in his future, too. He didn't want to ride into a new command looking like an orphan.

The savage had slashed the shirt but good, and his own blood had finished it off. Might be salvageable if he had it laundered and mended by someone who knew what they were doing. A spare, if he could get it fixed neat enough. He wasn't short of money, just careful with it.

Except when he threw away twenty dollars on a prostitute he hadn't even slept with.

He needed to focus on the assignment he was going

to. One he wasn't especially happy about. He'd spent a lot of years in the military and he'd served under many fine men—and some not so fine.

From all accounts, he was soon going to be scouting for a company led by a man who was concerned with his own advancement above all else—Colonel Wesley Ledbetter. The assignment didn't worry him all that much. He could leave any time he wanted if he couldn't abide Ledbetter's methods. And Cullen would be there to back him, either way, stay or go.

Nathan was fair-minded. He would give the colonel a chance to prove the rumors false. It was comforting to know he had the freedom to walk away if need be.

It went against the grain to quit, though. No one could say he was a quitter. He never had been and never would be, nor Cullen, either. They were a lot alike, in that respect.

The Sioux Nation was a definite threat to white settlers—it had been so for more than twenty years. Conflict had heated up to the boiling point once more. It was Nathan's job—scouting for the army to forge ahead into Sioux Territory, but he had a twofold purpose. He would not shirk either the job he'd been hired for or the duty he would fulfill in finding Rena—if he could locate her.

Leah's angry words rang in his ears as he shifted on the mattress. *My story is just that—mine. Something you won't know unless I choose to tell it.*

He thought of the way she'd looked at him as she'd spoken—the way her voice had trembled in remembrance. She had already told him a big part of her story. She just didn't realize it.

Nathan had learned to read people early on as a

matter of survival. Leah had a wall of protection erected against those memories that no one could tear down. But Nathan would be back at Statler's Mill eventually, and when he was, he'd find the truth about what Leah-with-no-last-name knew.

The next morning, Nathan rose early, despite having slept little the night before. Cullen was already up and around, but not looking chipper.

Nathan leaned over the washbasin and splashed some water on his face. He glanced at his friend in the chipped mirror that hung above the basin and pitcher. "You look like hell."

"Thanks. That's the pot callin' the kettle black, if I ever saw it." Cullen shrugged into his spare shirt with a grimace.

"We both need a doc to look at these cuts," Nathan said casually, knowing Cullen would never agree to see a doctor over something he considered minor. If he agreed to go, Nathan would know how serious his side was hurting.

Cullen's head jerked up. "The hell you say! I don't need a sawbones lookin' at me for somethin' this . . . this . . . Why, hell, this ain't nothin'! Little ol' cut, that's all."

Grinning, Nathan turned as he dried his face. "Yeah, you're feelin' better, though you don't look it. Guess we oughta ride on, if you're able."

"You ornery cuss," Cullen sputtered. "Of course, I'm able to ride."

"We'll get some grub first. Bet your stomach thinks your throat's been cut, doesn't it?"

"It does. Should've gone with you to eat last night, but I was too tired."

If Cullen had been with him, he never would've had that conversation with Leah. And that had been invaluable . . . maybe.

"I'm gonna go get clean before I do anything," Nathan said. "Believe me, that saloon food wasn't the best." He didn't explain the real reason he hadn't eaten it. "I'm hungry, but guess we better get presentable before we try going into a decent restaurant."

"S'pose you're right. I'd favor a bath right now. Might ease this cut some, too."

They settled up at the front desk, then headed for the recommended laundry, bath house, and barber.

Clean and shaven, they decided to take care of the business of selling the Creek ponies before eating breakfast.

"Been expecting you," Everett Anderson greeted them when they arrived at the livery. "John told me you men were lookin' to sell the five Injun ponies."

"That's true—if we can get a good price for 'em," Cullen said.

Anderson smiled and shook Nathan's hand, then Cullen's. "Let's do some horse tradin'. Looks like you're in a hurry to leave Statler's Mill behind."

Nathan nodded. "We're expected to report at Fort Randall next week."

"That a fact? You scouts? Don't see no uniform."

"That's right," Nathan responded. "But we did our stint in the army during the war."

"Oh? Which side?"

Nathan's voice hardened slightly as he said, "I disremember."

"Oh. Ah . . . of course." Anderson forced a chuckle. "I don't have a very good memory for those things myself. Well, you won't need to be keepin' up with five extra horses. That'll slow you down considerable. Let's see what kind of bargain we can come to so you men can be on your way."

Nathan spent more time than he liked bargaining with the livery owner, who was in need of some extra mounts and came close to paying them what they'd first asked for the animals.

From there, they went to buy supplies and the new rifle Nathan knew he couldn't leave without. It would be suicidal to start toward Fort Randall again with the older Winchester that had nearly cost him his life. A man could feel affectionate toward something that had stood him in good stead for years, but sooner or later the time came to move on.

The general store had one Winchester '73 that had seen very little use. The storekeeper knew the man who'd owned it—an older trapper who'd had it only a matter of weeks before he'd been hit by a stray bullet in a gun battle between two rival outlaw gangs who had both wound up in Statler's Mill at the same time.

"Just pur-dee old bad luck," Freeman, the store owner, told him. "I sold him this gun"—he took it from the rack on the wall behind the counter—"and he paid me half. Was s'posed to pay the other half the week after he got shot down in the street. I went right out to his place and took it. You know, before anyone else might get it in their heads to go in and loot. He still owed me twenty dollars for it, you know."

Nathan nodded, keeping his features neutral as Freeman handed the repeater to him to examine. It did look to be well cared for, almost as if the previous owner had never used it at all.

Nathan tried the action and found it to be smooth. The walnut stock was virtually flawless. Someone had carved a small double diamond symbol into the right side of it as a decoration, and the brass fittings and barrel had been polished.

"How much?" Nathan asked, showing no enthusiasm.

Freeman shrugged. "Forty bucks."

Nathan laughed and started to hand it back to the storekeeper. " No thanks, Mr. Freeman. I'm not looking to be robbed this early in the morning."

"Now see here, Mr. Stark. I'm a fair man, and—"

Nathan looked him squarely in the face. "You've sold this gun once. You got half your money at that time. Forty dollars is about twice what this piece is worth, even if it was brand spankin' new . . . which it isn't."

"We're remote from the commerce routes," Freeman said sullenly. "Ever'thang costs more out here."

"I'll give you twenty, considering you already made the first twenty from the old trapper."

"Thirty." Freeman's chin rose defiantly.

"Twenty-five, Mr. Freeman. That's more than fair, and we both know it." Nathan waited a beat, then said, "There are some other supplies I'll be needing, too. Maybe I should go on over to Alexson's"—he nodded toward the door as he mentioned the other general store down the street—"and see what they might have—"

"No, no, don't do that. I think we can do business." Freeman gave Nathan a hard stare. "All right. Twenty-five for the rifle." He put his hand out and they shook. "Want me to keep it up here while you look around?"

Nathan shook his head, glancing at Cullen. "No, we know what we need."

By the time Nathan and Cullen rode out of Statler's Mill, they were more than ready to be gone.

Two hours out of town, they were headed north again, but with all their business settled. With the extra horses sold, they were making good time once more. They should make Fort Randall by the end of the week, a couple days ahead of time.

They'd report to Colonel Ledbetter as soon as they arrived, but no matter what, Nathan planned to take at least one day—maybe two—to rest Buck before they did any more riding. Cullen needed a respite, too, whether he wanted to admit it or not.

The journey had not been an easy one, and Nathan had to admit that once or twice the thought of leaving the nomadic life behind had surfaced in his mind. But it was all he'd known for so long . . . though certainly not what he'd planned for his future, so many years past.

Those dreams of a long happy life with Camilla had ended abruptly—and that day had changed everything. When she had been taken from him, any compassion he might have had—or love—had been ripped away, too.

He'd become mercenary in every way. Life had held nothing but the single-minded purpose of revenge. He'd turned that into a lifelong job as a soldier—a man with a license to kill.

Now, he was even more dangerous. He answered to no one but himself. Even though scouts had certain expected protocols to abide by, the knowledge that he could walk away at any time gave him the freedom he couldn't live without. And the freedom to do what needed doing without having to answer to anyone.

Nathan Stark's responsibility was to himself—to his own ideals and heart—what there might be left of it.

CHAPTER 6

Four days later, a couple hours after sunset, Nathan and Cullen stopped at the gates of Fort Randall, already barred securely for the night. They waited for the familiar, "Who goes there?"

"Nathan Stark," he responded, adding "U.S. Army civilian scout," before the guard could ask him to state his business.

"Cullen Jefferson, the same," Cullen said.

In a few moments, one of the gates swung open to admit them, and they rode through.

"Hello, Mr. Stark, Mr. Jefferson," a young soldier greeted them as they dismounted. "Colonel Ledbetter's been expecting you"—he looked only at Nathan—"but he's already retired for the evening."

"That's fine, uh . . ." Nathan tried to read the soldier's rank in the dim light of the waning moon.

"Corporal. Corporal Sims, sir," the soldier supplied. "He will see you . . . uh . . . in the morning, at eight o'clock."

Nathan's eyes narrowed. *How would Ledbetter*

know . . . ? "Corporal, was the colonel aware I'd be arriving today?"

"No, sir. He gave us orders that whenever a guest or anyone with army business arrives, we are always to let them know they'll be expected to meet with the colonel at eight o'clock the next morning."

"Well, you can let the colonel know there'll be *two* of us at that eight o'clock meeting."

Sims nodded uncertainly. "I'll show you to your quarters, and someone else will escort you to your meeting with the colonel in the morning."

It was easy to see the young corporal's discomfort. Nathan and Cullen took a few steps toward the commons area. "Where are the stables? We'll need to see to our horses."

"I'll take them over, sir, and the Injun boys'll see to 'em right fine."

Nathan stopped and gave Corporal Sims a hard look. "Injun boys?"

Cullen held tight to his horse's reins, glaring at Sims as if he'd cursed them.

"Yes, sir. They live here. There's four of 'em and they . . . Well, sir, they're Sioux orphan boys. Real good with horses. Colonel Ledbetter feeds 'em, gives 'em shelter in the stables—"

"I'll see to my horse myself, Corporal. Thank you."

"As will I," Cullen said stonily.

Sims looked shocked at Nathan's announcement. "They're good boys, Mr. Stark, Mr. Jefferson. And they love the horses. You need not worry—"

"I won't, Corporal. I'll be seeing to Buck myself."

Cullen gave a decisive nod of agreement.

At that, Corporal Sims turned away stiffly and in utter silence, headed for the stables once more.

Once they reached the stables, Sims lit a lantern and pointed out where the oats and curry brushes were located. Fresh water was available in the nearby trough, buckets stacked beside it.

"Your quarters are ready. Second house on the left." Sims pointed it out from the stable doorway. "I'll stop by and light the lamp for you. Uh . . . and we'll ready another cabin for you, Mr. Jefferson. The one next to Mr. Stark's. We didn't know—"

"Much obliged, Corporal. We appreciate your help," Nathan interrupted.

Corporal Sims gave him a smart salute as he turned to go.

"No need for that, son," Nathan said.

"Sorry. I forget sometimes. Better safe than sorry. Good night, Mr. Stark. Mr. Jefferson." He turned back to Nathan for a moment. "Colonel Ledbetter's a stickler for bein' on time, sir."

Nathan rose soon after the 5:00 A.M. reveille call. He lit the lamp and washed, pulling on some of the new clothing he'd bought in Statler's Mill.

The little house wasn't much, but he wouldn't be spending a lot of time there. It was adequate. A cot with a mattress that had seen better days, but it still beat sleeping on the ground, as he'd spent so many nights. A nightstand nearby held the lantern. A wash table, containing a pitcher of water and a bowl, stood before the window. A chair and small rectangular table stood in the far corner of the room, obviously for studying maps and documents, possibly for reading or taking a private meal from time to time.

Three hooks were in place on the wall to hang heavy coats, saddlebags, or gun belts. A chamber pot was shoved beneath the cot. A chest of drawers completed the furnishings of his quarters.

He took the time to unpack his clothing and put everything away in the chest before strapping on his Colt. Then he stepped out the door, closing it firmly behind him as he headed for the latrine. He intended to search out the mess hall for breakfast in a bit, but first he wanted to get a look around and see how Cullen had fared.

The fort swarmed with soldiers going about their morning activities before their first call to assemble in the commons.

On the way back from the latrine, Nathan detoured to the stables. No matter how Corporal Sims had sung the praises of "the Injun boys" who lived in the stables, Nathan would never trust any kind of redskin with Buck's care. Those same Sioux orphans who offered so readily to take care of his horse would just as soon befriend the buckskin and ride off into the night, never to be seen or heard from again.

Nathan was a good judge of fine horseflesh, and he also knew the thieving ways of the red man, as well. He figured he'd shown them more mercy, in his own way, than they'd shown him.

Killing his parents and stealing Rena had been almost more than a man could take. But when he learned they'd murdered Camilla and their unborn baby, it had put a burning hatred within him that would never be quenched.

During all the years of blood and death that followed, he had never murdered children or women—pregnant or not. And truth to tell, he'd balk at killing the elderly. Maybe the last shred of his conscience was what had kept him from killing Black Sun. He was young . . . and though Nathan had no doubt that Black Sun would've killed him, no matter the circumstances, he still couldn't forget that look in the boy's eyes— probably much as he himself had looked on that fateful April day, fifteen years ago.

He walked into the stables and started for the stall where Buck had been secured last night, but something made him stop and listen in the dim morning light. Muffled voices drifted to him where he stood, next to the first stall.

"I'm going to ride him if the Indian Killer comes to see to him this morning!" The voice was young, the words heavily accented. Yeah, it was Sioux, all right. Nathan wasn't certain of the dialect, but from the inflection he believed the boy was Lakota.

"One of our number will be no more by the next moon," another voice answered in the Sioux language. Definitely Lakota, from the words he'd used for words *one*—*wanji*—and *moon*—*hanyewi*. Dakotas had a slight variation for both words—*wanzi* and *hanwi*.

Though Nathan often told himself the tribes were all alike, he knew better. Even the factions within the tribes themselves were different. He'd fought plenty of Indians in his lifetime. Had a reputation for being one of the best trackers and deadliest killers west of the Mississippi. And it was well-earned.

Along the way, he'd picked up some knowledge that had stood him in good stead. Things that could help. He had the advantage as long as he knew his enemy and understood a few bits and pieces about the likenesses and the differences.

"I don't intend to die, Hotah," the first boy said haughtily. "I only want to ride that beauty." His voice turned hard. "I want to say I rode the horse of the Indian Killer. He'll never know. Every time I look at him, I'll have a secret laugh."

Nathan's temper boiled over. He started forward then checked himself. The more he heard, the better he'd learn his enemies' weaknesses. He waited, barely breathing.

"Help me put the saddle on—"

"Oh, you need a saddle? Why don't you ride like our people, Matoskah?" The taunting tone was sure to do the trick.

Nathan found himself feeling the challenge as surely as would the young man who was so determined to ride Buck.

There was a silence, then, "I can do it. I will show you."

Nathan moved to the middle of the wide walkway and stood, not making a sound.

The two boys rounded the corner, leading Buck from his stall. The first one almost smacked into Nathan's silent, immovable form. He looked up in surprise, then fear crossed his features.

Nathan grabbed him by the ill-fitting army-issue shirt he wore and ripped the reins from his fingers. He pushed the boy up against the wall of a nearby stall while the other boy let out a small cry and hunkered down against a couple bales of hay stacked beside a stall.

"What in the cornbread hell do you think you're doing, boy?" Nathan growled as he held the boy tightly.

"Let me go!" The youngster had turned defiant, having let go of all his fear—or at least, having wiped his features clean of any sign of it.

The room had lightened to the predawn gray that allowed Nathan to look into the boy's eyes. Something in his own face must have urged the boy to speak to avoid any further rough handling.

"I wanted to ride him once. I would never hurt him."

Nathan grunted, releasing the boy's clothing. "Or ride away from here, either, I'm sure."

True confusion showed in the boy's eyes. "Why would I do that? Here, at least I have food, shelter, and"—he put his hands out to his sides in self-mockery—"clothing, such as it is."

Nathan gave him a long look. The boy appeared to be telling the truth, but Nathan had learned enough about the redskins to know they were masters of deceit.

"How are you called?" Nathan asked, more of a demand than a question.

There was a moment of sullen silence before the boy responded. "My name is Matoskah. The whites call me Billy." He fell silent once more and his taunting friend sniveled from behind Buck's back legs at the hay bales. "Stop bawling, Hotah. You shame yourself." Billy didn't look away from Nathan as he spoke to his friend.

If Nathan wasn't mistaken, Billy would have liked to cower in a heap alongside Hotah only moments earlier. But the boy had recovered nicely and had channeled his fear to angry defiance.

"Well, Billy, my name is Nathan Stark. But the redskins call me the Indian Killer."

The boy stared at him unflinchingly. "I've heard."

"I just rode in to Fort Randall late last night. Buck isn't done resting yet. We've had a long, hard journey. So you turn your little butt around and put him right back where you found him, understand? And don't touch him again. I'll see to him myself."

The boy reached for the reins, his fingers touching Nathan's for an instant. They both recoiled at the contact.

"Boy."

Billy stopped, but didn't turn back to face Nathan.

"Not resting a horse properly is a kind of mistreatment. Might be hard for you to understand, but horses—especially one as faithful and loyal as Buck here—deserve the best care we can give them. Being allowed to rest, eat, and drink is part of that."

Finally, Billy made a slow about-face. "I was raised with these animals. I know how to see to their care— *Indian Killer.*" He spat the words hotly, then walked away, leading the horse to his stall.

Hotah rose and followed, casting an apprehensive glance over his shoulder as he hurried away.

Nathan waited a few seconds, looking around the stables in the lightening day, then walked down to Buck's stall to be sure he had grain and water. He found a brush and began to rub the big buckskin down. He'd only given him a quick rubdown last night.

After his meeting with Colonel Ledbetter, Nathan

resolved to come back and do the job right. Buck deserved no less.

Casting a quick glance around, he saw no sign of the Sioux boys. They'd probably decided to steer well clear of him, after he'd put the fear of God in them.

He sighed heavily. The "Indian problem" had only gotten worse over the years, with no end in sight. Looked like fighting them had become his life's work.

It seemed his existence since the day of the raid had become nothing but hunting Indians, killing Indians, hating Indians—along with the determination he felt to find his sister. He owed that much to his dead mother and father, to find the cherished baby girl those renegade Pawnee had ridden off with.

Reid had left to join the army several years earlier. If he hadn't done that . . . if he had been home on that terrible day to help fight off the raiders . . . would it have made any difference? Nathan couldn't say for sure that it would have, but there was always that chance.

Jory, the youngest of the brothers, had been taken in by neighbors. Nathan had mixed feelings about that. He'd hated to leave Jory behind, but he couldn't tote a seven-year-old boy all over hell's half-acre while he searched for little Rena. And later, when he'd signed on with the Confederate Army to fight the damn Yankees . . . then after the war threw in with the bluebellies to fight the Indians . . . there was no way he could take care of a kid.

He supposed the better thing might have been to send Jory to New York City, where Reid had established a law practice after leaving the army. Jory could have lived there with Reid and his wife, but the

Thompsons, their neighbors, had nursed Jory back to health and then cared for him for years. Nathan knew none of them wanted to be parted.

Circumstances had rolled over all the surviving members of the Stark family, molding them into what they were today . . . for better or worse.

Nathan set the brush aside just as Cullen entered the stables.

"Nate," Cullen greeted as he entered, heading toward the stall next to where Nathan brushed Buck. "I was wonderin' where you'd got off to."

"Just taking care of business before we head up to eat and go visit with Ledbetter," Nathan said, turning back to his task.

"Yeah . . . I'm gettin' a real bad feelin' about Ledbetter," Cullen said grimly, giving the buckskin a pat as he passed by to the next stall. He picked up a nearby brush and began stroking his big bay.

"Sorry you threw in with me this time?" Nathan gave him a quick grin.

"No. You're gonna need me to watch your back."

Nathan laughed. "Cullen, I'm willing to give him a chance. But we've both been in this man's army from both sides—inside and out—long enough to know that where there's smoke, there's usually fire."

"Ain't it the truth," Cullen agreed with a dour look.

Nathan nodded toward the door. "C'mon. Let's go see if there's any food left."

Chapter 7

Colonel Wesley Stuart Ledbetter sat in his well-appointed office, tending to business at hand as he awaited his eight o'clock meeting with the new scout who'd been detailed to his command. Nathan Stark. Renowned killer of the red man . . . any and *all* red men, so the story went. Along with another scout he hadn't expected—Cullen Jefferson.

He didn't intend to see them together. For Jefferson to have the gumption to presume he would be welcomed, as well, was a bit brassy. No. He would interview them separately.

Ledbetter's aide, Corporal Winston Cahill, stood nearby, should the colonel need anything.

Ledbetter's mind wasn't on army business. He was already thinking about how to best handle Nathan Stark when he arrived in ten minutes.

And he better by damn be on time . . .

Once more, he glanced over Stark's dossier. Impressive, he had to admit, but why a man with Stark's talents wasn't in the ranks of the regular army was a mystery. Could it be he was too independent? Too much of an unreconstructed rebel? Didn't follow instructions well?

It was obvious to the colonel Nathan's traveling companion certainly didn't understand following commands. He wasn't even supposed to be there!

Ledbetter frowned. There were several ways to handle "problem" men, both in the ranks and outside those boundaries, and he wasn't above using whatever means necessary to bring about compliance in any recalcitrant soldier—or civilian.

Stark's hatred of and subsequent one-man war against Indians of any stripe was understandable— parents murdered, pregnant wife executed, and baby sister stolen. Younger brother wounded and unconscious for several weeks. Stark, himself, wounded and hovering near death for days on end . . .

That kind of loss could stir up a powerful hatred and need for vengeance in a man, for sure.

Ledbetter had not asked for Stark, but his superior, General Howard Sterling, had told him he needed Stark and was going to get him. That rankled. He didn't like having the scout shoved down his throat.

Especially one who seemed to be used to doing exactly as he pleased—obeying his own dictates and no one else's. And bringing along another defiant problem with him, in the person of the other scout, Cullen Jefferson.

Still, Stark had some admirable badges of merit. He had not yet given up the search for his little sister who'd been taken in the raid that had killed so many. He had earned praise from several of the officers under whom he had served. He had fought alongside

General George Armstrong Custer at the Battle of the Washita down in Indian Territory.

Word was that Stark knew every nook and cranny of Indian Territory—and why shouldn't he, having been born and raised near there? But even so, he was a formidable master of the land east of the Mississippi, including not only Indian Territory, but everything south and west of there into Texas and New Mexico and Arizona Territories, and north, into Kansas, Nebraska, and the Dakota Territory.

Ledbetter had to admit, he was somewhat in awe. He'd never excelled at geography, and though he had a high opinion of his own intellectual prowess, in his heart he knew he would never be able to learn the nuances and features of such a wide expanse of land. Committing it to memory as Stark had done would prove a virtual impossibility for Ledbetter.

No matter. There was plenty else he was good at.

A sudden rapping at the door brought Ledbetter out of his reverie. He nodded to Corporal Cahill, who walked to the door and pulled it open.

Cahill stepped aside, allowed the new scouts to enter, then asked, "Who shall I say is calling?" His eyes conveyed the ridiculousness of such a request that he could not allow into his tone.

Nathan looked at him, surprised. "Uh . . . Nathan Stark. Civilian scout." He played along, glancing at the man seated at the desk. The stripes on his sleeves told Nathan this was, indeed, a colonel—and most likely Ledbetter—but he waited for a formal introduction as indicated by the aide's demeanor. He glanced at Cullen, who was already looking disgusted by the whole display.

"Captain Stark, may I present to you Colonel Wesley Stuart Ledbetter." With a flourish, the aide gestured with open palm to where Ledbetter was seated.

"I don't believe I caught *your* name," Nathan said pointedly to the aide. It irked him that Ledbetter treated the man as his servant rather than with the respect due a soldier of any rank.

"Uh—" The aide looked toward Ledbetter.

Nathan put a hand out to the aide, and the man automatically took it and shook. Nathan gave him a questioning look.

"Corporal Cahill, sir. Corporal Winston Cahill. Aide to Colonel Ledbetter."

"Good to meet you, Corporal Cahill." Nathan stepped farther into the office toward Ledbetter's desk. "And this is my partner, Cullen Jefferson. Civilian scout, as well."

The rotund colonel rose from his seat, a look of surprise and anger mingling in his florid features.

Nathan ignored the expression, giving him a tight smile as he extended his hand.

After a brief hesitation, Ledbetter took Nathan's hand in a brief, limp shake that left Nathan feeling like he wanted to wipe his palm clean.

Ledbetter's look had hardened to one of severity. Nathan could hold his own. His father had been the headmaster at an all girls' school in Tennessee. Then, when they'd come west to Kansas, he'd opened a school of his own—and he had not spared the rod with any of his students; certainly not with his own children. If anything, he'd chosen to make examples of them.

Ledbetter shook Cullen's hand dismissively. "I will

interview you later, Mr. Jefferson. You're free to go
for now."

"Oh, by all means," Cullen answered mockingly. "I
can see we're gonna get along right well. Just open
the door and beller when ya need me, sir." The door
slammed behind him as he went out.

Nathan managed not to grin, but his attitude
changed as he turned his attention back to Ledbetter
and said coolly, "Colonel, good to meet you."

"Likewise, I'm sure."

The game was on. Neither of them meant a word of
their greeting. Nathan was there because it was his job
to be there. Colonel Ledbetter obviously felt the
same. A cloud of animosity already hung over them.

"Please, sit down," the colonel invited.

Trying to keep his reluctance hidden, Nathan sat
in the plush cowhide chair the colonel indicated.

"Welcome to Fort Randall, Mr. Stark."

Nathan noticed the colonel's intentional use of his
civilian title rather than the military one he'd earned.
Though Ledbetter was correct in his usage, among
military personnel and out of respect for having
served, civilian scouts who were former military officers were usually addressed by their previous rank.

Nathan didn't miss the vengeful gleam of satisfaction in Ledbetter's eyes. He wouldn't take the bait . . .
yet. "Thank you, Colonel."

"You have quite the reputation," Ledbetter said.

Nathan shrugged. "I'm glad to be of service wherever the Army sends me."

Ledbetter smirked at the insinuation. "Could be
worse, Stark. You might be in Texas . . . or back in
Indian Territory—godforsaken hole that it is."

Nathan gave an easy chuckle. "As compared to where, Colonel? *This* heavenly stretch of land the Sioux are hell-bent to hang on to?"

"At least we have a river here!"

Nathan only smiled at the colonel's pricked pride. "So you do." His superior look let Ledbetter know he could give him a geography lesson if he chose . . . but he wouldn't waste his time.

Ledbetter sighed. "It seems we've somehow gotten off on the wrong foot, Captain."

Nathan nodded. "I'm just here to do my job, Colonel. Don't know how long I'll be here, but while I am, we'd better both make the best of it, I reckon."

"We both want the same thing." Ledbetter pushed his spectacles up on his nose. "We *have* to hold this fort. We have to quell the Sioux. They're *always* ready to fight, and trouble is on the way with the western factions as well as the central bands."

"Why do you let those orphans stay here, Colonel?" Nathan asked, abruptly changing the subject.

Ledbetter shot him a look over the top of his glasses. "That's four less of the red bastards I have to worry about."

Nathan shook his head. "No. You're wrong. Once an Indian, always an Indian."

"They can be assimilated, as President Jackson decreed so many years past."

"That will never happen, Colonel."

Ledbetter regarded Nathan in silence then said, "At least that's one thing we agree on. I don't believe it, either . . . but we have to try. You may think what you will of me, Stark, but those boys were left behind as youngsters. They would've died out there if we'd not taken them in."

"They serve a usefulness, I suppose," Nathan said in a neutral tone. "Frees up your men from taking care of their own horses."

"It gives those boys purpose." Ledbetter glared at Nathan. "I suppose you, being the great Indian hunter that you are, would've let them starve or die of exposure. Are you that heartless, Stark? They were very young children."

After a moment, Nathan shook his head. He'd let Black Sun live, and he was much older than the orphans had been when Ledbetter had taken them in.

"I don't know what I'd 've done, Colonel. Just seems a shame to give them a home—however humble it may be—only to see them turn on you and possibly kill you in your sleep"—he broke off and shrugged— "but I don't know what I'd have done in your place."

"At least you're honest."

"Yes. I am. I don't want those boys around my horse while I'm here, Colonel. I'll see to him myself."

Ledbetter nodded. "Duly noted."

"You didn't want to see me to discuss this. Do you have specific orders for me?"

Ledbetter shook his head. "Not yet, Stark. It's been a while since you were up this way, has it not? Why don't you take a day or two to get settled in, reacquaint yourself with the lay of the land."

Nathan gave a short laugh. "I remember it well, Colonel. Rivers and all. But you're right. It has been a couple years since I was up this way. And I appreciate the reprieve. Cullen and I could both use a day off." Nathan rose, as did Ledbetter.

"Jefferson has no orders."

Nathan's smile faded. "He will, Colonel. Or we'll *both* be moving on."

Starting for the door, Nathan almost tripped over Corporal Cahill who rushed to get to it first. Nathan's hand collided with Cahill's arm as they reached for the knob at the same time.

"Sorry," mumbled the aide.

Nathan couldn't keep the pity from his expression. "I'll get it, Corporal," he murmured. He couldn't wait to take that first deep breath of fresh air.

CHAPTER 8

Nathan closed the door behind him, stepped down off the porch, and collided with a bundle of fury headed straight for Colonel Ledbetter's office. He managed to grab the petite woman who had run headlong into him and keep her from falling.

She looked up at him, her green eyes spitting fire.

Her expression changed as recognition dawned, warming her beautiful eyes and bringing a smile of unabashed delight to her lips. "Nate! Oh, my goodness."

"Delia? What in blue blazes are you doing here?" He realized his hands were still on her waist where he had steadied her, and that really wasn't proper . . . but he didn't get in a hurry to remove them.

"Is that any way to greet a lady?" she teased, hugging him close to her.

After a moment, he moved his hands to her shoulders and held her away from him, looking her up and down. In a cool mint-colored day dress that set off the emerald green of her eyes, she was a pure vision. Her auburn hair was done up on top of her head, and Nathan swore she didn't look a day past eighteen.

But he knew better.

Cordelia Blaine was closer to thirty, but she'd taken care of herself. Her face showed no sign of lines, though Nathan knew she'd had her share of worries and sorrow. She'd buried two children—a girl, dead of summer complaint at six months of age, and a boy at three years, of measles.

Delia was married to Stephen Blaine, a young officer who had been assigned to Fort Sill at the same time as Nathan. From there, Stephen had been sent to Fort Morgan in Colorado. And a few months later, Nathan had been reassigned to Fort Riley in Kansas, to help quell the Ponca and Pawnee unrest. Several years had passed since then, and Nathan hadn't seen Stephen Blaine or his lovely redheaded wife in that time.

As Delia stood looking at him, he shook his head to clear the cobwebs. "No, it's not. No way to greet a lady, for sure." He grinned at her. "You're looking as beautiful as ever, Mrs. Blaine." He wouldn't have been so informal with her a moment earlier if he hadn't been so surprised to see her.

"And you're ever the gentleman," Delia responded graciously, according to her upbringing.

Though she'd been born to Irish immigrant parents who had settled in Kentucky, her father had made a fortune with his eye for premium horseflesh and the spectacular horses he raised. And, Delia had mentioned once, from his equally fine Irish whiskey business that was every bit as lucrative as his horse farm.

"So Stephen is living the high life here under Colonel Ledbetter's reign, I take it?"

Delia shook her head and looked away. "You couldn't have known. Stephen was killed by the Sioux, Nate. He's been gone two years now, come August."

Nathan took a deep breath. "I'm so sorry, Delia. My deepest condolences. I had no idea. We'd lost track of each other."

She gave him a bittersweet smile. "He considered you a friend, always. We often spoke of you with fond memories."

"Delia, I feel badly I didn't know—"

"I should've written. Or sent a telegram . . ." Her voice trailed away.

Nathan shook his head and told her, "You probably couldn't have located me. Scouts are sent all over the place."

She smiled up at him. "Well, I'm certainly glad you're here now. Come for supper tonight. I've learned to cook a mean shepherd's pie over the years. And I actually have some fresh bison."

Nathan had taken quite a few meals with the Blaines while they were all at Fort Sill. It was true that Delia hadn't been much of a cook in those days . . . but a woman who looked like her didn't have to be. A part of him—a small part, since there wasn't much room for anything else besides the hatred and the desire for revenge he felt—had envied Stephen Blaine.

"I'd love to, but I don't want to put you out," he said. "Looks like you are a woman with a purpose right now."

"Before Stephen was killed, I'd begun to teach school. There are many of the families with children who benefit from going to school. I have a bit of education." She winked, and he was reminded that she had gone to one of the finest girls' academies for the best education her father's money could buy.

"I know you're good at what you do, Delia. No one loves children more than you—" He broke off, realization at his own unintentionally hurtful words hitting him like a blow.

She laid a hand on his arm in quick forgiveness. "It's all right. Nate. I *do* love children, even though my own were taken from me. You spoke the truth, nothing more."

He glanced over his shoulder at the door he'd just come out of. "Need help in there?"

She grinned. "Not one bit. The colonel knows to hide under his desk when I come through the door."

"What's the problem?"

"He's ordered my schoolhouse to be designated to store the extra rations and munitions! Why, there's no way on this earth I'd allow those children to literally sit on top of a powder keg. We'd all be nervous wrecks." She shook her head. "No, sir. We will not stand for this!"

"Well, let me get out of the way. I don't want to stop progress." He quickly stepped aside.

"Shall we eat at, say, six-thirty? Seven?" She was back in good humor once more, saving her anger for the colonel.

"Six-thirty all right? I haven't had a good shepherd's pie in I don't know how long. I'm sure looking forward to it."

"Oh, Nate, it's so good to see you again. My little house is at the end, next to the church." She pointed toward the opposite end of the street. "It's the one on the right side. Where the flowers are growing in the window box. I made that myself so I could keep my flowers out of the direct sunlight."

"They're mighty pretty, Delia." He tipped his hat. "I'll see you at six-thirty."

"Come hungry!" She breezed up the steps and knocked on the door.

"I will," Nathan answered, starting down the street again. He felt the slightest twinge of pity for Ledbetter. Delia had her Irish up.

"Well, ain't that sweet," Sergeant Seamus McCall muttered as he watched Nathan walk away from the woman half the men at the fort had in mind to woo, with Seamus leading the pack.

Delia Blaine was a beauty . . . well-born and a fine lady. Would she have him? Of course she would! Seamus was a prize in his own right. At least, in his own mind. He'd not yet declared his intentions to her, but by God, he wasn't going to stand by and let her be snapped up right out from under him, like a trout snapped up a choice minnow for his dinner.

Miss Delia was the only woman he had set his sights on. After her husband had been killed nearly two years past, Seamus had thought to give her time to grieve—and to miss having a man about the house—before he spoke up for her.

And here was this rough-and-tumble scout trying to step in and claim her! Dinner at the Widow Blaine's house? That should be Seamus McCall having dinner with the red-haired beauty—not the newly-arrived ex-Reb-officer-turned-scout!

Seamus stepped in front of Nathan. "I saw you speaking with the Widow Blaine just now."

The scout stopped and gave McCall an appraising stare. "That's right. We're old friends."

"Seamus McCall. *Sergeant* McCall." He extended a hand, and after a moment, Nathan took it firmly.

"Nathan Stark. I just rode in last night."

"I heard. Glad to have you—long as you understand the Widow Blaine is off limits."

Nathan slowly reached to push his hat back, his gaze hard as he studied this Sergeant Seamus McCall. "What makes you think that, McCall?"

"I don't *think* it, laddie; I *know* it. At least half the men in this company are moonin' after Miss Delia. The other half are married. None of us would take too kindly to you waltzin' in and tryin' to court her. You understand?"

Nathan stared at him a moment, then burst out laughing.

"I don't see nothin' funny about it, Stark," Seamus snarled, his temper boiling and making his face turn even redder than it usually was from the fierce Dakota Territory sun. "You best stop yer laughin' and heed my words."

"Or what?" Nathan challenged, still chuckling.

"I'll . . . I'll beat ya to a bloody pulp, that's what!" Seamus stepped back, putting his fists up.

"Now wait a minute, McCall. I told you Miss Delia is just an old friend of mine—"

"Oh, not good enough for you to court and marry, eh?"

"If I was looking for a wife—"

"Oh, and now you're too good for *any* woman. Well, ye sidewindin' yellow belly, take *that*!"

Nathan was ready for the punch when Seamus delivered it. He blocked the burly Irishman's clumsy haymaker and delivered a blow of his own, only to realize that the man's gut must be made of steel, rather than flesh and bone.

He followed the punch with a second. His first thought hadn't been incorrect. Instead of sinking in, his fist practically bounced off McCall's midsection.

And then, there was no more time for thought—only pure survival instinct, as McCall came at him with a vengeance and every ounce of strength he possessed.

CHAPTER 9

Nathan matched the man in height and muscle strength, but fighting McCall was like engaging in hand-to-hand combat with a full-grown grizzly bear. The sergeant had surprising speed for such a burly individual. He got the first punch in, a slamming left to the jaw that staggered Nathan. While he was off balance, McCall hit him with a right that caught him on the forehead and opened a cut.

Nathan felt warm blood running from the wound. The sensation sent rage coursing through him. A red haze seemed to drop over his vision. It came not from the blood but rather from the anger that filled him.

Nathan went after McCall, no holds barred. If he planned to survive, it was going to be necessary to use every trick in the book. And Nathan hadn't lived that long to be defeated by a human mountain of brawn.

He feinted with his right, and when McCall bit on it, Nathan stepped in and landed a couple swift left jabs to the sergeant's face. The punches rocked McCall's head back and Nathan realized the man's face was a better target than his belly. He sent in a right that scraped McCall's left cheekbone, but in return he took a punishing blow to the sternum that left him unable to catch his breath for a second. He hunched his shoulders, covered up, and absorbed a couple punches that didn't do much damage to his lean, rawhide-tough form.

When McCall launched a roundhouse right, though, Nathan ducked under it. That blow would have taken his head off if it had landed. While he had the chance, he tried another punch to McCall's belly, but with the same lack of success. He backed off as McCall recovered his balance from the missed haymaker.

Through the blood running from the cut above his eye, Nathan's glance caught the audience of soldiers of every rank who'd stopped what they were doing to watch the battle raging between the two men. Some of them shouted encouragement to McCall, since Nathan was an outsider as far as they were concerned.

McCall lumbered at him again like a runaway loco- motive. Nathan sidestepped quickly, giving McCall a shove to launch him forward into the dirt. Just then, a pistol shot sounded nearby, followed by the shouting of an officer as McCall clambered up.

"Sergeant McCall!" someone bellowed. "Cease and desist!"

Nathan stood ready to continue the fight, but he saw no reason for them to keep pummeling each other until both fell to the ground in bloody exhaustion. McCall evidently didn't feel the same way. Like a mad- dened bull, he charged at Nathan yet again, running full bore, his face a mask of fury.

The gun sounded again.

"Sergeant, the next one will be right through your thick Irish skull!"

McCall wasn't even trying to cover up anymore, just attacking blindly.

Nathan couldn't turn his attention away from the crazed Irishman for a second. To do so would be suicidal. Bracing himself, he threw a straight right into the man's nose, smashing it with an audible crack. The impact slowed McCall down long enough for three soldiers to tackle him to the ground and hold him while a fourth man cuffed his wrists behind his back. Then they hauled him to his feet.

"I'll kill the lot o' ye! I'll kill ye in yer sleep! Sorry bastards, the lot o' ye!" McCall shouted as they wrestled him toward the brig. His ranting faded as the soldiers forced him away.

"Stark!" Ledbetter barked from his front stoop. He was the one who had fired the shots and he held a revolver in his hand, pointed at the ground. "Are you all right?"

Before Nathan could respond, Delia moved past the colonel and hurried toward him, her eyes flooded with concern.

"I'm fine—" Nathan began quietly to Delia, not looking at Ledbetter.

"No, you are *not*," she interjected firmly. "You're bleeding, Nate, and—"

"Nothing the doc can't fix quick enough."

Just then, a soldier carrying a medical bag strode up to join them. "Get on over to my place and let's get you seen to," the man said briskly to Nathan.

"Where?" Nathan was breathing hard, trying to catch his breath. If nothing else, he wanted to get the bleeding stopped. It seemed to be pouring buckets down his face.

"Here, I'll—" Delia began.

But the doctor cut her off. "Don't get your hands all bloody, Mrs. Blaine. I'll walk him over to the infirmary myself. I haven't met our new scout . . . *yet*."

"I'm Doctor Isaac Lightner." He was a slender man with graying brown hair and brown eyes that seemed to have seen everything, good and bad, the world had to offer. Experience had made him appear somewhat older than he actually was. "I will shake your hand once we get you cleaned up," he added, putting his hand out in an indication for Nathan to lie on his examination table.

Nathan grimaced. "I'm all right, Doc."

Lightner frowned at him. "Oh? That's your diagnosis? When did you go to medical school? And where?"

Nathan grinned faintly, wincing at the twinge of a swollen lip. He didn't remember McCall hitting him in the mouth, but obviously the sergeant had caught him there with at least a glancing blow.

Nathan climbed up on the table and lay down gingerly. The doctor unbuttoned Nate's shirt and efficiently gathered the supplies he'd need, laying them out on the instrument table. He first began to wash the blood from Nathan's face, neck, and hands.

"McCall is a troublemaker," Lightner stated. "You're not the first man he's gone after for some slight, real or imagined. Just so you know, this wasn't your fault."

Nathan didn't respond. He sucked in a deep breath as the doctor probed for broken ribs. When Lightner nodded in satisfaction, relief washed through Nathan. He couldn't afford to be laid up with broken ribs from a ridiculous, unnecessary fight.

He was there to scout for Ledbetter. In his orders, he'd been told that he was to help find a way to deal with the various Sioux groups and clans. He understood the way their society was set up, but for years, unrest had simmered among them, always on the verge of boiling over.

He reviewed what he knew. The eastern Sioux—Santee, were most commonly called the Dakota, with four main bands. Collectively, they were known as the Isanti—or Knife Makers. They were at Fort Randall's back door, and would be the faction Nathan, Cullen, and the soldiers would have the most dealings with.

The central Sioux were the smallest, known as the Yankton, or Nakota, and consisted of only two bands. The Nakota were known as the Keepers of the Sacred Pipestone.

The western Sioux, or Teton, were by far the largest division with seven bands. They were called commonly the Lakota, also known as the Dwellers on the Plains.

Together, the *Oceti Sakowin*, or Seven Council Fires, comprised the entire Great Plains tribal system. But the bands in each of the three main divisions all spoke their own distinct dialects and were dealt with differently.

The western division had occupied the lands west of the nearby Missouri River, but they'd later migrated to settle the lands of what they called the *Pahá Sápa*—the Black Hills.

The Yankton, the middle division, occupied the

northwestern portion of Minnesota and eastern Dakota Territory.

Nathan was brought back to his current situation as the doctor cast a skeptical eye at the cut on Nathan's forehead and said, "That shouldn't need stitches, but I'll bandage it now that the bleeding's stopped. Try not to get hit in the head again for a while."

"I'll give it my best effort, Doc," Nathan said dryly.

Lightner bound up the cut, then the rough-healing gash on Nathan's right arm caught his eye. "What happened here?" He turned to prepare a swab to clean the wound properly.

"I ran into a couple Muscogee along the way."

Lightner raised an eyebrow. "Looks like you more than 'ran into' them, Mr. Stark—or do you prefer to be called by your previous rank?"

Nathan smiled. "I prefer *Nathan*, Doc. With friends, that is."

The doctor returned his smile. "Good enough, then, Nathan. Now, what happened here? And let me remind you, anything you tell me is strictly confidential. This may be nothing but a frontier wilderness post, but there are a few of us who adhere to the conventions of society and the professionalism that we hope to show as an example to others."

Nathan shot him a look as the doctor began to salve the cut and wrap it with clean bandaging. "Who are we talking about, Doc? Ledbetter?"

Lightner shook his head. "That would be unprofessional of me, wouldn't it, Nathan? Speaking out of turn about the esteemed supreme leader of our band of brave soldiers?"

Nathan gave a short nod as the doctor neatly tied off the bandage around his arm. "I suppose it might seem that way to some, Doc. But you know, I'm not really Army. My *compadre*, Cullen Jefferson, and I are in a somewhat precarious position. I need to know everything . . . and it saves me a world of time and trouble to learn it quick instead of having to find out about it from personal experience."

The doctor handed Nathan his dirty, torn shirt. "You may not want to put this on."

Nathan laughed. "Doc, that's where you're wrong. You don't ever show your wounds to the enemy. Gives 'em a place to aim for. If I could take this bandage off my forehead, I would—but the only thing that brings out bloodlust more than a white bandage is the sight of blood. So I'll leave it on, and hope my Stetson shades it enough so it's not too noticeable."

"You're smart. Couldn't have said it better myself."

"Anything you want to tell me about Ledbetter? Or any of the others?" Nathan sat on the edge of the table, looking at the doctor unwaveringly. He figured the doc wasn't ready to talk yet. Nathan was the new guy, and the doctor was every bit as savvy as he'd said Nathan was. "Okay, how about general information?"

Lightner broke eye contact, looking away briefly, then back at Nathan. "Do you hurt anywhere especially? If so, I can give you some laudanum—"

Nathan shook his head. "Don't need it. And frankly, I'd rather deal with pain than face the nightmares laudanum brings on."

"Understood." Lightner turned to put his supplies away. "If you change your mind, you know where I am."

Nathan stood and shrugged into his shirt. "Same

goes for you, Doc. When you're ready to talk, I'm ready to listen."

Lightner turned quickly, bending a cool stare on Nathan.

"Thanks for patching me up. What do I owe you?" Nathan asked as he finished buttoning his shirt and settled his hat on his head.

"Nothing. My services are courtesy of the U.S. Army."

Nathan nodded to the medico and went outside to find Cullen lounging in front of the building.

The older man grinned and said, "Hear tell you got yourself into a scrape while I was over at the sutler's store. When I heard the commotion I should've figured you'd be in the middle of it."

Nathan grunted. "It was nothing to worry about."

"That bandage on your noggin says different."

"You know how it is when you get a cut on your head. You bleed like a stuck hog, but it doesn't amount to anything. I'll be fine."

"If you say so. Also heard that the ruckus was about a woman."

"Cordelia Blaine," Nathan said.

Cullen raised a shaggy gray eyebrow. "The fair Delia. Her husband's posted here?"

"Her husband's dead." Nathan's voice was flat. Stephen Blaine had been a friend, but the life Nathan had led for the past fifteen years had accustomed him to never getting too close to anyone. He was sorry the Sioux had put Stephen under, but he wasn't overcome with grief. He didn't figure he had that capacity anymore.

"Too bad," Cullen said. "He wasn't a bad sort . . . for a Yankee officer."

"I'm having supper with Delia tonight." Nathan wasn't sure what prompted him to say that, but the words came out and lay there between him and Cullen.

Both of the older man's eyebrows rose in surprise. "Is that so? You reckon that's a good idea?"

"I don't see why not," Nathan said, his voice curt. "We're old friends, that's all."

"Yeah," Cullen drawled. "Old friends."

Nathan's eyes narrowed. "You mean something by that?"

Cullen grinned again and held up a hand, palm out. "Not a blessed thing."

Nathan wasn't sure whether to believe him or not.

"Our new scout is certainly cocksure of himself." Colonel Ledbetter let the curtain fall completely across the window once more, shutting off the view of the two scouts talking, then turned to face his aide. "Your opinion, Corporal Cahill?"

Cahill cleared his throat. "Begging your pardon, sir, but I don't know him well enough to say, yet."

Ledbetter gave a disgusted snort. "You never have an opinion of your own, do you, Corporal? Stark walked in the door and I knew within a minute what kind of man he was."

Cahill looked at Ledbetter, then stared stoically ahead. "What kind of man would that be, sir?"

Ledbetter crossed the room to his desk and seated himself in his plush cowhide chair. For a long moment, he toyed with the glass paperweight that his sister had given him when he'd made colonel, twisting it and turning it this way and that. The hollow thump it made came erratically as he repeatedly dropped it to the desk from a short distance.

"A dangerous one, Corporal. A very, very dangerous one."

CHAPTER 10

"Come in, Nate." Delia opened the door wide to admit him at six-thirty, as they'd agreed.

He had put on a clean shirt before coming over and knocked the dust off his hat, trousers, and boots. Removing his flat-crowned black hat, he stepped inside. She took it from him and hung it on the hat rack made from deer antlers that stood in the front entryway.

"Delia, dinner sure smells wonderful."

She led him into the small dining room where the table was set, including candles and some fresh flowers as the centerpiece, then turned a pretty pout his way. "Dinner smells good? I was hoping you'd have noticed this gardenia perfume I'm wearing rather than the smell of shepherd's pie."

Nathan hadn't been with a woman for a long time, but not so long he didn't recognize her bold flirtation for what it was. He forced a faint smile. He hated to be caught off guard, but realized he should have recognized there was more to this dinner invitation than what he'd expected.

The mouth-watering smell of the meal Delia had prepared soured in the air.

"My apologies, Delia. I guess I've been too long in my own company and that of other men. Of course, I should have complimented you on how beautiful you look—and the scent you're wearing. But you always were beautiful."

Delia smiled forgivingly, and Nathan realized belatedly he'd said something else offensive. Perhaps it was the phrase *should have complimented you*. He supposed he should have left it at *My apologies* . . .

"Everything's ready."

Nathan nodded, looking over the lovely table setting Delia had created in the middle of the savage prairie land.

She put her hand out toward the table. "Aren't the flowers gorgeous? I have my own flower and vegetable garden. It's my pride and joy. And it's good for my soul to be able to at least grow something to contribute to the community sometimes."

Nathan nodded. "They are beautiful. I'm sure it takes a lot of work. I remember, growing up, having to plant, and weed, and water. From an early age, I knew I wasn't cut out for farming. I had no choice, though, if we were gonna eat."

Delia gave him a somewhat forced smile. "Well, shall we? It's getting cold."

Nathan pulled Delia's chair out and seated her, then took his own chair directly across from her. Every square inch of the table was used somehow. It made him feel closed in.

"Would you say grace, please?" Delia asked quietly.

How he wished he could oblige her, but the words

weren't there. They'd never be there again, he figured. Not since God had seen fit to let Camilla and the baby be murdered by the Pawnee on that long ago sunny day. The day everything had been taken from him. How could he thank God for a meal when He'd taken everything else? He couldn't. *He wouldn't.*

Nathan shook his head. "Delia, I-I'm not able."

She gave him a questioning look but then smiled. "It's all right, Nate. I'm sure you have your reasons. Do you mind if I say a grateful prayer over our meal?"

Dumbly, Nathan shook his head, then managed to say, "No. I don't mind." The dull ache in his pounded ribs almost made him wish for the laudanum Doctor Lightner had offered.

Delia had as much right to her beliefs as he did to his own. As she began her blessing—"Dear Father, thank you for the bounty you have provided . . ."—he tried to let his mind wander.

Is there really something between Delia and the big Irish sergeant?

He glanced across the table at her, but her head was bowed, her eyes closed, as she continued her blessing.

No. Delia wouldn't have encouraged the attentions of someone as crude as Sergeant McCall. She is truly too lovely, too intelligent, and she'd been so in love with Stephen when they'd been married.

Yet something had been in Delia's expression. Something . . . hungry. *Stephen has been gone almost two years. Is it right having dinner with my good friend's widow? We're just friends. Just old friends. Having a meal together and catching up.*

Nathan had always perceived Stephen as one who

would never be killed . . . but he was gone . . . always a possibility in the life of a soldier. Or a scout. Nathan had always seen Stephen living to a ripe old age in his retirement, with Delia at his side.

"Amen." Delia raised her head and motioned to the dish of shepherd's pie. "Please, help yourself. I would ring for the serving maid, but she just stepped out." Her green eyes twinkled with humor at her poor joke.

Nathan returned her grin. "Sure you trust me to serve myself? I might eat the entire thing."

"Eat as much as you like, Nate. I know how a man prizes a good meal. Mother believed the way to a man's heart was through his stomach."

Nathan took a biscuit and put it on his plate. "Well, that may be true for most men, Delia. If they have a heart left to get to."

Her bright smile dimmed a bit, and she picked up a bowl of fresh tomatoes. "Care for any?"

"Maybe later. Thanks."

They ate in silence for a few moments, then Delia laid her fork down. "Are you sure you're all right? Sergeant McCall is a rough customer—"

"I'm fine," he answered, a little too curtly.

Anger flashed for a moment in her eyes. *"Really."* Delia knew how to cut a man to the quick with her tone, for sure.

Nathan inwardly winced. He'd managed to keep her at arm's length so far. "Delia, again, I apologize." He shook his head. "I guess I'm just not used to having someone fussing over me. Not for a very long time now."

Delia stared at him, then leaned forward. "Nate,

Stephen told me about what . . . what happened. And why you are so single-minded in your hatred of the Indians. I don't blame you. My Stephen was killed by them, just as your Camilla was. It's hard to forgive—"

"Forgive? Delia, the thought of forgiving them for what they took from me never even crossed my mind. My family—not only my pregnant wife, but my parents and my little sister. My little brother barely survived."

"And you, Nate?"

He waved a dismissive hand. "Forget about me. I was left behind to pick up the pieces." His voice had risen.

"It still bothers you so much?" Delia's eyes were filled with concern.

"Shouldn't it? Should it ever *stop* bothering me?"

Delia recoiled as if he'd struck her.

He grimaced. With his knack for saying the wrong thing in the wrong way, you could sure as hell tell that he hadn't been around women much in recent years. "Delia—"

"How long has it been?" she broke in. "Fourteen years? Fifteen?" Pity crept into her voice. "Yet your hatred is still eating you alive, Nathan Stark."

"You've never felt hatred for—"

"Oh, yes, I have!" She threw her napkin on the table where the edge of it trailed through the dish of shepherd's pie. "If you believe for one minute that Stephen wasn't as precious to me as Camilla was to you, you are sadly mistaken! I loved Stephen with all my heart. I gave up everything for him. *Everything!* So even though your parents were taken from you, I lost my family, too. You see, I was disinherited, Nathan, for loving a man so far *beneath my station*—but love him, I did. And I don't regret one blessed moment of it . . . of what I gave up to have him for the time I did. Why can't you remember the good times you were blessed with instead of making revenge your reason for living?"

"How can you forget what happened, Delia?"

"I haven't forgotten." She stood up, her green eyes blazing with righteous fire that burned him with a glance. "Don't you ever dare say that to me, Nathan! I will never forget what was taken from me. But by God, I refuse to let them steal the rest of my life, my happiness—*my future*—from me because of what happened in the past. You are soulless! Do you care about anything at all, Nathan? Anything, other than revenge?"

Nathan stood slowly. "No. I guess I haven't cared about anything else but seeing justice done for fifteen years."

She shook her head, an errant curl bouncing loose at the gesture. "I pity you, Nate. I pity you for thinking what you're doing is in the name of justice. Justice would be vindicating their deaths by seeing the perpetrators captured and lawfully punished, not by taking vigilante revenge on every Indian you come in contact with. What a horribly sad way to live out your life, never sparing a thought for your future, other than killing."

"My future was decided when everything was taken from me." His voice was as hard as flint.

"Oh, Nathan, you are so wrong. We each are the master of our own ship. I'm afraid yours has been set adrift in a storm of bitterness."

He gave her a sharp nod, biting back the retort he

wanted to make. "I'm sorry you see it that way, Delia. Thank you for the dinner, but—"

"I'll let you see yourself out," she responded stiffly, her hard stare pinning him for a moment until he turned away and headed for the front room to retrieve his hat.

Chapter 11

The guardhouse at Fort Randall stood at one end of the long parade ground bordered by cottonwood trees, in a row of buildings that included the sturdy brick powder magazine and the quartermaster's commissary and storehouse. The cells were at the rear of the structure, and that was where Sergeant Seamus McCall was lying on a bunk inside one of them. Every breath that rasped, wheezed, and bubbled through his broken nose fueled his growing hatred for the scout named Nathan Stark.

Doc Lightner, that smug bastard, had wrenched McCall's nose back into place, drawing a howl of pain from the sergeant. His reflexes made him try to strike out at the medico in reaction, but two soldiers holding his arms at the time kept a good grip on him. Probably a fortunate thing, if he ever wanted to get out of lock-up. Lightner had taped a plaster across McCall's nose to stabilize it. He probably appeared ridiculous with that stuck on his face and his eyes swollen and blackened. The Widow Blaine wouldn't want anything to do with him while he looked like that.

Of course, some of his so-called friends had told him that his quest to win the affection of Cordelia Blaine was doomed from the start, but he didn't believe those jealous spalpeens.

"Pssstt! Hey, McCall!"

The voice intruded on McCall's sullen brooding. He would have ignored it, but it repeated the insistent summons.

McCall growled a curse, sat up, swung his legs off the bunk, and stood. He turned to the small window and lifted his hands to grip the bars that closed it off. His knuckles were sore from banging them against Stark, but he ignored that.

"Is that you, Dockery?" McCall asked. Dusk had settled down on the post, and all he could make out was a dim shape outside the window. "What the devil d' ye want?"

"We just got back in from patrol," Sergeant Jeremiah Dockery said. "You got in another fight, didn't you?"

"What if I did?"

Dockery heaved a sigh. "If you keep getting in trouble, you're gonna get tossed out of this man's army, you damned fool. Then where will we be?"

McCall started to make some comment about how he'd be free of the army's damned rules and regulations at last, but he swallowed the words and sighed. He knew what Dockery meant.

"Sorry," he muttered. "It's just that I saw the new scout playin' up to the widow, and I could not stand it."

"The Widow Blaine? We've told you, Seamus—" Dockery stopped short. "What new scout?"

"Fella name of Stark," McCall replied. "Nathan Stark."

"The Indian Killer?" Dockery's startled exclamation made it clear he had heard of Stark. "That's the one you mean?"

"Aye, some call him that, I think. An ugly son of a gun. I dunno what the widow sees in him. Old friends, Stark claims they are, but I don't believe it. He's tryin' to weasel his way into her good graces, mark my word about that!"

Dockery's fingers rasped on beard stubble as he rubbed his chin in thought. "Bucher may know him. I'll talk to him and find out. Stark's got a reputation as a cold-blooded killer, as long as it's redskins you're talking about, but I don't know anything else about him."

"Are you worried about him horning in?" It hadn't even occurred to McCall until just now that Stark might represent a threat to the plans he had made with Dockery and Dietrich Bucher, one of the other scouts assigned to the fort. He had been too upset about what Stark could mean to his ambition regarding Delia Blaine.

"I worry about anybody knowing more than is healthy for us," Dockery snapped. "But I'll see what I can find out. In the meantime, McCall . . . for God's sake, keep your nose clean!"

McCall's big hands tightened on the bars. "What about my nose?" he demanded. "It's not my fault Stark broke it!"

"What? He . . ." Dockery's voice trailed off into a laugh. "I didn't know that. Well, all the more reason for you not to be sticking it where it don't belong, you big oaf!" He faded away into the shadows, leaving McCall to scowl after him.

After a moment, McCall turned from the window and sank onto the bunk again. Between his adoration for the Widow Blaine and the scheme that Dockery and Bucher had hatched together and brought him in on, sometimes there was just too much for him to keep up with. When he thought too much, it made his head hurt.

He sighed and stretched out. After a while as the darkness deepened in the guardhouse cell, he dozed off to dream about a beautiful auburn-haired woman with green eyes.

When Nathan stalked out of Delia's house, he had it in mind to get good and drunk. That impulse was fleeting, though, for a couple reasons.

For one, he wasn't sure where to get a drink around there. Cullen had mentioned a sutler's store, but Nathan didn't know exactly where it was located. He could hunt it up, of course—he wasn't a scout for nothing, after all—but it didn't seem worth the trouble.

For another, he had never been the sort to crawl into a bottle whenever something didn't go to suit him. If that had been the case, he would have drowned in whiskey long before now.

He headed toward his cabin instead. Might as well turn in and get a good night's sleep. The lack of supper might gnaw at his belly, but that would serve as a reminder he needed to keep a wall between himself and other people. He'd been foolish to think he could let that barrier down between him and Delia.

His and Cullen's cabins were located at the opposite end of the parade ground and on the other side from Delia's house. Nathan could have cut diagonally across the parade ground, past the flagpole and sundial that stood in the center, but he walked up the path between the row of cottonwoods and the buildings on Delia's side of the post. Even though he wasn't actually in the army, a certain sense of protocol reared its head from time to time, more a matter of habit than anything else.

Sort of like he was in the habit of killing Indians, he supposed.

Most of the enlisted men were in their barracks, and the officers—the married ones—were in their homes with their families. The junior, unmarried officers were probably in their quarters, as well. Nathan looked across the parade ground, between the buildings on the far side and saw lights burning at the stables, which lay southeast of the post. Dark shapes came and went between him and the lights, which meant men were moving around over there. A patrol might have just come back in. One wouldn't be going out after sundown.

Something ahead of him caught his eye, and his right hand drifted toward the butt of the Colt holstered on his hip. A man was walking toward him. In the dark, Nathan couldn't make out much about him, but his keen eyes told him something was odd about the man.

A second later, Nathan realized what it was—the

man wasn't wearing an enlisted man's cap or an officer's hat. The rounded shape on top of the man's head couldn't be anything except a derby. That stirred something in Nathan's memory, and so did the stranger's tall, brawny form. A name popped into his brain.

"Bucher?" Nathan called as he came to a stop. "Is that you?"

The other man stopped, too, about fifteen feet away, and muttered, "*Was ist los? Gott im Himmel*, is that Nathan Stark?"

"I didn't know you were assigned here, Bucher."

"*Und* I have had the distinct pleasure of not seeing your face for quite some time." Bucher scratched a lucifer to life and stuck a cigar in his mouth. When he held the match to the fat cylinder of tobacco, the harsh glare revealed heavy features dominated by a thick black mustache under a hawklike nose. Bucher puffed the cigar to life and dropped the lucifer, grinding it out under a boot toe.

Nathan had crossed trails with Dietrich Bucher half a dozen times in the past ten years. The son of German immigrants who had settled in Pennsylvania, Bucher had fought for the Union during the war, then become a scout for the army when hostilities moved to the frontier against the Indians. There was no love lost between him and Nathan, and it wasn't only because they had fought on opposite sides. They would have rubbed each other the wrong way even if they had both been Yankees—or Rebs.

Despite that, they had never had any real trouble with each other, had in fact worked together on several occasions. Nathan respected Bucher's abilities as a scout and believed that Bucher respected his.

Bucher and Cullen, on the other hand . . . those two didn't get along at all, hadn't ever since a knock-down, drag-out fight over a card game down at Fort Griffin in Texas a few years earlier.

Since Bucher was at Fort Randall, Nathan knew he needed to alert Cullen to that fact before the two of them accidentally came face-to-face. Cullen didn't go out of his way to start ruckuses, but he sure as hell wouldn't back away from one, either.

Those thoughts went through Nathan's mind in the time it took for Bucher to drag in a lungful of smoke from the cigar and exhale it. "So you have come to help us fight the Sioux, *ja?*"

"That's right," Nathan said.

"*Und* bathe your hands in more redskin blood."

"I won't deny that, but you've spilled a heap of it yourself," Nathan pointed out.

"*Ja*, of course. *Und* now hostilities loom again. Hanging Dog and his warriors would like nothing better than to ride down on this fort and wipe it from the face of the earth, annihilating everyone in it."

Nathan stiffened. He hadn't been aware that there was such an imminent threat. Delia was there, and so were other women and children. By God, if this Hanging Dog and the rest of the Sioux were about to go on the rampage, the army ought to be moving the innocents out so they wouldn't be in harm's way . . .

"But our noble commander believes the redskins are no match for the might of the United States army," Bucher went on.

The slightly scornful note in his voice when he referred to Colonel Ledbetter told Nathan that Bucher didn't have a very high opinion of the colonel, either.

That made the tension inside Nathan relax a little. They had that much common ground, anyway. "What's he planning to do?"

Bucher's thick shoulders rose and fell. "The colonel does not confide in me. I just came in with Lieutenant Pryor's troop from patrol. We encountered no hostiles. The lieutenant continues his report to Colonel Ledbetter even as we speak, but I was dismissed."

"Well, I reckon we'll find out soon enough," Nathan mused. He was debating whether to lie and tell Bucher it was good to see him again when the German spoke up.

"Come have a drink with me, Stark," Bucher said. "We will catch up on old times, *ja?*"

As far as Nathan was concerned, he and Bucher didn't have any old times to catch up on. He was about to say as much when he realized Bucher might prove the source of information that Doc Lightner had failed to be. "Sure. Why not?"

Bucher clenched his teeth on the cigar, making it tilt up at a jaunty angle, and grinned. "We go to the sutler's store," he declared. "Jake Farrow has the best whiskey in the Dakota Territory!"

CHAPTER 12

Some commanding officers allowed a civilian sutler's store on the actual grounds of a post, while others insisted that it had to be off government property. Given Nathan's initial impression of Colonel Ledbetter as an arrogant, stiff-necked, by-the-book officer, he wasn't surprised that the sutler's store at Fort Randall was located just past the fort's limits.

It was a large tent, with the half to the right of the entrance taken up by shelves full of merchandise—food, tools, guns, clothing, knives, pots and pans, candy, jewelry, harness, gunpowder, and all sorts of other things that soldiers and their families might find useful.

A canvas partition ran down the center of the tent to separate the right side from the left, which was the store's busiest part once the sun went down. That was where Jake Farrow, the proprietor, sold beer and whiskey. The bar consisted of planks laid over barrels along the tent's left-hand wall. Half a dozen tables had chairs around them, and in the back a small open area where soldiers could dance with Farrow's "hostesses."

Those women were pretty blatantly soiled doves, and Nathan knew several smaller tents would be out back where those camp followers could conduct their business.

He thought of Leah, back at Statler's Mill, which reminded him of all the bitter things she had said when he'd asked her about Rena. For the most part, Nathan had succeeded in forcing that encounter out of his mind so that he could concentrate on the business at hand, but it came flooding back and put a scowl on his face.

Bucher glanced over at him. "What is wrong, Stark? You look as if you would like to kill someone, but I see no redskins in here."

Nathan gave a little shake of his head. "It's nothing. Let's get that drink and be done with it." Suddenly he wanted to get out of there, but life at Fort Randall might go along more smoothly if he didn't offend Dietrich Bucher. He could tolerate one drink with the German.

Bucher led the way to the bar, past tables where soldiers sat drinking with the soiled doves and others where poker games were going on. There weren't many open spaces at the bar as soldiers who had permission to be there lined up to sample the sutler's whiskey. The two scouts stepped up to the planks and Bucher lifted a hand to signal the man behind the bar.

"Jake Farrow, meet Nathan Stark," Bucher said as the sutler came up to them.

"Stark, eh?" Farrow was a rugged-looking man with a shock of graying blond hair. He wore canvas trousers and a woolen shirt with the sleeves rolled up to reveal brawny forearms. He stuck a big hand across the bar and went on, "I've heard of you. I'm a little surprised we haven't crossed trails before now, as many forts as we've both been at over the years."

Nathan clasped Farrow's hand. The dry, muscular grip was a lot different from shaking with Colonel Ledbetter.

"You have my special bottle, *ja*?" Bucher said.

Farrow grinned. "Of course." He turned to pluck a bottle and a small glass off some lined-up crates that served as a makeshift back bar. "Here you go." He poured liquor into the glass.

Bucher picked it up and threw it back in one swallow, then licked his lips. "Ah, who would dream that one could find good German schnapps in the middle of a wilderness?" he said in satisfaction. He pushed the empty glass back toward Farrow, who filled it again.

"I can get whatever you want," Farrow said, "as long as there's a profit in it." He held up the bottle and cocked an eyebrow at Nathan. "Want to give it a try?"

"I'll just take a beer," Nathan said.

Bucher said, "You do not know what you are missing, *mein freund*."

Nathan knew well enough. From other bars and saloons in the past, he remembered Bucher's fondness for the fruity liquor. He also recalled how the big German had busted up a place or two because he couldn't get what he wanted. And for that matter, he and Bucher were hardly *freunden*, or however the Germans said it.

Farrow drew the beer and set the mug in front of Nathan, who placed a coin on the bar to pay for it.

Bucher pushed the money back toward him and said, "*Nein, nein*, I invited you. This is on me."

Nathan didn't waste breath arguing. He said, "Obliged," picked up the coin, and took a drink of the beer. It was warm but not too bitter. Went down easy enough. It would do in place of the supper he hadn't gotten.

He could kick himself for the things he had said to Delia. On the other hand, what right did she have to tell him he was soulless? Just because she had lost her family, too, didn't mean he ought to react to his own tragedy in the same way she had. She had lost her children to illness. In cases like that, there was nothing she could strike back against. And maybe she didn't go out and kill Indians to avenge Stephen's death because she *couldn't*. If she'd had the ability to pick up a gun and blow a few of the red devils to hell, who's to say she wouldn't do exactly that?

Nathan took another swig of the beer and then became aware of Bucher looking at him speculatively.

"You appear as if your thoughts are a million miles away," Bucher said.

"Not quite that far," Nathan said. *Just at the other end of Fort Randall's parade ground*. He finished his beer while Bucher and Farrow talked. When he was done, he turned to leave.

"You are going?" Bucher asked.

"Figured I'd turn in."

Farrow leered. "Got poker games you can sit in on, Stark, if you're of a mind to. Or other . . . *entertainments*, let's say . . . if you're more inclined that way. Take that little redheaded gal." He pointed. "I can personally vouch for her. She can turn a man inside out—" Farrow stopped in midsentence at the look on Nathan's face.

Nathan had swung back toward the bar, and his pulse hammered angrily inside his head. He wanted to reach across the bar, grab the front of Farrow's shirt, and jerk the sutler toward him so he could crack a couple blows across the man's face.

"*Was ist los?*" Bucher muttered. "Stark, what is wrong?"

Nathan didn't say anything.

Farrow lifted a hand. "Take it easy, Stark. Whatever I said to put a burr under your saddle, I didn't mean it that way."

"Forget it," Nathan snapped. He got control of himself and turned away again. His mind still raged, for a couple of reasons. One was the fact that the girl Farrow had pointed out had red hair, like Delia, and the other was that the soiled dove was no more than eighteen, which made her Rena's age. Those reminders of the two females most on his mind had been too much for him . . . but only for a moment.

He stalked away from the bar, toward the tent's entrance. He felt eyes watching him, not only Farrow and Bucher but also some of the soldiers who had seen him looking like he wanted to kill somebody. That didn't bother him. He had seen outright revulsion on the faces of so-called civilized people many times when they found out who he was—and what he was notorious for.

He paused at the entrance, realizing that he was too worked up to sleep. Ducking around the canvas partition, he went into the store side of the tent, rather than out into the night.

A single lantern burned over there. It sat on a

counter made from planks laid across stacked-up crates, rather than whiskey and beer barrels. A man stood behind the counter, shoulders hunched as he bent over an open ledger entering numbers into the columns with a scratchy pen.

He glanced up as Nathan approached. Peering over the spectacles that had slid down to the end of his nose, he seemed to have trouble focusing at first. He was a slight man, with thinning, lank, fair hair. But then he pushed the spectacles up and gave Nathan a friendly smile. "Hello. Something we can do you for?"

Nathan shook his head. "No, just looking around. I don't suppose you do much business after dark like this."

"None at all, to speak of," the man replied with a faint chuckle. He nodded toward the canvas partition. "All the nighttime business takes place on the other side of the establishment. Or out back."

"Not interested in any of that right now." Nathan saw some boxes of .44 cartridges sitting on the counter. "Might could use some ammunition, though. In my line of work, I expect I'll need it sooner rather than later."

"And that is?"

"Civilian scout." Nathan extended his hand. "Nathan Stark."

"Oh." The little man looked surprised, as if few men out here on the frontier offered to shake with him. But after a second he gripped Nathan's hand and said, "I'm Noah Crimmens. I work for Mr. Farrow."

"Pleased to meet you, Noah." The clerk's hand-shake was not as strong as Farrow's nor as weak as

Colonel Ledbetter's, but somewhere in between. Just average and unassuming, as he himself seemed to be.

Nathan went on, "I'll take a box of those .44s."

"Do you want me to set up a tab for you?"

"No, I'll pay cash. Always believed in paying as I go, since I never know if I'll be coming back from the next assignment." A wry smile twisted Nathan's lips. "Wouldn't want to leave some poor businessman hanging for what I owe him."

Crimmens returned the smile. "I wish all our other customers felt the same way. Usually, though, Mr. Farrow collects what's owed him . . . one way or another."

Having met Jake Farrow, Nathan could believe that. The hard-nosed sutler wouldn't let anything stand between him and his profit.

Something else caught Nathan's eye—half a dozen Winchesters hanging on a rack near the counter. He frowned slightly as he picked up one of them and took a closer look at it.

"Those are fine guns, if you're in need of one," Crimmens said. "The '73 model. You won't find a better rifle."

"I know," Nathan said. "I already have one." He tapped a finger against the double diamond design etched into the stock. "And it has this same marking on it."

"Really?"

"Yeah." Nathan looked at the other rifles. "All of these do."

"Yes, I know. It's a distributor's mark. These are all shipped out here from St. Louis through a company that Mr. Farrow and his partner own. You say that you have one?"

"Yeah. Bought in a settlement south of here after my old '66 let me down during a fight."

"Well, I know Mr. Farrow has sold a lot of them," Crimmens said. "He's set up stores at a number of different posts. And of course, weapons do get sold and traded quite a bit, so I'm not surprised that one found its way into your hands. Has your rifle worked well for you?"

"Haven't had any call to use it yet." Nathan thought about the looming threat of Hanging Dog and the other Sioux warriors champing at the bit to go on the warpath and added, "But I reckon there's a good chance I will before too much longer."

Somebody was waiting for Dietrich Bucher when he stepped out of the big tent a while later and started toward his cabin. A man who was shorter than him but just as broad through the shoulders stepped out of the shadows and said quietly, "Bucher."

The German stopped short. He carried a .44 caliber Smith & Wesson Model 3 in a cross-draw holster under his brown tweed coat. His hand instinctively wrapped around the butt before he realized he knew the man who had spoken to him. In fact, they had ridden into Fort Randall together, along with the rest of the patrol led by Lieutenant Pryor, less than two hours earlier.

"*Gott im Himmel,* Dockery, don't sneak up on a man like some skulking redskin. That's a good way to get yourself killed."

Sergeant Dockery let out a disdainful snort. "You're assuming I'd just stand here and let you kill me, you big dumb Dutchie."

Bucher was a little drunk from the schnapps, and on top of that, he didn't like Dockery. However, they had some very important interests in common, so he let the insult pass. "What do you want, Dockery?"

"Do you know a scout named Nathan Stark?"

In the darkness outside the tent, it was difficult for the two men to see each other, but Bucher stared at the sergeant in surprise anyway. After a couple of seconds he asked, "Why *der Teufel* are you asking me about Stark?"

"He's here, and earlier today he tangled with McCall. The stupid ox wound up locked in the guardhouse."

Bucher took off his derby, ran a hand over his coarse black hair, and let out a stream of colorful German obscenities. When his anger had calmed down a little, he asked, "What did they fight over?"

"A woman. The Widow Blaine."

"That is all?"

"As far as I know," Dockery said. "Now answer my question, damn it. Do you or don't you know Nathan Stark? Sometimes they call him the Indian Killer, if that helps."

"*Ja*, I know him. And I know perfectly that he is called the Indian Killer, and why he was given that name." Bucher put on his hat and inclined his head toward the tent. "He was in Farrow's place with me a while ago, having a drink."

"He's a friend of yours?"

"*Nein*, that I would not say. We have served at several

of the same posts. I have no fondness for the man, nor does he have any for me. But we have never been enemies." Bucher spat. "I cannot say the same for his partner Cullen Jefferson. That man is the size of a buffalo, just as stupid, and stinks just as bad."

"Well, I asked around, and Jefferson is here, too, although it seems he doesn't have any orders sending him to Fort Randall and the colonel wants to get rid of him. What I'm worried about is Stark holding a grudge against McCall and ruining all our plans."

"Ha!"

"What the hell do you mean by that?" Dockery sounded angry.

"I mean," Bucher said, "that Nathan Stark has room for only one grudge in his life, *und* that is the one he carries against Indians. Any and all Indians. So long as he has plenty of chances to kill them, he will show no interest in anything else." The big German paused. "We both know that very soon Stark will have all the opportunities to slay redskins that he could ever wish for."

"Yeah, well, if it doesn't work out that way, if he becomes a threat—"

"In that case, it is still nothing to worry about. I will just cut his throat and be done with it."

CHAPTER 13

Nathan had heard soldiers say that the only thing about the army worse than the fighting was all the waiting you had to do. He had seen plenty of examples of that, and his first week at Fort Randall was yet another. When he had gotten his orders to report, he had figured that action was imminent in Dakota Territory. When Bucher had told him about the Sioux war chief Hanging Dog stirring up trouble, it had seemed likely they would be marching against the hostiles in a matter of days.

Instead, he found himself sitting around the fort with Cullen, killing time rather than redskins. Rumor had it that another patrol would be going out in the near future, but nobody knew exactly when or which of the scouts would accompany it.

Nathan avoided the recently built post chapel, not only because he wasn't a religious man anymore but because Delia held her school classes in the library there. He was a rough man without the proper touch for dealing with women, he had concluded, so after their last encounter it was best just to stay away from her. He knew he'd probably run into her now and then around the fort, but he wouldn't go out of his way to do so.

By keeping his distance from Delia, he also insured that he was less likely to bump into Sergeant Seamus McCall. The burly Irish noncom had been released from the guardhouse with a stern warning to stay out of trouble, but Nathan had a hunch that if he, Delia, and McCall were in the same vicinity at the same time, the hotheaded sergeant would lose his temper again. The cut on Nathan's forehead was healing up, and he didn't want another ruckus with McCall.

He and Cullen spent a considerable amount of time at the sutler's store, nursing drinks and playing cards. Nathan was surprised to find that he enjoyed talking to Noah Crimmens, as well. The clerk was so mild-mannered that he tended to blend into the background, but he was smart and had a dry sense of humor. He confirmed Nathan's opinion of Colonel Wesley Stuart Ledbetter: the commanding officer was a stuffed shirt, a martinet when it suited him, and harbored visions of glory.

"You've seen the colonel," Crimmens said to Nathan and Cullen one day when they were alone in the store area of the tent. "And I'm aware that you both served with General Custer."

"Mighty big difference there," Cullen drawled. "With that long yellow hair, the ladies all swoon over Custer. Ledbetter looks more like a frog with spectacles on. Ain't nobody gonna be swoonin' over him, no matter how many Injuns he kills."

"I think he's aware of that, too, but he feels that his greatest chance for advancement, socially as well as militarily, lies in running up a record of successful engagements with the hostiles. If he were to return to Washington for duty at the War Department, say, and had a chestful of ribbons and medals, there would be at least a chance his superiors *and* the ladies might look upon him differently."

Nathan was sitting on a keg with his back propped against a stack of crates. He stretched his legs out in front of him and crossed them at the ankles. "I suppose that's all right, if that sort of thing is important to you."

"I know what's important to *you*," Cullen said. "At least I used to think I did, until the business with that Creek down by Fort Smith."

Crimmens looked interested. "What's this?"

"None of your damn business," Nathan said. He saw the way Crimmens reacted to his sharp tone and harsh words and bit back a curse.

"Nathan didn't mean to bite your head off, Noah," Cullen said. "That's just a sore spot with him. He let some Injun go instead of killin' him. It ain't the way we usually go about our business."

"Did these hostiles ambush you?"

"More like the other way around."

Crimmens frowned in confusion. "They weren't trying to kill you?"

"They would have sooner or later, if they got the chance," Nathan said. "Killing white folks is all any of those red devils ever think about. And if it hadn't been us, they would have killed somebody else. More than likely, somebody a hell of a lot more innocent than Cullen and me."

"Oh. I . . . I suppose I understand."

Nathan looked away. He wished Cullen hadn't brought up that incident. Over the past couple weeks, he had succeeded in shoving Black Sun out of his thoughts, but now the Creek youngster was back.

Was he out there somewhere, tracking them, looking for an opportunity to take his revenge on the white men who had killed his father and brother and friends? Part of Nathan hoped that was the case. It would give him a chance to correct the mistake he had made . . .

One of the soldiers poked his head through the tent entrance and looked around on both sides of the canvas partition. When his gaze fell on Nathan, Cullen, and Crimmens, he said, "There you are."

Nathan sat up straighter and asked, "You looking for me, Corporal?" He had recognized Corporal Winston Cahill, Colonel Ledbetter's aide. Maybe a summons from the colonel would mean that something was about to happen at last.

Cahill seemed a little uncomfortable as he replied, "Ah, no, sir, Captain Stark. I was looking for Mr. Jefferson."

During the war, Cullen had never held a higher rank than sergeant, and civilian employees of the army who were noncommissioned officers weren't referred to by their former rank.

Cullen had been whittling on a chunk of wood and had fashioned it into a rough semblance of a grizzly bear standing up on its hind legs. He sheathed his knife and tossed the carving to Crimmens. "Here you go, Noah. You hang on to that for me."

"Ah . . . thank you?" the clerk said uncertainly.

"I reckon my orders finally came through," Cullen

said to Nathan as they stood up. "Come on. Let's go see the colonel."

"I was only supposed to find you, Mr. Jefferson," Cahill said. "Not Captain Stark."

"We ain't got no secrets from each other. Been partners for nigh on to ten years. Anything Ledbetter says to me, I'm just gonna tell Nathan anyway."

Cahill sighed and didn't try to argue. He sensed that it would be like arguing with a force of nature.

Nathan and Cullen followed Corporal Cahill to "The House," the big frame structure that served as the commander's quarters and post headquarters. Nathan hadn't set foot in there since the day they had arrived at Fort Randall, nor laid eyes on Colonel Ledbetter in that time except at a distance.

Cahill ushered them into the building and opened the door of the colonel's office. "I have Mr. Jefferson, sir," he announced, then added, "and, ah, Captain Stark."

"What?" Ledbetter's voice came from inside. "Corporal, I specifically said—"

"I'm here, Colonel." Cullen brushed past Cahill and strode into the office with Nathan trailing behind him. "What is it you want? My orders finally come through?"

Ledbetter's face turned red, and the way his cheeks puffed up put Nathan in mind of the way Cullen had compared him to a frog a short time earlier.

The colonel controlled his anger, though, and said, "There are no orders, because you were never assigned to this post to start with, Jefferson. But Colonel Bixby down at Fort Sill knew where you were, so he passed along this dispatch for you." Ledbetter picked up a folded and sealed piece of paper from his desk and held it out. "*Letter*, I should say, since you're a civilian."

Both of Cullen's shaggy brows drew down in a puzzled frown. He looked at the letter almost as if it were a rattler like the one he had blasted down in Indian Territory. "Who in Hades would be writin' to me?"

Ledbetter shook the paper impatiently and suggested, "Why don't you take it and find out?"

Cullen reached out, took the letter from the officer, and then clumsily broke the seal. He unfolded it and started to read.

Nathan saw the way his partner suddenly drew in a breath. Cullen's weather-beaten features tightened. Whatever was in that letter, it was bad news.

Cullen read all the way through the message at least twice, then lowered the hand holding it to his side. His fingers clenched, crumpling the paper. He turned and stalked past Nathan, out of the office. His eyes looked stunned and didn't seem to be seeing anything.

Nathan looked at Ledbetter and said, "What the hell!"

The colonel spread his hands and smiled smugly. "Honestly, I have no idea. You'll have to ask your friend yourself, Mister Stark."

"That's damn well what I figure on doing." Nathan went after Cullen.

He caught up to the older man on the porch of The House. Cullen had stopped at the top of the stairs and stared unseeingly out over the parade ground.

Nathan came up beside him. "Cullen, what's wrong?"

At first, Cullen didn't seem to hear him, but then

he frowned, gave a little shake of his head, and said, "What?"

"I asked you what's wrong. You read that letter and looked like somebody walloped you over the head with a singletree."

Slowly, Cullen lifted the crumpled piece of paper and stared at it as if surprised to find it in his hand. Then he smoothed it out, folded it, and tucked it away inside his buckskin shirt.

"My ma died."

"Your . . . I didn't know either of your folks were still alive. You never talked about 'em."

"My pa's still alive," Cullen said. "Near as old as Methuselah, I reckon, but he's still kickin'. The letter's from him, tellin' me about my ma's passin'. And askin' me to come home while there's still a chance for him to see me one more time."

Nathan knew that Cullen was from Texas, although he wasn't sure exactly where in that massive state. Cullen had always been tight-lipped about his family history. From a few things he had said, Nathan had gotten the idea that there might be one of those notorious Texas feuds in Cullen's background. They were friends, so he didn't pry. On the frontier, everything that had happened in a man's life before he rode over the most recent hill was nobody's damned business, if he wanted it that way.

"Are you going?" Nathan asked simply.

"I got to. When I left home, all those years ago, there were some hard feelin's. My pa and my brothers thought I ought to stay and help with the ranch, but I was too fiddle-footed. They told me to go and never come back." Cullen drew in a deep, ragged breath.

"It's hard when your own kin feels that way about you. Maybe that's why . . . you and me hit it off so good, Nate. You was like a brother to me. A better brother than any o' my own."

"I've thought the same thing about you more than once, Cul," Nathan said honestly.

"Yeah." Cullen smiled. "I guess a couple old codgers like us, we're just too rough for normal folks to put up with. Good thing we run into each other durin' the war. But now, with my pa tellin' me he's sorry and that he made a mistake and wants to see me again . . ."

"You've got to go," Nathan finished for his friend as Cullen's voice trailed off. "No two ways about it."

Cullen looked at him. "It'll take some time to ride all the way down to Texas. Maybe my pa will last until I get there."

"I hope so."

"Whether he does or not, I reckon it won't be long. Then I'll be headed back up this way." Cullen grunted. "Don't go and get yourself killed while I'm gone."

"I don't reckon there's much chance of that," Nathan replied with a shake of his head. "Unless all this blasted boredom does me in."

CHAPTER 14

Fort Randall seemed a lot emptier with Cullen gone. Nathan liked Noah Crimmens, but the two of them didn't really have enough in common to be considered close friends. Dietrich Bucher was around, but Nathan would have to get a lot more lonely than he was, before he sought out the big German's company. Doc Lightner kept up a professional reserve when he changed the dressings on Nathan's wounds, finally pronouncing them healed sufficiently that they didn't need to be bandaged anymore.

That left Delia Blaine, and Nathan still wasn't convinced that spending much time around her was a good idea. For one thing, he didn't even know if she would *want* him around. Their last parting hadn't been on the best of terms, after all.

So he was thankful when he stepped out of his cabin a few days after Cullen had ridden away, heading south, to see that a new air of activity gripped the post. Soldiers were moving here and there with purposeful strides. Several pack mules were lined up in front of the quartermaster's storehouses with hostlers holding them. Bags of supplies were brought from the building and attached to the pack saddles on the mules' backs.

A patrol was going out, Nathan realized, and from the amount of provisions they were taking with them, it looked like they were expecting to be gone from the fort for several days.

He walked toward headquarters. Colonel Ledbetter hadn't sent for him, but that didn't mean someone else would be going along to scout for the patrol. Maybe the colonel just hadn't gotten around to letting him know yet.

He wasn't going to sit around waiting and let that ass Bucher snatch up the job. Nathan felt like he would go mad if he had to spend much more time at the fort.

Cahill was at his desk in the outer office when Nathan strode in. "Captain Stark," the corporal said. "I was about to come looking for you, as soon as I finish writing up the official orders for Lieutenant Pryor."

"Pryor's taking out another patrol?" Nathan was a little surprised. Other junior officers were posted at Fort Randall, and Pryor had been in command of the previous patrol. But maybe Colonel Ledbetter trusted him more than the other shavetails.

"That's right, and you'll be assigned to it as one of the scouts."

"One of the scouts?" Nathan repeated as a frown creased his forehead. "You mean Bucher is going along, too?"

"No, there's a, ah, new man," Cahill answered. "The colonel is talking to him now."

Nathan jerked his head in a curt nod and stepped

over to the door of Ledbetter's office. If he was going to be working with someone else, he wanted to find out who it was. There was a pretty good chance he would know the man, even if they had never been assigned to the same patrol before. He would have preferred to have Cullen with him, of course, but at least he could hope that whoever the other fellow was, he would be better than Dietrich Bucher.

"Captain Stark—" Cahill began.

Nathan ignored Cahill, grasped the knob, and opened the door. He knew the corporal was going to tell him that he couldn't go in just yet. He took one step inside, then stopped short.

His hand dropped to the butt of the Colt on his hip and clawed it halfway out of the holster before Colonel Ledbetter yelled, "Stark! What the hell are you doing?"

The man standing in front of Ledbetter's desk had half-turned toward Nathan when the door opened. He wore a battered old brown hat with a high, creased crown that matched the vest he wore over a loose cotton shirt. An eagle feather was tucked into the hat's snakeskin band. A loincloth, fringed buckskin leggings, and high-topped black boots completed his outfit. Under the hat, his thick, raven-black hair was twisted into two braids that hung on the front of his shoulders. His coppery face was as sharp as an ax blade. He carried a Henry rifle in the crook of his left arm, and a revolver and a knife were stuck behind the sash tied around his lean waist.

The Indian seemed completely at ease, untroubled by the fact that Nathan had started to draw on him. But he had an air of alert competence to him as well, which seemed to say that he would have done more than just stand there if Nathan had continued his draw.

Nathan felt himself trembling inside as his gaze locked with the dark, deep-set eyes of the Indian. The urge to kill raged inside him. With an effort, he controlled it. He allowed the Colt to slide back down into its holster, but he didn't release his grip on the weapon.

Ledbetter was on his feet. "By God, Stark, you can't just burst into my office like this, and you certainly can't threaten this man."

"This ain't a man," Nathan said through clenched teeth. "It's a redskinned heathen. Not much better than an animal."

"You are the one called the Indian Killer," the man said unhesitatingly, in excellent English. "In other words, a madman."

Nathan's hand tightened on the walnut grips of his revolver. As it did, the Indian turned more toward him, which swung the Henry's barrel in his direction. The strong-muscled red hand slid up the stock toward the trigger.

"Both of you, at ease!" Ledbetter bellowed.

"We're not *in* the army, Colonel," Nathan said.

"We follow orders only so far," the Indian said.

"You're both insubordinate wretches! Cahill! Corporal Cahill!"

The aide nervously poked his head through the open door and said, "C-Colonel?"

"I want you to summon the sergeant of the guard. I intend to have these two men clapped in irons!" Ledbetter tapped a fingertip on top of his desk and glared at Nathan and the Indian. "Unless you'd both prefer to listen to what I have to say."

Nathan didn't take his eyes off the Indian. "I'm listening, Colonel, but I don't know what in blazes you can say to explain the way this red devil is standing in your office like he belongs here."

"He *does* belong here. His name is Moses Red Buffalo. He's one of the new Crow scouts who has signed up to help us deal with the Sioux."

Nathan had already seen enough to tentatively identify the stranger as a Crow. To most people, all Indians looked alike, and they couldn't tell one tribe from another. Nathan had spent years studying the savages, though—the more you knew about your enemy, the easier it was to kill him—so he'd learned the small but significant differences in the way the various tribes wore their hair and decorated their clothing set them apart.

"I haven't heard anything about using hostiles for scouts," he said.

"As I just told you, it's a new development. The Crow are traditional enemies of the Sioux. They would like to see the Sioux brought under control. What more natural way to accomplish that end than to work together with us? We have a common goal, you see."

"There's no way white men and redskins can work together," Nathan said. "You can't ever trust them. All they want to do is kill us. If the Crow say they're on our side, it's a trick. They'll lie and then betray us. Lead us into a damn ambush!"

Moses Red Buffalo kept his eyes locked on Nathan. "Red men have been lied to by whites much more often than the other way around. And white men and Indians have fought on the same side many times in your country's past." A smug smile tugged at his lips. "Perhaps you never went to school to learn these things, Stark."

"You sound like you went to school somewhere."

"Mission school. The missionary's wife taught us."

"I expect you raped and murdered her as soon as you got the chance." Nathan practically spat the accusation.

Red Buffalo moved half a step toward him. "She was one of the finest women I have ever known," he grated. "How dare you—"

Ledbetter slapped a palm on the desk. "Enough! I can still send for the sergeant of the guard."

"You don't need to do that, Colonel," Nathan said. "Just tell this heathen to go back where he came from. He can sit in the dirt with the dogs and the worms, where he belongs."

"This man is a murderer," Moses Red Buffalo said. "If there was any truth to the so-called justice you white men profess to believe in, he should be hanged."

"If I hang anybody, it'll be both of you!" Ledbetter threatened. "I need to know where Hanging Dog is, how strong his forces are, and what he plans to do with them. Lieutenant Pryor's job is to find out, and I expect the two of you to accompany him and do your utmost to see that he carries out his mission successfully!" Spittle flew in front of the colonel's face. "Do you understand?"

"If the job needs two scouts, send Bucher with me," Nathan said. Hard to believe that he would seek out Dietrich Bucher's company, but even a German was better than an Indian. Nathan sure wished that Cullen was still there. The two of them could have done a bang-up job on the assignment.

Ledbetter turned back to his desk and picked up a piece of paper that he waved toward Nathan. "Do you know what this document is, Stark?"

"You are assuming he can read, Colonel," Red Buffalo said.

"I can read just fine," Nathan snapped, "but not with you slinging it around like that, Colonel."

"This document is a dispatch from the War Department informing me of the new Crow scouts and instructing me to make full and proper use of them immediately. As it happens, Moses Red Buffalo is the first one to arrive, so it falls to him to carry out the first assignment. Mr. Bucher went with the last patrol, so it's your turn, Mr. Stark."

That comment momentarily distracted Nathan from his anger at Red Buffalo's very presence that close to him. "You've only given Lieutenant Pryor a short rest. Shouldn't someone else lead this patrol?"

"The lieutenant volunteered. Very insistently, I might add. I won't hold back a man who seeks to do his duty."

"All right. I don't know Pryor, but I haven't heard anything bad about him while I'm here. If he wants to go, I reckon that's his business." Nathan looked at Moses Red Buffalo. "But not with this . . . this . . ."

"I believe I can come up with more creative insults than you," the Crow said coolly, "if you wish to waste time trading them."

"Nobody's wasting any more time," Ledbetter said.

"I've made my decision, and it's final. You're both going."

Nathan knew the colonel's overbearing pride wasn't going to allow him to back down now that he had declared himself so plainly. Ledbetter would have both him and Red Buffalo thrown in the guardhouse if they continued to defy his will. He might even have them put in the same cell, just to aggravate them.

But there might be a way to bring the colonel around to his way of thinking. Nathan said, "Are you gonna let some paper pusher in Washington tell you what to do, Colonel? You're the one who's out here on the frontier, risking your life every day to pacify those savages, not some fella sitting at a desk in the War Department who's never been west of the Potomac!"

The veiled flattery—telling Ledbetter he was risking his life when so far he hadn't done any such thing, as far as Nathan knew—appeared for a second that it might work. Ledbetter lifted his head and jutted out his chin, looking for all the world like he was posing for a statue that would go on the town square back home, honoring the local hero.

Then reality set in, and Ledbetter said, "There's such a thing as the chain of command, Stark. Even a former Rebel like you ought to know that." He sneered. "I have no choice. My orders are clear. Both of you will accompany Lieutenant Pryor's patrol and assist him in locating the hostiles and obtaining the information required. That . . . is . . . all."

Nathan and Red Buffalo glared at the colonel, not at each other.

"Dismissed!" Ledbetter shouted.

At that moment, Nathan came mighty damned close to quitting. He wanted to tell Ledbetter what he could do with those orders from the War Department, then tell him to go to hell and stalk out of the office. But before he could do any of those things, he saw the self-satisfied smirk on the face of Moses Red Buffalo and realized that if he quit, it meant the Indian *won*. Red Buffalo would still go along on the patrol, and Dietrich Bucher would be forced to ride with him.

Bucher was an idiot. He wasn't nearly smart enough to catch on to the tricks that Red Buffalo would no doubt try to pull. He would go along without any objections while the Crow led the soldiers into a trap and would die along with the others when the heathens massacred them. Nathan didn't care all that much what happened to Bucher, but Lieutenant Pryor and the other men on the patrol didn't deserve that fate.

Nathan reached a decision. "All right," he said, tight-lipped. "I'll go."

The surprise on Moses Red Buffalo's face was almost worth putting up with the stinking savage.

Chapter 15

Lurking near the door so he could listen to what was going on in Ledbetter's office, Corporal Cahill scuttled back to his desk as Nathan and Red Buffalo emerged and headed for the outer door. Neither scout looked at the other or acknowledged his presence in any way. Each acted as if he were alone.

"Ah . . . Captain Stark?" the aide said.

Nathan stopped and wheeled toward the desk. "What?"

Cahill flinched from the curt tone, but he held out a piece of paper. "Would you mind giving this to Lieutenant Pryor?"

"His orders for the patrol?"

"That's right."

Nathan took the document. "All right." He started again to leave, then paused. "Corporal, how long has the colonel known about the"—he looked around and saw that Red Buffalo had gone on outside—"savages being forced on us?"

"You mean the Crow scouts?" Cahill swallowed. He glanced at the door to the colonel's office, which was closed. "The dispatch rider came in two days ago. Mr. Red Buffalo arrived late yesterday afternoon."

Nathan grunted. He wondered how he had missed seeing an Indian ride into the fort. Sitting around this place with nothing to do must have dulled his senses.

"It never occurred to Ledbetter to let the *real* scouts know what was going on?" As soon as the words were out of his mouth, Nathan realized what a ridiculous question it was. Ledbetter would never feel that he had to share anything with anybody unless it suited his own purposes. Nathan waved a hand. "Never mind. And don't call that heathen *mister*. He's a redskin, not a human being."

That was funny in a way. Most tribes' name for themselves translated as *the human beings.* They considered themselves the only true people, with everyone else being lesser somehow. The irony of what he had just said without thinking put a scowl on Nathan's face as he left the building.

That scowl deepened when he saw Moses Red Buffalo standing on the porch of The House, one shoulder leaning against a post holding up the roof.

The Crow said, "Perhaps I should deliver the orders to Lieutenant Pryor. An uneducated man such as yourself might forget what they are and use the paper to wipe when you visit the privy."

"Not that it's any of your damn business, redskin, but I was educated just fine. My pa was a schoolmaster."

Red Buffalo raised an eyebrow. "A surprise. I took you for a brute who could not read or write."

Nathan started past him to go down the steps. "Stay the hell out of my way," he said without looking over.

"The colonel wouldn't like it if I killed you, but push me too much and I'll do it anyway." He paused. "From here I could make it to Canada without any problem. It's a big country up there. Nobody would ever find me if I didn't want them to."

"Exactly the sort of threatening bluster I would expect from a man such as yourself."

Nathan blew out a disgusted breath, clattered down the steps, and started along the edge of the parade ground toward the area in front of the quartermaster's storehouse where the patrol was assembling. He didn't look around to see if Red Buffalo was following him.

Lieutenant Alfred Pryor was a medium-sized young man with curly dark hair. He had grown a mustache, probably in an attempt to make him look older, but if that was true, the effort wasn't too successful. He still looked like he was barely out of West Point. Nathan didn't know it for a fact, but he suspected Fort Randall was Pryor's first posting.

The lieutenant was inspecting the packs on the mules as if he knew what he was doing. Maybe he did.

Nathan waited until Pryor finished then extended the orders when the lieutenant turned toward him. "From Colonel Ledbetter, Lieutenant," he said coolly.

"Thank you, Captain Stark," Pryor said. "I'm told that you'll be accompanying us on this patrol."

"Yep."

Pryor looked past him. "As well as, ah . . ."

"Just call me Red Buffalo," the Crow said as he stepped up beside Nathan. "Christian name's Moses, but only my friends back at the mission ever use it."

Pryor's eyes widened in badly concealed surprise. "You're a Christian?"

"I am," Red Buffalo said simply.

Nathan wouldn't have believed he could hate Red Buffalo more than he already did, but hearing the man profess a belief in the Christian faith accomplished that very thing. Nathan's own faith had been gutted by the tragedy that had shaped his life. Still, he found it deeply offensive to hear such a claim from a redskin. Nor did he believe for a second in its sincerity. Deep down, all Indians were heathens. That was just a fact.

"Well, I see that you're going to be riding with us as well," Pryor said as he glanced over the official orders Corporal Cahill had written up. "I'll be very grateful for any assistance you and Captain Stark can provide." The lieutenant's jaw tightened. "I failed to locate the hostiles the last time. I will *not* fail this time."

Nathan understood now why Pryor had volunteered to lead this patrol. The young man's pride was at stake. Not many things were more important to an ambitious young officer than his pride. Nathan had ridden with many of them. He knew it was his job to temper that overarching self-importance with a healthy dose of reality now and then, just to keep them all from getting killed.

"What the devil is this?" a new voice demanded harshly from behind Nathan. He thought he recognized it but looked over his shoulder anyway and saw Sergeant Seamus McCall standing there with bulky fists planted on his hips and an angry glower on his flushed face.

"These are our scouts, Sergeant," Pryor said. "I believe you know Captain Stark, and this is Moses Red Buffalo."

"I know Stark, all right," McCall said. "And an Indian? Where the hell's Bucher?"

"Mr. Bucher isn't coming with us this time." Pryor's voice sharpened. "And watch your tone, Sergeant. I won't tolerate any insubordination."

"Sorry, sir," McCall muttered, obviously not meaning the apology. "I just ain't sure—for the good of the patrol, I mean—that we ought to be relyin' on these two . . . *scouts*." He made the last word drip with venom.

"We have our orders, Sergeant. Are the men ready to ride?"

"Yes, sir. Whenever you give the word."

Pryor looked at Nathan and Red Buffalo. "Gentlemen?"

Nathan said, "Give me ten minutes to saddle my horse."

"I will be ready, as well," Red Buffalo said.

"Very well. Ten minutes."

Nathan headed for the stables to get Buck. He knew Red Buffalo was going in that direction, too, but he didn't say anything. He was going to ignore the redskin for the entire duration of the patrol, but it wouldn't be easy.

He waved off the hostler who came toward him when he entered the stable, preferring to see to Buck himself. He went to the stall where the big, rangy buckskin was, unlatched the gate, and swung it open. Buck tossed his head in greeting.

"Yeah, I know," Nathan said. "You've been getting stale hanging around this blasted fort, too, just like me. Well, we're gonna be back out on the prairie soon, and I'll bet you get a chance to run some while we're gone."

Buck let out a little whicker of what Nathan took to be agreement.

He threw the saddle blanket over Buck's back and adjusted it precisely the way both of them liked it. He didn't know where Red Buffalo had gotten off to and didn't care. He heard some horses stomping around elsewhere in the cavernous barn and assumed it was because they smelled an Indian.

Nathan had just lifted his saddle into place when he heard a soft footstep nearby. He glanced around quickly, his muscles stiffening in alarm. It would be just like one of those damned red heathens to try to sneak up on him and knife him while he was busy with something else—

Delia Blaine stood there, one slender hand resting on the stall gate. "Nathan, I heard that you are going out on patrol with Lieutenant Pryor."

He jerked his head in a nod, glad to see her but at the same time wary after what had happened the last time they were together. "That's right. We're supposed to locate Hanging Dog and the rest of the Sioux."

She moved a little closer. "You've been avoiding me."

"Figured that was what you wanted." He looked away from her as he tightened the cinches on Buck's saddle. "We didn't exactly part as friends."

"Nonsense. Just because we disagreed doesn't mean we're not still friends. And speaking honestly, as your friend, I was hurt when you chose to stay away from me."

Nathan frowned. He bristled a little at the chiding

tone in her voice, but at the same time he felt an unexpected surge of relief at knowing she wasn't angry with him. "I didn't mean to hurt your feelings. Just didn't want to cause any more trouble."

"Why don't we just put that behind us?" Delia suggested. "You're leaving, and I . . . I wouldn't want any hard feelings between us . . ."

"In case I don't come back?"

"Don't say that!" she cried softly. "Of course you're coming back. You're Nathan Stark. You're . . . indestructible."

He finally turned to look at her. "I used to think the same thing about Stephen. Seemed to me like he'd always be around . . . with you."

"I felt the same way," she whispered. "But fate . . . fate doesn't always pay attention to our feelings, Nathan. It just goes ahead and does what it pleases, and we're left to pick up the pieces." A sad smile curved her lips. "You're one of the pieces left in my life. I don't want to lose you."

"Don't worry about that," he said gruffly. "If there's one thing I know how to do, it's take care of myself."

Without him really being aware of it, she had gotten close enough for him to smell the soft scent of her, even with the stronger smells of horseflesh, straw, manure, and piss that filled the air of any stable. Shafts of light slanted through gaps in the boards, struck reddish-gold glints in her hair, and caressed the soft curve of her cheek.

Nathan's heart slugged in his chest as he realized he wanted to lift a hand and stroke her cheek as well.

He drew in a breath and turned back to Buck. "I'll be fine. You look after yourself and your school."

"Nathan—"

"I need to go get my rifle and the rest of my gear." He picked up the horse's reins. "Come on, Buck." He led Buck out of the stall, forcing Delia to step aside.

She said to his back, "Good-bye, Nathan."

"So long."

He had just reached the stable's open double doors when Moses Red Buffalo led a high-stepping paint up alongside him and Buck.

The Crow scout said, "You really are a damned fool, Stark. That woman wanted you to kiss her."

Nathan's head jerked toward him. "You keep your filthy red tongue to yourself. You go near that woman, you even talk about that woman, and I'll kill you."

"You can try," Red Buffalo said coolly. "But don't worry. I have no interest in white women. Not everything you believe about my people is true, Stark."

"It's true that you bleed when I blow a hole in you or cut your throat. That's all that matters to me."

CHAPTER 16

The patrol rode out of Fort Randall a short time later, heading northwest along the Missouri River. On the other side of the broad, slow-moving stream, a range of hills rose. Nathan glanced toward them and wondered if hostile eyes were watching from those heights. Certainly, it was possible. A cold feeling in the pit of his belly told him it was even likely.

Hanging Dog and the Sioux probably wanted to know what the army was doing, just as much as Colonel Ledbetter desired information about the hostiles.

Nathan rode next to Lieutenant Pryor at the head of the patrol. Red Buffalo, on his paint pony, was off to one side about twenty yards. Sergeant McCall and forty soldiers rode behind. They were mounted infantry, not cavalry. If it came to a fight, they wouldn't do battle on horseback but would dismount and form up in a skirmish line with the horses behind them or arrange themselves in a square with the horses in the middle, depending on the circumstances.

Nathan had served with many such companies and

found that they varied widely in discipline and fighting ability, depending on their experience and the quality of their officers. These men didn't appear to be green recruits, at least for the most part, but he wouldn't know what they actually were made of until he saw how they handled themselves in a fight.

And there might not *be* a fight during this patrol, he mused. They might ride around for four or five days and never see a single Indian, the way it had been on Pryor's last patrol. The lieutenant took that as a personal failure, but he didn't realize that out there, you only saw redskins when they wanted you to see them.

"Which way did you go the last time you were out, Lieutenant?" Nathan asked.

"We rode due west," Pryor replied. "There were some Sioux villages in that direction several months ago, but they don't appear to be there any longer."

Nathan nodded slowly. "They move around some. There's a place a few miles upriver where we can ford and then strike north into the hills. Might be more likely to run into Hanging Dog's bunch up that way."

"You're the scout, so I'm certainly disposed to listen to your advice, Mr. Stark. I mean, Captain Stark."

"Either way," Nathan said with a shrug. "It doesn't really matter to me. The war was a hell of a long time ago."

"Yes, I heard a great deal about it from my father and uncles."

Nathan let a little grunt of laughter escape at that reminder of Pryor's youth.

The lieutenant heard it and flushed. "Perhaps you should consult with your fellow scout about our best course," he suggested.

"No," Nathan said, his voice flat and hard now. "I don't need any advice from the likes of him."

"Officially, the two of you have the same status, you know. You're both civilian employees of the army."

"You listen to whoever you want to, Lieutenant. Just remember that it's a redskin's nature to lie. And to kill."

"The War Department wouldn't have sent Mr. Red Buffalo to us unless the men there believed he could help us."

"One thing you might ought to learn about politicians and bureaucrats, Lieutenant . . . they have a lot of reasons for the things they do, but being helpful usually isn't one of 'em."

"That's bold talk, Captain."

"Just what I've seen with my own eyes," Nathan said.

They rode along in silence for several minutes then Nathan asked, "Where are you from, Lieutenant?"

"Ohio. And I believe you're from . . . Indian Territory?"

"Not exactly. Right over the line in Kansas. I've spent a lot of time there over the years, though."

"According to the stories I've heard, you've spent a lot of time just about everywhere west of the Mississippi."

Nathan shrugged. "A fella works for the army, he gets around. I never had much interest in staying in one place."

That wasn't strictly true. There had been a time in

his life when he would have been happy to stay in the same place . . . as long as Camilla and their children were there.

"There was a great difference of opinion in Kansas during the days before the war, wasn't there?"

Nathan gave an outright laugh. "If you're asking whether it's true that I fought for the Confederacy, Lieutenant, it is. Don't think too badly of my family, though. My older brother fought for the Yankees. That's the way it was in the border states. Some fellas went one way, and their fathers and brothers and sons went the other."

"It doesn't matter now. The Union was preserved, and we're all countrymen again."

"One way to look at it," Nathan said.

With that subject apparently exhausted, silence reigned again for a spell, until Pryor said quietly, "I heard that you had trouble with Sergeant McCall."

"He gave me this scar on my forehead, and a heap of bruises, to boot."

"I trust that that animosity won't affect the two of you being able to serve together on this patrol."

"I don't hold any grudges," Nathan lied. "I'm just here to do my job." He pointed toward the river. "And part of it is leading you to this ford, which I've done."

Nathan and Pryor reined in.

Red Buffalo turned his paint and loped over to them. "You do not intend to cross the river here, do you, Lieutenant?"

"That's what Captain Stark suggested."

Red Buffalo shook his head. "Bad mistake. The water is shallow, but the bottom is too muddy. In a few places, it's almost like quicksand. You'll have some horses bog down if you try it."

"I've forded here before," Nathan said. "It's been a while, but the river doesn't look like it's changed."

"That buckskin of yours is lighter than those army mounts. Probably more sure-footed, too."

"Buck's a damn fine horse."

"That's my point," Red Buffalo said. "It will be safer to cross the river at a spot I know farther upstream, Lieutenant."

Nathan's first instinct was to argue. His pride didn't want to let himself be corrected by a redskin. But then he thought about how he had considered Colonel Ledbetter's pride to be foolish and stubborn, and he didn't want to be like Ledbetter.

Besides, he considered himself a practical man. Red Buffalo had a point about the difference between Buck and the army horses, and the soldiers weren't necessarily the most skilled riders, either. "Maybe we ought to have a look at the place Red Buffalo is talking about, Lieutenant."

"Really?" Pryor responded, looking and sounding surprised.

Red Buffalo just narrowed his eyes, as if having Nathan agree with him made him suspicious.

"Well, it can't hurt anything . . . unless he's leading us into an ambush."

"If we are ambushed by the Sioux, they will be more eager to kill me than to kill you," Red Buffalo said. "You know that, Stark, whether you care to admit it or not."

Stark just shrugged. It was true that the Sioux and

the Crow were enemies of long standing. That didn't mean he was going to *trust* Red Buffalo or anything crazy like that.

"We'll take a look," Lieutenant Pryor decided. He raised a gauntleted hand and waved the troop forward.

Red Buffalo was right. The spot he'd picked out three miles upstream *was* better for fording. The river bottom was more solid and there wasn't as much risk of the horses getting stuck. Nathan knew that as soon as he rode Buck out into the muddy water. He hipped around in the saddle and nodded to Lieutenant Pryor.

"Sergeant, move the men across single file," the junior officer ordered McCall. "I want five men standing watch, rifles at the ready at all times while the others are crossing. Once half the men are on the other side, some of them can take over that duty."

"Aye, sir." McCall turned and barked commands at the soldiers.

Nathan had been about to suggest that very thing to Pryor, but the lieutenant had beaten him to it. Pryor was young, but he had the makings of a decent officer—if he lived long enough.

Water splashed up around Buck's legs as Nathan rode on across the broad river. When he reached the northern bank and turned around, he saw Moses Red Buffalo fording behind him. The Crow scout wore a satisfied smirk that made Nathan want to smash a fist into that red face.

Red Buffalo rode out onto the bank. "You never forded the Missouri here?"

"Not right here, no," Nathan answered tightly. "But I never had any problem getting from one side to the other when I wanted to."

"It is a good thing Colonel Ledbetter sent both of us, then."

"We'll see about that." It was a particularly weak response, and Nathan was annoyed that he had made it. He turned his horse away and looked up into the hills.

When Lieutenant Pryor joined them a few minutes later, Nathan said, "I reckon I need to ride on ahead now and have a look around. The terrain's more rugged on this side of the river. More places for hostiles to hide."

"I will go, too," Red Buffalo said.

"I didn't ask for company."

"We are both scouts. I know my duty."

Pryor held up a hand to stop the wrangling. "I don't want both of you gone at the same time. Mr. Red Buffalo, you stay here while Captain Stark reconnoiters."

"I'm just as good a scout as he is—" Red Buffalo began.

"I'm not doubting that," Pryor broke in. "Next time, you'll go ahead. This time, it's Captain Stark's job."

Nathan nodded and raised a hand to his hat brim to acknowledge the lieutenant's orders. It wasn't a military salute, but he wasn't in the army. He turned Buck and heeled the horse into motion. A grin stretched across his face, because the last thing he had seen as he turned away was Moses Red Buffalo scowling.

The cottonwoods along the river fell behind him. Several miles of rolling grassland lay between the Missouri and the hills. Nathan knew that out in the open like he was, anyone watching from higher ground would spot him easily, but he couldn't do a blasted thing about that. Once he got into the hills, he would have to rely on his eyes and ears and most important his instincts to warn him of any lurking danger.

Thoughts of Delia Blaine and the way she had come to the stable to say good-bye to him kept trying to crowd into his brain, now that he was away from the rest of the patrol. As much as it pained him to admit that the Crow could be right about anything, he knew Red Buffalo had pegged *that* correctly, too. Delia had wanted him to kiss her. She'd been waiting for him to put his hands on her shoulders and press his lips to hers . . .

A growl sounded deep in his throat. There was a time for pondering such things—maybe—but it sure as hell wasn't while he might be riding under the watchful, hostile eyes of a Sioux war party.

He shoved Delia right out of his head.

His keen vision constantly swept the countryside around him. The weather had been fairly dry for months, and it would be difficult for a large group of riders to move around much without raising some dust. He knew the soldiers' horses had kicked up plenty so far. The huge, arching vault of blue sky was clear around him, though. If Sioux were in those parts, it wasn't a big bunch of them.

Or if it *was* a big bunch, they weren't going anywhere.

He didn't see any smoke, either, or any other signs of a village. Was it possible that all the rumors about Hanging Dog were just that? Nothing but rumors? According to what Dietrich Bucher had told him back at Fort Randall, large groups of Sioux had been spotted by previous patrols for several months, but the hostiles hadn't attacked and in fact had disappeared whenever the soldiers tried to close with them. They were supposed to be on reservations and by being out on the plains and in the hills they were asking for trouble . . . but did Hanging Dog really want trouble? Or did he and his people just want to be left alone?

Nathan frowned disapprovingly at his own thoughts. That sounded almost like he was excusing the savages' being in violation of the treaties. Nothing could be further from the truth. The heathens deserved to be pushed onto reservations and kept there where they couldn't hurt innocent people. If they didn't want to go, then whatever happened was on their own heads. He was just annoyed with Red Buffalo and tired of the inaction that had laid heavily on him for weeks. He needed something to happen.

Let the Sioux try to jump him. He would match Buck's speed against their ponies any day. They could chase him right back to the river . . . where the soldiers' rifles would be waiting to cut down the red savages.

By the time he reached the base of the hills, it was becoming obvious that he was the only human for miles. He saw a herd of elk grazing peacefully. They bolted when they smelled him coming. An eagle wheeled gracefully through the sky. Nathan reined in when he was halfway up the first hill, turned in the saddle, and looked northwest along the river. A dark smudge several miles away would be a small herd of buffalo, come to drink. Peaceful, yeah, and beautiful.

Nathan grimaced and heeled Buck into motion again. They rode the rest of the way to the top of the hill. He reined in and swung down from the saddle before he reached the crest, then led the buckskin along the slope until he found a place where they could slip over without being skylined too much. Something stirred inside him, an indefinable sense that some men had to start with or developed if they lived very long out on the frontier. Earlier, he had been absolutely certain that he was alone.

Suddenly, he was equally sure that he wasn't.

The far side of the hill dipped down, then rose again. Brush choked the little valley between the hills. Somebody could be hidden down there, watching him. When he mounted up again, he pulled the Winchester '73 from its scabbard, levered a round into the chamber, and held it across the saddle in front of him as he rode slowly down the hill.

Since buying the rifle at Statler's Mill, he had tried it out several times to familiarize himself with it. The action was smooth as it ought to be and had been used enough to be broken in but no more than that. Nathan had adjusted the sights until it fired true each and every time. He trusted the weapon as much as he could, considering that he had never fired it in anger.

Until that happened, he could never be completely confident in the Winchester.

Maybe today . . .

He reached the brush at the bottom of the slope

and reined in. Still nothing to go on except his instincts, but he cocked his head slightly to the side as he listened. He heard water flowing somewhere nearby—a little creek somewhere in the thicket.

Something made a small splash. A horse's hoof? Had somebody stopped to let his mount drink, maybe wet his whistle himself?

Nathan slid his feet out of the stirrups, swung his right leg over Buck's back, and dropped lightly to the ground, making only the faintest of sounds. He gripped the rifle in both hands. Buck wouldn't go anywhere with his reins hanging loose, and Nathan knew it. He crouched forward, moving slowly and cautiously as he eased the branches aside to penetrate deeper into the brush.

Some men would get nervous in a situation like that, would rush and make too much racket and announce their presence. Not Nathan Stark. He had been in such circumstances many times and was cool-nerved.

Minutes ticked by before he reached the tiny creek winding through the hills. He dropped to one knee, leaned forward, and parted the brush to look along the narrow stream to a clearing on the other side where an Indian stood with a brown pony while the horse drank. The redskin was young but still a warrior grown. He was a Sioux. His face was not painted for war, but as he rested his left hand on the pony's shoulder, his right hand held a Winchester.

Nathan lifted his own repeater and drew a bead. There might be a hundred of this warrior's friends just over the next hill. Hell, there might be five hundred of the bastards. Nathan didn't know, and at the moment, he didn't care. He settled his sights on the young Sioux's chest.

Before he could pull the trigger, he heard a faint *snap!* somewhere behind him, and the next instant a gun blasted.

CHAPTER 17

With blinding speed, Nathan reacted to the almost inaudible sound of a twig breaking. He twisted to his left and brought the Winchester around. At the same time he heard the shot, he felt the hot breath of a slug pass close to his cheek. The bullet would have gone through his head if he hadn't moved so fast.

He returned the fire, aiming at the sound of the first shot. He cranked off three rounds as fast as he could work the rifle's lever, then went to ground, bellying down in the brush. More shots roared. Bullets whipped through the brush a couple feet above his head. He didn't move.

Acutely aware that he had an enemy at his back in the person of the young Sioux warrior watering his pony at the creek, Nathan was caught between two forces and didn't like the feeling.

He heard a swift rataplan of hoofbeats from the other side of the stream. Sounded like the redskin was lighting a shuck. The shooting must have spooked him. But that left the bushwhacker on Nathan's side of the creek.

More hoofbeats drifted to his ears. The bushwhacker was leaving, too. Maybe it was a trick to draw him out into the open. He stayed where he was for long minutes before moving. When he heard birds flitting around again and small animals moving in the brush, he knew he was alone.

He stood up and looked across the creek. The Indian was gone, all right, and other than a few unshod hoofprints on the bank, there was no sign he had ever been there.

It was a different story back up the hill. Nathan looked around until he found the spot where the bushwhacker had knelt to take aim at him. He rooted around in the brush and came up with three empty cartridges. The man who'd tried to kill him hadn't taken the time to collect his brass.

.44-40, Nathan noted as he studied the spent cartridges. Probably from a Winchester much like his own . . . and the one carried by the Sioux on the other side of the creek. He wondered briefly where the redskin had gotten that rifle. From a dead white man, almost surely.

He walked back to where he had left Buck. The horse was out of the line of fire, so he hadn't been harmed. Nathan swung up into the saddle, rode down the hill, and splashed across the creek. No doubt Lieutenant Pryor and the rest of the patrol had heard those gunshots and were wondering what had happened to him, but he still wanted to take a better look around before he returned.

He had proof that Sioux were in the area, although that warrior could have been a lone hunter. The only way to be sure was to follow him and see if he had hurried back to rejoin a larger party. Nathan's experienced eyes picked up the trail with ease. To a man such as him, a broken branch, an overturned rock, a bit of crushed grass, were just as good as bold markings on a map.

He tracked the Sioux for more than a mile, up and down hills, until he came to a place where a lot more unshod horses had passed recently. Nathan reined in and studied the welter of tracks. They led toward a rocky ridge about a mile away. He studied it with narrowed eyes for a long moment, then clicked his tongue at Buck and pulled the horse around.

The Sioux had headed for what was probably more rugged country on the far side of that ridge. The patrol had a good place to start now. One thing puzzled Nathan, though, as he rode back toward the river.

Only one set of hoofprints had joined the larger party, so the man who had taken that shot at him from behind hadn't circled around and rendezvoused with the redskin Nathan had seen.

That left him wondering just who the hell the bushwhacker could have been.

Lieutenant Pryor rode out to meet Nathan as he approached the patrol waiting beside the Missouri River.

"Thank God!" Pryor said as he reined in. "We heard shooting and were worried that you might have been killed."

Nathan cast a skeptical glance toward Moses Red

Buffalo, who was pointedly not looking his way. "I'd bet a new hat not all of you were worried. I've got a hunch that redskin would've been downright pleased to find my body and leave it for the buzzards to feast on."

"Mr. Red Buffalo is a fellow member of this patrol," Pryor said stiffly. "We should all be loyal to each other."

Nathan just grunted at that.

"What did you find?" the lieutenant went on. "What was the shooting about?"

"Somebody tried to part my hair with a .44-40 slug." Nathan reached into his shirt pocket and took out one of the empty cartridges he'd found, then handed it to Pryor. "I don't suppose Red Buffalo happened to wander off for a spell while I was gone, did he?"

Pryor frowned at the cartridge and shook his head. "He was here the entire time. We all were. No one left."

"You know that for a fact?"

"I saw it with my own eyes." Pryor handed the cartridge back to Nathan. "What else did you find?"

"The Sioux are up there, all right. I spotted one of them watering his pony just before I was ambushed." Nathan didn't mention that he'd been about to shoot the Indian just before that dangerous interruption occurred. "He took off when the shooting started. Once I was sure the bushwhacker was gone, I followed the redskin and found where he joined up with a bigger bunch on unshod ponies. They headed north."

"We have to follow them," Pryor said with excitement creeping into his voice. "They could lead us right to the main body of Hanging Dog's forces. Once we locate them, I'll send a rider back to the fort with word for Colonel Ledbetter to bring the entire company. The hostiles will be forced to either capitulate or be wiped out."

Nathan thought the lieutenant was getting a little ahead of himself. "Let's just see what we find."

"Of course." Pryor turned his horse and shouted to McCall, "Sergeant, get the men mounted and ready to ride!"

Nathan stayed where he was while Pryor hurried back to supervise the preparations. He dismounted to give Buck a chance to rest for a few minutes.

Red Buffalo rode over.

Before the Crow scout could say anything, Nathan asked him, "Sorry to see that I came back alive?"

"I am not surprised. You white men have a saying about how the good die young, and since that description does not fit you . . . I am curious what all the shooting was about, though."

Grudgingly, Nathan repeated the story he had told Lieutenant Pryor.

Red Buffalo frowned. "I know the ridge you speak of. The land beyond it is rough and broken, and then it rises to a mesa. If Hanging Dog is going up there, it will be difficult to reach him without losing many men."

Nathan rubbed his chin, caught up in thinking about the situation and forgetting for the moment that he was discussing it with a hated redskin. "Is there any way down from up there?"

"Not a good one. The mesa is surrounded on three sides by a deep gorge. A man might be able to climb down into it and back out again, but not a horse."

"I can't see Hanging Dog abandoning his ponies. I don't believe he would take women and children up there, either. He'd be moving his whole band into a trap if he did that."

Red Buffalo nodded. "But why would he and his warriors retreat there?"

"Maybe he's trying to lead *us* into a trap," Nathan said.

"That makes no sense," Red Buffalo replied, shaking his head. "We would have him penned there. We could lay siege to his forces."

"Yeah, that's what it looks like," Nathan admitted. "But who can ever tell how a savage's brain is going to work?"

Red Buffalo glared and turned his horse away. Nathan didn't try to stop him as he rode away. He had tolerated the redskin's presence for as long as he could manage.

The questions they had raised in their conversation were interesting ones, though, and he continued mulling them over as the patrol got ready to move again.

Nathan led the way, while Red Buffalo dropped back to make sure no enemies were coming up behind them. Even Lieutenant Pryor's inexperienced eyes were able to see the tracks left by the large party of Sioux when Nathan pointed them out. Nathan could tell that the young officer's excitement was growing. Pryor's orders were only to locate the hostiles, not to engage them, but Nathan was starting to wonder if Pryor would be able to hold himself back when the time came. Visions of battlefield glory were dancing in the youngster's head.

They hadn't reached the ridge by nightfall. With obvious reluctance, Pryor called a halt and ordered his men to make camp. "Should it be a cold camp?" he asked Nathan. "Can we risk building fires?"

A humorless laugh came from Nathan. "I promise you, Hanging Dog knows where we are. You won't be giving away a thing by building fires, and the men might as well have hot food and coffee. I know I could sure as hell use some. Probably be a good idea to double the guard tonight, though."

Pryor nodded. "I'll do that. Definitely. Will we catch up to them tomorrow?"

"Depends more on what *they* want than anything we do," Nathan said with a shrug. "Anyway, Lieutenant, I thought you weren't looking for a fight. Didn't you say something about sending for the colonel and the rest of the men back at the fort?"

"Well, yes, of course. I'll follow my orders. But I'm allowed *some* discretion, you know, in the event that the savages initiate hostilities."

Clearly, that was exactly what the lieutenant was hoping for.

Nathan saw to Buck's needs, then enjoyed a supper of beans, bacon, biscuits, and coffee after making do with jerky for the midday meal. The patrol had made camp just outside some trees at the edge of a meadow. Nathan sat on a log, nursing a second cup of coffee that he had sweetened with a slug of bourbon from a flask he had taken out of his saddlebags. He had never been a heavy drinker, but a dram like that was a comfort after a long day in the saddle.

He frowned as Red Buffalo came over and sat down on the same log, several feet away. "I don't recall saying I wanted any company," he told the Crow scout.

"I don't recall asking," Red Buffalo replied. He had a cup of coffee in his hand, too.

"I'd offer you something to give that coffee a mite more punch, but I know how you redskins are about firewater. Just can't handle it, probably because of your weak mind and moral fiber."

Red Buffalo sipped from his cup. "I would say it's more a case of the white man's puny brain not being able to function without the crutch of liquor."

"You talk mighty fancy for a savage."

"And you talk like an uneducated lout . . . which you claim not to be."

Nathan sighed. "What the hell do you want, Red Buffalo?"

Without looking at Nathan, Red Buffalo drank some more coffee. "The lieutenant is young."

"Is that supposed to be some sort of revelation?"

"Young . . . and eager."

"You think he's going to get us into trouble."

"I think it is possible. I do not know Hanging Dog, but he would not have risen to a position of power among the Sioux unless he was a cunning warrior. Based on what you said about your encounter, he did not show himself to us deliberately, but by now he knows we are following him and is taking no pains to conceal his trail."

"Which means he's trying to take advantage of the situation."

Red Buffalo nodded slowly. "When we get closer, we will have to make sure the lieutenant listens and heeds our counsel, otherwise we may be doing exactly what Hanging Dog wants us to do."

"Pryor gives the orders," Nathan said. "Once he

makes up his mind, there's not much we can do about it."

"We can do our best to convince him to do what is wise."

"Sure. That's our job." Nathan swirled the mixture of coffee and bourbon that was left in his cup. After they had traded insults to begin the conversation, he and Red Buffalo had been talking like any two scouts would in this situation. Nathan could imagine him and Cullen saying pretty much the same things, or even him and Dietrich Bucher. But Red Buffalo wasn't a white scout. He was an Indian. And it was damned odd—not to mention annoying—that Nathan seemed to have forgotten about that for a moment.

Won't forget again, he told himself.

He downed the rest of the spiked coffee and stood up. "You trust these soldiers to keep a good enough watch?"

"Do you?"

"Not really. I'll take the first half of the night." He didn't ask Red Buffalo which shift he would prefer. Nathan didn't give a damn what the Crow wanted.

Red Buffalo just grunted assent. Nathan went and checked on Buck one more time, then took his rifle and faded back into the shadows under the trees, ready to spend the next few hours silent, motionless, and with every sense alert for any indication of danger.

CHAPTER 18

Nothing happened during the night, but somehow that lack of trouble didn't ease Nathan's mind. A sense of unease still gnawed at his guts the next morning, and a breakfast of flapjacks and bacon washed down with more strong coffee didn't make it go away.

By sun-up, the patrol was moving on toward the ridge. The trail left by the Sioux was still plain to see. In fact, as the morning went on the tracks became even fresher, telling Nathan that Hanging Dog and his warriors were taking their time and not really trying to get away from the soldiers.

"Lieutenant, this doesn't look good," he said. "Those redskins *want* us to catch them."

"That seems unlikely to me, Captain. How big would you say their force is?"

"Judging by the number of ponies . . . fifty men. You're outnumbered."

"Barely. And we're well-armed, with a more than adequate supply of ammunition. Can the Sioux say that?"

"The one I saw yesterday was carrying a Winchester

every bit as good as this one of mine," Nathan pointed out. "And a fifteen-shot repeater beats those single-shot trapdoor Springfields of yours any day of the week."

Pryor shook his head. "You don't know how many of the hostiles are armed with such weapons. Why, most of them are probably carrying bows and arrows! Perhaps a few old trade muskets. You're overestimating their capabilities, Captain."

And the lieutenant was allowing his ambition and pride to blind him to the possibilities, Nathan thought.

Red Buffalo nudged his pony up on Pryor's other side. "Stark is right. And even though we haven't been out here for long, you should already know how much it pains me to say that, Lieutenant. Hanging Dog wants us to follow him. Actually, he wants us to catch up to him. There has to be a good reason for that. Good for *him*, that is. Not us."

"I appreciate your caution, gentlemen. I really do. But when it comes to tactics and strategy, the final decision is mine, and I assure you, I'm well-equipped to make it."

"High in your class at West Point, eh?" Nathan said. He knew it was a mistake as soon as the words came out.

Judging by Red Buffalo's glare, the Crow scout did, too.

"That will be enough, sir," Pryor snapped. "You may be a civilian, but I won't stand for such displays of insubordination in the field."

"Sorry," Nathan muttered through clenched teeth.

"I'm gonna have a look up ahead." He dug his heels into Buck's flanks.

"I will go, too," Red Buffalo declared. He urged his pony to a faster pace before Lieutenant Pryor could give him any orders to the contrary.

Red Buffalo caught up with Nathan and asked from the corner of his mouth, "Are you trying to get us killed, Stark? That boy will never listen to reason now."

"He wouldn't have, anyway. He wants a fight, and he's bound and determined to get one. Ledbetter probably dressed him down when he didn't find anything on his last patrol, so he's going to come back from this one with some Sioux scalps . . . or die trying."

"I'm not worried about him dying," Red Buffalo said. "It's my own hide I'm worried about."

"Maybe he's right. Maybe Hanging Dog's warriors have only a few of those Winchesters and we'll have them outgunned. The numbers are close enough that superior firepower would swing the advantage our way."

"How will we know until it's too late to do anything about it?"

A cold grin stretched across Nathan's face. "That's the problem, all right."

The mesa rose ahead of them. Its southern face was a long slope that wasn't too steep for horses to climb. Sure-footed Indian ponies wouldn't have any trouble with it, Nathan thought.

Then the ground leveled off for a half-mile or so before dropping off into the gorge that surrounded it on north, east, and west. It was a trap for any mounted force that ventured onto it, every bit as much as a box canyon would be.

Maybe Lieutenant Pryor wasn't the only commander in the field with a thirst for glory, Nathan reflected. Once the patrol reached the bottom of the slope leading up to the mesa, Hanging Dog might intend to lead his warriors back down in a last-ditch charge. More than likely, the result would be to get himself and all his followers killed . . . but the rest of the Sioux would sing songs about his courage from then on.

Nathan's jaw tightened. No. That was the sort of courageous but crazy thing a white man would do. Redskins were more practical than that. They fought for glory and the excitement of battle, sure, but more than anything else, they fought to win. They wouldn't throw their lives away in some grand but ultimately meaningless gesture.

"I've heard stories about you, you know," Red Buffalo said after they had ridden along for a few minutes in silence.

"Yeah, I know. They call me the Indian Killer. I'm not particularly proud of it, but I've never denied it."

Red Buffalo shook his head. "No. I mean about what started you on that path in the beginning. About what happened to your family when the Pawnee raided the town where you lived."

Nathan's backbone went stiff as an iron ramrod. "You've got no call to talk about that. It was a long time ago. Years."

And yet there were moments when it seemed like

only yesterday, when the pain was as fresh and strong as if the wounds had just been inflicted . . .

"When I was a young man, the Blackfeet came to steal our ponies and kill our warriors and capture our women and children to make slaves out of them."

"I didn't ask you to tell me any of this."

As if he hadn't heard what Nathan said, Red Buffalo went on. "I was to be married soon to a young maiden called Bright Meadow. When the Blackfeet attacked our village, she was killed in the fighting. So were my mother and my father and my brother. I was left alone."

"If you're waiting for me to tell you how sorry I am, you're gonna have a long wait. You savages kill each other all the time." Nathan warmed to the subject. "Those stuffed-shirt idiots back east like to talk about the poor Indians and how they all get along with each other. You and I both know that's a lie. All you different bunches have been killing each other ever since you got here. You're all bloodthirsty heathens."

Red Buffalo surprised him by saying, "You're absolutely right." The Crow paused. "And the white men have been killing each other for centuries because one group worships a god, or group of gods, different from another group. You cannot deny that, Stark. Hatred and killing are human conditions. They do not belong to anyone based on the color of one's skin."

"The hell with this," Nathan said. "I'm not gonna waste my breath arguing with a savage." He reined in. They had reached the base of the slope leading up to the mesa. The tracks of Hanging Dog's ponies were still visible.

"Well, hell. They went up there, all right. No doubt about it. You can tell by the depth of those prints that the ponies had riders. Hanging Dog's not trying to fool us."

"You should go back and let the lieutenant know," Red Buffalo suggested.

Nathan squinted at him. "And let you ride up and parley with the Sioux? Strike some deal with Hanging Dog to double-cross us?"

"You know better," Red Buffalo said sharply. "If I rode up there, the Sioux would take great delight in torturing me. I would be staked out, my eyelids cut off, my genitals mutilated, and my guts pulled out and piled on my chest."

"Quit painting pretty pictures and go report to the lieutenant."

Red Buffalo made a sound of pure disgust, yanked his pony around, and galloped away, back toward the patrol.

Several clumps of boulders on the slope led up to the mesa, and Nathan kept a close eye on them while he waited for Red Buffalo to return with the soldiers. He wouldn't put it past the Sioux for a few to crawl down and take some potshots at him. The range was fairly long, but a lucky shot could kill a man just as dead as a well-aimed one.

Nothing happened, though. After a while, he heard hoofbeats in the distance and saw dust rising. A few more minutes passed, and then the patrol came into view. The men were running the horses hard, revealing the lieutenant's eagerness to close with the enemy. Nathan wondered if Pryor had sent a rider back to the fort to carry the news to Colonel Ledbetter, like he was supposed to.

With Red Buffalo trailing a short distance behind him, the lieutenant galloped up and reined in. "Are they really up there, Captain?"

"Unless their horses sprouted wings and flew off, they are," Nathan replied. He gestured toward the gorges several hundred yards away that cut off the approach to the mesa. "With that surrounding them, there's nowhere for them to go."

"Excellent!" Pryor clenched a gauntleted hand into a fist. "We'll keep them penned up there until the colonel arrives. Then Hanging Dog will have no choice but to surrender and return to the reservation—or be wiped out!"

Red Buffalo said, "We don't know for sure that Hanging Dog is with this bunch. It could be some other war chief leading them."

"Either way, they're hostiles, and what we do here today will send a message to all the other savages that the United States Army is not to be trifled with."

Yeah, that's what the Sioux are thinking about, Nathan reflected wryly. *Trifling with the United States Army.*

"How quickly do you think the colonel will arrive?" Pryor went on.

Nathan said, "Well, if the messenger you sent kills his horse getting back and Ledbetter is ready to move out right away, he might get here by nightfall . . .

but it's a lot more likely it'll be the middle of the day tomorrow before they show up."

"We can keep the Indians pinned down for that long, can't we? They can't possibly get out past us—"

The sharp crack of a rifle shot interrupted the lieutenant.

Nathan heard a bullet whine overhead, and a split second later one of the soldiers cried out. Nathan jerked his head around and saw a man toppling off his horse as blood spurted from a neck wound. Several soldiers near him shouted in surprise and anger.

More shots rang out. Bullets whipped around the patrol. Nathan glanced toward the rocks on the slope and saw gray powder smoke hanging over some of them. Just as he had thought might happen, the Sioux had crawled down there to ambush the soldiers.

What it was going to gain them was beyond him, though. For a second it had appeared that the soldiers' discipline would break and they would scatter across the prairie in an attempt to get away from the attack. But then Lieutenant Pryor and Sergeant McCall began bawling orders. Months of training stiffened the soldiers' spines. Horse holders fell back with the animals while other men formed ranks and began returning the fire on Pryor's command.

Nathan and Red Buffalo dashed on horseback to one side. While Buck was still moving, Nathan swung down from the saddle and dragged his rifle from the scabbard. He threw himself to the ground behind a little hummock of dirt that would give him some cover.

To his disgust, Red Buffalo landed right beside him.

"Damn it," Nathan rasped as he levered the Winchester, "you keep showing up when I don't want company!"

"I'm not pleased with this development, either," Red Buffalo replied. He ducked his head as a bullet struck just in front of the hummock and kicked dirt over both of them. "But this was the closest cover!"

Nathan raised himself on his elbows, thrust the rifle over the hummock, and squeezed off a shot at one of the clusters of boulders. He couldn't see any of the hidden Sioux, but he aimed so the bullet would bounce around in the rocks and maybe give the red bastards something to think about, anyway.

Beside him, Red Buffalo's rifle spat flame and lead. "See?" the Crow scout said as he worked the weapon's lever. "The Sioux are not my friends!"

"I reckon not," Nathan admitted. He fired again. "What the hell are they doing? This ambush doesn't gain them a damned thing!"

"They killed at least one soldier."

"That's not worth throwing all their lives away."

The members of the patrol had settled down and were concentrating a heavy fire on the slope. The single-shot Springfields couldn't fire as fast as Winchesters, but with different groups of soldiers taking turns while others reloaded, they were able to keep up an almost constant bombardment.

Nathan and Red Buffalo fired several more rounds toward the rocks, then Red Buffalo pushed himself a little higher as he exclaimed, "They're running!"

It was true. The Sioux ambushers had abandoned their positions and were dashing back up the slope toward the top of the mesa. Since they were already at the outer edges of accurate rifle range, most of the bullets fired by the soldiers fell short, but one of the Indians suddenly arched his back as a .45-70 round from a government-issue trapdoor Springfield smashed into it. The warrior staggered on several more steps before collapsing. Cheers went up from the soldiers at the sight.

"We've got them on the run!" Lieutenant Pryor shouted. "Advance! Advance! Close with the enemy!"

"No!" Nathan and Red Buffalo shouted at the same time. Both scouts knew the lieutenant was making a bad mistake by committing his forces to a charge.

In the tumult of battle, though, Pryor either didn't hear them or ignored the warning. He led the advance himself as the soldiers swarmed up the slope on foot, still firing sporadically after the fleeing Sioux. A handful of men were left behind to hold the horses.

Those were the first ones slaughtered as more Sioux warriors came at them from both flanks. Nathan was already swinging the barrel of his Winchester to the left as he realized what Hanging Dog's plan had been all along. The Sioux war chief had lured the soldiers, just as Nathan thought he was doing, then left a handful of men in the rocks to keep the patrol busy and goad them into charging, while the rest of the war party left their horses on top of the mesa, climbed down into the gorge on both sides, and circled around to attack from the flanks and the rear.

At the same time, the warriors who had been hidden in the rocks stopped their retreat, turned around, and went on the attack again, firing into the suddenly confused mass of soldiers as they realized they were under fire from all sides. Judging by the rate the Sioux were spraying bullets down the slope, they were all armed with repeating Winchesters, just as Nathan had worried about.

With slugs whining around their heads, the members of the patrol were the ones who were neatly trapped—not the Sioux.

CHAPTER 19

Nathan and Red Buffalo surged to their feet and fired at the closest group of Sioux warriors charging toward them.

As he levered the Winchester, Nathan shouted, "Lieutenant! Lieutenant Pryor!" He had to get the officer's attention. The surviving members of the patrol were out in the open, partway up the slope, and if they stayed there they would be massacred.

The rocks where the Sioux sharpshooters had been hidden a short time earlier were the closest cover. The soldiers had to reach them or die.

Firing on the run, the two scouts headed up the slope. Nathan felt a bullet pluck at his shirt but ignored it. He had been in many such fights, so he knew to zigzag and make himself a more difficult target. He also knew that a lot of what happened was just the luck of the draw. If there was a bullet with his name on it today, there probably wasn't a whole hell of a lot he could do about it.

He called out, "Lieutenant!"

The shout caught Pryor's attention, and he looked

around, wide-eyed with fear, as he tried to reload the revolver he had emptied at the Sioux. He was on his feet, but the soldiers around him knelt as they fought.

Nathan waved at Pryor and yelled, "Go! Go! Head for the rocks!"

Pryor's eyes got even bigger, but he turned his head and shouted at McCall, "Sergeant! Advance to the rocks! Everyone! Advance!"

The soldiers leaped to their feet and got moving again. Nathan and Red Buffalo carried on a rear-guard action, spraying lead into the Sioux and slowing down their assault. If the two scouts had been a few seconds slower in their realization of what was going on, the patrol would have been surrounded and wiped out. At least they had a fighting chance—even if it wasn't much of one.

Red Buffalo took Nathan by surprise, grabbing his arm and jerking him off his feet. Nathan's first thought was that Red Buffalo was sacrificing him to give himself a better chance of reaching safety, but then from the corner of his eye he spotted a Sioux warrior lunging toward them from the side. Red Buffalo jerked the pistol from the sash tied around his waist and fired. The .44 slug knocked the screaming Sioux off his feet and sent him rolling down the slope.

"Come on!" Red Buffalo snapped. "Can't sit here all day, white man." He jammed the gun back behind the sash and extended that hand to Nathan.

Normally, Nathan would have spat on a redskin's outstretched hand rather than take it, but with half a dozen kill-crazy Sioux no more than twenty yards away, he didn't hesitate. He grabbed Red Buffalo's hand and let the Crow scout help him to his feet. As he came upright, Nathan saw one of the warriors drawing a bead on Red Buffalo's back and fired the Winchester one-handed at the man.

The recoil almost ripped the rifle out of Nathan's grasp. The hastily fired shot missed, but it came close enough to throw off the Sioux's aim. Red Buffalo ducked a little as the bullet passed close by his head then they started running for the rocks again.

The first of the soldiers had reached the boulders and thrown themselves down behind the protection. Shots began to blast from them, aimed upslope and down.

As Nathan felt the wind-rip of a bullet passing close to his ear, he exclaimed, "Damn bluebellies better watch where they're shooting!"

"You don't get along with anybody, do you?" Red Buffalo asked, puffing a little from the exertion of running uphill.

Nathan ignored the question and concentrated on lunging toward the rocks. Close enough, he leaped, rolled over the top of a boulder that stood about four feet high, and fell to the ground behind it. Red Buffalo sprawled behind another rock a few feet away.

Slugs spanged wildly off the boulders. Nathan kept his head down for a moment while he caught his breath, then raised it to look around. A dozen soldiers had sought shelter in that particular cluster of rocks, including Lieutenant Pryor and Sergeant McCall. The other survivors from the patrol had hunkered down behind boulders scattered across the slope.

They wouldn't make it, Nathan thought bleakly. Their cover wasn't good enough. They would be picked off one by one. He and the others nearby had a better chance, since there were enough boulders to provide at least some cover from all directions.

But more than likely, ricochets would kill all of them, too. It just might take a little longer. Or the Sioux would get tired of waiting and would overrun the position with their superior numbers.

Red Buffalo lay on his side as he thumbed fresh cartridges through the loading gate of his rifle. "We should have figured out sooner what Hanging Dog was up to. I knew there had to be a reason he was leading us on like that."

"You think it would have done any good if we had?" Nathan asked. "Once we were on their trail, the lieutenant wasn't going to turn back or even wait."

"You're probably right."

"Do you know if he actually sent a rider back to the fort with the news?"

"He did," Red Buffalo said. "I saw the man ride off. The lieutenant ordered him to get to the fort as quickly as he could." A grim smile curved the scout's lips. "Of course, he might have run into more of the Sioux along the way."

"We'd better hope not. Him getting through is the only chance we've got."

Red Buffalo frowned. "Do you actually believe Colonel Ledbetter can get here with reinforcements in time to help us?"

"I don't know. But if he doesn't, we're dead men, no doubt about that." Nathan had reloaded, too. He came up sharply on his knees, thrust the Winchester over the top of the rock, and sent three swift shots at the Sioux, all of whom had gone to ground.

Return fire made him duck. His eyes stung and his

nose and throat burned from the clouds of powder smoke hanging over the rocks.

And it was going to get worse before it got better. A hell of a lot worse.

Heat and the lack of water added to their problems. The canteens were still on the patrol's horses, all of which were either scattered or had been captured by the Sioux. The sun beat down fiercely on the slope during the afternoon, causing the temperature to climb. Skin blistered and sweat dried as soon as it sprang out. For relief, men panted like dogs.

Since the siege began, Nathan had killed one of the Sioux that he knew of, with another couple wounded although he hadn't been able to tell how badly. To pass the time, he called to Moses Red Buffalo, "What's your score over there, redskin?"

"Score?" Red Buffalo repeated. "This is not a game of dice, white man."

"Sure it is. The stakes are life and death, that's all."

Red Buffalo snorted. "I have heard that you whites keep count of such things. Have you carved a notch in the butt of your pistol or the stock of your rifle for every Indian you have killed?"

"Hell, if I did that, I'd have whittled them down to nothing by now."

"I'm curious. Has the Indian Killer murdered any white men as well? What about Mexicans? Or Negroes?"

"I never killed anybody who didn't need killing," Nathan snapped, wishing he hadn't started the conversation. "Let's leave it at that."

"What about men you have shot from ambush? They were doing you no harm at that moment."

"They had harmed plenty of others. And they would have again, if I'd let 'em live."

"You know this for a fact? Without any doubt? There is no possible chance you have gunned down men who did absolutely nothing to deserve it?"

"You know who got what they didn't deserve? My wife. My unborn child. My father and mother and everybody else who was killed that day!" Nathan raised up and pegged another shot in the direction of the Sioux so they wouldn't think he had forgotten about them. He muttered, "Go to hell, Red Buffalo."

"I believe you may be there already," the Crow said.

The faint tone of pity in the other scout's voice made fury well up inside Nathan. He felt like rolling over and shooting the redskinned son of a bitch. But like it or not, at that moment fate had made them allies. Anyway, Nathan heard a noise behind him. He turned to look and saw Lieutenant Pryor crawling toward him, keeping his head down because of the occasional slug that flew over the rocks or bounced among them.

Pryor's face was so pale under the powder smoke grime, his features so haggard and drawn, he already looked almost like the dead man he likely soon would be. He swallowed, wiped a hand across his face, and asked, "Do you have any idea how we can get out of here, Captain?"

"I'm not a captain anymore," Nathan said. "Haven't been for a long time. You're in command of this patrol, Lieutenant. What'd they tell you to do at

West Point if you ever found yourself in a fix like this?"

That wasn't fair and Nathan knew it, but he was still angry at Red Buffalo, frustrated with himself, and unwilling to die before he got the chance to settle more of his score with the Indians . . . a score that would never really be settled, of course, because he couldn't bring his loved ones back to life no matter how many redskins he put under.

"If . . . if we advance on the hostiles below us—"

Red Buffalo said, "We get up from these rocks and they'll cut us to pieces in a crossfire, Lieutenant. Our only chance is to hold on here."

"But the men who took other positions . . . only a few of them seem to be firing anymore. I don't know if they're running low on ammunition—"

"They're dead." Nathan interrupted that time. "That's why they're not shooting, Lieutenant. The Sioux have picked them off." He couldn't resist adding, "Sounds to me like all of the redskins have Winchesters. Not many bows and arrows or trade muskets among 'em."

Anger put a little color back into Pryor's strained pallor. "I suppose I deserve that, Stark, but I don't appreciate it. You warned me, and I'll mention that fact in my report when we get back to the fort." He glanced at Red Buffalo. "You both warned me. I acknowledge that, but it doesn't get us out of here."

Nathan said, "Like Red Buffalo told you, we're not getting out of here. We're pinned down. The only way we'll make it is by holding on until Colonel Ledbetter gets here. *If* he gets here."

Pryor stared at him for a moment, then sighed.

"You're right. I don't suppose there's any possibility one of you could slip out and try to find the colonel, maybe hurry him along . . ."

"We may not have much of a chance, Lieutenant," Red Buffalo said, "but I don't think I want to throw away what little of my life may be left."

Nathan didn't even bother responding to the lieutenant's suggestion.

Pryor backed away on his belly and resumed his previous position behind a boulder with a jagged top. Sergeant McCall was a few yards away from him. The sergeant had a smear of blood on the right side of his face from a wound where a bullet had nicked him. McCall would have a scar there much like the one on Nathan's forehead from their battle over Delia Blaine . . . assuming that McCall survived, which was pretty unlikely.

That thought conjured up an image of Delia in Nathan's mind. He wondered if she would cry when she found out he was dead. She probably would shed a tear or two, he decided. After all, she had known him longer than she'd known anyone else at Fort Randall.

Somehow, the idea of Delia mourning him didn't make him feel the least bit better.

More time went by. His tongue was so swollen it seemed like it completely filled his mouth. He let his thoughts drift to a cold, clear mountain lake, and he could imagine plunging his head into it and gulping down swallow after swallow of the life-giving water . . .

"The Sioux are tired of waiting!" Red Buffalo exclaimed, breaking into the pleasant reverie that filled Nathan's brain. "Here they come!"

CHAPTER 20

The Sioux attacked from both directions. If that wasn't bad enough, the ones atop the mesa were mounted on their nimble, fast-moving ponies as they charged down the slope at the soldiers forted up in the rocks.

"Bring down those horses!" Nathan shouted as he twisted around and opened fire in that direction. If anybody questioned the idea of a scout giving orders, no one brought it up at that moment, not even Lieutenant Pryor.

The embattled soldiers banged away with their Springfields while Nathan and Red Buffalo sprayed bullets across the slope with their Winchesters. Four horses went down. Mortally wounded, they rolled on down the hill with legs flailing wildly. Nathan hated to see that, but he would hate to die even more. Since some of the ponies threw their riders and then rolled on them, breaking bones and crushing flesh, there was that to consider, too.

He couldn't neglect the Indians attacking from below. He rolled over again, dropped his empty rifle, and came up with the Colt in his fist. Earlier, he had slid a cartridge into the normally empty chamber where he carried the hammer, so the revolver had a full six rounds in it as he knelt and fired past the boulder at the onrushing warriors.

A Sioux's head jerked back as Nathan's first shot left a red-rimmed hole above his nose. The slug drilled on through the man's brain and left him stumbling, dead on his feet, before momentum toppled him forward. The two men right behind him leaped over his body and ran smack into Nathan's second and third bullets. The slugs punched into their chests and drove them backwards. Those three deaths in a pair of heartbeats slowed the charge.

That hesitation gave Red Buffalo the chance to drill two more men with his Winchester. The four who were left dived to the ground, suddenly eager to avoid the deadly hail of lead from the two scouts.

Nathan and Red Buffalo had blunted the attack from below, but the Sioux charging down from above continued their assault even though several men and ponies were down. A couple warriors leaped their mounts right into the cluster of rocks and opened fire at close range. One of the soldiers screamed as bullets tore into him.

Nathan spun. He still had three rounds in the Colt and triggered them all in a deadly burst of muzzle flame. One bullet caught a Sioux under the chin and flipped him backwards off his pony. Another shattered the second man's shoulder, and the third slug went through his yelling mouth and exploded out the back of his head in a grisly pink spray.

"The red devils are pullin' back!" Sergeant McCall shouted.

Nathan hated to agree with the sergeant about anything, but he had referred to Indians as *red devils* many times himself. McCall was right about the Sioux retreating, too. They hurried back up the slope toward the top of the mesa, firing over their shoulders as they fled.

Nathan hunkered down and reloaded the Colt and the Winchester, his fingers moving swiftly and efficiently without conscious thought, carrying out a ritual of sorts he had performed thousands of times over the years. Echoes of battle rolled away across the hills, but other than that an eerie silence had fallen over the scene. Everyone on both sides was lying low again, waiting for the next outbreak of killing.

When the Colt had a full wheel, Nathan pouched the iron and looked around. Three of the soldiers who had taken cover near him lay bloody and motionless on the hot ground. A couple others were wounded, and their comrades were tying makeshift bandages around arms and legs to try to stop the bleeding. Lieutenant Pryor was still unwounded somehow, and Sergeant McCall had only the minor gash on the side of his face.

Neither Nathan nor Red Buffalo had been hit in the latest skirmish. Both knew that luck wouldn't continue to hold.

Movement caught Nathan's eye and he turned his head to see Pryor starting to get to his feet. Nathan lunged at the lieutenant, grabbed his shoulder, and pulled him back down just as a rifle cracked somewhere up the slope.

"Damn it, Lieutenant! Are you trying to get your head blown off?"

"I . . . I thought it would be safe to look around. To assess our situation."

"Our situation is that we're still in a damn mess," Nathan said.

"But we fought them off. We made them retreat. And they suffered heavier casualties than we did. I'm sure of it."

"They had more men than we did to start with," Red Buffalo said. "And they hold the high ground."

"And the low road, too," Nathan added dryly. "They may think twice before attacking us head-on again, but that's the only way we're any better off now than we were before. Our only chance is still for the colonel to show up while some of us are still alive."

Pryor swallowed so hard it was practically a gulp, and Nathan had a pretty good idea why the lieutenant reacted that way.

Their lives were in the hands of Colonel Wesley Stuart Ledbetter—and that was not a good place to be.

Things settled back down to desultory sniping at the rocks by the Sioux, with the trapped soldiers returning the fire now and then.

Nathan would have killed for a drink of cold water. He had sucked on a pebble at times during the long, dry afternoon, and that helped some, but not enough. The soldiers were in even worse shape, the wounded men moaning and calling out for water even though there was none to be had.

Red Buffalo's hatchet face remained expressionless. Nathan had heard people talk about how Indians never displayed emotion, a belief worth every bit as much as a steaming pile of mule droppings. Indians displayed plenty of emotion—usually savage glee as they were killing some innocent white person. Red Buffalo seemed determined not to show how he felt, probably because of the company he was in. He wouldn't want to give Nathan the satisfaction of seeing that he was scared.

Nathan knew that. He felt the same way about Red Buffalo. He'd be damned if he was going to display any weakness in front of the Crow.

As the sun dipped closer to the western horizon, Red Buffalo said quietly, "You know that once night falls, everything changes, Stark."

"Damned right I know," Nathan responded. "We won't be able to see the sons of bitches anymore. They'll sneak in on us and be among us before we know what's happening. Before anybody except you and I know, that is. And that won't be enough to save us."

"Ah, well. It was a good fight. We killed many of them. I wish I knew for sure that Hanging Dog was the leader of this war party."

"What does it matter?"

"A man should know who is responsible for ending his life."

"That doesn't make him any less dead."

"No," Red Buffalo agreed. "His spirit is still unshackled from his body either way. His soul journeys on to what waits beyond."

"You claim to be a Christian. You reckon you're

going to Heaven, Red Buffalo? You think St. Peter will let you in?"

"Nothing in the Bible says a red man cannot enter the kingdom of Heaven."

"Guess it's been too long since I read it," Nathan said. "I disremember what it says about redskinned heathens."

Red Buffalo shook his head. "Why are you trying to annoy me in the last hours of our lives, Stark? Do you hate me that much? Do you hate all Indians that much? Even the ones who have never done anything to harm you?"

"Like I always say, if it's not me some savage comes after, sooner or later it'll be some other innocent."

"As innocent as the women and children in Black Kettle's camp on the Washita? You were there, weren't you, Stark? How many did you kill that day?"

Nathan bristled at that. "I didn't kill anybody who wasn't trying to kill me. Every warrior I shot had a weapon in his hand."

"Has it always been that way?"

Nathan thought back to the encounter with the Creeks down in Indian Territory. It was hard to worry about whether he had done the right thing by leaving the young man called Black Sun alive when he was surrounded by Sioux warriors who wanted to kill him. He shoved that aside. "You didn't answer my question. You reckon you're going to Heaven when the Sioux get through with us?"

"I hope so," Red Buffalo replied. "But I would say the chances are better that you will go to Hell."

"I'll see you there. You won't be hearing Gabriel blow his trumpet—"

"Stark!"

"What?" Nathan tensed. "You want to fight me now? You don't reckon we can just leave it to Hanging Dog and his bastards?"

"Listen," Red Buffalo said.

Nathan frowned and tilted his head a little to one side. He didn't hear anything except the wind sighing over the prairie and the hills, and then . . .

"Son of a bitch," he breathed as he heard the blaring notes of a brass instrument. "Gabriel?"

"That's not an angel's trumpet," Red Buffalo said. "That's an army bugle."

The notes were very faint, but clear enough to realize that Red Buffalo was right. Somewhere in the distance, a mile away or maybe more, a bugler was blowing.

Nathan had heard that tinny sound often enough in the past fifteen years that it was unmistakable. "Colonel Ledbetter. It has to be."

"You told the lieutenant that if the messenger rode his horse to death and the colonel came on immediately, it was possible. That is the only explanation."

The bugle was getting louder, which meant the party from the fort was coming closer. Nathan knew that if he and Red Buffalo could hear it, so could the Sioux who were lower down on the slope. Their numbers were already depleted. The odds of them wanting to wait around and face a larger force from Fort Randall were small.

"Lieutenant," Nathan said. "You hear that?"

Pryor was sitting with his back against a rock, his head drooping forward. He wasn't asleep, but clearly he was so filled with despair and dread that he could barely stir himself. He lifted his head slowly and asked in a vague voice, "What? What are you talking about, Stark?"

No more *Captain,* Nathan thought. He and Pryor had clashed too often, and the lieutenant was sunk too deeply in the grim prospect of his impending death to care about anything else. Nathan supposed he couldn't blame the young officer for that.

"Lieutenant, listen. Somebody's blowing a bugle. It has to be Colonel Ledbetter and the rest of the troops from the fort."

Pryor's eyes widened in the twilight. "The colonel?" he said in a tone of hushed disbelief. "It can't be—"

"It is, Lieutenant!" Sergeant McCall said. "I hear it, too, now!"

Excitement swept over the men. In a second, they had gone from almost certain death to at least a chance for survival.

"Check your guns!" Red Buffalo said sharply. "The Sioux above us on the mesa will hear the bugle, too, and they won't want to be trapped up there. They'll try to break out—"

A sudden rumble of hoofbeats drowned out Red Buffalo's words. Several dozen ponies had been left up on the mesa when their owners climbed down into the gorge to flank the patrol. Those animals were stampeding down the slope toward the rocks, driven by yipping and shouting mounted warriors.

"Stop them!" Lieutenant Pryor cried as he twisted around and aimed his pistol over the rock he had been leaning against a moment earlier. "Don't let them get away!"

CHAPTER 21

Nathan came up on one knee and brought the Winchester to his shoulder. With a full fifteen rounds in the repeater, he fired at the onrushing Sioux, aiming over the heads of the stampeding ponies in an effort to pick off some of the warriors driving the horses downhill. Not far away, Moses Red Buffalo did likewise, emptying his Winchester at the charge.

When both rifles ran dry, the scouts leaped to their feet and yanked out their revolvers. Nathan darted aside to avoid being trampled as the first of the riderless ponies reached the rocks. He lifted the Colt and triggered it at one of the warriors. The man slewed to the side and clutched at his arm where Nathan's bullet had struck him. He lost his grip with his knees and slid off the pony. When he hit the ground, he tried to struggle to his feet but Nathan shot him again, that time in the head.

"Stark, look out!" The warning shout came from Red Buffalo.

Nathan twisted to his left and saw a Sioux aiming a rifle at him from horseback. Muzzle flame spurted from the repeater. Nathan felt the flat *whap!* of the bullet passing within inches of his ear as he fired the Colt and saw the Indian pitch the rifle into the air as he threw his arms up. He fell off the horse as it galloped on by.

Nathan fired again and again as the Sioux ponies swarmed around him. More than once, he narrowly avoided getting trampled. Then the charge was past and his gun was empty. Two or three Sioux warriors were still on horseback. They were going to get away and there was nothing he could do about it. That knowledge made a bitter taste form under his tongue. He would have liked to kill them all.

A groan made him look around. Red Buffalo lay on the ground, struggling to get up. Nathan figured the Crow had been shot, but when he looked closer, he didn't see any blood on the scout.

"What the hell happened to you?" he asked as he stepped closer.

"One of those ponies hit me and knocked me down." Red Buffalo held his left shoulder with his right hand. "I don't believe any bones are broken, but it hurts like blazes."

Nathan holstered his Colt and stuck his hand out. "Well, here. You helped me before, and you yelled that warning just now, so I reckon I can help you up."

"Are you sure you wouldn't rather just kick me while I'm down?"

"Don't tempt me, redskin. Now, are you gonna let me give you a hand or not?"

Red Buffalo let go of his injured shoulder and reached up. He clasped Nathan's wrist while Nathan took hold of his. With a grunt, Nathan hauled the Crow to his feet.

"I am obliged to you."

"Don't worry about me trying to collect," Nathan said. "Where's the lieutenant?"

He heard swearing from elsewhere in the cluster of rocks and turned to see what it was about. His jaw tightened as he spotted Sergeant McCall on one knee next to a motionless figure on the ground.

"Hell," Nathan said. "Is that—?"

"Aye. One of those bullets flyin' around caught him right in the head." McCall sounded more annoyed than sorry that Lieutenant Pryor was dead.

The young officer lay on his back, his eyes wide open and a surprised look on his face. Judging by that, he might have had just enough time before life fled to realize that he'd been killed. Blood had trickled from the hole in his head above his right ear, but not much.

McCall stood up. "I reckon that leaves me in command—"

"Someone is coming," Red Buffalo interrupted. "Just one rider."

Nathan looked around. The sun was below the horizon, but there was plenty of light left for him to make out the rounded shape of the derby shoved down on the approaching rider's head. "That's Bucher."

"One of the other scouts?" Red Buffalo asked with a frown.

"Yeah. I don't guess you've met him yet, since you weren't at the fort very long before the colonel sent you out on this patrol." Nathan frowned. "I wonder what the hell he's doing here."

While Bucher was riding toward them, Nathan scanned the countryside to the south, toward the river. He could no longer see any of the Sioux—not the ones who had escaped on horseback nor the ones on foot who had climbed down into the gorge to flank the patrol and get behind the soldiers. All of the hostiles had faded away into the dusk.

Nathan, Red Buffalo, Sergeant McCall, and the rest of the soldiers who could stand were on their feet when Bucher rode up and reined in.

"*Mein Gott,*" the German said. "Is this all of you who are left?"

"There might be some wounded men behind those other rocks," McCall replied. He turned to the soldiers. "Harney, go take a look around. See if any of the other lads are still alive."

"Sure, Sarge," the private responded. He trotted toward the nearest rock where one of the patrol had taken cover.

"Where's Colonel Ledbetter and the rest of the men?" Nathan asked.

Bucher waved a hand toward the south. "The colonel sent Captain Jameson and a company to pursue the savages we saw fleeing, while he stayed back with another company in reserve."

That didn't surprise Nathan. He had no trouble believing that Ledbetter would send somebody else to chase the Sioux while he remained safely in the rear.

"Captain Lucas and Company H stayed at the fort," Bucher went on. "Colonel Ledbetter thought it wise not to leave it undefended. The messenger who brought word to the fort said it was believed the enemy force numbered only approximately fifty, so two companies were more than enough to handle the threat."

"And we'd already whittled 'em down quite a bit by the time you got here," Nathan said. He still didn't like Colonel Ledbetter, but he had to admit the man had reacted swiftly and appropriately. "I reckon he decided to bring you along as well, Bucher?"

"A wise officer does not venture into the field without the services of a good scout, *ja*? It is fortunate I was there. I did not expect to be needed, so I did a bit of hunting yesterday." Bucher looked at Red Buffalo. "Speaking of scouts, this must be the Crow I have heard about."

"Moses Red Buffalo, meet Dietrich Bucher," Nathan drawled.

Both men nodded curtly. Neither offered to shake hands.

Private Harney had made the rounds of the other rocks on the slope where members of the patrol had taken cover. He looked a little sick as he reported back to McCall, "They're all dead, Sarge. Every one of 'em."

"Well, don't just stand there," McCall said. "Form a burial detail. We're not haulin' all those carcasses back to the fort with us."

As night fell, the wranglers who had come with Colonel Ledbetter rounded up as many loose horses as they could find. Many of the animals were Indian ponies, while others were mounts that belonged to the original patrol. Some of the army horses were lost. But the wranglers found enough mounts that everyone would be able to ride back to Fort Randall.

Nathan was relieved when he saw Buck among the animals driven in by the soldiers. He hadn't figured that Buck would let himself be captured by redskins, but it was good to see for himself that the horse was safe.

Since Sergeant McCall was the only officer left alive, albeit a noncommissioned one, Colonel Ledbetter spoke to him at length, getting his report on everything that had happened. Ledbetter didn't ask to talk to the scouts, which didn't surprise Nathan. As far as the colonel was concerned, civilian scouts might be useful but had no official standing.

Ledbetter also assigned men to walk around the battlefield and check the bodies of all the fallen Sioux to make sure they were dead and to bring back their rifles, along with anything else of value or interest. Scavenged Winchesters were piled near the campfire. Nathan looked idly at the repeaters, then frowned and hunkered on his heels to study them more closely. He reached out and moved a couple around to get a better look.

Red Buffalo came up behind him and asked, "What are you doing, Stark?"

"Nothing." He straightened. "Just thinking it's a damned shame those redskins ever got their hands on guns like those."

"Bows and arrows against firearms would not be a very fair fight."

"Who the hell said anything about fair? Anyway, like I told the lieutenant, Winchesters have a lot more firepower than those army Springfields. If all the Plains Indians wound up being armed with them—"

"It would make no difference in the long run," Red Buffalo said. "There are too many white men. They swarm like ants, an endless number of them in the eastern cities." The Crow shook his head. "The Indian's way of life is doomed. Some of us know this, so we work with the white men to help our people survive the best they can."

"If the numbers were even, you'd fight to the death, though," Nathan said.

Red Buffalo's silence was an eloquent response to that statement.

The burial detail finished its grim work by lantern light, well after dark. Colonel Ledbetter said a brief prayer for the men being laid to rest, and the bugler played "Taps."

When that was done, Nathan looked up Captain Jameson and said, "Best double the guard tonight, Captain. The chances of any of those Sioux coming back are pretty slim, but it won't hurt to be careful."

Bucher was standing nearby, smoking a cigar. "*Ja*, I have already made the same suggestion to the captain, Stark. We will not be taken by surprise."

"In that case, then," Nathan said, "I'm going to turn in. It has been one hell of a long, hard day."

That was true, and thinking about all the Indians he had killed didn't lift his spirits or ease his weariness, as it might have under normal circumstances. Maybe he had done too much killing, he mused as he stretched out in his bedroll, just before exhaustion claimed him. Was such a thing possible? Could he ever kill too many redskins . . . or even enough?

He didn't find any answers to those questions in his dreams, because he didn't have any. His sleep was numb, almost stunned. And when he awoke in the morning, he didn't feel rested, just ready to get back to the fort.

Something was nagging at the back of his brain, and he thought he might find an explanation for it there.

Dietrich Bucher was getting his horse ready to ride that morning when he sensed someone behind him. His hand dropped to the big hunting knife sheathed at his waist. He was fast and deadly with the blade and could gut a man in the blink of an eye.

It was Sergeant Seamus McCall who stood there, however, not an enemy. Of course, he wasn't a completely trusted ally, either, Bucher reminded himself. Bucher made it a habit not to trust anyone all the way except himself.

"Damn it, Bucher, what's the idea?" McCall demanded in a low voice.

"I don't know what you mean, Sergeant."

McCall pointed to the gash on his cheek left behind by a bullet from one of those Winchesters used by the Sioux. "Look how close I came to dyin'," he grated. "There's no tellin' how many slugs almost got me. The damn redskins weren't supposed to be shootin' at *me*!"

"Serving in the frontier army is a dangerous profession, Sergeant, and those Sioux had no way of knowing you were among the soldiers who happened upon them. When we entered into this enterprise, we knew there would be risks. But the rewards have been great, *nicht wahr*?"

"A fella can't spend money if he's dead," McCall snapped. He blew out a sigh and shrugged. "I suppose you're right. We got to keep up a good front, and that means goin' about our usual business. I just don't like bein' shot at with guns the blasted heathens wouldn't even have if not for us!"

Bucher leaned closer and motioned for the sergeant to keep his voice down. "Hanging Dog suffered a setback here yesterday, but he still has warriors flocking in from all over the territory. Once he has the next shipment of rifles, he will be able to scour the plains clean of white men . . . for a while. But you *und* I and our other two *freunden* will be long gone by then, Seamus, hopefully enjoying our riches somewhere the weather is warm and the *frauleins* are beautiful and willing. Is such a destiny not worth taking a few chances?"

"I suppose," McCall admitted. "I just don't like the sound of bullets passin' that close to my ears! I didn't like the way Stark was looking at those rifles we gathered up, either."

"Stark," Bucher breathed. "That is a problem I have tried to solve once already. Next time, I will have to try harder."

CHAPTER 22

They took their time getting back to the fort and reached it late that afternoon. Nathan was glad to see that nothing had happened while Colonel Ledbetter was gone with two companies. It would be just like a bunch of tricky redskins to attack the fort while most of the garrison was occupied elsewhere. The fact that Lieutenant Pryor's patrol had encountered the Indians largely by accident meant the possibility of such a sneak attack wasn't very likely, though.

As the force rode in, Nathan saw Delia Blaine come out of the chapel where she had her school. She took a couple hurried steps as if she were about to break into a run that would carry her out to greet him but then stopped and just smiled in his direction. He gave her a nod as he rode by, twenty yards away. A warm tightness filled his chest. It wasn't a particularly welcome feeling. He had a mission in life. It was really *all* he had. Getting involved with Delia would just complicate things.

No matter how gratifying such a complication might be in some ways, he didn't need anything distracting him from his goal. He was plagued already by too many doubts stemming from the encounter with Black Sun and the difficult questions Red Buffalo had asked him while they were squatting in those rocks, waiting to die.

There was nothing like the looming specter of death to clarify a man's thoughts and make him be honest with himself.

After the ride around the parade ground—showing off by Colonel Ledbetter, Nathan thought, even though the colonel hadn't done anything except chase a few Indians off—they went to the stable and turned their horses over to the hostlers.

Nathan walked to his cabin and found Delia waiting on the little porch.

"Thank God you're back," she said as she put her arms around his neck and hugged him tightly. She had given him a few hugs when she'd said good night after meals he had shared with her and Stephen, but not like that. Those embraces had been friendly, that was all. This one was tinged with desperation and need and relief.

"When I heard that the patrol had been trapped by the Sioux, I . . . I was so worried about you, Nathan."

"You had every right to be," he told her as he slid his left arm around her waist and patted her rather awkwardly on the back with his right hand. He moved his right hand to her auburn hair and touched it lightly as she rested her head against his shoulder. "This, uh . . . I'm not sure how proper this is, hugging like this right out in the middle of the open."

"If you think I care about propriety right now, Nathan Stark, you're sadly mistaken."

"Well, in that case . . ." He continued to hold her. He had been with a number of women during the past fifteen years, all of them soiled doves or saloon girls who had slaked a basic physical need no more meaningful than hunger or thirst, but that was all. Delia was the first respectable lady he had held in his arms since his wife. It was a sensation rewarding and disturbing.

After a moment he stepped away and put his hands on her shoulders. "Just so you won't worry anymore, I'm fine. Not even a scratch."

"Quite a few men were killed, though, weren't they?"

Nathan leaned his head to the side. "I'm afraid so."

"And next time, you could be one of them."

"We all know the risks." Thinking about Stephen, Nathan added, "You as well as anybody, I reckon."

"That doesn't make it any better. I wish . . . sometimes I wish I could go back east and live somewhere I never had to hear about such dreadful things again."

"You can go any time," he told her. "There's nothing holding you out here."

"I wouldn't want to go alone."

Nathan wasn't going to travel any farther along that trail. He said, "I reckon I ought to clean up. Not sure I'll ever get all the powder smoke grime off of me."

"You'll come to supper tonight," she said. "I won't take no for an answer."

"I don't suppose I'll try to give it, then." He put even more distance between them. "So long, Delia."

"Come to my house at seven."

Not seeing any way to avoid it, he nodded his head and promised, "I'll be there."

He wasn't sure where the evening would lead, but he didn't figure it would be anywhere good.

There was still an arch of reddish-gold light in the western sky when Nathan went up the two steps onto the porch of Delia's house. She must have been watching for him as she opened the door before he could reach it.

He had washed up, put on a clean blue bib-front shirt and a pair of fringed buckskin trousers. He'd brushed the dust off his black hat and had it cocked at a sort of jaunty angle on his head. While he was getting ready, he had asked himself why he was going to so much trouble to make himself look respectable. The last time he had gone to Delia's for supper, the evening hadn't ended well. This one might not, either, although she was obviously glad to see that he had gotten back to the fort safely. He assumed she was glad for the other survivors from the patrol, too, but she hadn't invited them to eat with her.

She wore a dark blue dress, had her hair pinned up, and looked lovely. She held out a hand to him and said, "Come in, Nathan. Let me take your hat."

He handed it to her and she led him into the foyer. As she turned and hung the hat on one of the hooks of a hat tree, he noticed another hat hanging there. It was black, too, but with a high, creased crown and an eagle feather stuck in the band. Nathan's breath caught in his throat as he recognized it. His heart pounded and made his pulse thunder inside his head.

"What the hell!" he exclaimed, not giving a hang about cussing in front of a lady.

Delia took hold of his arm. "Let's go into the parlor." She hung on and steered him in that direction, and since he didn't want to jerk roughly away from her, he went with her.

He came to an abrupt stop just inside the door to the parlor, though. He couldn't go any farther. Moses Red Buffalo stood beside the fireplace with a pipe in his hand.

Nathan glared at the Crow. "I hate to tell you this, Delia, but you're never gonna get the stink of redskin out of here."

"Shame on you, Nathan! I didn't invite you here to insult my other guest."

He turned his head to look at her and tried not to glare. "Why did you invite me, then? And why in blazes did you invite *him*?"

Her chin lifted defiantly as she said, "Because I thought the two of you should talk, and I'm hoping that you'll regard this as neutral ground, so to speak."

"There's no such thing as neutral ground where Indians are concerned," Nathan snapped.

"You're right, Stark," Red Buffalo said, "because wherever there are Indians, white men are trying to take their land and everything else away from them."

"Stop it, both of you," Delia said calmly. "You're on the same side. You're both assigned to this post, whether you like it or not, and from what I've heard, you saved each other's life more than once during the past few days. So there's no reason why you can't stop insulting each other and sit down to supper at the same table like civilized human beings."

Nathan started to make some comment about how redskins weren't human beings and sure as hell not civilized, but the way Delia was looking at him, he couldn't bring himself to do it. He supposed that if she could put up with having Red Buffalo there, after what had happened to her husband, he could, too.

He took a deep breath and said, "All right. But you'd better behave yourself, Red Buffalo."

"I'll try not to jump onto the table and break into a war dance in the middle of the meal," the Crow said.

That wry comment made Delia smile, which just increased the resentment Nathan felt.

"You two gentlemen can keep each other company while I go check on the food one last time." She swept out of the room.

"Our hostess is quite charming," Red Buffalo said when Delia was gone.

"I've told you before, don't talk about that woman."

"Not even to pay her a compliment? A richly deserved compliment, I might add."

"Just—" Nathan broke off what he'd been about to say. He closed his eyes for a second, forced himself to breathe regularly, and then said, "Mrs. Blaine is an old friend of mine. I believe I've already explained that to you. I don't want to do anything that might distress her."

"I've only just met the lady, and I feel the same way. Don't worry, Stark. I'm going to be on my best behavior this evening, and I suggest you do the same. I was . . . surprised . . . by Mrs. Blaine's invitation, and I'd just as soon not give her any reason to regret it." Red Buffalo smiled. "She might even issue another one, one of these days."

"I wouldn't count on it," Nathan said.

"We'll see."

Red Buffalo stood there by the fireplace smoking his pipe. He had put on a clean shirt, too, Nathan noted, and wiped away the powder smoke grime.

An awkward silence hung between them until Delia came back into the room. "We're ready to eat," she announced. "Gentlemen, if you'll follow me."

Nathan and Red Buffalo started toward her at the same time. They might have bumped into each other if they'd both kept going, but Red Buffalo paused. With a little mocking smile, he motioned for Nathan to go first. Nathan scowled, feeling that the Crow had gotten the better of him somehow, but went ahead anyway.

Delia led them into the dining room. The table had a white linen cover on it, with settings of fine crystal and china and silver. A platter of fried chicken was in the center of the table, surrounded by bowls of potatoes and corn and greens, a tureen of gravy, and a plate stacked with fluffy biscuits. Delia filled the glasses with lemonade from a pitcher. Cups and saucers had been placed at every setting, too, and a pot of coffee stood ready.

Nathan held the chair at the head of the table for her, then moved to the chair on her right. Red Buffalo took the one on her left.

As the men sat down, Red Buffalo said, "Mrs. Blaine, I hope it will be all right if I say grace before we eat."

"Why, that would be just fine, Mr. Red Buffalo," she replied. "Are you a Christian man?"

"Yes, ma'am. I was educated at a mission school and became a believer while there."

"That's splendid. Go right ahead."

Red Buffalo bowed his head and closed his eyes.

Delia did likewise. Nathan lowered his head but left his eyes slitted. He couldn't bring himself to close them completely while he was sitting across the table from an Indian. Not that he expected Red Buffalo to lunge across and attack him or anything like that, but where redskins were concerned . . . well, you just couldn't tell.

"Father, please accept our thanks for this meal and the gracious lady who has prepared it," Red Buffalo said, "along with all the other blessings You have bestowed upon us. Watch over everyone in this vast frontier which You have provided as a home for us. We ask these things in Your name, amen."

"Amen," Delia said. "Lovely sentiments, Mr. Red Buffalo."

"Thank you, ma'am."

She beamed. "Now, to be plain about it, let's dig in. I imagine after the past few days, both of you can really use a good meal!"

She might be wrong about a lot of things, Nathan thought, but she wasn't wrong about that.

The stable was dark and quiet. All the hostlers had returned to their quarters, and the only sounds inside the cavernous building were the faint noises of horses' tails swishing and the occasional thump of a hoof as the animals shifted around.

Three men were in one of the tack rooms with a single candle burning dimly. Dietrich Bucher lifted a jug and took a swig from it, then held it out to Sergeant Jeremiah Dockery. "Not as good as schnapps, but I suppose this . . . what do you call it? Who hit Johann? It is better than nothing."

Dockery took a drink and licked his lips. "You mean nothing is better than some good corn squeezin's like I used to get back in Tennessee."

"None of it can hold this candle or any other to good Irish whiskey," Seamus McCall insisted as he took the jug from Dockery. "But soon we'll be able to afford whatever we want to drink, boyos. The next shipment of rifles will be here within a week, and it's the biggest one yet."

The three conspirators—two sergeants and a civilian scout—continued drinking for a while, not saying much.

Finally Dockery got back to the subject of the clandestine meeting. "The boss has men lined up to deliver those guns?" he asked.

"*Ja,*" Bucher replied. "I spoke with him a short time ago. Crates loaded with rocks will be delivered to the fort *und* checked off the freight manifest, while wagons with the real crates will meet Hanging Dog at Weeping Woman Rock."

McCall said, "I'd still like to know where the savages are getting the gold to pay for those rifles."

"What does it matter?" Dockery snapped. "They've got it, and they're giving it to us. That's all I care about."

"They believe themselves to be getting a good deal," Bucher said. "To them, gold is just a useless yellow rock, too soft to make arrowheads or knives. That attitude is fortunate for us, *nicht wahr?*"

"I wish ye'd talk good English," McCall complained. "I know ye can do it, because I've heard ye."

"You understand me, *ja?*" Bucher reached out and prodded a blunt fingertip against McCall's chest, causing the Irish noncom to glare at him. The German sounded a little drunk as he went on. "Now understand this—I do not trust Nathan Stark. The man is obsessed with killing Indians, but other than that he is honest . . . and smart. It will be better for us if he is dead."

"You claimed you were gonna kill him," Dockery said.

"I tried. He moved, just as I pulled the trigger. He should have died then and there, but fate protected him for some reason."

It wasn't fate, and Bucher knew it. It was his own damned fault Nathan Stark was still alive. He had stepped where he shouldn't and made a little noise, and Stark's keen ears had caught the warning just in time to save him. But those *dummkopfs* Dockery and McCall didn't have to know that.

Dockery said, "You missed your shot at him, Bucher. And you had a chance to bust his head open but didn't do it, McCall."

"I thought I was fightin' to keep the spalpeen away from my Delia," McCall said with a glower. "I didn't know he was gonna wind up bein' a threat to our business! If I had, I never would've let him get away."

Bucher doubted that. McCall outweighed Stark by a good fifty pounds, but he was slow and Stark was cat-quick, not to mention surprisingly strong considering his wiry frame. Bucher was sure, of course, that he could defeat Stark in a brawl, if it ever came to that.

But maybe it wouldn't . . .

Dockery took the jug back, downed another slug of liquor, and said, "You two have had your chance. It's my turn now." He shoved the jug into Bucher's hands. "I'm gonna make damn sure Nathan Stark is dead long before that next shipment of rifles ever gets here."

CHAPTER 23

The food was very good. As Delia had intimated when she first greeted Nathan at Fort Randall, she hadn't been renowned for the quality of her cooking when he had been friends with her and her husband. She had gotten better, though. The chicken was fried just right.

"This is a delicious meal," Red Buffalo complimented as they ate.

Nathan couldn't let that pass. "A lot better than a hunk of raw dog meat on a stick, isn't it?"

"Nathan, that was uncalled for," Delia scolded him, frowning. "You should apologize to Mr. Red Buffalo."

"Please, call me Moses," the Crow scout said.

Nathan didn't like the idea of that at all.

Delia just smiled and said, "Of course, Moses." She looked at Nathan. "We're still waiting for that apology." There was a hint of iron in her voice.

He could imagine her speaking to unruly school kids that way. "Sorry," he muttered, clearly not meaning it.

Red Buffalo waved a hand in nonchalant dismissal,

angering Nathan that much more. It just wasn't right for a damned redskin to talk and act like a white man.

Delia made small talk about life at the fort as the meal continued. For dessert, she brought out apple pie with cream. It was a shame Red Buffalo had to be there and ruin an otherwise perfectly fine supper, Nathan thought.

When they were finished, Delia poured coffee for all of them and then leaned back in her chair, cradling her cup in both hands. Solemnly, she said, "Nathan, I believe you should tell Moses about what happened to your family."

Taken by surprise, Nathan bristled. "What? I'm not gonna . . . It's none of his business what happened to them." His upper lip pulled back from his teeth as he grimaced. "It was the Pawnee who raided Badger Creek that day, not the Crow. If it had been his relatives, I would have killed him by now, scout or not."

"You might have tried." Red Buffalo cocked an eyebrow and raised his cup to sip from it.

"The two of you have a great deal in common," Delia insisted. "You both lost loved ones to violence."

"A lot of people have, out here on the frontier," Nathan said. "That doesn't mean this savage and I are anything alike."

"You know perfectly well Moses isn't a savage. I couldn't have done as good a job of educating him as that missionary lady did."

Red Buffalo looked surprised. "You know more about my background than I expected, Mrs. Blaine."

"If I'm going to call you Moses, you should call me Delia. And I'll admit, I did some asking around about you." She smiled. "Corporal Cahill was very helpful when I asked him what he could find out."

I'll just bet he was, Nathan thought. Delia had always been able to wrap any man she wanted to around her little finger. A meek little fellow like Winston Cahill wouldn't be any challenge at all for her.

"For instance," Delia went on, "I know that your village was attacked by the Blackfeet when you were a young man, Moses. You had already been to school at the mission, but you had gone back to your people to resume your life with them. I don't know all the details, but I'm sure you lost loved ones that day."

The slightly smug look Red Buffalo had been wearing earlier was gone, replaced by a frown. "The young woman I was going to marry was killed, and so were several members of my family, along with a number of friends. And this is not really something I wish to discuss, especially after such a pleasant meal."

"Good food can ease the way to difficult things that need to be said. Perhaps you weren't aware that Nathan also lost friends and family to an Indian raid."

"I told him already," Nathan said harshly. "He doesn't care."

"A Pawnee war party attacked the town of Badger Creek in Kansas near Indian Territory," Delia pressed on. "Nathan lived there along with his wife Camilla, who was carrying their first child. She was . . . how old, Nathan? Eighteen?"

"Seventeen," he managed to choke out. The food he had eaten was becoming a sickening lump in his stomach due to all the terrible memories Delia insisted on stirring up.

"Only seventeen years old. Just on the threshold of

life, really. His parents were killed as well, and he and his brother were both badly injured."

"My little brother was unconscious for days." Now that Delia had dredged all it up, he couldn't stop himself from letting it pour out. "I didn't figure he'd ever wake up. I didn't think I'd ever see him alive again or ever talk to him. But he made it. The folks who took him in made sure of that. They looked out for him like he was their own."

"What did you do?" Red Buffalo asked.

Nathan shrugged. "Soon as I was fit to travel, I lit out after those red bas—those Pawnee renegades. I never found the ones who were responsible for what happened . . . at least I could never be sure of it . . . but I found plenty of others who needed killing."

Delia leaned forward, crossing her arms on the table. "Does anyone actually *need* killing?"

Without hesitation, Nathan and Red Buffalo looked at her and said in unison, "Yes."

That strong response seemed to take her a little aback. She frowned. "I'm not sure I really believe that, but . . . let's say you're right. Surely you can see by now how very much alike the two of you are. Both of you have suffered terrible tragedies in your lives. Both of you have set out to avenge the ones you lost. Really, the two of you should be friends."

The men looked at each other in disbelief.

It was Red Buffalo who shook his head and spoke first. "That will never happen."

"Not hardly," Nathan agreed.

Undeterred, Delia turned back to Red Buffalo. "You haven't heard the entire story, Moses. Nathan had a sister, too. The Pawnee took her. Carried her off with them when they fled that day."

Nathan's face might have been carved out of stone. He didn't dare let his iron control slip, even for a second. He didn't know what would happen if he did.

"What was her name, Nathan?" Delia went on. "I want to say Rena—"

"Renata, but we all called her Rena. Three years old. Prettiest little girl you ever saw. She had"—a swallow forced its way through his throat—"she had long red hair. My ma would braid it every morning and wind it around Rena's head, then pin it in place. Every night she unwound it and combed it out. The two of them always laughed and talked while they were doing that."

"I am sorry, Stark," Red Buffalo said. "Truly."

"You being sorry doesn't change a damn thing," Nathan said.

"You said you went after the renegades who raided your town. You searched for your sister, too, didn't you?" Delia asked.

"For fifteen years now," Nathan said. "She's never far from my thoughts. One of these days I'll find her." In truth, he had no way of knowing if Rena was even still alive.

If she was, there was a good chance the things Leah had said down in Statler's Mill were true. Rena wouldn't be the sweet little girl he remembered. He might even look at her and not recognize her, not see anything except another filthy Indian squaw . . .

And it would be bucks like Red Buffalo that made her that way.

Abruptly, Nathan scraped back his chair and stood

up. He felt himself trembling inside from the rage that filled him. He forced himself to sound halfway calm as he said, "Thank you for supper, Delia. It was delicious. But I have to go now, and so does Red Buffalo."

The Crow leaned back in his chair. "I have nowhere I need to be."

"Yeah, you do," Nathan said. "Anywhere but here."

"Nathan, you're being very rude—" Delia began.

Red Buffalo lifted a hand to stop her. "No, it's all right. Stark doesn't want to leave you here alone with me. He's afraid of what a redskin might do to you."

"You're damn right," Nathan said.

Red Buffalo got to his feet and turned to Delia, saying, "Thank you. It was a noble gesture on your part, trying to make the two of us see that we should be friends instead of enemies, especially since circumstances have forced us to work together. But it was doomed to failure. Stark can't see anything good in any of my people, I'm afraid."

Nathan jerked his head toward the door. "Let's go."

"Good night, Mrs. Blaine."

They reached the hat tree in the foyer at the same time and once again could have collided. Red Buffalo didn't back off. Nathan slowed down because the alternative was to tackle the Crow and have a knock-down, drag-out fight with him right there in Delia's parlor. Nathan wasn't willing to do that despite the anger he felt.

He was mad at both of them, he realized. Red Buffalo for being, well, an Indian, and Delia for refusing to see how that made all the difference.

He felt Delia's eyes boring into him and knew that

once again he was leaving her house with hard feelings between them. Maybe it would be a good idea not to go there anymore. He was sure he could manage to forget how good she smelled, and how nice it had felt when she'd hugged him a few hours earlier and rested her head against his chest.

When he was outside, he put his hat on and just stood there, breathing deeply. The air had cooled off slightly since the sun went down. The temperature was pleasant. Far off in the distance to the south, lightning flickered as a thunderstorm rolled across the plains. It was far enough away that he couldn't hear the thunder, only see the bursts of illumination dancing through the darkness.

Red Buffalo paused nearby. "We should tell Colonel Ledbetter it would be wise not to pair the two of us on the same assignments anymore."

"If you think it'll do any good to talk to that stuffed shirt, you go right ahead. We made it back from that patrol without killing each other. I reckon we can do it again, no matter how we feel about it."

"Why, Stark." Red Buffalo chuckled. "That's the nicest thing you've ever said to me."

"Go to hell." Nathan turned on his heel and stalked away, heading for his cabin at the other end of the parade ground. He didn't look back to see where Red Buffalo was going. He didn't care.

He thought about stopping by the sutler's store to say hello to Noah Crimmens. He hadn't seen the clerk since he'd been back. It could wait until morning, he decided. He liked Crimmens but didn't feel like being friendly.

Delia is like all women, he told himself.

She believed she knew what men were thinking and feeling. Even more important, she believed she knew what they *ought* to be thinking and feeling. She had gotten it into her head that he and Red Buffalo had enough in common to be friends. Nothing would sway her from that belief, no matter how many times she butted her head against that particular brick wall.

Just try to avoid her, he told himself again.

That was the best solution . . . even though a part of him knew that he would really miss her.

With those thoughts going through his head as he walked past the night-deserted granary, a third of the way down the parade ground, he didn't notice the dark shape shifting position in the thick shadows behind the building. Nor did he see the twin barrels of the shotgun that thrust out of the gloom and centered directly on his back.

CHAPTER 24

Something slammed into Nathan's back and knocked him forward off his feet. At the same time, a roar like the unheard thunder from that distant storm exploded through the night. The impact and the sound combined to leave him stunned for a second.

The part of his brain that was always working recognized the blast as that of a shotgun going off. He didn't think he'd been hit, but the weight on his back pinned him down and as long as he couldn't move he was in danger. He bucked up from the ground as hard as he could and as the weight fell away from him he rolled to his left, closer to the parade ground. He came up on his knees and balanced with his left hand, filling his right hand with the butt of the Colt.

A dark shape, long enough and thick enough to be human, lay motionless on the ground a few feet away. Nathan heard the swift thud of running footsteps next to the granary. Instinct told him that was the shotgunner getting away. He lifted the revolver and triggered two quick shots. Colt flame bloomed in the darkness, but the garish flash didn't reach far enough to light up the fleeing figure. Nathan caught a glimpse of movement, that was all.

Knowing there could be more than one bushwhacker lurking in the shadows, he stayed low as he hurried over to the granary and planted himself with his back against the building. His enemies would have to come at him from the front, if there were any more around.

In the distance, men called urgently to each other. That would be the soldiers posted on guard duty, Nathan thought. A light bobbed along the edge of the parade ground. Somebody with a lantern was headed his way, moving quickly.

A groan came from the man still lying on the ground. Whoever it was, he had tackled Nathan from behind and knocked him out of the way of that shotgun blast. The man must have spotted the twin barrels of the Greener and acted instantly to save Nathan's life at the risk of his own. Nathan wondered if the man had caught both charges of buckshot in the back.

The soldier with the lantern came trotting up, followed by two more guards with rifles. The circle of yellow light from the lantern spread out over the ground and washed over the man lying there. Nathan's jaw tightened as he spotted the black, high-crowned hat with the eagle feather in the band a few feet away. It had come off when its owner had knocked Nathan out of the way.

Moses Red Buffalo groaned again and tried to get to his feet.

"Damn it," Nathan muttered under his breath as he holstered the Colt and stepped into the light. Kneeling beside the Crow scout, he told the soldiers, "Take it easy, boys. The excitement's all over."

Red Buffalo turned his head enough to look up at Nathan. "Stark, were you hit?"

"Just by you. How bad are you hurt?" Nathan told himself he didn't care how badly an Indian was wounded, but Red Buffalo had saved his life . . . again. There was no denying that.

"I think I'll live. Seems most of the charge went above us. The fellow must have jerked the barrels up a little when he pulled the trigger. But it feels like I caught a couple buckshot in the back."

In the lantern light, Nathan saw the pair of blood-stains on the back of Red Buffalo's vest and knew he was right. He looked up at the two soldiers who'd accompanied the man with the lantern and said, "You fellas help him up and get him over to the infirmary. Doc Lightner needs to take a look at him."

"We, uh, we can't leave our posts," one of the men said.

"You already have," Nathan snapped. "Now get moving. This man needs medical attention."

With a grim chuckle, Red Buffalo said, "I suppose I should be glad you called me a man and not a dirty redskin. Thanks, Stark."

I'm the one who ought to be thanking Red Buffalo, Nathan thought. He knew that but couldn't bring himself to say the words.

Standing up, he glared at the soldiers until they stepped in to grasp the Crow's arms and help him to his feet. Steadying him, they started across the parade ground, the quickest, most direct route to the infirmary.

"What happened here, Mr. Stark?" the remaining soldier asked.

Nathan took out the Colt and began reloading the chambers he had emptied. "Somebody tried to ambush me with a shotgun. Red Buffalo knocked me down so the shot missed."

Crazy thoughts swirled. Why had Red Buffalo been so close? Had the Crow been following or just going in the same general direction? Maybe Red Buffalo had been sneaking up to put a knife in his back and had acted so swiftly to save him because he didn't want anybody else to have the satisfaction of killing the white man. Delia would scold him for having such an ungenerous thought, but he couldn't rule out the possibility. Where redskins were concerned, no treachery could ever be ruled out completely.

"He saved your life," the soldier said.

"That he did."

"But who tried to kill you, Mr. Stark?"

Nathan shook his head. He couldn't answer that question. He had a vague idea, but the picture in his head was still far from clear.

"When you make your report to the sergeant of the guard, tell him he can come see me tomorrow if he wants to know anything else. I don't reckon I'll be able to tell him anything I haven't already told you, though. Right now I want to see how Red Buffalo is doing." Nathan started across the parade ground before the soldier could say anything else.

Doc Lightner had turned in already. He was wearing a nightshirt when Nathan went into the infirmary and found the post surgeon digging buckshot out of Red Buffalo's back.

It was the first time Nathan had seen the Crow scout without a shirt on. The number of scars scattered around Red Buffalo's torso testified to the adventurous, hazardous life the man had led. His face was set in stony lines as Lightner went after the buckshot using a probe and a pair of forceps. The doctor had cleaned the blood from around the wounds, but more crimson continued to seep out while he was working on them.

"How bad is it, Doc?" Nathan asked.

"The shot struck at an angle, so neither of them penetrated very deeply." Lightner nodded toward a pan sitting on the table next to Red Buffalo. "I've already extracted one of them, and I'll have this one any time now . . . Ah, there it is." He extended the forceps over the bowl and dropped the second piece of buckshot into it.

The small, bloody lead ball rolled a little and dinged against the other one before it stopped.

"Now, I'll clean these wounds a bit more and apply dressings to them. You'll be fine, Moses."

Red Buffalo grunted. "Thanks, Doc."

Lightner looked over his shoulder at Nathan. "Moses was rather reticent about how he got shot. Maybe you can explain it."

"He knocked me out of the way of a double-barreled shotgun blast," Nathan answered honestly. "You'd have had more trouble patching up the hole that would have left in me, Doc."

Lightner cocked an eyebrow and commented, "I daresay you're right about that."

"So he's in no danger?"

"Very little, as long as he keeps those wounds clean."

Nathan nodded "All right. Reckon I'll go, then."

Lightner stopped him by asking, "Have you expressed your gratitude, Nathan?"

"It's all right, Doc," Red Buffalo said. "I don't expect Stark to thank me. That wouldn't set well with all the hatred he feels toward Indians."

"I'm obliged to you," Nathan said stiffly. "I haven't denied that you saved my life."

Red Buffalo looked back over his shoulder. "What I'd like to know is who was trying to kill you."

"That does seem like an important question," Lightner agreed.

Nathan shrugged more casually than he felt. "I've made my share of enemies over the years."

"Someone who's posted here at Fort Randall?" Lightner asked.

"There are several hundred soldiers here. I haven't seen all of 'em . . . so I don't really know."

Both of the other men appeared skeptical of that answer.

Nathan didn't offer any other explanation. He left the infirmary and walked toward his cabin, circling the parade ground and staying in the cover of the cottonwoods instead of cutting across. He didn't want to make himself a target in all that open space. The person who wanted him dead might try with a rifle or a pistol next time.

Nathan was accustomed to risking his life in battle, but he didn't like the idea that somebody was skulking around and trying to kill him. That was harder to defend against. He'd been shot at from ambush twice in the past few days and didn't believe the would-be killer was somebody with an old grudge against him, as he had hinted to Red Buffalo and the doctor. He thought the attempts sprang from something more recent.

Sergeant Seamus McCall didn't like him, and after the ruckus they'd had over Delia when they first met, Nathan wouldn't put attempted murder past the brutal Irishman. The problem was that when he'd been shot at while on patrol, McCall had been with Red Buffalo, Lieutenant Pryor, and the rest of the soldiers. He couldn't have done that . . . but he could have wielded the shotgun tonight.

That would mean *two* bushwhackers, not one. For two different reasons, or did they share a motivation?

Nathan didn't know, but he didn't like the murky waters in which he found himself swimming. It was much simpler to hate Indians and kill as many of them as he could. That had been his life for a decade and a half, and while it wasn't much, he preferred it to all the complications plaguing him at the moment— dealing with a beautiful, strong-willed redhead, being forced to work with a savage, and having some unknown person trying to put him under. He would rather handle problems that he could put right in the sights of his gun.

He made it back to his cabin without anything else happening, undressed, and turned in right away, but sleep was a long time in coming.

He waited for it with the Colt right on a chair, close to the side of the bed where he could reach it in a hurry.

CHAPTER 25

The next morning, Colonel Ledbetter summoned the three scouts assigned to Fort Randall to his office.

"Come in, gentlemen," the stocky, bespectacled officer greeted them. With a smile, he waved them into chairs that Corporal Cahill had lined up in front of the desk.

Nathan didn't believe for a second that Ledbetter's cheerfulness was genuine, but the colonel had some reason for acting like it was. Nathan figured that if he was patient, he'd find out what it was sooner or later.

Ledbetter pushed a wooden box across the desk. "Cigar?"

"I do not mind if I do," Bucher said as he took a cigar. "*Danke schön*, Colonel."

"Thanks anyway, but I prefer my pipe," Red Buffalo said.

"A peace pipe, eh?" Ledbetter said with a chuckle.

The Indian scout explained, "Briar, actually, with a meerschaum bowl."

"Ah . . . of course." Ledbetter got over his momentary fluster and went on. "How about you, Mr. Stark?"

"Thank you, Colonel." Nathan leaned forward and plucked one of the cigars from the box. He smelled it and then tucked it in the pocket of his shirt. "I'll save it for later."

"Very well." Ledbetter closed the box and clasped his pudgy hands together on the desk in front of him. "We dealt quite a blow to the Sioux yesterday, didn't we? For all we know, Hanging Dog himself was among the dead out there."

"I would not count on that, Colonel," Bucher said. "That *verdammt* savage is tricky. I would wager that he got away—if he was even among the members of that war party to start with."

Nathan said, "Calling it a *war party* might be stretching things a mite. They weren't painted for war. Could be they were out hunting or just having a look around."

"With numbers like that?" Bucher shook his head. "If they were looking for anything, it was trouble."

Nathan couldn't dispute that. The Sioux might not have known they were going to run into a patrol, but once they did, they acted quickly to take advantage of the situation. More than twenty soldiers had been killed in the fighting—a pretty hard blow—even though more Sioux had lost their lives.

"What I want to do," the colonel said, "is to strike while we have the hostiles off balance and on the run. I propose to take two companies out again and track those savages back to their village and wipe them out."

Red Buffalo frowned. "That might be difficult to do, Colonel."

Ledbetter's tone sharpened as he replied, "I didn't call you here to ask your opinion. I summoned you to tell you what we're going to do. We *will* accomplish this task. All three of you will accompany my command. You will pick up the trail of the Indians who fled yesterday and follow it to wherever the rest of them have gathered. They *do* have a village somewhere out there, don't they?"

"I reckon they do," Red Buffalo admitted.

"If we attack that village and deal out severe punishment to the hostiles, that will break the back of their resistance," Ledbetter said with arrogant certainty. "They will have no choice but to obey the treaties and move onto the reservations the way they're supposed to."

"What will make the white men obey their treaties?" Red Buffalo muttered.

Nathan understood what the Crow scout meant, but he wasn't sure either of the other two men in the room did.

"What was that?" Ledbetter snapped, proving that he hadn't understood.

Stark said, "Nothing, Colonel. When you attack the Sioux village—if we can find it—do you intend to spare the women and children?"

"Scouts don't decide tactics. They go where they're told and follow orders." Ledbetter shrugged. "But Captain Jameson and Captain Lucas will instruct their men to spare noncombatants to a reasonable extent. If a woman picks up a weapon and threatens our men, she will be dealt with the same as any of the male savages."

That sent Nathan's mind back to the Battle of the Washita. Some people, especially those back east who didn't know what they were talking about, called it a massacre, but it hadn't been, not to his way of thinking. Some of the women in Black Kettle's village had grabbed weapons to put up a fight, and they had been shot down before they could harm any of the soldiers. Although he hadn't killed any women in the battle, Nathan couldn't fault General Custer's troopers for that. A man had a right to defend himself.

Of course, to some people's way of thinking, the Cheyenne had been defending *themselves* when the Seventh Cavalry rode down on their village. Deep down, Nathan couldn't argue with that position either, but he had picked his side in the war—or rather, had it picked for him by those Pawnee renegades who attacked Badger Creek—and there wasn't a damned thing he could do about it.

"The real question," Ledbetter went on, breaking into Nathan's thoughts, "is whether the three of you can do your jobs and locate that village."

"Certainly we can, Colonel," Bucher said. "Those Sioux just wanted to get away. They were not concerned with covering up their trail. Later, after they'd escaped, they may have been more careful, but we can follow them." He looked over at Nathan and Red Buffalo. "Is this not true?"

Red Buffalo said slowly, "It's a good chance to find Hanging Dog's main bunch, that's right. I can't make you any promises, Colonel, but I believe we can locate the village, if that's what you want."

"Of course it's what I want!" Ledbetter thumped a fist on the desk. "Hanging Dog and the rest of those savages have been out there for weeks now, harassing wagon trains, murdering government surveyors, slaughtering innocent settlers, and *laughing at me*." It was clear from the colonel's voice which of those things he considered the most heinous crime. "I want them brought to heel." He came to his feet. "We leave at first light tomorrow. Be ready for a long and dangerous mission, gentlemen . . . as long as it takes to bring those red miscreants to justice!"

Dietrich Bucher stood on the front porch of The House and puffed on the cigar Colonel Ledbetter had given him. After blowing out a cloud of smoke, he said to Nathan and Red Buffalo, "The colonel is putting all his chips in this pot, *ja?*"

"A man who bets everything had better be prepared to lose it," Nathan said. "I'm not sure he is. He seems to think this is going to be an easy job."

Red Buffalo said, "Nothing is ever easy about fighting the Sioux. They are good warriors."

"You sound like you admire them," Bucher said.

"I find something to admire about all the tribes. Except the Blackfeet." Red Buffalo had a personal grudge against the Blackfeet, so his comment wasn't surprising.

If Nathan felt the same way, he would have gone after just the Pawnee instead of all Indians, but he had heard enough firsthand accounts of atrocities committed by all different breeds of redskins to know that it didn't make any difference. They were all guilty as far as he was concerned.

Slaves were no better than ponies, there was no

telling which bunch might have Rena by now. That was another reason to hate all of them.

He had to admit, though, it was getting a mite wearying, toting around that much hate. He went down the steps and started to walk off.

Red Buffalo called after him, "Where are you going, Stark?"

"We're not pulling out until in the morning, the colonel said," Nathan replied without looking around. "Until then, where I go and what I do is none of your damn business." He started to add *redskin* but didn't bother. Red Buffalo knew what he was.

Honestly, Nathan wasn't sure where he was going, but he found his steps carrying him toward the chapel. The night before, he had resolved to stay as far away as possible from Delia Blaine, for both their sakes, but he had an undeniable sense of leaving something unfinished between them and knew that was going to gnaw at his innards.

Especially with him setting out on a major campaign against the Sioux the next day. On such a mission, the odds were no better than fifty-fifty that he would come back alive. He figured he couldn't actually *settle* things with Delia—they were too far apart on what they believed—but maybe he could leave things on a better footing between them.

He heard singing as he approached the chapel—the sweet voices of children, but they weren't singing a hymn. Rather, it was a sweet, wholesome popular song from a few years earlier. Nathan had never had much interest in music, but he vaguely recognized it. He supposed those were the children in Delia's classroom doing the singing.

He hadn't been in too many houses of worship

during the past fifteen years, so he felt a little uncomfortable walking into that one. His footsteps echoed hollowly from the sanctuary's high ceiling as he walked between the two sections of pews to an open door at the front of the room. Looking through the door, he saw a smaller room with eighteen children sitting at tables while they sang. He propped a shoulder against the door jamb to watch them.

There were a few more girls than boys, and they ranged in age from six or seven up to the middle teens. Delia stood facing them, with her back to Nathan, and clearly didn't know he was there as the tune reached its conclusion.

"That was very good," she told them. "I think singing a song in the middle of the morning's work breaks it up nicely. That keeps us from getting too tired . . ." Her voice trailed off as some of the younger children giggled. Most of them were looking at Nathan, and the ones who weren't had to make an obvious effort not to.

Delia looked back over her shoulder, making a half-turn. "Nathan, I didn't expect you."

"I shouldn't have bothered you," he said, straightening. "I can go—"

"No need, now that you're here." Delia smiled as she turned back to the youngsters. "Children, this is Mr. Nathan Stark, an old friend of mine and one of the scouts assigned to the fort. Some of you may know who he is."

One of the younger boys asked, "Is he your beau, Mrs. Blaine?"

"What? No, no . . . not at all. We're . . . old friends, like I said."

The kids might have come closer to believing her if

she hadn't been acting so flustered. Oddly enough, he *wasn't* her beau, even though they might have liked that if things had worked out differently.

"Why are you here, Nathan?"

"I wanted to talk to you for a minute, but it's nothing that can't wait until later today. I shouldn't have interrupted your class." He shrugged. "Just acted without thinking, I reckon. I do that sometimes."

She smiled and shook her head. "No, it's all right. The children are going to be working in their copybooks for a while now. I can step out for a moment." She looked at the oldest of the girls. "Janey, you can watch the class for a few minutes, can't you?"

"Of course, Mrs. Blaine," the girl said.

Delia took Nathan's arm and led him out of the classroom, which caused more giggles and snickers behind them until Janey shushed the other children. Nathan and Delia walked through the sanctuary and stepped outside.

Pausing in the shadow of the chapel, she said, "Is something wrong?"

"No, I meant it when I said it was just thoughtless of me to bust in like that. What I wanted to tell you is that I'll be leaving in the morning, maybe for a pretty good spell. The colonel's taking two companies out to chase down Hanging Dog, and all three scouts are going with him."

A solemn expression came over Delia's face. "This sounds like a major campaign."

"Well . . . it's not like some of the ones I've been on with Custer and Crook, where the column stretches for dang near a mile or more. It's not a big deal compared to those. But if we find Hanging Dog's village, it'll be a good fight, sure enough."

"Do you think you will? Find it, that is."

"Well"—he smiled—"I wouldn't have a very high opinion of my skills as a scout if I said no, now would I?"

She looked down at the ground. "I know I should wish you success . . . but there's a part of me that hopes you fail, Nathan. If you don't find the Sioux, there won't be a battle. And there's been enough killing . . . on both sides."

"That won't be true until it's safe for innocent folks to live out here, Delia. And I'm not sure that'll ever be possible as long as any of those savages are still alive. At least, not until they're beaten so bad they go back to the reservations and stay there where they belong." Nathan paused, then plunged ahead. "It seems to me you ought to feel the same way, considering everything they've taken from you."

"If all the Sioux die . . . and all the Cheyenne and the Kiowa and the Comanche . . . and . . . and all the rest . . . it won't bring Stephen back, will it? Or Camilla, either."

Nathan turned and smacked the side of his fist against the chapel wall. "Every time," he said bitterly. "Every dang time I try to talk to you, I just get you all upset. I admire you more than any other woman on this earth, Delia, and yet I keep opening my big ol' mouth and causing trouble."

"Then, damn it, quit talking!" Delia put her arms around his neck, drew his face to hers, and kissed him with an urgency that shook Nathan right down to his boots.

CHAPTER 26

Those kids in the schoolroom would have been giggling for sure if they had seen their teacher kissing the hard-bitten scout. Delia had taken Nathan by surprise, but he didn't pull away from her. Instinctively, he embraced her. She tasted too intoxicating and felt too good in his arms.

He couldn't help but realize they were right out in the open, though, and in broad daylight, to boot. It pained him, but he broke the kiss and stepped back. "You're gonna ruin your reputation if you keep doing impulsive things like that, Mrs. Blaine."

"It would probably be healthy for people to follow their impulses more."

Nathan shook his head. "I don't know. As sweet as that was, it didn't change a blasted thing, did it? I'm still going with the colonel tomorrow to chase down Hanging Dog, and you're still gonna think we ought to be making peace instead of war."

"Isn't peace better?"

"Not if it means you just stop fighting and wait for the other fella to kill you."

"You don't think the Sioux would leave us alone if we left them alone?" she challenged.

Nathan sighed, took off his hat, and wearily scrubbed a hand over his face. "I don't decide these things, Delia. You should be talking to the folks in the War Department back in Washington. All I do is follow orders."

"Which happen to coincide with your need to fight and kill Indians."

Nathan wasn't going to argue with her. Obviously she was right about that. He had defended himself to her before, and it was a waste of time.

"There's a saying about how sometimes folks just have to agree to disagree," he told her. "I reckon that's what we're gonna have to do. Neither of us is likely to change the way we feel about things, are we?"

"No," she said softly. "I suppose not."

"But there are some things we *can* agree on. I care about you, Delia, and I believe you honestly care about me. Maybe for us it'll never be like it is for some people, but what we do have is a good thing." He smiled. "I can always use another friend."

"Do you really have any friends, Nathan?"

"Cullen Jefferson," he answered without hesitation. "But I guess when you come right down to it, he's the only one."

"Until now."

"Until now," he agreed.

"And we're . . . more than friends, Nathan."

"Maybe. One of these days . . . maybe we can be."

She hugged him again, not passionately but with deep affection radiating from her. Stepping back, she rested her hands on his arms and said, "You're coming to supper tonight."

"Now, dang it, Delia, we keep beating our heads against that wall. It's not gonna work out well, and you know it."

"We won't talk about Indians or the campaign or anything else that we've argued about."

Nathan shook his head. "It's not a good idea. Let's just go ahead and say good-bye now."

"But it's nearly twenty-four hours until you leave!"

"Then I'll have twenty-four hours of a mighty good memory in my head instead of maybe twelve hours of reliving over and over another argument I didn't want."

She glared at him for a long moment, but he didn't believe she was actually that upset at him.

Finally, she said, "You are a stubborn, infuriating man, Nathan Stark. But I suppose you have a point. There's only one thing . . ."

"What's that?"

"If this is the memory you're going to take with you, we need to make sure it's a very good one." With that she kissed him again.

Nathan decided that if she wasn't overly concerned about her reputation, he wasn't going to be, either. And it felt mighty good to hold her.

Good enough that when she finally murmured, "I have to get back to the children," and slipped away into the chapel, he felt like he had lost something he might never get back.

The fort buzzed with activity all day as preparations were made for the campaign against Hanging Dog and the Sioux. The soldiers would need plenty of food and ammunition, so the men assigned to the quartermaster were kept busy packing those supplies. The packs would be loaded on mules early the next morning, starting well before dawn.

Three men met under the trees beyond the stables, each of them arriving at different times so people would be less likely to notice them getting together. Sergeant Jeremiah Dockery arrived first, followed by Dietrich Bucher and then Sergeant Seamus McCall.

"Anybody watching you?" Dockery asked once they were all there.

"No one paid attention to me," Bucher said. "I know how to make sure I am not seen."

"Are ye sayin' I don't?" McCall demanded.

"Do not take offense where none is intended," Bucher snapped.

"Listen, none of us can afford to get touchy right now, what with the colonel getting this crazy idea in his head." Dockery frowned at McCall. "If you hadn't gotten into that scrape with the Sioux, Ledbetter might not have such a burr under his saddle about Hanging Dog."

"That wasn't my doin'," McCall said. "And I didn't want to be there any more than anybody else did. Damn it, I *knew* those redskins had Winchesters. Do ye think I would have put me own neck on the line like that if I'd had any choice in the matter?"

Bucher said, "The colonel's mind is made up. We are going out after the Indians, and there is nothing we can do about it."

"I'll not be goin'," McCall said. "Since that last patrol came from Company K and we're undermanned right now because of the casualties, we're the ones stayin' behind to guard the post while the colonel is out glory-huntin'. I'll be here to keep an eye on things, if that's what you're worried about."

"I'm more worried Ledbetter will blunder right into the wagons delivering those rifles to Hanging Dog at Weeping Woman Rock," Dockery said. "If he does, that'll ruin everything." The Tennessean looked at Bucher. "It'll be your job to make sure that doesn't happen."

"I will not be the only scout on this campaign," Bucher pointed out.

"That means one of us, you"—Dockery pointed to Bucher—"or me, needs to take care of Stark and Red Buffalo the first chance we get."

"Ye had your chance last night," McCall said with a sneer. "From what I hear, ye didn't do a very good job of it."

"*Ja*, as it turned out, both of them were there," Bucher added. "You could have gotten rid of Stark and the Crow at the same time. How could you have missed them both with a shotgun?"

Dockery's face darkened with anger. "Neither of you were there," he snapped. "You don't know how close I came to getting them."

"Close does not count." Bucher smirked. "We must not allow ourselves to get distracted. I will keep the column well away from Weeping Woman Rock if at all possible. The colonel knows nothing. It will not be difficult to lead him around in circles. Even if we cannot get rid of Stark and Red Buffalo, they are new here. They can be fooled as well."

"I hope you're right," Dockery said. "If you're not, this whole thing might blow up in our faces."

With nothing left to say, the three conspirators left the woods one by one, each being as casual as possible.

None of them noticed a slight rustling in the brush nearby after they were gone. A slender figure slipped into sight, stood there for a moment breathing heavily, and then broke into a run toward the stables. His heart pounded, and uncertainty was etched on his young face.

He had never been more unsure of what to do in his life. Or more afraid.

Those at the fort who weren't going along on the campaign gathered at sunrise the next morning to watch the column move out. Wives and children stood outside the chapel, waving to the husbands and fathers who rode past.

Nathan noted Delia was with them. Although it had been difficult, he had managed to avoid her for the rest of the previous day, and he carried with him that good memory she'd wanted to instill in him.

More than he would have expected, he found himself wanting to get back safely from the mission. He had never cared much about that before. He didn't fear death, as long as it came in service to the vengeance he had sought for so long. If he died in action, his only regret would be that he'd never found his sister and brought her back to civilization.

In the past twenty-four hours he'd come to realize that if destiny caught up to him on the campaign, his last thoughts would be not only of Rena but of Delia Blaine, as well.

The four Sioux boys were standing with the regular hostlers as the column passed. Nathan recognized the two he'd had the run-in with over Buck not long after arriving at Fort Randall. One was known as Billy, he recalled, but he couldn't remember either of their redskin names. They all watched with sullen expressions on their faces, resentful.

Nathan noticed Billy appeared worried about something and then immediately forgot about it, since he didn't give a damn about any of the little heathens. He still thought Colonel Ledbetter was making a mistake by letting them remain at the fort. Nathan wondered if Delia had had anything to do with that. The possibility seemed likely.

The sun had just peeked over the eastern horizon. The light washing over the prairie in front of the column was garish and the shadows cast by the men and horses and mules were long.

Nathan rode with Red Buffalo and Bucher well behind Colonel Ledbetter, who was leading the column, flanked by Captains Jameson and Lucas. Lieutenants Barkley, Hanover, Williams, and DeBrett were with the column, as well.

Doc Lightner was traveling with the column, too, since the campaign was expected to produce a considerable amount of fighting and a surgeon's services were bound to be called for. He had two medical orderlies with him, one of whom drove the ambulance wagon. Lightner himself was on horseback, dressed in his regular captain's uniform, not the long duster he usually wore while working in the infirmary.

Company H was first in the column, followed by the pack train and the ambulance, then Company G brought up the rear. Lieutenant Allingham was back at the fort, in command of the remains of Company K left behind as garrison troops.

Nathan glanced back over his shoulder. Although he had ridden with much bigger columns, it was an impressive force. He didn't know how many warriors Hanging Dog had with him. From previous scouting missions, Bucher had estimated the number of Sioux at a hundred and fifty, but Nathan didn't have much faith in the German's judgment. Ledbetter had more than two hundred and fifty troops with him, however, and that seemed like it ought to be enough to handle whatever force Hanging Dog could muster.

Nathan said, "With this many men, we ought to be able to whip the Sioux if we can find them."

"We can find them," Red Buffalo said, "but we may wish that we hadn't. Sooner or later, the Sioux, the Cheyenne, and the rest of the tribes are going to realize that the only way they can truly defeat the army is to band together. It will take strong leaders to accomplish . . . men such as Crazy Horse and Sitting Bull . . . but someday such an alliance will happen."

"You're insane," Bucher said with a cocky grin on his face. "The savages will never work together like that. They hate each other too much . . . just like they hate the whites."

"In the end it wouldn't matter," Nathan said. "There might be enough of them to wipe out a column of cavalry, but they can't wipe out the whole United States Army. And that's what it would take."

Red Buffalo nodded solemnly. "You're right, Stark. The ending is foretold." The Crow scout stared straight ahead as he rode. "But no one can foretell how much blood will be spilled before that day ever gets here."

CHAPTER 27

The column moved northwestward along the Missouri River as the patrol had done several days earlier. It crossed the broad, slow-moving stream at the same ford and proceeded in a more northerly direction into the hills. The soldiers didn't follow the route all the way to the mesa where the patrol had found itself trapped, however. Before they got that far, Red Buffalo found the trail the Sioux had left when they fled.

The three scouts had been ranging in front of the column in a broad half-circle, searching for that trail. When Red Buffalo located it, he rendezvoused with Nathan and Bucher and took them back to have a look at the tracks.

"Got to be them, all right," Nathan agreed as he studied the sign. "The size of this bunch matches up with the ones who got away from that fight, and they look like they were in a hurry. Mostly unshod ponies, too, with a few shod horses being the army mounts they gathered up along the way."

Red Buffalo grunted. "We can follow them from

here. Sooner or later, they will have tried to cover their tracks—"

"But not good enough to hide them from our keen eyes, *ja*?" Bucher said with a cocky grin.

"A couple of us ought to keep on following this trail while the other goes back to fetch the colonel," Nathan said. "It doesn't matter to me who does what."

"I will ride back to the column," Bucher declared. "We can return here by nightfall, perhaps."

Red Buffalo nodded. "If we are not here, you can follow these tracks in the morning. We'll rejoin you somewhere up ahead."

"*Ja*, it sounds like a good plan to me." Bucher lifted a hand in farewell as he tightened up on the reins with his other hand. "Be careful. Until the column gets here, you will be on your own out there, *und* there is no telling how many savages you might encounter."

"We'll keep our eyes open," Nathan said dryly. "Don't worry about us."

Bucher nodded, swung his horse around, and loped off toward the southeast.

"I can't say that I'm sad to see him go," Red Buffalo commented when the German was out of earshot.

"Me, either," Nathan replied, then frowned as he realized he had just agreed with an Indian.

Judging by the smile lurking around the corners of Red Buffalo's mouth, the same thought had occurred to him. Nathan grimaced, pulled Buck's head around, and nudged the horse into motion, following the tracks left by the fleeing Sioux several days earlier.

Only an hour of good light was left. Nathan didn't

expect the soldiers to arrive in time to take up the trail. He and Red Buffalo could follow the tracks for a while, then make camp. In the morning one of them would ride back while the other forged ahead. Nathan didn't mind the idea of being on his own. He had handled such missions many times in the past. Usually he and Cullen had worked together, but sometimes circumstances had forced them to split up for a while.

And Moses Red Buffalo was no Cullen Jefferson, that was for damn sure. Although . . . if somebody had put a gun to Nathan's head and forced him to admit the truth . . . having Red Buffalo around had come in pretty handy a few times. Nathan glanced at the Crow. He was still moving a little stiffly from those two buckshot in the back he had caught while saving Nathan's life.

Nathan didn't allow himself to think too much about that.

As dusk settled over the landscape, they rode into a grove of aspen along a creek. The trees would give them a good place to camp and plenty of cover if any hostiles came along. No fire tonight, Nathan reflected. A large, well-armed force like the column from Fort Randall could build cooking fires when they called a halt, but two men out on their own in Sioux country couldn't afford to take that chance.

They picketed their horses, unsaddled the animals, and spread blankets on the ground underneath the trees. In the morning they would refill their canteens from the creek, but they had enough water to wash down the jerky and hard biscuits in their saddlebags.

Nathan propped his back against a tree trunk and stretched his legs out in front of him, crossing them at the ankles. The shadows were thick enough that he could still see Red Buffalo but not make out many details. He swallowed a bite of biscuit, then said, "You're eating like a white man. How come you're not gnawing on a hunk of pemmican?"

"I like white man's food. Couldn't you tell that from our supper at Mrs. Blaine's?"

"Don't remind me of that," Nathan said with a scowl. Knowing Red Buffalo probably couldn't see his face any better than he could see the Crow's, he glared anyway.

"You are the one who asked the question. Truly, though, I have never cared for pemmican. Are there no foods eaten by white men that you find unappetizing?"

"Plenty of 'em." Nathan thought about it for a moment. "I never have understood why anybody would ever think it was a good idea to eat brussels sprouts."

Red Buffalo laughed softly. "I do not know what that is, but I admit, they don't sound very good to me."

"But I do like a good buffalo steak."

"So do I."

Nathan asked himself what the hell he was doing, sitting there talking to Red Buffalo almost like he and the savage were friends. Sure, they had been thrown together and forced to fight side by side, and more than likely Red Buffalo was his only ally within ten or fifteen miles, but that didn't mean he had to be pleasant toward the redskinned son of a bitch.

"How long have you had that horse?" Red Buffalo asked, taking Nathan by surprise.

"Buck?"

"That's what you call him . . . because he's a buckskin, I suppose."

"What the hell else would I call him?"

Red Buffalo said, "I once met a man who named all his horses Horse and all his dogs Dog. He claimed it was simpler that way, and since it worked, he saw no reason to change the habit."

That sounded familiar to Nathan, and after a moment he realized why. "You're talking about that old mountain man, the one they call Preacher."

"You know him?" Red Buffalo asked.

"Never met the man, which is sort of surprising, since to hear folks tell it he's done everything and been everywhere out here on the frontier. But our trails have never crossed. I'm not surprised yours have, though. I seem to recall hearing that he never got along real well with the Blackfeet, either."

"They have long been his mortal enemies. Years ago, when I was a young man, I met him and another mountain man, a fellow named MacCallister. They were tracking down some outlaws." Red Buffalo grunted. "I would not want to have those two on my trail."

"No, I reckon not. I've heard of MacCallister, too. Pretty salty hombre."

"For a man to survive out here, often he has to be." The Crow paused. "You did not answer my question about your horse."

"Buck and I been together, oh, five years now, I'd say. I bought him off a fella in Colorado who couldn't handle him. Buck was young and pretty high-spirited in those days. The man who owned him took a whip to him. Buck didn't take kindly to that, and neither did I."

"So you came to the horse's aid."

"Let's just say I showed that fella the error of his ways," Nathan drawled. "Then I dropped a couple double eagles on his chest while he was out cold and took Buck in return." Nathan snorted. "Hell, that bastard should've paid me for saving his life. If he'd kept on mistreating Buck like that, Buck would've killed him sooner or later."

"You are kind to animals, then."

Nathan said sharply, "Animals never did me any harm. Never saw a point to shooting any of them except to eat, or to make a coat or a robe out of."

"Another way in which we agree."

Anger sparked inside Nathan. He knew good and well what Red Buffalo was up to. The Crow was goading him by pointing out the ways in which they were alike, along with the contradiction between Nathan's kind heart toward animals and his burning desire to kill Indians. Red Buffalo was like Delia—he thought he could sort of steer Nathan around to feeling differently about things.

Not gonna happen. Nathan's voice was curt when he said, "I'll take the first watch."

"All right. I do not believe we are in any danger from the Sioux . . . yet . . . but we cannot ignore that possibility."

Nathan didn't say anything. He finished his sparse meal, drank some more water from his canteen, and tried not to think about how good a cup of hot, black coffee would taste. He picked up his Winchester, which he had placed on the ground beside him when he sat down, and stood up to move deeper into the trees, where the thick shadows would conceal him.

The night was quiet enough that within a few minutes he heard deep, regular breathing as the Crow scout slept. Red Buffalo had the frontiersman's knack of being able to fall asleep almost right away when the opportunity presented itself.

Nathan tucked the rifle under his left arm and leaned his shoulder against a tree. After a long day in the saddle, he was weary but not particularly sleepy. His brain was too full of thoughts, most of them about everything that had happened since he'd come to Fort Randall. Cullen's departure, the alternately happy and strained reunion with Delia, the forced and unwelcome partnership with Moses Red Buffalo, the mysterious attempts on his life . . . and the quite possibly ill-advised campaign against the Sioux.

Nathan didn't necessarily believe it was a mistake for the army to go after Hanging Dog. The war chief needed to be brought to heel before he could stir things up even more. It was the fact that Colonel Wesley Stuart Ledbetter was in charge that worried Nathan. He had seen the combination of ambition, inexperience, and downright incompetence before. When a commanding officer like that marched out into the field against the enemy, he nearly always got men killed.

Nathan didn't trust Dietrich Bucher, either. To be honest, Nathan had never witnessed the German doing anything to question whether he could handle the job of a scout. It was more a matter of how Bucher just rubbed him the wrong way. Nathan's gut said not to trust the German. And Nathan had learned to rely on his gut's wisdom.

His forehead creased as another worry occurred to him. While he was at the fort, he had done his best to avoid and ignore those four Sioux boys who worked in the stables. They had seldom even crossed his mind.

But in the quiet of the night their presence at Fort Randall was more troubling. With a depleted company of around a hundred men left there to protect the place, the post would make a mighty tempting target if Hanging Dog ever found out just how few defenders were on hand. It wouldn't be any trouble at all for Billy or one of those other young heathens to slip away and ride upriver in search of his people. All he'd have to do was find Hanging Dog and tell him what was going on, and then Hanging Dog could lead a horde of bloodthirsty savages down on the fort where Delia and all those other helpless women and children were.

Son of a bitch, Nathan thought as his jaw clenched so tight it was painful. He should have told Colonel Ledbetter that he wasn't going along on the campaign. He should have stayed at the fort to keep an eye on things, and if Ledbetter didn't like it, well . . . Nathan could have told him to go climb a stump.

He'd had just about enough of the army, anyway.

Those thoughts filled his head, but his senses were still fully alert, working at a high level without conscious awareness. He realized suddenly that something was wrong. A hint of a smell caught on the night breeze, a tiny sound . . . he couldn't pin it down, but whatever it was made him turn sharply toward the place where he had left Red Buffalo sleeping.

He had just started to move when the roar of a gunshot filled the night.

CHAPTER 28

Nathan ran through the woods with the Winchester held at a slant across his chest. More shots boomed, and he could tell by the sound that they came from two different guns. Muzzle flame licked back and forth in the darkness. Nathan thought he knew which of the flashes marked Red Buffalo's position, but it was hard to be sure and he didn't want to blunder right into an enemy.

He stopped, put his back against a tree trunk, and during a lull in the firing called, "Red Buffalo! Sing out!"

"Here, Stark!" the Crow replied, confirming Nathan's guess about his position.

"Who's that shooting at you?"

"I have no idea, but he missed!"

Two more shots hammered out from the unknown gunman and thudded into a tree trunk. Nathan had him spotted and dropped to one knee. He brought the Winchester to his shoulder and squeezed off three rounds one after the other, working the rifle's lever quickly between shots. He placed them around the spot where he had caught a glimpse of orange flame from the ambusher's gun.

It seemed like there were a lot of cowardly back shooters in that part of the country, and he was getting damned sick and tired of it. The life he had led had made him accustomed to people trying to kill him, but most of the time his enemies were right in front of him, not behind him.

More booming shots blasted from Red Buffalo's revolver. Return fire spurted from the shadows. Nathan snapped two more rounds in that direction.

The bushwhacker had had enough. As echoes died away, Nathan heard something splash through the creek, then the rapid drumming of a horse's hooves as the hidden gunman fled.

Waiting until the sound had faded away into the distance, Nathan finally called to Red Buffalo, "You reckon there was only one of them?"

"I saw muzzle flashes from only one gun," the Crow replied.

"Were you hit?"

"No. The first bullet came close, but shooting in such bad light is tricky."

Nathan knew that from experience, all right. He thought about the situation. If there had been *two* bushwhackers, one could have opened up first to draw the fire of their quarry, then fled to make Nathan and Red Buffalo believe they were safe. There could be another man lurking in the shadows in absolute silence, just waiting for a good shot at them.

Even though that was a possibility, Nathan knew he and his companion would have to move sometime.

After another five minutes had passed with no sign of danger, he stood up and walked toward Red Buffalo's position. "Don't get hasty on the trigger. It's me."

Red Buffalo stepped out from behind a tree. "You are unharmed as well?"

"That's right. I'm gonna take a look around and see if I can find anything that'll tell us something about that varmint."

"I will check on the horses. Neither of them made any noise of being hurt, but there were quite a few bullets flying around."

That was true, and Nathan was grateful that Red Buffalo was going to make sure Buck hadn't been hit. He moved quietly toward the spot where he had seen the ambusher's muzzle flashes, and when he thought he was in the right place, he slipped a lucifer from his shirt pocket and snapped it into life with his thumbnail.

Nathan had his eyes squinted against the light before he ignited the match, so it didn't blind him. He held it up high enough for its flickering glow to fall over the ground and caught a glimpse of a reflection in the soft duff under the trees. He leaned his rifle against a trunk and bent to pick up the object he had found. It was an empty .44-40 cartridge, which told him exactly nothing since there were thousands, maybe millions, of them around on the frontier. It was the most common load for Winchester repeaters. Nathan's own rifle carried them.

The lucifer burned down and he struck another as he hunkered there, studying the ground. Catching sight of something else, he leaned forward and frowned. The bushwhacker had left part of a footprint behind, and from the sharp edges caused by the foot pressing down into the earth, he knew the track was left by a man wearing a boot, not a moccasin. That wasn't absolute proof the ambusher had been a white man, since some of the Sioux wore boots they had stolen off the bodies of slain settlers, but it was more likely the lurking gunman hadn't been an Indian.

Nathan found a few more empty shells but no other footprints. He went back to the camp where Red Buffalo waited for him. "Horses all right?"

"Both fine," was the reply. "What did you find?"

"Just some .44-40 shells, and we both know the hombre was using a rifle from the sound of it. And some boot tracks."

Red Buffalo drew in a sharp breath. "Boot tracks," he repeated. "A white man."

"We don't know that for sure." Grudgingly, Nathan went on. "But shooting at a fella in the dark isn't usually the way a redskin does things."

"My people prefer to attack their enemies openly, other than skulking dogs such as the Apaches."

Nathan laughed.

"Something amuses you?" Red Buffalo asked coolly.

"You look down on some of the tribes, too. You so-called noble red men aren't really any better than anybody else, are you?"

"We are all people, good and bad alike. But I believe our history displays less treachery and dishonor than that of the whites."

"Believe whatever you want," Nathan said. "I believe I'd like to know who it is that keeps trying to kill me."

"Those shots were aimed at me," Red Buffalo pointed out.

"Only because you're with me. That varmint wanted to kill both of us, and you know it."

After a moment, the Crow admitted, "You are probably correct. We have more enemies out here than just Hanging Dog and his warriors, Stark."

Nathan just grunted. He was getting tired of agreeing with Red Buffalo, but he knew the other scout was right.

The rest of the night passed without incident. In the morning they ate another cold, unsatisfying breakfast, filled their canteens at the stream, and saddled up.

"Who goes on and who rides back to find Bucher and the rest of the column?" Nathan asked. That was different, he realized. In the past, he had simply decided such things based on what he wanted, without caring what Red Buffalo's opinion was.

"I will go ahead," the Crow said. "If any of the Sioux see me, they will be more likely to believe I am some lone brave passing through this area, and no threat to them."

Nathan frowned dubiously, but he supposed Red Buffalo was right. Any Indians who spotted a lone white man would go after him with no hesitation, figuring it would be an easy kill.

"If you find Hanging Dog's village, backtrack and let us know," Nathan said. "Otherwise the column will just continue to follow these tracks."

Red Buffalo nodded. He wheeled his pony and rode along the creek at a leisurely pace without looking back, following the tracks left several days earlier.

Son of a bitch didn't even say good-bye, Nathan thought, then asked himself why he would care about such a thing. He turned Buck and rode back the way they had come.

By midmorning, he saw the dust haze hanging in the air ahead of him and knew that marked the column's location. Sure enough, half an hour later a man on horseback came into view. Nathan recognized Dietrich Bucher's derby hat and burly shape. Both scouts reined in as they rode up to each other.

Bucher said, "The column is half a mile behind me. Red Buffalo has continued tracking the Sioux?"

"That's right."

"You did not locate their village?"

"Not yet," Nathan said. "We probably still have a ways to go."

"No trouble, then."

That was an odd thing to say, Nathan thought. Almost like Bucher expected something to have happened. Nathan shrugged a little and shook his head. "Nope. We didn't run into any problems."

Bucher scowled, but only for a second then he forced a grin and said, "*Das ist gut.* Come on. We will report to Colonel Ledbetter."

Nathan lifted his reins and nudged Buck into motion. Bucher had looked puzzled and confused for a moment, and that was mighty interesting. Nathan glanced over at the German as Bucher fell in alongside him. Bucher didn't seem to be paying much attention to him, but that could easily be a ruse.

Within minutes they came in sight of the column. Colonel Ledbetter saw them coming and raised a hand in a signal to stop. As the column ground to a halt, Ledbetter rode on out to intercept the scouts, accompanied by Captain Lucas.

"We're still on the right trail, Stark?" the colonel asked without any greeting.

"We are, Colonel," Nathan replied. "Red Buffalo's gone ahead. He'll be trying to locate the Sioux village or at least make sure we haven't lost the trail."

"The sooner we find those hostiles and deal with them, the better," Ledbetter snapped. "Deal with them harshly, I might add."

"I figure they'll be trying to deal harshly with us if they find us first," Nathan drawled.

Ledbetter frowned. "No ragtag band of savages will ever be a match for the best fighting men and the finest officers the country can muster."

The problem with that boastful declaration was that while Companies G and H were, for the most part, experienced soldiers, there was no guarantee they were the best fighting men in the country. Despite his hatred for the redskins, Nathan was pragmatic enough to know that most of them didn't suck hind tit to anybody when it came to fighting.

He was damned sure that particular assemblage of soldiers wasn't being commanded by the finest officer the army had to offer, but there was no point in saying that to Ledbetter's face. Such an opinion would run smack-dab into the brick wall of the colonel's arrogance.

Nathan turned in his saddle and pointed. "Anyway, that's the direction we're headed. All we have to do is push on. Red Buffalo will ride back and find us if there's anything we need to know."

"Very well." Ledbetter lifted his stocky form in the stirrups and waved the column forward. Lieutenants and then sergeants bawled orders and got the soldiers moving again.

Nathan turned his horse to ride alongside the leaders in the column, but he gradually dropped back and let the first company pass him. Neither Bucher nor Ledbetter and the captains seemed to notice what he was doing.

Nathan kept up his slow pace until Doc Lightner and the ambulance wagon caught up with him.

The surgeon nodded to him and said, "Hello, Stark. Any new developments?"

"No, we're still on the trail of those hostiles. I'd like to ask you a question, though, Doc."

Lightner frowned. "We've already discussed how it wouldn't be professional of me to offer any opinions on Colonel Ledbetter's competence or tactical decisions."

"Not asking you to, Doc." Nathan chuckled, but there wasn't much genuine humor in the sound. "Reckon I've already come to my own conclusions on those matters. No, what I want to ask you about is Dietrich Bucher."

Lightner looked surprised. "I don't know what I can tell you. I haven't really had any dealings with him. He hasn't required medical attention."

"Here's what I'm curious about. Did you happen to notice when he rejoined the company yesterday evening? It should have been sometime around dusk, maybe a little later."

Lightner thought about it for a moment and then shook his head. "I don't believe that's the case,

Captain. I had supper last night with the colonel and Captains Jameson and Lucas. I'm sure Mr. Bucher would have reported to them immediately when he rode in. In fact, when I noticed that he was in camp this morning, I recall thinking that he must have come in very late, because there'd been no sign of him by the time I turned in."

"So you're saying he didn't turn up until the middle of the night or later?"

"It appears that way," Lightner replied. "Why? Is there something important about what time Mr. Bucher arrived?"

"I don't know how important it is, but it's curious." Nathan waved a hand. "Don't trouble yourself over it, Doc. And it would probably be better if you didn't mention to Bucher that I'd been asking questions about him . . . if that's all right with you."

"Whatever this is about, unless it has some bearing on medical issues, it's no business of mine. I'd just as soon keep it that way."

"That's good, Doc. Thanks."

Nathan heeled Buck to a faster pace and rode back toward the head of the column. He kept thinking about what he had just learned. If Dietrich Bucher hadn't rejoined the column until late in the night, that meant his whereabouts for several hours were unaccounted for.

He would have had time to follow Nathan and Red Buffalo to their camp in the aspens and open fire on them. Nathan thought back to the day when he had been ambushed while scouting for Lieutenant Pryor's patrol. Supposedly, Dietrich had been back at Fort Randall on that day . . . but did anyone really pay enough attention to the German to guarantee that he hadn't slipped off and trailed the patrol without anybody noticing? It was possible that had happened, Nathan decided, which left an even more important question.

Why would Dietrich Bucher want him dead badly enough to keep trying to bushwhack him?

CHAPTER 29

The tracks left by the Sioux were easy enough to follow, and since the column had Nathan and Bucher to read sign, it was simple to stay on the trail of their quarry. As the day went on, Nathan expected to see Red Buffalo riding toward them to deliver the news that he had found Hanging Dog's village, but the Crow scout didn't appear.

Nathan was also keeping a close eye on Bucher. Even if his suspicions about the German were correct, it was pretty damned unlikely that Bucher would try to kill him right out in the open, in plain sight of two companies of mounted infantry and more than half a dozen officers. Nathan watched him closely anyway.

With those two concerns occupying his mind, he didn't really have much time to think about Delia Blaine and what was going on back at the fort, but she kept sneaking into his thoughts anyway. He wouldn't stop worrying until he and the rest of the men were back at Fort Randall and he could see with his own eyes that she was safe.

By late afternoon, there was still no sign of Red

Buffalo, and the trail had gotten more difficult to follow, indicating that the Sioux hadn't been fleeing headlong anymore but rather had slowed down to cover their tracks.

"I don't like this," Colonel Ledbetter complained. "Shouldn't we have found the savages by now?"

"We've only been looking for them for two days, Colonel," Nathan said. "I've been out on campaigns that lasted for weeks or even months."

"*Ja,*" Bucher said. "Sometimes these things cannot be hurried, Colonel. We are still on the hostiles' trail, so there is every chance we will locate them eventually."

Ledbetter scowled. "We didn't bring enough supplies to stay out for a month, even if we're able to find game to supplement our rations. If we don't find the Sioux in a week, we'll have to turn back." His face darkened and puffed up like a toad again. "I will *not* return to Fort Randall empty-handed and in disgrace. I simply will not have it."

Ledbetter seemed to be having trouble with the idea that sometimes, things were out of a man's control. That no matter what he did, now and then fate was going to rear up and kick him in the teeth. Pain and failure were inevitable. How a man handled life when that happened was what really told the story about him.

When it happened to Nathan, he had set off on a killing spree that had lasted fifteen years. So far. What would make him call a halt to it at last, he wondered? If he found Rena, if he was able to return her to a normal life—assuming that was even possible—would that be enough to satisfy him?

All the blood he had spilled hadn't been, that was for sure. Was there enough Indian blood in the world to do that?

Bucher spurred his horse ahead of the column. Nathan went with him, unwilling to let Bucher stray too far because he wanted the German where he could keep an eye on him.

When they were out of earshot of the column, Bucher slowed his mount. With a frown, he said, "The trail is becoming more difficult to follow, Stark. Are these *verdammt* savages going to give us the slip?"

Nathan had pulled Buck back to a walk, as well. He studied the rolling prairie ahead of them, broken up here and there by ridges, hills, buttes, and ranges of small mountains. Farther north and west lay the Black Hills, from that distance just a low, dark line on the horizon. There were plenty of hiding places in the vast, untamed land. The frontier could swallow up hundreds of Indians as if they had never been there. He had seen it happen.

But . . . if a man knew what he was looking for, there were always things to point him in the right direction.

He said, "We'll find them. I'm not worried about that. I'm a mite concerned that Red Buffalo may have found them already, though. Or *they* found *him.*"

A harsh laugh came from Bucher. "If I did not know better, Stark, I would say that you are worried about the Indian. Have you decided that you no longer hate all redskins?"

"I never said that," Nathan snapped. "Red Buffalo's our partner. We've got to work with him. Besides, he knows the column is coming along behind him. If the Sioux grabbed him and went to work on him, he might tell them where to find us." He had a hunch Red Buffalo wouldn't give up much information, even if he was being tortured but figured he'd rather not find out for sure.

"Only about an hour of daylight remaining," Bucher commented. "We should start looking for a place the column can make camp. They will catch up to us as the sun is going down, I think."

Nathan agreed. They rode on, stopping a short time later atop a broad, shallow ridge. Trees had become scarce, but at least the ridge would give the soldiers some high ground to hold if they came under attack.

The two scouts waited there for the column to arrive. To pass the time, Nathan gathered up buffalo chips to use as fuel for the cook fires, since they weren't likely to find any firewood. Bucher watched him with a faintly mocking smile on his face.

"You too good to gather buffalo droppings?" Nathan asked as he dumped another load of the chips on the ground.

"I prefer not to eat food cooked over *scheiss*," Bucher said.

"Nobody's gonna force you to, I reckon. You can dig out some jerky and gnaw on it."

"Perhaps I will do that."

The whole time, Nathan had been watching Bucher from the corner of his eye, thinking it would be easy enough for the German to yank out his gun, put a bullet through him, and then claim that he'd been shot from a distance by one of the Sioux. It would have been easy for Bucher to *try* that, anyway.

Nathan was more than willing to match his gun-handling skill against that of the other man.

Bucher didn't make a play, though. Maybe he was concerned that the column was too close and someone would be able to tell what really happened. Maybe Bucher just preferred to attempt his killing from ambush. Nathan wouldn't doubt that for a second.

The soldiers came into view a few minutes after sundown. Dusk had begun to gather by the time they reached the ridge.

"Still no word from Red Buffalo?" Colonel Ledbetter asked in an obviously impatient tone.

"Haven't seen him," Nathan replied.

"This is an empty land," Bucher said. "For hours nothing has moved except for Stark and me. And a few birds in the sky and animals, of course."

"We didn't see any dust, either," Nathan added, "so it's safe to say Hanging Dog's whole bunch isn't on the move. My hunch is that they've gone to ground ever since tangling with the patrol. We gave 'em plenty of wounds to lick."

"Not enough," Ledbetter snapped. "Not if there are still Indians alive to cause trouble."

That sounds familiar, Nathan thought.

A moment later he realized why. It reminded him of something he might say. The idea that he and Colonel Wesley Stuart Ledbetter were thinking along the same lines put a frown on his face. Of course, just because some horse's ass shared an opinion didn't make it wrong.

Some of the soldiers built fires while others broke

out provisions. Most of them had been on previous campaigns in Dakota Territory and knew how to use the buffalo chips for fuel. That was better than having a cold camp.

Captain Jameson established a guard perimeter. The men who weren't on duty lined up to fill their tin plates and cups. Nathan got a cup of coffee for himself, along with a plate of beans, salt pork, and hardtack, and carried the food over to sit on the lowered tailgate of the ambulance wagon with Doc Lightner.

"I'm not sure how much longer the colonel's gonna be able to put up with this," Nathan said. "He thought chasing Indians was going to be easy. Ride out, win a great victory, ride back. Get his name and maybe even in a woodcut in the illustrated weeklies."

"Does it ever work that way?" Lightner asked.

Nathan laughed. "Not that I've seen. And when the journalists back east write about how it is here, somehow they never get around to mentioning the mud, the rain and snow, the blue northers that cut a man to the bone, the sun that bakes him dry . . . or all the blood and the dying."

"Why would anyone ever volunteer for such a life, eh?"

"It's a good question, Doc," Nathan answered.

They ate in silence for a few minutes, and then Nathan said quietly, "Might be a good idea to keep an eye on Bucher."

"You're suspicious of him. I could tell that this morning. Why? What do you think he's done?"

Nathan hesitated for a second, then said, "Two of the times I've been shot at in the past week or so, Bucher's been around and could have done it."

"What about when someone tried to kill you with a shotgun?"

Nathan shook his head. "He wouldn't have had time to get in position to do that."

"So you have more than one enemy."

"Looks like it."

Lightner frowned and gestured with his fork at the camp around them. "Do you believe it has something to do with this campaign or is it personal? Someone carrying an old grudge against you, perhaps?"

"Can't rule it out, but it doesn't seem very likely."

"No one has sworn to kill you in recent months?"

Nathan took a deep breath. "When Cullen and I were on our way up to Randall, we had a run-in with some Creek warriors down in Indian Territory." Calling it a *run-in* was maybe too generous, he thought fleetingly. "Four out of the five of 'em wound up dead. I could've killed the fifth one. Cullen full expected me to. But I didn't. We rode off and let him live. Young fella name of Black Sun. Two of the others who died were his father and brother. He claimed he would find me and settle the score for them, one of these days."

"Then this Black Sun could have been one of the people who tried to ambush you," Lightner said.

Nathan shook his head. "I just don't see that happening, Doc. That boy hates me worse than anybody or anything he's ever hated in his life. It wouldn't satisfy that hate to shoot me from a distance. He'll want to kill me close up, so he can watch me suffer. He'll want to look into my eyes while I'm dying so he can be sure I know why."

The surgeon said, "You sound like . . . you've had

some experience with that sort of thing yourself, Nathan."

Suddenly the coffee and the food didn't taste as good. Stark finished off the meal anyway. "Just consider it a friendly warning, Doc. Watch Bucher and be on the lookout for trouble."

"I will," Lightner promised.

Nathan left the ambulance wagon, dumped his cup and plate in a pan with others to be washed, or at least scoured with sand, and then walked to the area on the ridge where the command's horses were picketed and guarded. One of the sentries challenged him, then let him pass when he identified himself.

Nathan found his horse, patted the buckskin's shoulder, and murmured soft words as Buck nudged his shoulder in return.

"You worked hard all day, old son," Nathan said. "I hate to ask more of you, but I don't know these army mounts and aren't sure which ones are fresh, anyway. You think you got any sand left in you?"

As if he understood the words, Buck bumped Nathan's shoulder again.

"Yeah, I thought so." Nathan found his saddle, got it on Buck without making much noise, and pulled the picket pin. He knew where the guards were posted, and the horses were snorting and moving around enough to cover the sound of Buck's hoofbeats as Nathan slowly led him clear of the herd. They went down the far side of the ridge between two of the sentries who never knew what was happening.

Nathan didn't mount right away. He continued leading Buck away from the camp as their legs swished through the knee-high grass. He still didn't swing up into the saddle, even after he judged that they were far enough away from the column not to be heard if he rode. He could walk for a while, and that would make it easier on Buck.

A vast darkness was all around, broken by the campfires behind them and the sweep of millions of stars in the heavens above. After a while, Nathan looked back and could no longer see the fires—they had dropped below the horizon—but he could still see a faint orange glow from the flames. He looked at it for a moment, then turned and studied the sky ahead of him.

There. Was that the dimmest smudge of light to the northwest? He couldn't be sure, but he believed it was.

One way to find out, he told himself. He put his foot in the stirrup, swung up into the saddle, and nudged Buck forward. He let the horse set his own pace.

Nathan knew where he was going. It didn't matter if they took most of the night to get there.

CHAPTER 30

Nathan judged that the hour was well after midnight by the time he approached his destination. As he had ridden through the night, the orange glow in the sky continued to shrink as the fires causing it died down, but he had marked out a course and could guide himself by the stars as well as any sailor out on the vast oceans.

Buck was holding up well. Nathan hadn't pushed him, but he knew the horse really needed more rest . . . especially if all possible speed was called for sometime in the near future.

Nathan reined in as he heard something. When he listened closer, he knew his first impression was right. That was a dog barking. Not a wolf or a coyote, but a dog. And out there, that could only mean one thing.

An Indian village.

Had the dog caught his scent and started barking to announce that a stranger was nearby? Nathan checked what little breeze was blowing and decided that wasn't likely. He and Buck were still too far away. But dogs didn't need much of an excuse to bark.

Maybe the cur was just bored. After a few minutes, it fell silent.

Nathan nudged the buckskin into motion and rode half a mile closer to the village before he halted Buck in a grove of saplings. He tied the reins to one of the little trees and patted Buck on the nose.

"I'm gonna leave you right here for now, old son," he said quietly. "I'll be back, though. If I'm not, I didn't tie those reins so tight you can't get loose after a while . . . but I'm not planning on getting caught."

He left the Winchester where it was in the saddle boot and started toward the village on foot. If any shooting was to be done, likely it would be at close range, and he didn't need the rifle weighing him down. Close quarters work was meant for a revolver.

He paused, slipped the Colt out of leather, and thumbed a cartridge from one of the loops on his shell belt into the gun's empty chamber. A man sneaking up on a whole village full of hostile Sioux stood a good chance of needing a full wheel before the night was over.

Of course, if he did need to use the gun, he'd probably be dead pretty soon after that. In the dark in an Indian village, stealth was more important than anything else.

He hadn't gone much farther when he smelled the tang of wood smoke. The fires in the village might have all burned down to embers, but that scent would linger in the air for hours. He approached through loosely grouped aspen, being careful not to brush against the low-hanging branches too much and make them rattle together.

The ground began to slope down gently under his

feet. He paused, rested his hand on a tree trunk, and looked down into a little valley visible by starlight. A dark, meandering line of vegetation marked the course of a creek. In one bend of the stream, he saw the lodges of the Sioux, several score of them. A dark mass farther on was the pony herd, grazing in a field.

Nathan had no proof that this was the village of Hanging Dog's band, but he was sure it was. This was what Colonel Ledbetter was looking for. Nathan could back away, pick up Buck, and gallop back to the column, confident in the knowledge he could lead the soldiers right back there in the morning.

But if he did that, he might not find out what had happened to Moses Red Buffalo.

If Nathan had been able to locate the village, he had no doubt that Red Buffalo had, too. But if that was true, why hadn't the Crow scout returned to the column with news of the discovery?

Nathan could think of only one reason that made sense. Red Buffalo hadn't come back because he couldn't.

That meant he was either dead or a prisoner right down there. Either way, Nathan wanted to know the answer.

For a moment, however, he stayed where he was and thought about what would happen when the soldiers got there. Colonel Ledbetter claimed he wanted to negotiate with the hostiles and demand their return to the reservation. Maybe the colonel told himself that was the plan, but Nathan doubted it was what Ledbetter would actually do.

No, it was a lot more likely that Ledbetter would order an attack without even hesitating. More than two hundred men would open fire on the village without warning, and their bullets would rip through everyone—men, women, and children alike. After killing as many of the Sioux as they could in that initial barrage, the troops would mount up again and go thundering down to finish off any adult male survivors. They would probably spare the women and children . . . the ones who hadn't been killed already.

Nathan had seen it all before at Black Kettle's camp on the Washita. He had been right there with the soldiers during the fighting, and he had killed a good number of the Cheyenne warriors that day. Never lost a minute's sleep over it, either. The way he saw it, they'd had it coming. With every pull of the trigger, he had gotten a little bit more revenge for what had happened to his parents and to Rena.

As he watched in the dark, though, he felt numb when he thought about the column attacking the Sioux village and wiping out everyone. Such slaughter wouldn't change anything. It wouldn't bring his folks or Rena back.

Had all the years of killing finally started to wear the hatred off his soul, like a constant touch of fingertips rubbing away the gilt letters on the cover of a book? He never would have guessed that such a thing was possible, but he was unutterably weary, and he knew it had nothing to do with not getting any sleep while he searched for the village.

You came to find out what happened to Red Buffalo, he reminded himself. It didn't matter that Red Buffalo was an Indian. Didn't matter that Nathan disliked him. Red Buffalo was his partner, and never before, not once, had Nathan Stark turned his back on a partner.

He started carefully down the slope toward the Sioux camp.

Halfway to the big cluster of lodges, a dog began barking again. Nathan froze where he was crouched next to some brush. After a few minutes, a man shouted at the dog, and a second later there was a yelp, then some whimpers that trailed off as the dog fled.

The cur had just gotten a swift kick in the ribs. Still, that was better than winding up in a stew pot.

As soon as things quieted down again, Nathan resumed his cautious approach to the village. If the savages had caught and killed Red Buffalo, there was no telling where they might have thrown his body. Likewise, if he was a prisoner being kept in one of the lodges, Nathan would never be able to find him. His only chance of rescuing the Crow lay in the possibility that Red Buffalo was still alive and tied up somewhere outside.

As far as Nathan could see, no one was moving around in the village. The place was quiet and dark. There might not even be any guards out, since the Sioux probably considered themselves safe in the camp. As long as he didn't make any noise or literally trip over one of the Indians, Nathan believed he stood a good chance of not being discovered.

He could see no rhyme or reason to how the village was laid out. Each family had put up its lodge wherever the notion struck. Reaching the edge of the dwellings, all he could do was slip along the open areas between them, winding his way deeper into the camp as he searched for Red Buffalo.

He paused frequently to listen for any sounds of alarm, but so far everything remained quiet. But all it would take was one warrior waking up at the wrong time and stumbling outside in the wrong place. Every time Nathan passed one of the buffalo-hide flaps that covered the entrances to the lodges, he eyed them warily, ready to duck back into the shadows.

He hadn't seen any sign of Red Buffalo.

As he neared the center of the village, the smell of burned wood grew stronger. Each lodge had a fire pit in its center, but Indian villages often had large open cooking fires, as well. Nathan saw a cluster of glowing orange embers ahead of him and knew he was approaching the remains of such a fire.

A dark shape stirred, passing between him and those embers.

Nathan dropped to one knee and held his breath as he tried to make out what was going on. Footsteps shuffled in the dirt. Somebody was moving around.

Nathan waited, hoping whoever it was would go away.

He wasn't that lucky. His eyes were well enough adjusted to the starlight that he was able to make out a vague man-shaped figure sinking down on the ground to sit cross-legged near the remains of the fire. The figure rested something across its lap. A rifle?

Nathan peered at the area near where the man sat and realized someone else was there, stretched out motionless on the ground. No one would be lying there with a guard sitting nearby except a prisoner.

And of all the people who might be a prisoner in

that Sioux village on that night, Moses Red Buffalo was the most likely.

A grim smile tugged at Nathan's mouth in the darkness. If he was wrong, what he was about to do would give away his presence in the camp, but he wouldn't know for sure until he tried. He went to hands and knees and started creeping up on the guard.

The Indian muttered to himself. Nathan couldn't hear him clearly enough to understand the words, but he got a definite sense that the guard wasn't happy about being given the job. He would have preferred being curled up in a buffalo robe with his woman, instead of sitting on the hard ground watching over a prisoner.

Nathan was close enough to be sure the sentry was sitting with his back toward him, watching the still shape beside the remains of the fire. Nathan grimaced as he wondered if the Sioux women had pulled burning brands out of that fire earlier and used them to torture Red Buffalo. That was the sort of thing those harpies would do. Anyone who spent much time on the frontier quickly learned that no matter how fierce the warriors were, the Indian women were even more cruel and vicious.

Nathan emerged from the shadow of a tipi. Ten feet of open ground separated him from the guard. He tried to move in absolute silence as he started closer.

A guttural voice suddenly spoke, shocking him into immobility. The words were in the Sioux tongue, but spoken with an accent that told him the speaker belonged to a different tribe.

"The birds will come and peck your eyes out, dog, if you continue to make war on the white man," the voice said. "You will be left dead on the battlefield, and the wolves will tear the flesh from your bones and feast upon it."

"Be quiet, filthy Crow," the guard snapped. "You call me *dog*, but it is you who cower before the white man and lick his hand as you beg for scraps."

The first voice belonged to Red Buffalo. Nathan saw him shift slightly.

The Crow scout said, "The whites are as many as the pebbles in the beds of every stream from here to as far as a man could ride in many moons. And there is no end to them. You can kill every one on this side of the Father of Waters, and more will come. The Sioux can never drive them away."

"The Sioux *will* drive them away," the guard insisted. "When we have spilled enough blood, the whites will grow weak in the belly and turn away, leaving the true people to live their lives again the way we always have since the world began. Our medicine men have promised that this is so."

"Your medicine men promise what your people want to hear," Red Buffalo said. "Always it has been so, and always it will be. Even though many of the whites are *foolish and slow to act*, the time will come when they do what needs to be done."

Nathan realized with a shock that Red Buffalo was talking to *him.* The scout was talking to the Sioux guard to distract the man and keep him from noticing that Nathan was creeping up behind him. Nathan started forward again as Red Buffalo continued insulting and harassing the sentry.

Don't get too carried away with that, Nathan thought. If Red Buffalo angered the guard enough to make the man shout at him, that could rouse the warriors in the nearby lodges and ruin everything.

Nathan was almost within arm's reach of the guard and paused long enough to slip his Colt from its holster. The sound of steel against leather was only a faint whisper, covered up by Red Buffalo's haranguing of the sentry.

Nathan crawled a little closer as he shifted his grip on the revolver. Holding it butt forward, he raised his arm over back of the Sioux warrior's head.

CHAPTER 31

In spite of Red Buffalo's distracting conversation, as the gun in Nathan's hand streaked toward his head, some instinct warned the guard. He started up and twisted around. Instead of a solid blow that would have knocked the Sioux cold or even cracked his skull and killed him, the Colt glanced off.

The impact was still enough to knock the man over. As he rolled, he tried to bring the gun around toward Nathan. Even if the shot missed, it would wake up the whole camp . . . and thus prove fatal to him and Red Buffalo.

With his left hand, Nathan grabbed the rifle's barrel and yanked on it as hard as he could. The Indian's finger was already on the trigger, and Nathan heard him pull it desperately.

Nothing happened.

In that split second, Nathan realized the guard had failed to work the Winchester's lever and throw a cartridge into the chamber before he sat down to keep an eye on Red Buffalo. At the late hour, the man was probably the second or even the third warrior to stand guard, and his grogginess had betrayed him and made him careless.

Nathan suddenly threw his weight against the weapon and drove it backwards, ramming the stock into the man's belly. That forced the air out of the guard's lungs and kept him from shouting as Nathan threw himself forward again and slashed at the guard's head with the gun butt. The blow landed the way he wanted it to . . . with a solid thud that rippled back up his arm.

The guard quivered once as he stretched out on the ground, then lay silent and motionless. There was a good chance he was dead, or at least out cold, and Nathan didn't care which. He intended to be out of there with Red Buffalo before it was even possible for the guard to regain consciousness.

Nathan flipped the gun around, shoved it back in the holster, pulled his knife from its sheath on his left hip, and crawled quickly over to Red Buffalo, who was squirming around and trying to sit up.

"Just stay still," Nathan told him in a whisper. Strips of rawhide had been used to lash Red Buffalo's ankles together, and he went to work on them with the knife he kept sharpened to a razor keenness. Although those bindings were tough, he was able to saw through them fairly quickly.

Red Buffalo's wrists were tied together behind his back. Nathan told him to roll onto his side so he could reach them.

"Try not to slash my wrists," Red Buffalo whispered.

"Try not moving, and I'll be less likely to." Nathan worked the blade under the rawhide strips and moved the edge back and forth. "How bad are you hurt? Can you walk?"

"I can run, if I have to. Hurry."

"First you tell me to be careful, now you tell me to hurry. There just isn't any satisfying you, is there, redskin?"

"If you handled a knife like an Indian instead of a white man, I would be free by now."

The bindings came apart.

Nathan said, "Well, there you go. Let's get out of here."

Red Buffalo sat up and brought his arms around in front of him. He rolled his shoulders and flexed his hands to get the blood flowing properly again. "I have to find my horse. It should be with the rest of the ponies."

"How about you just grab *a* horse? We don't have time to sort out all of 'em while you look for a particular one."

"That horse and I have ridden many trails together," Red Buffalo snapped. "Would you want to leave your buckskin?"

Nathan supposed he had a point about that, although he still didn't like the idea of hanging around the Sioux camp any longer than was absolutely necessary. He sheathed the knife, straightened to his feet, and extended a hand to Red Buffalo. "Come on."

If the Crow was surprised that Nathan would offer to help him up, he didn't show it. Old hostilities had a way of receding into the background when a fellow was surrounded by enemies. He and Nathan clasped wrists.

Red Buffalo stumbled a little as Nathan hauled him

to his feet. "Feet still feel like chunks of wood. The Sioux tied me too tight."

"I doubt if they were worried about making you comfortable."

The horse herd was on the far side of the camp from where Nathan had left Buck, which chafed at him even more. On the other hand, as tired as the buckskin was, Nathan couldn't expect him to carry double for any length of time, and certainly not with any speed. Maybe they could find Red Buffalo's pony fairly quickly. All he knew for sure was that he was itching to get away before they were discovered.

They weaved through the camp quickly but carefully, staying in the shadows wherever possible. There was still a chance they would run into some early riser. Dawn was several hours away, but the eastern sky was beginning to lighten in places.

"You should have cut that guard's throat, just to make sure he was dead," Red Buffalo said. "If he wakes up, he will raise the alarm."

"I hit him hard enough he won't be waking up any time soon, if ever."

"You still should have cut his throat."

"You sound like a bloodthirsty Injun," Nathan said, grinning in the darkness.

"I didn't like the Sioux to start with. After the way they've treated me, I'm even less fond of them."

"Well, hell, they didn't kill you."

"No, they were enjoying themselves too much working up to it."

They reached the edge of the village. The nearest of the grazing ponies was about fifty yards away . . . fifty yards of open ground along the creek bank that

Nathan and Red Buffalo would have to cross. If anyone in the camp happened to look in that direction, they were bound to be spotted.

There was also the chance that the horses might spook as the two men approached and make enough racket to rouse the village. That couldn't be helped.

"There," Red Buffalo said, pointing. "That's my horse."

"How can you tell?"

"He still has the saddle on. Sioux ponies don't wear a white man's saddle."

Even under the desperate circumstances, Nathan couldn't resist a gibe directed at the Crow scout. "So you're saying that something the white men came up with is a good thing?"

"Stay back. I don't want you upsetting those ponies with your white man's stink."

Nathan almost laughed. He had to give Red Buffalo credit. He could give as good as he got.

While Red Buffalo drew closer to the horse herd, Nathan turned and kept an eye on the camp. Everything appeared to be quiet and peaceful back there. Difficult as it was to believe, they were getting pretty close to a successful escape.

Just as Nathan was thinking they'd get away, someone in the village let out an angry shout. More yelling followed immediately. Either the guard had regained consciousness sooner than Nathan expected, or else somebody had discovered him.

Either way, the Sioux would realize in seconds that their prisoner was gone, and they would fan out to look for him.

The horses stirred behind him, blowing and snorting.

Nathan looked over his shoulder and saw the animals spooking as Red Buffalo lunged toward his pony and reached out for the trailing reins. He missed with his first grab.

If the horse stampeded away—

Red Buffalo snagged the reins on his second attempt. He tightened up on them and grasped the saddle horn as he tried to steady the horse. His foot found the stirrup and he swung up.

At a distance of twenty yards, Nathan saw that and kept glancing back and forth. Men with torches moved around the Sioux village. Some of them ran toward the horse herd, no doubt suspecting that the escaping prisoner would try to get his hands on a mount.

In the other direction, Red Buffalo wheeled his pony around to face away from Nathan. All he had to do was jab his heels into the animal's flanks to send it galloping away. Nathan might be able to catch one of the other horses, but it was doubtful.

He could pull his gun and keep the Sioux occupied while Red Buffalo got away. He would sell his life dearly, by taking as many of the savages with him as he possibly could.

Before he could make any decisions, hoofbeats pounded nearby and Red Buffalo called, "Stark! Come on!"

Nathan turned and saw the Crow scout riding hard toward him. Red Buffalo's right hand was extended as he leaned from the saddle. Nathan didn't waste any more time thinking. He ran to meet Red Buffalo and reached up. They caught at each other's wrists.

Nathan's feet came off the ground as he leaped and Red Buffalo pulled at the same time.

Nathan came down astride the pony's back, behind Red Buffalo. As he started to slide off on the other side, Nathan got his arms around the Indian scout's midsection in time to catch himself. He hung on tightly as Red Buffalo turned the pony and urged it into a run away from the Sioux village. Nathan kept his head down so his hat wouldn't blow off as they galloped.

Red Buffalo called, "Where did you leave your horse?"

"Around on the other side of the camp, in some aspens on top of a hill."

"I know the place. I watched the camp from there when I found it."

"You mean before the Sioux found *you.*"

Red Buffalo didn't make any reply to that. Both men leaned forward as the pony lunged ahead. Behind them in the distance, rifles began to crack. Nathan didn't hear any bullets whining close to them, however. The Sioux were firing almost blind, aiming at the swift rataplan of the pony's hoofbeats.

Red Buffalo circled to the north, taking them around the camp and back to the spot where Nathan had left Buck. They couldn't hope to outrun any pursuit riding double. It wouldn't be easy, even with the buckskin.

"How far away is the column?" Red Buffalo asked.

"About five miles, I reckon."

"Once you'd found the village, why didn't you go back and tell the colonel? He could have had the men in position for an attack at dawn."

"I didn't know if you were down there, but I figured there was a good chance they'd grabbed you. I wanted to know for sure."

For a moment, Red Buffalo didn't say anything. Then, "If the colonel *had* attacked, the first thing my captors would have done was cut my throat."

"Yeah, I know."

"So you risked your life, not even knowing if I was still alive."

"Stop wasting breath on all this talking, damn it! They'll be coming after us, and if they figure out what we're doing, they'll try to cut us off."

Red Buffalo hadn't slowed the pony's racing stride, and he urged even more speed out of the mount as they swung wide around the Sioux camp. The hill where Nathan had left Buck was directly ahead of them, a dark bulk in the night. The pony hit the slope and began to struggle under the weight of both men.

"I'll find Buck," Nathan said. "You get back to the column as fast as you can and let the colonel know where those hostiles are."

"Stark, what are you— Wait!" Red Buffalo cried as Nathan slid off the pony's back and landed running on his feet.

Momentum tripped him. He went down but rolled and came right back up, snatching his hat off the ground and clapping it on his head as he angled off through the trees. Behind him, Red Buffalo kept moving.

It was important that at least one of them make it back to the column with the location of the Sioux camp, and they increased the odds of that by splitting up. Red Buffalo wasn't armed, but his pony was fast and had had a chance to rest some. Buck might have a little left, but not much.

"Buck!" Nathan called. "Buck, where are you?"

An answering whinny turned him in the right direction through the trees. A moment later, he spotted the buckskin, still tied to a sapling. Nathan jerked the reins loose and was in the saddle in a flash.

He pulled Buck around and heeled the horse into motion. Nathan bent forward over Buck's neck so that no low-hanging branch would sweep him out of the saddle as he rode through the thick shadows under the trees. Down along the creek, men still shouted. A rifle cracked now and then, but the Sioux were shooting at phantoms.

Nathan and Red Buffalo had gotten away. All they had to do was stay ahead of any pursuit until they got back to the column. The Sioux wouldn't have time to break camp and move away before the column arrived. The savages were doomed, but they would put up a hard fight, Nathan knew. A lot of redskins would die in the next ten or twelve hours.

In the past, that would have filled him with exultation.

Tonight he just kept riding, acting on instinct alone, glad only that he had penetrated the Sioux village and gotten out alive . . . with Red Buffalo.

CHAPTER 32

Nathan had gone less than half a mile when a mounted figure suddenly loomed up on his left and made him reach for the gun on his hip as he hauled back on the reins.

"Don't shoot, Stark," Red Buffalo snapped. "It's just me."

"Damn it," Nathan barked right back at him. "You ought to be a mile closer to the column by now. What the hell did you do, hang back to make sure I found my horse?"

"Yes," the Crow scout answered simply. "Did you really believe I would abandon you?" He grunted. "We may not like it, Stark, but we are partners on this mission. I do not betray my partners."

Nathan's jaw tightened. He wasn't about to admit that same thought had crossed his mind earlier in the night. "Let's just get the hell out of here while we still can, all right?"

"Is that buckskin of yours up to a hard run?"

"Buck can hold up to anything he needs to!" Nathan hoped that was true. He hated to think of the valiant buckskin running until his heart burst . . . just because Nathan had asked him to.

They rode southeast, moving at a fast clip but not a full-out gallop.

After a while, Red Buffalo said, "That was a damned foolish thing you did, Stark."

Nathan laughed harshly. "I thought redskins didn't cuss."

"I've been around you profane white men too long. You've corrupted my spirit. But that doesn't change the fact that you shouldn't have come into the Sioux camp like that."

"Shouldn't have risked my life to save you, you mean?"

"Shouldn't have risked not being able to let the column know where to find the camp. You didn't know that I was still alive. Strategically, it was a foolish thing to do." Red Buffalo paused, then added, "Even if, in the end, it doesn't really matter."

"What in blazes do you mean, it doesn't matter? If the colonel moves fast, he can be in position to put an end to all the hell Hanging Dog's been raising."

Red Buffalo shook his head. "Hanging Dog is not there."

"Now what the hell are you talking about? Are you trying to tell me that's not Hanging Dog's camp after all?"

"It is Hanging Dog's camp, but he is not there. And there are only a dozen or so of his warriors left in the village. He and all the rest . . . nearly three hundred men . . . rode out yesterday. I heard much talk about it while I was their prisoner."

"They've gone out raiding again?" Nathan guessed.

"Worse. They are on their way to a place called

Weeping Woman Rock to meet some white men with several wagons full of rifles and ammunition. By tomorrow evening . . . this evening, actually . . . every warrior riding with Hanging Dog will be armed with a new or nearly new Winchester and hundreds of rounds for it."

"Good Lord!" Nathan muttered. "And you say there are three hundred of 'em?"

"Close to it."

"That's enough to— Hell! They could wipe out Fort Randall!"

"That is exactly what Hanging Dog intends to do."

Alarm rampaged through Nathan as he thought about Delia Blaine and all the other women and children at the fort. What was left of the company that had remained at the fort wouldn't be enough to fight off an attack such as the one Red Buffalo described. The Sioux could sweep in without warning, kill all the soldiers, and then take their time with the women and children.

The very thought of it made Nathan's blood run cold. "The colonel's got to forget about the village and get back to the fort as quick as he can."

"The column cannot move fast enough to arrive in time, not without riding all day and then all night. Hanging Dog will be in position to attack by early tomorrow morning. At least, that is what I gathered from the talk I overheard. I do not know exactly where this Weeping Woman Rock is."

Nathan forced himself to put aside his fears for Delia and the others and make his brain work. He had been to Weeping Woman Rock, a huge formation of weathered sandstone that, from a distance, looked like a woman on her knees with her head bent forward as she wept. Like a lot of geographical features on the frontier, the name it had been given was a bit of a stretch.

He never had figured out how come the Tetons had reminded the Frenchman who'd named them of a woman's bosoms. That Frenchy must have *really* been missing female companionship.

None of that was important at the moment, and he banished the thoughts. "Weeping Woman Rock is about fifty miles northeast of the fort. When is Hanging Dog supposed to meet those damn gunrunners?"

"Sometime today. That is all I know."

Nathan frowned. White men . . . selling guns to the Indians so the weapons could be used to slaughter innocent people. It was hard to conceive of anything more despicable.

A thought suddenly blazed through his brain. "I don't reckon you heard any of those hostiles mention the names of the men selling those guns to them."

"No. Why does it matter now?"

"It doesn't, I suppose." Nathan couldn't stop thinking about that double diamond pattern etched into the stock of the rifle he carried, as well as on the Winchesters he had seen that were gathered up from the dead Sioux. Noah Crimmens had told him that mark meant the guns had been distributed by the company belonging to the sutler, Jake Farrow.

Farrow had to be up to his neck in the gunrunning, Nathan thought. He suddenly wondered if Dietrich Bucher might be, as well. If Bucher was crooked, he wouldn't want Nathan nosing around the fort. That would explain the ambushes. And Farrow could have been the man with the shotgun . . .

Red Buffalo spoke, yanking him back to more pressing problems than figuring out who was responsible for the gunrunning. "Depending on when those men turn over the rifles to Hanging Dog, the column *might* be able to get back to the fort in time to save some of the people there. I don't believe they could arrive in time to stop the Sioux attack entirely."

"They have to try. There's nothing else we can do."

"If anyone back there does survive, Stark, it will be thanks to you. If you had waited and not found Hanging Dog's camp when you did, it would have been too late. The column would not have gotten back to the fort until long after the attack." Red Buffalo paused, then said, "So by saving me, you may have saved others as well. You did not risk your life simply for a filthy redskin after all."

"Yeah, well . . . maybe some redskins aren't quite as filthy as others."

Red Buffalo laughed. "Keep it up, Stark, and you may become positively enlightened."

"Don't hold your damn breath."

The eastern sky gradually turned red and gold with the approach of the sun.

In the light, Nathan could see better, so when he glanced over at Red Buffalo and noticed the raw, ugly marks on the Crow's face, he stiffened in surprise. "Damn it, what happened to you? It looks like those Sioux squaws took coals from that fire and put 'em right on your face." He had wondered earlier if Red Buffalo had been subjected to such torture.

"That is exactly what they did. They wanted to hear me scream. I did not."

"Yeah, I believe that."

"They would have gotten around to doing worse today, if you had not come along and freed me. For that, I am obliged to you, Stark."

"We've helped each other out enough times I reckon we ought to just consider it square between us from now on. Wasn't necessarily what I wanted, but hell, a man can't just keep banging his head against a wall forever, can he?"

Red Buffalo grunted. "Some men do. Hanging Dog will never change. He is too full of hate. Perhaps he has good reason to feel that way. We don't know everything that has happened to him in his life, or to those he loved."

Nathan didn't say anything. He couldn't bring himself to defend any of the hostiles, no matter what their motivations might be. But there was no point in wasting his breath vilifying them.

Delia would probably regard that slight change in attitude as progress. That reminded him of Delia and sent a renewed sense of urgency coursing through him. "Blast it, where's that column? We ought to be getting there any time now."

"This is the right trail?"

Nathan blew out a scoffing breath. He hadn't been lost in years, and he damn sure didn't intend to start now.

Sure enough, just a few minutes later the higher

ground where the soldiers were camped came into view. Smoke from cooking fires rose into the early morning air. Somebody was bound to have noticed that he wasn't there. Seems they would be wondering what had happened to him.

They surely wouldn't be expecting him to show up with Red Buffalo, along with the shocking news about the gunrunning and Hanging Dog's plan to attack Fort Randall.

Some sentries spotted them coming, and Captain Jameson rode out to meet them, accompanied by several troopers.

As the men reined in, Jameson frowned. "The next time you're going off on your own, Stark, you need to let someone know."

"In case you haven't noticed, Captain, I found Red Buffalo," Nathan replied coolly. "I've also got news for the colonel."

"You found the hostiles' camp?" Jameson's voice betrayed his eagerness.

"We'd better just make our report to the colonel," Nathan said. "Saves time that way."

"I concur," Red Buffalo said.

Jameson looked irritated, but he jerked his head in a curt nod. "Very well. I don't know if he's awake yet, but we'll go and see."

"Sun's over the horizon," Nathan pointed out.

Jameson ignored the comment and turned his horse back toward the camp.

A few minutes later, he, Nathan, and Red Buffalo walked up to Colonel Ledbetter's tent. Nathan had turned Buck over to one of the hostlers and told the man to take good care of the horse. Buck had been on his last legs by the time they got there, although Nathan felt like he would be all right with plenty of rest. Red Buffalo's pony had been worn out, too, although still in better shape than Buck.

The colonel had left Corporal Cahill back at the fort, but a private had been posted at the tent's entrance to serve as a combination guard and aide. The soldier came to attention and saluted Captain Jameson.

"Civilian scouts Stark and Red Buffalo have returned and have a report for the colonel," Jameson said.

Ledbetter was awake and heard what Jameson said. He called, "Captain! Bring them in here, immediately!"

The private held the canvas entrance flap aside. Jameson led the way into the tent and saluted the colonel. Nathan and Red Buffalo followed.

Ledbetter was sitting at a camp table eating breakfast. He was fully dressed, and even in the rugged Dakota Territory badlands, his uniform was clean and creased and the glass in his spectacles sparkled. He looked like he was ready to step out onto the parade ground back at Fort Randall and review the troops. He took a sip of coffee and then patted his lips with a napkin as he set the cup down.

"Mister Stark, I intend to write a letter to the War Department reprimanding you for your actions during this campaign and recommending that you be relieved of your post as a scout for the army. You seem totally unwilling to acclimate yourself to military discipline."

Nathan stared at the officer, completely taken aback

by Ledbetter's harsh words. "What are you talking about, Colonel?" he demanded. "The fact that I rode off last night without telling anybody where I was going?"

Ledbetter tipped his head back slightly and thrust his jaw out. "For all anyone knew, you deserted."

"Well, that would be a good trick, since I'm not actually *in* the army."

"I have nothing more to say to you, sir." Ledbetter turned his head to look at Red Buffalo. "Where have *you* been?"

"Captured by the Sioux and held prisoner in Hanging Dog's camp."

"Then you located the hostiles," Ledbetter said as he leaned forward. "Excellent work."

"Yes, I located them. And they would have killed me if not for Stark. He risked his life to steal into the camp and free me, and then we were able to get away."

Ledbetter glanced at Nathan again and grunted. Clearly, he couldn't bring himself to offer any congratulations.

"But none of that is important now," Red Buffalo went on.

"I should say not." Colonel Ledbetter stood up from the chair where he'd been sitting. "We have to get ready to move. Red Buffalo, you will lead us back to the enemy camp, where we will fall upon and destroy Hanging Dog and his forces if he refuses to surrender. Captain, pass the order to have the men ready to ride as quickly as possible."

Jameson started to salute again but stopped when Nathan said, "Wait just a damned minute, Colonel."

"I'll listen to no more of your insubordination, Stark—"

"You can't destroy Hanging Dog and his men *because they're not there*," Nathan broke in. "They've gone to meet with some gunrunners, take delivery of another shipment of Winchesters, and then attack the fort. They figure on wiping Fort Randall and everybody in it right off the face of the earth!"

CHAPTER 33

Ledbetter stared at Nathan for a long moment and then sniffed. "Nonsense."

"What?" Nathan couldn't believe what he was hearing—and seeing, because the colonel had started to shake his head stubbornly.

"You're mistaken, Stark. Not even Hanging Dog would dare to attack a fort of the United States Army."

Red Buffalo said, "Stark is right, Colonel. He knows this because I told him, and I know it because I heard the Sioux talking about it while I was their prisoner."

"Then you misunderstood what you heard. You are, after all, a Crow and not a Sioux. Perhaps some of the nuances of their language escape you."

Red Buffalo's burned face was set in stony lines. Nathan thought he looked like he was about to leap right over that fancy little table and go after Ledbetter. Nathan felt like doing the same thing himself.

Captain Jameson said, "Colonel, perhaps we should give some consideration to their story. We haven't actually seen for ourselves what the situation is—"

"I know what the situation is, Captain," Ledbetter snapped. "I ordered this campaign in order to locate Hanging Dog's camp and pacify him and his followers. Their camp has been located. The next step is to subjugate the hostiles or, failing that, exterminate them like the vermin they are."

Nathan was so torn between wonderment and rage that it was all he could do to stand there and gaze at Ledbetter's serene arrogance. The colonel had made up his mind to attack the village, that was obvious, and nothing was going to turn him aside from that goal. At the same time, Ledbetter knew he couldn't have the full amount of glory accrue to himself unless he defeated the notorious war chief Hanging Dog, so in the colonel's mind, Hanging Dog had to be there in the village in order for him to achieve his goal. It was simple.

Utterly wrong, but simple.

"Colonel, you're right. You've got to get this column moving immediately, but you need to head back to the fort. Hanging Dog won't get his hands on those guns until later today, which means he probably won't attack the fort until tomorrow morning. If you push the column as hard as you can—"

Ledbetter ignored Nathan's heartfelt plea and barked, "You have your orders, Captain Jameson. Carry them out."

Red Buffalo tried to get through to him. "Colonel, Stark is right. You may not be able to stop Hanging Dog from attacking the fort, but you can get there in time to keep him from wiping everyone out. I know the men who were left there will put up a fight—"

"Mister Red Buffalo," Ledbetter interrupted again, "you will prepare to lead us back to the hostiles' encampment right away. We'll waste no time in dealing with the savages and teaching them the lesson they so richly deserve."

Red Buffalo frowned and stood straighter. "Colonel, you're wrong. If you persist in this course, you're dooming everyone back at the fort to an ugly death. When word of this gets out, your career will be ruined. You'll be a pariah—"

"Silence!" Ledbetter roared. "Captain, place these two men under arrest and send for Mister Bucher. He's a competent scout, I'm sure he can follow the trail to the Sioux village."

Jameson frowned and shifted his feet uneasily on the dirt. "Colonel, with all due respect, sir, I don't see any reason why Stark and the Crow would lie about this—"

"Because they're obstinate!" Ledbetter shouted. He wasn't going to let anyone finish a sentence. "Stark is . . . is a Rebel, and Red Buffalo is a savage himself! Lying is second nature to them, Captain, you know that. I'm not sure what they hope to gain with this mad story about gunrunning and an attack on the fort, but I'm not going to be deceived by it. This campaign will achieve its end, by God!"

Jameson tried one last time. "Colonel—"

"You have your orders, Captain!" Ledbetter bellowed, spittle flying from his mouth. "Carry them out!"

With a sigh, Jameson rested a hand on the closed flap of his holster and started to turn toward Nathan and Red Buffalo. "Gentlemen—"

Stark didn't let him finish, either. He swung a hard, fast right that caught Jameson on the jaw and knocked him against the tent's sidewall.

"Guards!" the colonel roared.

Nathan's first impulse was to hurdle the table, grab Ledbetter by his fat neck, and choke the life out of the crazy bastard . . . but something more important had to be done, and he knew it.

The private who was on duty right outside the tent rushed in, eyes wide in shock at the commotion that had broken out. Red Buffalo was waiting for him. He drove a left into the soldier's face, rocking the young man's head back and making his eyes roll up in their sockets. At the same time, Red Buffalo's right hand closed around the guard's Springfield and jerked the rifle out of his grasp. The guard stumbled and sat down hard.

With Jameson and the guard both momentarily stunned, that left only Colonel Ledbetter to try to stop Nathan and Red Buffalo. The officer stood there sputtering and red-faced with rage. He didn't come out from behind the table, though.

Nathan and Red Buffalo glanced at each other. Nathan read agreement in the Crow's eyes. They would never convince Ledbetter to head back to the fort in time. Nor would Jameson or Lucas defy his orders and take over the column.

The only thing the two scouts could do was try to reach Fort Randall before Hanging Dog did and warn the soldiers there about the attack. With even a little time to prepare, they might be able to hold off the Sioux, at least for a while. In order to do that, Nathan and Red Buffalo would need fresh horses.

They dashed out of Colonel Ledbetter's tent and Nathan practically ran into Doc Lightner. The surgeon reached out and closed his hand around Nathan's arm in an urgent grip.

"Doc, let me go!" Nathan said as he tried to pull away.

"Stark, wait! I heard you were back and came to make sure you were all right. I was outside the tent and overheard everything you and Red Buffalo had to say. Are you going back to the fort?"

"Damn right."

"Then I'm coming with you. I'll be needed there more than I am here!"

Nathan didn't want to waste time arguing, and anyway, Lightner was probably right. Nathan jerked his head toward the horse herd. "Come on!"

The three men ran past startled soldiers and noncoms, but without orders, no one tried to stop them. They reached the picketed horses, some of which were already saddled in preparation for the column to move out shortly. The hostlers were saddling the others.

Lightner grabbed the reins of one of the saddled mounts. "This is my horse." That fact was obvious from the black medical bag tied to the saddle. "He's sturdy and fast and won't slow us down. I don't know about the others."

Nathan had a good eye for horseflesh and so did Red Buffalo. Each of them selected a mount from among those already saddled, and untied the reins.

One of the hostlers ran toward them, calling, "Hey! What are you fellas doin'? Nobody's given the order to mount up—"

Nathan, Red Buffalo, and Lightner were already swinging into the saddles.

As they yanked the horses around, Colonel Ledbetter finally stumbled out of his tent and shouted, "Stop them! Stop those men! Shoot them!"

No one immediately obeyed those commands, especially the last one. The idea of shooting at the post surgeon and two civilian scouts was so unexpected, the soldiers failed to grasp it at first.

Nathan, Red Buffalo, and Lightner jammed their heels into the horses' flanks and sent them leaping away from the rest of the herd. Finally, as they thundered down the slope, guns began a sporadic popping behind them. None of the bullets came close. It was possible the soldiers were shooting wild on purpose, unwilling to kill men they had all along thought of as allies.

Lightner bounced a little in the saddle and hung on to his hat with one hand while he gripped the reins in the other. His face was pale and drawn. He wasn't used to galloping, and he certainly wasn't accustomed to being shot at by fellow members of the United States Army. "I hope you're right about this!" he called over the pounding hoofbeats. "Otherwise I'll be court-martialed!"

"I don't reckon a court-martial would be enough to satisfy the colonel!" Nathan replied. "He'll want to string us all up and strip the hide off of us, inch by inch!"

The four young men had been working in the stables since before dawn, mucking out stalls and feeding the horses. Matoskah had been forking clean straw into one of the stalls, but he stopped and leaned on the pitchfork with a worried frown on his face. It was the same sort of expression he had been wearing most of the time for the past several days.

Hotah, his best friend, came up and poked him on the shoulder. "What's wrong with you?" he asked in the Sioux tongue. "You've been moping around, not doing your work, and making it harder on the rest of us."

"My mind and my heart are both heavy," Matoskah answered. He had kept what he knew to himself while he tried to figure out what to do about it, but the weight of it was beginning to wear him down. He needed to share the burden with someone.

But not Hotah. Although he considered the other young man to be his brother, Matoskah knew that Hotah could not be relied upon. He was boastful, and he panicked easily. Sad to say, Matoskah would not have wanted to go into battle with Hotah at his side.

"What's heavy is that pitchfork with a pile of straw on it, and that's why you don't want to use it," Hotah said. "You don't fool me, *Billy*. Living around these white men has weakened you."

Matoskah bristled. He had gotten used to the soldiers calling him Billy, and he didn't mind when Miss Delia used the name. But the scorn he heard in Hotah's voice angered him. So did the contempt for the whites implicit in his friend's tone.

"The soldiers have not treated us badly," he said. "Some whites would have killed us out of hand when they found us, rather than taking us in and giving us food and a place to live."

Hotah sneered. "Better that they *had* killed us. We would have fought them and would have died as Sioux warriors should die, but not before we killed some of them."

"We were children. We could not have counted coup on any of them, let alone killed them. You are a fool, Hotah."

Hotah glared at him. "Someday the white men will be gone. This fort will lie in ruins, rotting away until it is like the white men were never here. And when that day comes, I will ride with our true people once more, proud and free, lords of the plains."

Hotah's grandiose bragging annoyed Matoskah, but what he said about the fort being empty and falling into ruins stirred the worry inside the young man. The boastful prediction might come true a lot sooner than Hotah expected . . . unless someone acted to prevent that from happening.

Matoskah shoved the pitchfork into Hotah's hands, who grasped the wooden handle without thinking. Then as Matoskah turned away, Hotah exclaimed, "Wait! What are you doing?"

"What I should have done before now," Matoskah said over his shoulder as he stalked out of the stable.

Every morning, Delia always enjoyed the time before the children arrived, when she could sit in the classroom inside the chapel and think about what the day would bring. She loved the children—their laughter, their smiling faces, their sheer innocence and exuberance in life—even though being around them was an always sharp reminder of the son and daughter she had lost. Her young ones were gone, but others in the world needed her.

When she had first seen Nathan Stark at the fort, for a second an almost forgotten hope had flared to life inside her . . . the hope that someday she might have more children of her own. She remembered the fondness she had felt for Nathan, the sense that somewhere inside him was a good man, buried under all those layers of hate and bitterness. If she could just peel away those layers and reach the man he truly was, no telling what might happen.

Unfortunately, those efforts hadn't accomplished much. And he was gone again, somewhere out in the wilderness trying to track down the Sioux so there could be more killing, more death that wouldn't solve anything.

Delia swallowed hard as she moved some of the books on her desk. Her good feelings and looking forward to the day had almost evaporated. She had to learn not to allow herself to dwell on the things she couldn't change.

A tentative footstep made her look up.

One of the Sioux youngsters who worked in the stable stood just inside the classroom door. His unkempt, raven-black hair hung around his face. He wore cast-off army trousers and a buckskin shirt. He was clearly nervous and kept swallowing.

Delia smiled as she recognized him. She didn't teach the Indian youths in the classroom, but she had helped all of them learn to speak better English since she had been at Fort Randall. She had tried to communicate to them some sense of the bigger world that was out there, too, not just the plains and the mountains to which they were accustomed. Most of them accepted her help only grudgingly and remained sullen, but not this one. He had seemed eager to learn.

"Good morning, Billy," she said. "What can I do for you?"

"Miss Delia." He came a step farther into the room, then hesitated and looked around, like a wild animal with the urge to bolt.

"It's all right," she told him. "You can come closer to the desk. No one is going to hurt you."

Billy swallowed again, harder than before. The sound was almost a gulp. "I have to tell you something, Miss Delia."

"Anything, Billy. You know that."

"A few evenings ago, I . . . I was out in the woods, east of the stables. I like to go there . . . to get away from the fort . . . to listen to the animals . . ."

Delia nodded. "I understand. Everyone needs a bit of peace and quiet and privacy sometimes. You certainly don't get much of that around the fort!"

"Yeah, I, uh, guess that's right, ma'am. Anyway . . . while I was out there . . . some other fellas came out there, too. One by one, but they met and talked. It was a . . . rendezvous, I guess you'd call it."

"Men from the fort, you mean?" Delia asked with a faint frown. She didn't understand why Billy would be upset about such a thing. From what he had said so far, it seemed harmless enough to her.

But then he blurted out, "Yes, ma'am. Two of the sergeants and . . . and Mister Bucher, the scout . . . and they were talking about selling guns to Hanging Dog! They're gonna deliver a whole bunch of Winchesters to him, Miss Delia, and even though they didn't say anything about it, I just know he's going to take them and attack the fort!"

CHAPTER 34

Nathan and Red Buffalo kept an eye on their back trail, but no dust rose into the sky to signify that Colonel Ledbetter had sent pursuers after them. That didn't come as a complete surprise to Nathan. No matter how furious the colonel was about his orders being defied, he wouldn't want to split his forces. Probably wouldn't want to spare even a small patrol to go after the "renegade" scouts, as Ledbetter would think of them. To the colonel's way of thinking, he would need all of his men to insure his glorious victory over Hanging Dog and the Sioux.

Though all the while, Hanging Dog and his warriors would be at the fort, trying to slaughter everyone there.

After they had ridden several miles, the three men pulled their horses to a walk. They had a long way to go and couldn't afford to ride the animals into the ground. As the day went on, they would have to stop several times to let the horses rest.

Though each of those delays were necessary, they

were going to gnaw viciously at them, Nathan knew. Otherwise the horses would collapse, he and his companions would be left afoot with no chance at all of reaching the fort in time to warn the people.

While they were proceeding at a slower pace, Doc Lightner looked over at Red Buffalo and said, "My God, man, what did they do to your face? Those burns should be treated."

"Later, Doc," the Crow scout said. "No time for that now."

"But burns like that are going to leave scars."

"So he'll be uglier than he is now," Nathan said, "but only a little. When skin's that red to start with, it can't get much worse."

"Captain Stark, that's not at all appropriate—"

"It's all right, Doc," Red Buffalo interrupted. "I'm used to this white man's feeble insults."

"Still, there's no need for it." Lightner frowned. "Oh, I see. That's your odd way of showing affection for each other."

Nathan and Red Buffalo glared at the surgeon.

Nathan said, "You couldn't be more wrong, Doc. I mean every word of it."

"He does," Red Buffalo agreed. "He is a cruel, vicious man, more badger than human. In fact, he *looks* a bit like a badger, wouldn't you say?"

"He *did* risk his life to save you," Lightner pointed out.

"Everybody makes mistakes," Nathan said.

The doctor just sighed and shook his head, as if to say that he couldn't figure out his two companions and wasn't going to waste any more effort trying.

After a few more minutes of walking the horses, they pushed the mounts back into a ground-eating lope.

Nathan pointed out, "We didn't have a chance to grab any supplies. It's gonna be a long, hungry ride back to the fort."

"Since this is my horse, I have some jerky in my saddlebags," Lightner said. "I'll be happy to share it, although it's not really enough for all of us. Better than nothing, though."

"You don't happen to have any cartridges for that Springfield Red Buffalo's carrying, do you?"

Lightner shook his head. "No, I'm afraid not."

"Might as well throw that rifle away," Nathan told Red Buffalo. "It's just weighing you down."

"I will if it becomes apparent I need to," the Crow replied. "But for now, there's one shot in it." He chuckled. "You never know when one shot might come in handy."

Nathan sighed. "I reckon not. And you can use it as a club when it's empty. I know you savages are primitive enough you like your war clubs."

"As long as I'm using it to break open the right heads," Red Buffalo said.

Colonel Ledbetter had left Lieutenant Marcus Allingham in command at the fort. Allingham was a tall, thin young man with sandy hair and a straggling mustache that he labored to grow without much success. He had been born in England, but his parents had moved to the States when Marcus was six years old. He still had a trace of a British accent, especially when excited. Although regarded as a competent junior officer, he had never been under fire. And although he fully expected to rise in the ranks, he harbored some lingering doubts about his own abilities. He would never admit that to anyone, but he looked forward to the day when he would finally find out just what sort of mettle he actually possessed.

He wasn't expecting it to be *that day*, but when Corporal Cahill appeared in the doorway of the office Allingham occupied temporarily as the commanding officer and said, "Uh, Mrs. Blaine wants to see you, Lieutenant. And she's got an Indian with her," a tiny shiver went up Allingham's spine.

"An Indian," he repeated. Not really a question, just a surprised comment.

"Yes, sir. One of those Sioux boys from the stables."

Allingham knew who the Sioux boys were, of course. Not individually, because all Indians tended to look alike to him, but he had seen them working with the horses. It was odd, having four hostiles right there in the fort, but as far as he knew they had never caused any trouble. He nodded and motioned to Cahill. "Show them in, Corporal."

"Yes, sir." Cahill backed out, and a moment later Delia Blaine marched in, followed with obvious reluctance by the young Indian.

Allingham got to his feet and came around the desk. Like every other unmarried man on the post— and many of the married ones, he would wager—he had looked at Mrs. Cordelia Blaine in the past and struggled with the impure thoughts that tried to worm their way into his head. She was a beautiful woman.

Older than him, to be sure, but that wasn't always a drawback. Older women were more . . . experienced . . . in certain matters.

But as an officer and a gentleman, Allingham had never behaved toward Mrs. Blaine in any way that could be considered even remotely improper. He smiled, nodded, and said, "Mrs. Blaine, how lovely to see you. What can I do for you this morning?"

She nodded toward her companion. "Billy and I have to talk to you."

"Ah . . . Billy. One of the lads from the stables, is that correct?"

"Yes. His real name is Matoskah . . . but that's not important right now." Delia stood up straighter, fixed Allingham with a grim, solemn gaze, and went on. "A large, well-armed force of Sioux warriors led by Hanging Dog is going to attack the fort within twenty-four hours. Probably tomorrow morning at sunrise. You'll be outnumbered, Lieutenant—I don't know exactly by how much—so you should begin making preparations right away to defend the post."

The lieutenant could not have been more surprised if she had walked into the office, ripped her garments off, and thrown herself down on the desk to be ravaged. He stared at her, unable to speak for a long moment. When he finally found his voice again, he said, "An attack? An imminent attack?"

"Within the next twenty-four hours," she said again. "Hanging Dog is meeting a gang of gunrunners *today* to take possession of a shipment of Winchester repeating rifles, to go with the rifles he already has.

such wild flights of fancy. If you set out to cause trouble for someone else, you'll most likely wind up causing it for yourself."

The Indian looked angry.

You could never fully trust any savage, Allingham thought. He put his hand on the flap of the holster where his sidearm rested.

Delia turned to the boy. "Go on, Billy. I'll talk some more to the lieutenant."

"No," he said with a stubborn shake of his head. "He will not believe you. But I speak the truth!"

"I know you do," she told him quietly, "but it's not going to do any good to keep arguing right now." She rested a hand on his shoulder—which rubbed Allingham the wrong way, a white woman touching a savage like that—and urged him toward the door. "I'll speak to you again later. For now, please don't say anything about this to anyone else."

The Indian looked like he wanted to continue arguing, but after a moment he nodded, gave Allingham a sullen glare, and turned to leave.

As soon as he was gone, Allingham began. "Really, Mrs. Blaine—"

"No, you listen to me, Lieutenant. I've been out here on the frontier considerably longer than you have. I trust Billy, both in his honesty about what he overheard and what he believes Hanging Dog will do as soon as he has those rifles. By refusing to even consider the possibility that he may be right, you're putting everyone here at risk."

"I'm in command here," the lieutenant said stiffly, "and I must use my best judgment in these matters.

There's simply no evidence of this conspiracy other than the word of a savage. That's not enough, and it never will be." Something occurred to Allingham. "However, if it will make you feel better, I can call in Sergeant McCall and question him. I'm certain he'll deny any wrongdoing, but—"

"You'd tell him what Billy said?"

"Well, of course. He'd have the right to know who was accusing him, wouldn't he?"

Delia stared bleakly at him for a couple heartbeats, then shook her head. "No. No, don't do that. There's no need."

"I agree, but if it will make you feel better—"

"No. Just forget anything was said. Forget we were here."

"Oh, there's no need to go that far—"

"Please. It was a mistake."

Allingham shrugged and ventured a smile. "I always try to oblige a lady. Especially such a lovely one."

As if she hadn't even heard the compliment, she turned and left the office.

Allingham heaved a sigh. He'd never had any sort of chance with Mrs. Blaine anyway, he told himself. Besides, if she believed such a story as that one, she was obviously mad!

Delia was so angry she felt herself trembling inside as she left The House. She went down the steps from the porch and saw Matoskah waiting for her.

"He does not believe," the young man said. "He will never believe."

"Not until Hanging Dog and his warriors are here." She didn't tell him that Lieutenant Allingham had offered to call in Sergeant McCall and tell him what Billy had said. Delia had realized instantly that she couldn't allow that. Allingham still wouldn't change his mind, and McCall would know that Billy had tried to inform on him. Delia knew how brutal Seamus McCall was. She had no doubt that McCall would go after Billy and hurt him, maybe even kill him.

Another worry occurred to her. "If you're right about Hanging Dog attacking the fort, what will he do to you and the others?"

Billy smiled, but there was no humor in the expression. It was as cold as the grave. "He will kill us. We have lived with the whites for years. To Hanging Dog, we are no longer Sioux. We are worse than white in his eyes, because once we were part of his people."

Delia nodded. "I was afraid that was what you were going to say. Tonight, while it's still safe, I want you and your friends to leave. Take horses and ride away from here."

His eyes widened as he shook his head. "The army would call us horse thieves and hunt us down. They might even blame us for what is going to happen here."

"Perhaps, but you'll still be alive. You can lose yourselves somewhere. Start over."

"There is no starting over for ones such as us. We have cast our lot with your people."

"But if you stay, you'll die."

"There is no place for us in the world. No home but here. And maybe we can help. When the attack comes, go to the chapel. That will be the safest place. I will come to you there and protect you the best I can, as long as I can."

A chill gripped Delia as the young man spoke. She understood what he meant. If he was right about Hanging Dog, the battle that was coming would be a fight to the death.

A fight that the inhabitants of Fort Randall couldn't win.

CHAPTER 35

By late afternoon, Nathan estimated that he, Red Buffalo, and Doc Lightner were more than halfway back to Fort Randall. But their mounts were played out. They had been careful not to push the horses too hard for too long at a time and had stopped for brief rests numerous times during the day, but the horses' flagging condition made it imperative that they call a halt for several hours.

Nathan didn't know if he would be able to stand a delay that long—not when he thought about Delia and all the other innocent people back at the fort.

The men reined in at the edge of some trees. A grassy meadow lay in front of them. The horses would be able to graze for a while. They had drunk their fill at a stream a few miles back.

The men took the saddles off, wiped down the sweaty animals, and picketed them loosely to allow them to roam a little in search of the most succulent shoots of grass. Doc Lightner sat down, leaned his back against a tree trunk, and sighed wearily.

"After riding all day, I think I'd rather stand up for a while," Red Buffalo commented.

"We still have a long way to go." The nervous energy Nathan felt had him pacing back and forth, even though he couldn't remember the last time he had slept.

Lightner said, "That's right. We still have to ride all night, don't we? So you really should get some rest, Nathan. Both of you should. If you're worried about dozing off, I'll stay awake and make sure you don't sleep too long." He pulled out his pocket watch and opened it to check the time. "Will a couple hours be long enough for the horses?"

"It should be," Nathan said. "Longer would be better, but we can't afford it. There's no point in me trying to sleep. I don't reckon I could do it, the way I feel now."

"You might be surprised. Moses, is there anything I can do to help you with those burns? I have some ointment in my medical bag."

"That's all right, Doc," the Crow said. "I'll make a poultice when I get the chance. No offense, but Injun herbs are better than some patent-medicine nostrum."

"None taken," Lightner assured him. "Since coming out here to the frontier, I've learned a great many things they never taught us at medical college. My philosophy is that the best cure is the most effective one, whether the learned academicians are familiar with it or not."

Nathan laughed. "It figures the two of you would get along. You both talk the same lingo—and I don't mean Crow!"

Stalking back and forth isn't going to do me any good, he told himself, *but it might not hurt to sit down, take a few deep breaths, and try to clear my mind.*

He found a tree to his liking, sat down, and leaned against it.

We've made good time so far and should reach Fort Randall before dawn. At least then we can warn the soldiers. We'll be greatly outnumbered, of course, but if all the women and children are herded into the chapel—probably the sturdiest building on the post—and what's left of Company K holed up there, as well, we might . . . just might . . . be able to hold out until Colonel Ledbetter got back.

Assuming, of course, that once the colonel sees the Sioux village is practically empty of warriors, he realizes we were right and lights a shuck for the fort.

And if we were wrong . . . if Hanging Dog didn't attack the fort . . . then I will thank my lucky stars that Delia and all the other folks are safe and take my chances with a vengeful Colonel Ledbetter.

Those thoughts were going through his brain, and then suddenly his head jerked up and he saw that most of the light was gone. He bolted to his feet. "What the hell!"

Red Buffalo and Doc Lightner were nearby, saddling their horses. Nathan's mount was already saddled.

The surgeon turned his head to look at him. "You were asleep, Nathan, but don't worry. It's only been a couple hours, like I said. The horses needed the rest, and obviously, so did you."

Nathan ran his fingers through his dark hair, making it stick up wildly, then rubbed his face. "Who saddled my horse?"

"I did," Red Buffalo said.

A thought sprang unbidden to his mind about how he'd better check the cinches, since you couldn't trust a redskin to do anything right, especially a white man's job. But it was just a matter of habit, he realized.

He bit back the words and said, "Thanks."

From the corner of his eye he saw Red Buffalo give him a surprised look, but he ignored it. He picked up his hat, swatted it against his thigh a couple times, and put it on, then cleared his throat and went over to his horse to pick up the reins.

A few minutes later, the three men were riding through the gathering dusk toward the fort.

Delia sent the children home early that day. Knowing what she knew, she couldn't look at their sweet faces and think about how they might be under attack by the time the sun came up the next morning.

Of course, there was always danger on the frontier, at least to a certain extent. In the well-manned fort, she had felt safe, but at the same time, she knew that forts had been attacked. Hostile Indians were hardly the only things that could prove deadly on the frontier. Blizzards roared down out of the northern climes every winter. Spring and summer thunderstorms often spawned cyclones that could destroy a building in seconds and kill everyone in it with hardly any warning. Rattlesnakes could be lurking behind every rock.

There were a million ways to die on the frontier, she thought. The only way not to go mad . . . was to not think about them. To go on living life and hoping for the best. But that wasn't easy to do, given the tragedies she had suffered in the past . . . and the knowledge that she possessed now.

So she gave the children a bit of a holiday and sent them home to their mothers. They could pick up their school work the next day. Or the day after that, if there was one.

Delia walked from the chapel back to her house and went inside. In the bedroom, she opened the trunk at the foot of the bed and took out an oilcloth-wrapped bundle. She carried it out of the room and set it on the kitchen table, then unwrapped it to reveal a wooden box. She unfastened the latch and lifted the lid.

Inside was a .44 caliber Model 3 Schofield revolver, along with a dozen cartridges. It was the gun Stephen had carried as his sidearm for the last few years of his life. The metal's dull finish and the plain wooden grips reflected its owner. Stephen Blaine had been a good man who did his duty, nothing fancy or flashy about him. Delia had loved him dearly, but he didn't like to call attention to himself. It was easy to forget that he was around . . . until he was needed.

Much like his revolver.

He had taught her how to fire the gun, and how to clean it, as well. She had kept it in good repair, though it hadn't been used in a long time. She picked it up, pushed the little lever that broke it open at the top, and tilted the barrel and cylinder down to inspect the chambers. Satisfied, she took six of the bullets and slid them, one at a time, into the gun. Then she closed it with a firm snap.

The revolver weighed a bit less than three pounds and was a foot long from the tip of the barrel to the end of the butt. Too big for her to go carrying it around openly in the fort, but she had a canvas bag that she sometimes used to bring back supplies from the commissary, so she slipped the gun into it and put the extra six rounds in the pocket of her dress. She was going to keep the Schofield with her, or at least close at hand, until she saw what was going to happen.

Wouldn't Nathan get a laugh out of that, she thought. All the times she had hectored him about how violence and killing didn't solve anything, and what did she do as soon as really bad trouble loomed? She loaded a gun and was very glad that she had it and knew how to use it.

That put a wry smile on her face as she left the house and started walking toward the stables. It would be dark soon, and she wanted to talk to Billy—*Matoskah*—again before night fell.

Even though the sun had just set, the shadows were already growing thick inside the stables. Matoskah knew he could light a lantern if he needed to, but he was almost finished with his chores and didn't want to go to the trouble if it wasn't necessary.

Everything would have been done by now if Hotah and the others had stayed to help him. But they were tired and hungry for their supper and had wandered off, leaving him to make sure all the water troughs were filled. Carrying a bucket, he went to the pump outside, filled it, then stepped back into the gloomy, cavernous building carrying the full bucket when a burly figure stepped out of the shadows in front of him. He had to stop short to keep from running into the man.

"Just hold it right there, ye little redskinned heathen."

The angry voice with its unmistakable Irish accent made Matoskah catch his breath. Sergeant Seamus McCall was blocking his path, and the brutal noncom didn't sound happy.

In fact, he sounded like he was mad enough to kill.

Matoskah tried to step around him. "I have to finish my chores, Sergeant—"

McCall put a big hand on the young man's chest to stop him.

It was like running into a wall, Matoskah thought. He and the sergeant were roughly the same height, but he would never be able to budge McCall.

"Your chores can wait. I've got somethin' to say to ye, lad, and you're gonna listen to it. Or rather, I have a question to ask ye."

Matoskah swallowed hard. "A . . . a question?"

"Aye. Just why in the hell are ye goin' around accusin' me of runnin' guns to the filthy Sioux?"

The fear inside Matoskah went up another notch. Somehow, McCall had found out about the conversation he and Mrs. Blaine had had with Lieutenant Allingham. That wasn't too surprising when he thought about it. Corporal Winston Cahill had been in the outer office, and Cahill was as big a gossip as an old woman. He had eavesdropped and then told someone what he'd heard, and that person told someone else . . .

Until it came to the ears of Sergeant Seamus McCall, and McCall had headed for the stables to confront Matoskah.

Gathering up his courage, the young man said, "I am not one of your soldiers, Sergeant. I take orders only from the stable master, and I do not have to answer your questions."

"No?" McCall seemed more puzzled than angry. "That's the way it is, is it?"

"Yes, I—"

McCall took Matoskah by surprise. His left hand came up fast and cracked across the young man's face in a backhanded blow that jerked Matoskah's head around. He staggered backwards and almost fell. Water sloshed from the bucket in his hand, but he held on to its bail and didn't drop it. When McCall charged him like a maddened bull, Matoskah swung the bucket without thinking about what he was doing. Its wooden side cracked hard against McCall's head, and more water flew over both of them.

McCall grunted in pain, but his momentum carried him into Matoskah. The sergeant's weight was too much for the young man to withstand. Matoskah lost his balance and went over backwards. He landed on his back with McCall on top of him. Unable to breathe because of the bulk pressing down on him, he flailed desperately at McCall with the bucket.

The noncom raised his left arm to shield himself from the blows, then struck Matoskah on the inside of the elbow with his forearm. Matoskah's arm went numb, and the bucket slipped from his fingers and clattered away. With it went his last chance of being able to defend himself.

The next moment, both of McCall's hands wrapped around Matoskah's throat and began to squeeze. McCall leaned over, bringing his face so close to Matoskah's face that the Sioux youth could feel the man's hot breath and smell the firewater he had drunk sometime recently.

"Go around spreadin' lies about me. I'll teach ye!" McCall laughed. "But you know, and so do I, that they ain't lies. Ye heard me and Dockery and that Dutchie, Bucher, out there in the woods one night, didn't ye? Didn't ye!"

Matoskah didn't think McCall actually wanted an answer to that question, but he managed to move his head a little anyway in a semblance of a nod.

Amazingly, some of the terrible crushing pressure on Matoskah's throat was relieved. McCall didn't let go of him, though. "Rumor has it ye told the lieutenant ol' Hangin' Dog is liable to attack as soon as he gets his hands on those guns. We had a deal with the red bastard! He wouldn't bother the fort until a time when Dockery an' Bucher an' me were all away from here. But you're sayin' he's gonna wipe out the whole place when the sun comes up in the mornin'!"

McCall's grip was loose enough for Matoskah to talk. In an agonized whisper, he said, "I . . . I do not know . . . but I believe . . . it is what he will do."

"You know what, lad? I believe it, too. Do ye know why? Because it's just my luck! Dockery an' Bucher are gone, the sons o' bitches, but here ol' Seamus sits, waitin' to be massa-creed by the dirty heathens. Well, I'm not gonna stand for it, do ye hear? By mornin', I'm gonna be far away from here. I'll give up my final share of the money to keep me hair!" His fingers began to tighten again. "Now all I have to do is shut ye up, so ye can't tell anyone where I've gone . . ."

Matoskah tried to thrash around enough to get free, but McCall weighed too much. He couldn't dislodge the burly noncom. And McCall was choking him tighter and tighter, until red balls of fire began erupting behind Matoskah's eyes and he knew that in seconds he would be dead.

Then the entire world seemed to explode.

CHAPTER 36

Delia heard grunting inside the stable as she approached, then a clatter as if someone had dropped a bucket. She had thought at first she was hearing someone working in there, but as the noises continued, she realized a struggle was going on.

She walked faster, but her steps were light on the hard ground, almost silent.

Just inside the door, she paused to let her eyes adjust to the gloom. She heard a harsh voice speaking quietly and moved closer to an irregular dark shape she spotted in the aisle between the rows of stalls.

No, not one shape. Two. One man was kneeling on top of another, and from the look of his arms, he had his hands around the second man's throat. The only reason for him to be doing that was if he were trying to choke the second man to death . . .

That shocking realization was followed instantly by another. The voice she heard belonged to Sergeant Seamus McCall . . . and the second man had to be Billy, which meant McCall had found out about the visit she and Billy had paid to Lieutenant Allingham, and he intended to dispose of the witness. As she reached into the bag and closed her hand around the Schofield's grips, she heard him admit that he was part of the gunrunning scheme along with Sergeant Dockery and Dietrich Bucher.

She had the proof she needed but had to stop McCall from murdering Billy!

She dropped the bag, pointed the gun at the ceiling, pulled back the hammer until it locked into place, and squeezed the trigger. The boom was deafening, and the recoil might have torn the revolver out of her grip if she hadn't been using both hands to hold it.

"Let go of that boy!" she cried. Her ears were still ringing so badly from the Schofield's report that her own words sounded muffled and distant to her.

She saw McCall rise and start toward her. "Damn it, Delia, why'd ye have to go an' stick your pretty little nose in where it don't belong? Gimme that gun—"

He would kill her, too, in order to protect himself, she thought. The shot would bring more of the soldiers to the stables, so McCall would have to act quickly. If he murdered her and then killed Billy, he could claim that Billy was the one responsible for her death.

All McCall would have to say was *Yeah, I came in and saw that the savage had killed poor Mrs. Blaine, so I grabbed him and done for him, 'fore he could murder me, too. Some people might suspect he wasn't telling the truth, but no one would be able to prove it. And since it was always easy to blame an Indian for killing a white, in the end everyone would accept McCall's story.*

That knowledge flashed through Delia's mind in less than a second. Her thumb was already on the

Schofield's hammer. As McCall lunged at her, she drew it back and pulled the trigger again.

He was so close the flame licking out from the gun muzzle touched his chest. He flung his arms out to the sides and went over backwards as the slug drove deep into his body. Delia screamed, unable to control the reaction, and staggered backwards. The Schofield slipped from her fingers and thudded to the ground.

Billy was beside her quickly, one hand holding his throat. "Mrs. Blaine," he croaked, the tortured voice showing how close McCall had come to choking him to death. "Are you all right?"

Before Delia could answer, a man yelled, "Mrs. Blaine! Get out of the way! Kill the Indian!"

"No!" she cried. She flung her arms out, much like McCall had done when she'd shot him, and threw herself in front of Billy. "Don't shoot! He hasn't done anything!"

A soldier with a lantern appeared in the stable's open doors. The light revealed two more soldiers with rifles who had rushed up in response to the first shot.

When the lantern's glare fell over McCall's body, the man holding it up shouted, "Good Lord! The savage has killed Sergeant McCall!"

"No!" Delia insisted. "I shot him! I shot him! He was going to kill me and Billy!"

"Step out of the way, ma'am," one of the riflemen ordered. "This mad dog needs to be put down."

"Aren't you *listening* to me? Billy didn't hurt anybody. McCall was trying to murder him. McCall's a gunrunner—"

The three soldiers suddenly stepped aside as a

fourth man strode into the stable. Delia recognized the tall, slender figure of Lieutenant Marcus Allingham.

The lieutenant had arrived in time to hear what she was saying and exclaimed, "Not this blasted gun-running business again! Mrs. Blaine, I thought I had made you understand that such a thing just isn't feasible." Allingham stared in shock at McCall's body. "And now the Indian boy has killed poor Sergeant McCall!" He gestured curtly to the other men. "Take him into custody and lock him in the guardhouse."

"Lieutenant, listen to me! You can't—"

"Sure you wouldn't rather us just shoot him, Lieutenant?" one of the soldiers asked.

"We're going to handle this matter in a proper fashion. That means a trial." Allingham's voice hardened. "And then a hanging."

Delia looked down at the ground. The Schofield lay near her feet. She thought she could pick it up before any of the soldiers could reach her . . .

"Mrs. Blaine, no," Billy said in a low voice. "Do not make more trouble for yourself."

She turned to him, saw that his expression was strained, but oddly enough, he seemed fairly composed.

"Billy . . . Matoskah . . . we can't let them lock you up—"

He stopped her by shaking his head. "It does not matter." He glanced at Lieutenant Allingham's stern, angry visage. "There will be no trial until Colonel Ledbetter returns to the fort."

"That's right," Allingham snapped. "The colonel will want to handle this terrible affair himself, I'm sure."

Everyone in the stable knew what he meant. Colonel Ledbetter would want the credit for trying and hanging an Indian who had killed a white soldier. It would make him look that much better back in Washington.

But as Delia met Billy's dark eyes, she knew what it really meant. Waiting for Ledbetter to return insured that whatever was going to happen with Hanging Dog would have occurred by then. The whole thing might well be moot . . . rendered so by hordes of well-armed Sioux warriors pouring into the fort and slaughtering everyone they saw.

The two soldiers with rifles strode over and grabbed Billy by the arms.

As they shoved and dragged him roughly toward the entrance, he glanced one last time at Delia and said, "Remember . . . the chapel."

Then they were gone.

Lieutenant Allingham started to pick up the revolver. "That's mine," Delia said sharply. "Or rather, my late husband's."

"Why did you bring it out here?" Allingham asked. "If you hadn't done that, the Indian wouldn't have been able to take it away from you and use it to slay Sergeant McCall."

Delia didn't answer him. She bent, grasped the gun, and slid it back into her bag. As soon as possible, she would replace the rounds she had fired with a couple of the extra cartridges. She had ten shots left. That wouldn't be enough if Hanging Dog attacked, but the other two bullets wouldn't have made any difference.

As long as she had one left at the end, that was all that mattered.

* * *

With Nathan and Red Buffalo to guide them by the stars, it was next to impossible that they and Doc Lightner would get lost during the night as they rode toward Fort Randall. They couldn't go as fast as they had been during the day for a couple reasons. Despite the rest, the horses were still tired and could only be pushed so hard, and the darkness made it more difficult to see the ground ahead of them. If a horse were to step in a prairie dog hole and snap a leg, that would be disastrous.

Because of the slowed-down pace, Nathan's impatience grew steadily. They had to stop completely now and then to let the horses blow, and every time they did, he lifted his head and listened intently, dreading to hear the sound of gunfire in the distance. However, the night was quiet, and the world seemed to be asleep.

That tranquility would not last, he sensed.

The stars wheeled through the night sky, and it was well after midnight by the time he and his companions reached the ford across the Missouri River.

As they rode across with the muddy water splashing quietly around their mounts' legs, Nathan said, "Another couple hours and we ought to be there."

"We will arrive before dawn," Red Buffalo said. "If Hanging Dog doesn't attack until then, we'll have a chance to warn everyone and get ready."

Doc Lightner said, "To tell you the truth, I wasn't sure we'd make it. It seemed like, with so many things having gone wrong already, something else was bound to."

"We're not there yet, Doc," Nathan said, "and don't say anything else, or you're liable to jinx us."

"I'm a man of science, Captain, not of superstition."

Red Buffalo chuckled. "Well, I'm just a redskin who believes in bad medicine and bunk like that, but I agree with Stark, Doc. No need for us to tempt fate."

"Fine," Lightner said as they came up out of the river. "Let's just get back there."

"Couldn't agree more," Nathan said.

They set a little faster pace now that they were in the last stretch. Horses and men alike were exhausted, but urgency drove them on. Nathan saw a thin, pale line of gray on the eastern horizon and knew what it meant. They were in a race now—a race against the onrushing dawn.

Finally, Nathan spotted what looked like a light far ahead. At least one lamp was kept burning all night in the guardhouse. Since there were no farms or ranches between where they were and the fort, he knew that had to be Fort Randall. They had made it.

A few minutes later, Doc Lightner asked excitedly, "Is that a light I see? Is that the fort?"

"It sure is, Doc," Red Buffalo replied. "I spotted it a ways back, and I'm sure Nathan did, too."

"Yeah, but that's all right, Doc," Nathan said. "You're not a scout. You're not supposed to be eagle-eyed like us."

The surgeon said, "I don't hear any shooting. That's a good thing, isn't it?"

"It sure is," Nathan agreed.

The night was quiet, and that was indeed a good thing. But if what Red Buffalo had overheard back in the Sioux village was true—and there was no reason to think it wasn't—the sounds of gunfire and war cries would soon fill the air.

Nathan urged his borrowed army mount on, asking the animal for its last reserves of strength.

They slowed as they neared the fort, not wanting to spook some trigger-happy green recruit on sentry duty into shooting them. The guardhouse was at the northern end of the parade ground, so that was where the riders approached. Not surprising, as they slowed their horses to a walk someone called the usual challenge, "Halt! Who goes there?"

"It's Dr. Lightner," the surgeon replied, "along with the scouts, Captain Stark and Moses Red Buffalo."

"Advance and be recognized, Doctor."

A match scraped to life as Nathan, Red Buffalo, and Lightner walked their horses forward. Its flaring light illuminated them enough for the sentry to know that Lightner had told the truth. He shook out the match and dropped it, then straightened and saluted Lightner, since the post surgeon was also a captain. Lightner returned it with as much precision as he could manage, considering how exhausted he was.

"Is the rest of the column with you, Doctor?" the guard wanted to know.

"It's just the three of us. We need to speak to Lieutenant Allingham immediately."

"I imagine he's still asleep—"

"We'll wake him up." Lightner reined his horse past the sentry and headed along the edge of the parade ground toward the headquarters building at the other end. Since Allingham was in command of the fort temporarily, he should be sleeping there.

They dismounted in front of The House. Nathan's legs betrayed him for a second, but he caught himself.

Red Buffalo and Lightner weren't too steady, either. The horses stood with their sides heaving and their heads drooping. Nathan felt like doing that himself, but their chore wasn't over yet.

The three of them made it up the steps to the porch. Lightner pounded a fist on the door.

After a couple of minutes, a sleepy-looking Corporal Cahill, wearing a hastily pulled on pair of uniform trousers over his long underwear, answered the summons and peered out at them with bleary eyes as he held a lamp. "Doctor?" he said in astonishment. "What—"

"We need to speak to Lieutenant Allingham right away," Lightner interrupted.

Cahill looked past the surgeon at Nathan and Red Buffalo and grew even more confused. "Where's the colonel?"

"Chasing phantoms," Lightner snapped. "Step aside, Corporal."

Cahill backed away. "I'll fetch the lieutenant." He placed the lamp on the desk in the outer office and went along a hall that led to guest quarters, in this case used for the officer left in command while Colonel Ledbetter was gone.

Two more minutes went by while Cahill was gone, minutes that gnawed at Nathan. He didn't know Allingham at all, had seen the junior officer a few times, that was all. He hoped the lieutenant was the sort who would listen to reason. Hanging Dog and the rest of the Sioux could be closing in on the fort while time was wasted.

Lieutenant Allingham stumbled into the office wearing a dressing gown. His hair was askew and he looked totally flustered. "What's going on here?" he demanded. "Doctor—"

"Captain," Lightner broke in, correcting him.

Nathan hadn't thought about that earlier, but it was true—Lightner outranked the lieutenant. "There's no time for a formal report, but the fort is in great danger. We have information that Hanging Dog and a large war party numbering close to three hundred men armed with repeating rifles will soon attack the fort—"

"That business again?" Allingham blurted out.

Nathan edged forward tensely. "You know about it? Then why in hell is the whole fort asleep?"

Allingham sighed with an air of exaggerated patience. "One of the Sioux boys from the stables told some wild story to Mrs. Blaine about an attack, but it was clearly a fabrication and I put no stock in it. Why, he even claimed that two of our sergeants, as well as that German, Bucher, are involved in selling guns to the Indians. To make matters worse, the young buck killed Sergeant McCall."

"McCall," Nathan breathed. "He was one of the men mixed up in the scheme?"

"So the Indian claimed, but it was an obvious lie."

Nathan didn't think so. He had no trouble believing that McCall would do such a thing. And he was already suspicious of Bucher, so that tied in with what he knew.

"Where's this Indian kid now? You didn't execute him, did you?"

"He's locked up safely in the guardhouse where he can't get into any more mischief," Allingham said.

"When Colonel Ledbetter gets back, I'm sure there'll be a trial. Where *is* the colonel?"

Lightner ignored that question. "Everything that Sioux lad told you is true, Lieutenant. You need to alert the post right now and order the men to prepare for an imminent attack."

"But Doctor—"

"Captain," Lightner said again with steel in his voice. "That's an order, Lieutenant. I'm relieving you of command. Now get out there and get busy, son, before Hanging Dog and all his bloodthirsty friends get here!"

CHAPTER 37

Allingham had said something about Delia being involved with the Sioux youngster who had tried to warn folks about the attack. Nathan didn't wait to find out what that was all about. He just wanted to see Delia with his own eyes and make sure she was all right. How Sergeant Seamus McCall had wound up dead could be hashed out later.

Nathan left Lightner and Allingham to make what plans they could for the fort's defense and ran along the parade ground until he came to Delia's house. Weariness forgotten, he bounded onto her porch and banged a fist against the door. "Delia!" he called. "Delia!"

She opened the door, surprising him by being fully dressed—and having a gun in her hand. "Nathan!" she cried and threw her arms around his neck.

He recognized Stephen's old Schofield revolver. "Careful there with that hogleg," he murmured as he embraced her. She felt fine in his arms, damned fine. Their mouths found each other and clung together.

When Delia finally broke the kiss and pulled back a little, she asked, "Is the rest of the column with you?"

Nathan shook his head. "No, just me and Moses and Doc Lightner. The colonel's an even bigger damned fool than I thought he was. I hope he's on his way back by now, but I can't guarantee it."

Delia moaned and rested her head against his chest. "The Sioux are coming . . ."

"I know. I reckon we've both got stories to tell each other, but that can wait. You got to get ready."

"I've been up all night, just waiting. I have Stephen's gun. It's loaded—"

"Not near enough. I'll take you to the chapel. It's the sturdiest building on the post, and it's got that bell tower. We'll put some riflemen up there and they'll have a field of fire over the whole post. Not even Winchester rounds will make it through those thick stone walls. It'd take a cannon to knock them down . . . and Hanging Dog doesn't have a cannon."

At least, Nathan hoped that was true.

Since Delia was already dressed, he put his arm around her shoulders and walked with her toward the chapel. The enlisted men had built it out of thick blocks of sandstone and heavy wooden beams. It was a large, L-shaped building with the two-story bell tower rising where the two legs came together. Nathan thought there would be room inside for all the women and children on the post, as well as the remainder of Company K. With riflemen at every window and in the tower, they ought to able to hold off the Sioux and keep the savages from overrunning them. That would be true for a while, anyway.

Of course, it would also mean leaving the rest of the fort undefended. Lieutenant Allingham probably wouldn't want to do that, but since Doc Lightner had taken command, Nathan hoped the surgeon would think the sacrifice was worthwhile.

It appeared that was what was going on. Soldiers carrying lanterns rushed here and there. Men carried supplies from the commissary and the quartermaster's storehouse into the chapel. Women herded sleepy, complaining children behind the protection of the thick walls.

Nathan and Delia were almost there when she stopped and looked around sharply. "Billy. I mean Matoskah. He may still be locked up in the guardhouse. They can't leave him there."

"He's the one who found out McCall was part of the gunrunning ring?"

"Yes, along with Sergeant Dockery and Dietrich Bucher."

"And Jake Farrow."

Delia shook her head. "I don't know about that. But it certainly seems likely."

Nathan glanced around and didn't see Farrow anywhere. Maybe the sutler had cut and run because he knew the attack was coming. His clerk, Noah Crimmens, was unaccounted for, too.

Nathan liked the mild little man. "You go on inside," he told Delia. "I want to find a friend of mine, and I'll check on the Indian boy while I'm at it."

"If Hanging Dog finds Matoskah in the guardhouse, he'll kill him. He'll kill all those boys."

"I'll do what I can," Nathan promised. "Now, you go in there and find you a nice safe place. They'll probably pile up some of the pews in the sanctuary. You get behind them. And keep that Schofield handy, just in case."

"I will. Be careful, Nathan."

He grinned even though he didn't feel like it. "Why, it's my middle name, darlin'." With that, he was off at a run toward the far side of the post where the sutler's store was located.

The commotion had roused everyone, including, to his surprise, Jake Farrow.

The man was ushering the handful of soiled doves out of the building. "Stark! You brought the word that the redskins are on their way?"

"That's right. What are you doing still here, Farrow?"

The man frowned at him. "What do you mean? Where the hell else would I be?" Farrow waved a hand. "Never mind. Is there room over there in the chapel for my girls?"

"Should be. Some of the officers' wives might object to their kids being exposed to such immorality as your gals represent, but I reckon they'll just have to get over it for a while."

"Damn right. Move, ladies!"

Nathan caught hold of Farrow's sleeve. "Where's Noah?"

"I already sent him over there with my ledgers. Got to keep them safe, you know. *And* my strongbox."

Nathan nodded. Farrow didn't lose sight of business, even in the face of an Indian attack. He sure didn't act like a man who should have been expecting trouble. The news seemed to have taken him completely by surprise.

No time to ponder that. Nathan left Farrow ushering his "ladies" toward safety and hurried to the guardhouse. The soldiers who had been on duty there were gone, already pressed into jobs elsewhere.

"Billy!" Nathan called as he stepped into the outer room. A lamp still burned on the desk usually manned by the sergeant of the guard. "Hey, kid!"

"Back here!" came the response from a hallway leading to the cells. Nathan picked up the lamp and walked along it. The light splashed into the only occupied cell.

The Sioux youngster stood at the door, clutching the bars. He looked surprised to see Nathan. "It's you."

"Yeah, it is," Nathan drawled. "You and your friend been riding any bad horses lately, Billy?"

"You're going to leave me in here, aren't you?"

"I promised Mrs. Blaine I'd get you out. Where are the keys to unlock that door?"

Billy shook his head. "I don't know. In the sergeant of the guard's desk, maybe?"

"Hang on. I'll have a look."

"I'm not going anywhere," the youngster said bitterly.

Nathan went back to the outer room. He didn't see any keys lying on the desk or hanging on hooks, so he started jerking open the desk drawers. He found a ring of keys in the second one he opened. A moment later he was trying them in the lock on the cell door. The fourth key made it click.

Nathan swung the door open.

Billy hesitated for a second, as if he feared that somehow this was a trick, but then he stepped out.

"Let's go," Nathan said.

They stepped into the outer office. He was about to set the lamp back on the desk when it suddenly exploded in his hand. His brain registered several things almost instantaneously. He'd heard a shot, the whine of a bullet, and then the lamp's chimney had shattered. Somebody had just tried to kill him again and hit the lamp instead.

Flames erupted when the shattered lamp hit the desk. Nathan knew the oil had spilled from the reservoir and ignited. The fire would reveal them to whoever was outside. He grabbed Billy's arm and went to the floor, taking the youngster with him. At the same time, his other hand palmed the Colt from its holster.

Another slug whipped through the open door as a rifle cracked. Prone on the floor, Nathan saw the muzzle flash and triggered two shots in its general direction. A quick glance over his shoulder showed the desk burning. The flames would spread to the rest of the guardhouse in a matter of moments. It was time for him and Billy to get out of there.

"Stay behind me!" he told the young man as he surged to his feet and headed for the door, firing the Colt as he ran. He didn't figure he would hit anything, but he wanted to keep the would-be killer occupied. He heard Billy right behind him.

They burst through the door. Nathan ducked left and dived off the porch. No shots came. On the other side of the post and halfway along the parade ground, men were shouting around the chapel, no doubt alarmed by the gunfire and thinking the Sioux attack had begun.

Nathan didn't figure that was the case. If the Sioux were there, a lot more guns would be going off. War whoops would fill the air, too.

The shots were another ambush intended to kill *him*, he realized. Or Billy. He couldn't rule out that possibility, either. Had the bushwhacker fled again, like in the past?

The sky was gray. Dawn wasn't far off. They were running out of time . . . unless Red Buffalo had been wrong about Hanging Dog's plans, in which case the whole thing was nothing but a false alarm.

Wouldn't they all feel foolish then?

Nathan looked around, saw Billy climbing shakily to his feet. "You all right, kid?" he asked as he got up, too.

"Y-yeah. Thanks, Mr. Stark. We'd better— Look out!"

Billy leaped toward Nathan, rammed a shoulder into him, and knocked him off his feet. Another shot blared, followed by a high-pitched cry somewhere on the prairie not far from the fort. More shots rang out.

Nathan and Billy rolled to their feet and ran toward the chapel as bullets continued to whine around them.

Hanging Dog and his men were there. Nathan didn't have to worry about looking foolish . . . just dying.

CHAPTER 38

Some of the soldiers provided covering fire while others carried the last of the supplies into the chapel. One of the blue-clad troopers staggered and fell with blood gushing from his bullet-torn throat as Nathan and Billy approached the building's front door. Shots came from every direction. The burning guardhouse threw a hellish glare across the parade ground. Chaos reigned.

As soon as he was inside, Nathan darted to the right and put his back against the stone wall. The sprint under fire across the parade ground had left him winded. He stood there trying to catch his breath as Billy did likewise beside him.

When Nathan could talk again, he said, "Why'd you knock me down like that?"

"I caught a glimpse of movement just outside the fort and knew it had to be one of Hanging Dog's warriors. I just guessed he was about to shoot at you."

"It was a good guess. That slug came close enough I felt the wind of it. Reckon you saved my life, kid."

"You saved mine by taking me out of the guardhouse."

"We'll call it even." Nathan had said just about the same thing to Red Buffalo the day before. *Getting mighty friendly with the damned heathens,* he thought.

Facts were facts, no matter how galling, and Nathan was hardheaded enough to realize that.

"Get those doors closed!" Doc Lightner bellowed.

Shots were still coming in through the chapel's open doors and ricocheting around the room. A couple soldiers sprang to obey the order. They shoved the heavy wooden doors shut, but a last bullet came through the narrowing gap and struck a man in the shoulder. He went down howling in pain. Another man stepped up and dropped the bar across the doors to keep them from being opened from outside.

Lightner knelt to check on the wounded man. Lieutenant Allingham dispersed riflemen to all the windows and ordered others up into the bell tower. The stained glass was already shattered in most of the windows in the sanctuary, and it wouldn't last long in the others. The soldiers began firing back at the Sioux attackers.

Nathan looked around for Delia but didn't see her. Alarm jumped up his throat. If she hadn't managed to get inside . . .

He spotted Red Buffalo and hurried over to the Crow. He noticed Billy trailing him but didn't say anything to the youngster except, "Keep your head down, kid."

"Are you all right, Nathan?" Red Buffalo asked.

"Yeah. Came close a few times, but not hit yet. How about you?"

Red Buffalo still had the Springfield he had brought with him when they escaped from the column. He smiled grimly. "Fine. Just waiting for the right moment to fire my one shot."

"Have you seen Delia?"

"Mrs. Blaine is with the women and children inside her classroom. The soldiers upended some of the benches and placed them in front of the windows to block them, so it should be relatively safe in there."

Nathan felt relief course through him. It was such a strong sensation that for a second it made him weak in the knees. Then he stiffened and said, "We've got a fight on our hands."

"Yes . . . but thanks to our long ride yesterday and last night, perhaps not a massacre."

Nathan jerked a thumb at his companion. "This is Billy . . . or rather, Matoskah. Right?"

"For now, I am just Billy," the youngster said.

"This is Moses. You stay with him. Look after the kid, all right?"

"This is no kid," Red Buffalo said. "I can tell by looking at him, he is a warrior."

Billy stood a little taller at that.

Nathan said, "You two ought to get along, even if one of you is a Sioux and the other's a Crow. Try not to scalp each other."

"If I have not taken *your* hair by now, I think this young man's scalp is safe," Red Buffalo said as he arched an eyebrow.

Nathan just grinned to himself and hurried toward the classroom. He wanted to make sure Delia was all right.

She had been watching for him, and ran to him

and threw her arms around him as soon as he stepped into the room. "There was so much shooting outside," she said quietly as she hugged him. "I was so worried about you, Nathan."

"It was a real hornet's nest, all right, but I managed not to get stung. And neither did Billy."

She pulled back a little and gazed up at him with a look of gratitude on her lovely face. "You were able to get him out of the guardhouse in time?"

"That's right. He's out there with Red Buffalo . . . but don't worry, I told 'em not to go on the warpath against each other just because they're from different tribes."

She laughed. "You never change, do you, Nathan?"

"I got to be who I am," he said, even though he knew her comment wasn't completely true. He *had* changed over the past couple weeks. Maybe not much, and the change had been mostly involuntarily . . . but he was beginning to see a few things a little differently . . . and there didn't seem to be anything he could do about it.

The room was crowded with women and children and a handful of soldiers who had been ordered to watch over them. Some of the children were crying, and a few of the women wept in fear, too. Most seemed to have stern resolve on their faces, though. A woman didn't marry a soldier without knowing that she and her family might face trouble someday.

"You'll be all right in here," Nathan went on to Delia. "I don't think you'll need that Schofield, but better keep it handy just in case."

"I intend to. Do you think we'll be able to survive this attack, Nathan?"

"I've got to believe we will. I've still got scores to settle."

"Aren't there more important things in life than that?"

"For most people, I reckon."

"But not for Nathan Stark?"

"Maybe someday."

He knelt at one of the windows with a Springfield he had picked up from the floor where it lay next to a dead soldier. Nathan had scavenged the unlucky trooper's extra rounds, too, and they were lined up on the windowsill, ready for him to load them as he needed to.

The sun was up. Black smoke billowed into the sky here and there from the buildings the Sioux had torched, but so far the savages hadn't wreaked much destruction. Most of the fort was intact because the Sioux were using the buildings for cover as they continued attacking the chapel. The closest structures were officers' quarters and one of the enlisted men's barracks. Most of Hanging Dog's forces were concentrated there. A smaller group had encircled the other side of the chapel to keep everyone pinned inside . . . not that anyone behind those thick stone walls actually wanted to venture out.

Nathan had his cheek resting against the Springfield's stock as he watched intently over the loaded rifle's sights. When he saw one of the attackers pop into view for a second, he squeezed the trigger. The Springfield cracked and bucked back against his shoulder. The Sioux warrior jumped and then flopped out into the open, half his head blown away by the powerful .45-70 round.

Nathan had killed half a dozen attackers over the past couple hours as the siege continued, but that wasn't nearly enough. In the beginning, Hanging Dog's forces had outnumbered the defenders slightly more than three to one, and Nathan doubted if they had whittled down those odds very much. A dozen soldiers were dead or wounded badly enough to be out of action.

No women or children had been hurt so far, at least that he knew of. He opened the trapdoor mechanism of the Springfield's breech and slipped another of the long, sharp-pointed cartridges into the rifle.

A sound made him look over. He saw that Billy had crawled up to the window.

The youngster dropped another dozen cartridges onto the floor next to Nathan and explained, "Doc put us to work resupplying ammunition."

"You and your friends?"

"That's right."

"Are any of them hurt?"

Billy shook his head. "Not so far. When they got here from the stables, during the preparations for battle, some of the soldiers didn't want to let them in. But Doc made them."

Nathan nodded. "Good."

"You trust us, even though we are Sioux?"

"I know that you're men who walk between worlds," he said, using the Indian phrase for those who were red but lived with the hated whites. "Betraying us now wouldn't do you any good. You'd always be tainted where Hanging Dog is concerned. He'd kill you without blinking."

"Yes, and all of us know it. Fate has given us a bitter brew to drink."

"At least you're alive to drink it," Nathan said. "Thanks for the ammunition."

Billy nodded and crawled away. Nathan went back to keeping his eyes open for another Sioux to kill.

By the middle of the day, it was hot enough inside the chapel that the defenders were all drenched in sweat. A little breeze came through the broken windows, but not enough to cool things down or disperse the clouds of powder smoke that hung in the air, stinging the eyes and nose of everyone. Billy and his friends crawled around the sanctuary offering canteens to the men. Nobody seemed to care anymore that they were Sioux. They were just the boys with the water.

Red Buffalo went over to the window where Nathan was posted. "I will take your spot for a few minutes," the Crow offered. "Sit down and rest."

"Was a time I'd have said I didn't need any help from a stinking redskin," Nathan replied as he turned and sank down gratefully with his back against the stone wall. "Today is not one of those days."

Red Buffalo laughed as he slid his Springfield over the windowsill. "You have learned that weariness is sometimes more powerful than hate."

"I'm tired, all right. Plumb worn out. And honest enough to say that you haven't given me any reason to hate you."

"What about my red skin?"

"I won't ever *like* it, mind you . . . but you're not a bad sort, for a filthy savage."

"And I have known worse white men. Not many, you understand, but a few."

"Like Bucher and Dockery and McCall."

"Yes," Red Buffalo agreed. "Those three, without a doubt."

Nathan looked over at the other side of the room where Jake Farrow knelt at one of the windows with a rifle, potting away at the Sioux on the west side of the chapel. The sutler had been in the thick of the fight right from the start. Of course, even if he was involved in the gunrunning, his life was still in danger just like everybody else's. Once Hanging Dog had gotten what he wanted, he hadn't hesitated to betray his partners, so it made sense that Farrow would fight.

Nathan still had the nagging feeling that Farrow hadn't known a damned thing about the attack or the gunrunning. If they survived, Nathan intended to get to the bottom of that. He already had a vague idea stirring in the back of his brain.

"Nathan!" Red Buffalo's voice was sharp. "Listen!"

Nathan listened for a moment, then shook his head. "I don't hear anything except guns."

"No, it's there, I tell you. A bugle!"

Nathan grunted. "You're just wishing for things now. I don't—" He stopped and drew in a breath as the distant, brassy tones reached his ear. "Well, son of a bitch."

If Colonel Ledbetter had ridden down on the Sioux camp the day before, as he had been bound and determined to do, even he would have realized he'd been wrong . . . and that meant what Nathan and Red Buffalo had told him more than likely was right. The thing to do then was to head back to the fort as quickly as possible. That was the only way for Ledbetter to salvage any glory from the fiasco. Nathan had been counting on the colonel's vanity and ambition to make him do the right thing, even if it was for the wrong reason.

As the familiar strains of "Charge!" from the bugle grew louder, Nathan knew his hunch had been right.

"They're running!" Red Buffalo exclaimed. "Hanging Dog wants to get out of here before he's trapped, but it's too late!"

Nathan got up hurriedly and knelt at the window beside the Crow scout. He saw the Sioux fleeing across the parade ground. Bringing the Springfield to his shoulder, he drew a bead on one of them and pressed the trigger. The rifle boomed. Nathan saw his target pitch forward on his face as the slug smashed into his back between the shoulder blades.

For several moments, Nathan and Red Buffalo reloaded and fired again and again, as many times as they could before the Sioux were out of sight. They dropped more of Hanging Dog's warriors, and Nathan felt a fierce exultation with each of the savages who fell. Maybe, just maybe, it didn't make sense to hate all Indians equally . . . but he figured it was just fine to hate these raiders who had intended to slaughter everyone in the fort, women and children included.

Soldiers on horseback swept around the northern end of the fort to cut off Hanging Dog's escape route.

The men of Companies G and H might not be cavalry, but they rode down the Sioux anyway. Some of them dismounted and formed ranks, and their devastating rifle fire scythed through the scattering remainder of the war party. Some of the Indians would get away, Nathan had no doubt of that, but it would be a long time before they tried to attack a fort again, especially if Hanging Dog was one of those killed. Without his leadership, this threat to peace along the frontier would evaporate . . . at least for a while.

Inside the chapel, the soldiers whooped and congratulated each other on surviving. Lightner and Lieutenant Allingham tried to maintain order and discipline, but it wasn't easy when the men had come so close to death.

Nathan stood up, sighed, and leaned the empty Springfield against the wall next to the window. "Finally used that bullet of yours, eh?" he said as Red Buffalo set his rifle aside, too.

"That was gone a long time ago," Red Buffalo said. "I gave it to one of the Sioux."

"Generous man." Nathan started walking across the sanctuary.

"Where are you going?" Red Buffalo asked as he came up alongside. "Shouldn't you check on Mrs. Blaine?"

"Yeah, but there's one more thing I need to do first."

He walked toward Jake Farrow. Noah Crimmens was there with the sutler, looking pale and drawn but relieved. Nathan had seen Crimmens huddled in a corner several times during the battle, obviously frightened. He was a clerk, not a fighting man.

But that didn't mean he wasn't dangerous.

Farrow grinned at Nathan. "Glad to see you came through it alive, Stark."

"Yes, I am, too," Crimmens said, his Adam's apple bobbing as he swallowed hard.

"We were lucky, all of us." Nathan's gaze tracked over to Crimmens. "But you're the luckiest one of all, Noah."

"I . . . I don't understand why you'd say that, Nathan."

"Well, it seems like fate would've had a bullet with your name on it today, since it was you who supplied those rifles to Hanging Dog. You didn't know he was gonna double-cross you and attack the fort before you had a chance to slip off and head back east with the money you made betraying everybody who trusted you."

Crimmens' eyes widened while Nathan was talking, until they seemed about to bulge out of their sockets. Everyone else around was listening intently, including Farrow, Doc Lightner, and Lieutenant Allingham.

"What?" Crimmens ventured. "That's crazy talk! I didn't— How in the world would I even go about doing such a thing?"

"You handled the paperwork on all the freight your boss brought in. It would have been easy enough for you to account for extra rifles, make it look like you took delivery of them when really the men you hired turned them over to Hanging Dog instead. To make it work, though, you had to know everything the army was doing in these parts, and that's why you had to bring Bucher, McCall, and Dockery in on the scheme. We know all about it now, Noah. A witness heard McCall admit before he died that you were behind the whole thing."

That was an outright lie. Delia hadn't heard McCall say anything about Crimmens . . . but the clerk didn't know that. From the way Crimmens' face suddenly twisted with hatred and rage, Nathan knew his shot in the dark had found its target.

"You son of a—!" Crimmens cried as his hand darted under his coat and came out holding a small pistol. "You've ruined everything!"

Crimmens had drawn first, but that didn't matter. Nathan's hand flashed to his Colt. He was no gunslinger, but his shot was faster—and more accurate. The slug crashed into Crimmens' narrow chest and flung him back against the stone wall behind him. His gun popped, but the bullet went into the plank floor at his feet. He hung where he was for a second, his mouth opening and closing and his throat working, then he slid down to a sitting position and died. His head slumped forward over his chest.

"Sorry," Nathan muttered to a staring Doc Lightner. He holstered the Colt. "Figured if I pushed him a mite, he'd confess. Didn't really expect him to put up a fight."

Lightner regained his composure. "I'd say what just happened is as good as a confession, Captain Stark. You'll need to make a full report about this to Colonel Ledbetter, though."

"You reckon he'll believe me this time?" Nathan asked, smiling faintly.

"He'll believe you. He won't have much choice."

Red Buffalo put a hand on Nathan's shoulder. "Somebody's looking for you."

Nathan didn't shrug it off, as he would have a couple weeks earlier. Looking around, he saw Delia coming toward him across the sanctuary with a smile on her face, and hurried to meet her.

CHAPTER 39

Colonel Ledbetter, for all his flaws, had proven to be a halfway decent tactician in his first major engagement with the hostiles. He had split his forces, encircled the enemy, and inflicted devastating losses. The Sioux suffered more than two hundred killed and another fifty wounded and/or captured. Only a couple dozen escaped. Hanging Dog's body was found among the dead.

The story of the battle would be featured in *Harper's Illustrated Weekly*, that was certain.

There had been fifteen fatalities among the defenders of Fort Randall, a fact that probably wouldn't be mentioned prominently in journalistic accounts. In addition, nine men from the column under Colonel Ledbetter's command had been killed in the fighting. One of them was Sergeant Jeremiah Dockery, originally from Tennessee.

Fate might have spared Noah Crimmens—momentarily—but it hadn't been that kind to Dockery.

Of Dietrich Bucher, the German scout attached to the column, there was no sign. Somewhere amidst all the bloody commotion, Bucher had slipped away, and his whereabouts were unknown. That bothered Nathan, but there was nothing he could do about it.

Several days after the battle, Nathan showed up at the chapel to walk Delia back to her house after her class was dismissed for the day. The building's broken windows were boarded up until they could be replaced. Men were already at work rebuilding the guardhouse and the other buildings that had been burned. The sound of hammering floated over the prairie as Nathan and Delia strolled, arm in arm.

"The racket of progress," he commented.

Delia laughed. "I hear the colonel called you in again today."

Nathan laughed. "Yeah. Poor varmint can't figure out what to do with me. He hates my guts, but too many people know that if Moses and Doc and I hadn't done what we did, things might've turned out a whole lot different."

"And much worse. You saved the lives of everyone here, Nathan."

"Just doing my job."

"With an Indian partner." She smiled. "I noticed that you call him Moses now. If I were to invite the two of you to dinner again, would you still be at each other's throats?"

"I wouldn't bet against it. We may have to work together. That doesn't make us friends."

"Small steps," she said as she squeezed his arm.

He shrugged. Let her think what she wanted to. It wasn't going to change things.

"So what *is* Colonel Ledbetter going to do with you?" Delia went on.

"He'd planned on asking the War Department to fire me or at least send me somewhere else. But since that might look bad now, he says he's stuck with me. He's not much fonder of Moses, but for the time being, we're going to keep on working together. Until Cullen gets back, anyway."

"What will happen then?"

"I reckon we'll find out," Nathan said. "Right now, I'm more interested in finding out what you've got planned for supper tonight. You *are* planning on asking me, aren't you?"

Delia laughed. "You're very sure of yourself, aren't you, Nathan Stark?"

Nathan just smiled. He was less sure about a lot of things than he had been at any time during the past fifteen years . . . but nobody had to know that.

He wished he knew, though, why he had a sudden prickling on the back of his neck as he and Delia walked on toward her house.

Half a mile away, bellied down at the crest of a small rise, Dietrich Bucher peered over the sights of a Sharps Big Fifty buffalo rifle and adjusted them slightly for windage and distance. The German's eyes were keen enough to pick out the two figures strolling unconcernedly across the parade ground.

Stark might believe he could come in and ruin everything, cost Bucher a lot of money, and ruin his reputation, all without paying any price for what he had done. The *verdammt* American was about to find out that wasn't true. The Sharps was perfectly capable of making the shot, especially in the hands of an expert such as Dietrich Bucher. He centered the sights on the tiny shape that was the back of Nathan Stark's head.

Concentrating so much on the killing shot he was about to make, he never heard the grass whisper under moccasin-shod feet. Never knew that anyone else was around until fingers tangled in his thick dark hair and jerked his head up. Bucher barely had time to feel the razor-sharp blade being drawn across his throat, biting deep, before his life began to wash away on a red tide.

The killer rolled the dying man onto his back. Consciousness was fading fast in the man's eyes, but the killer wanted him to know *why*.

Black Sun smiled coldly, shook his head, and said, "Mine."

TURN THE PAGE FOR AN EXCITING PREVIEW!

**Johnstone Country. Where Two Guns Kill
Better Than One.**

*Once upon a time in the Old West, Slash and Pecos were
two of the wiliest robbers this side of the Rio Grande. Now
they're fighting on the side of the angels—against three of
the nastiest killers this side of Hell . . .*

SLASH AND PECOS . . . IN THE SOUP AGAIN
Not many men get a second chance at life. But thanks
to a chief U.S. marshal who needs their help, the
bank-robbing duo of Jimmy "Slash" Braddock and
Melvin "Pecos Kid" Baker are on the right side of the
law. As unofficial marshals, they've agreed to pick up
three prisoners from a Milestown jail and escort them
to Denver. Sounds easy enough—until they learn who
the prisoners are: an unholy trio of sadistic cutthroat
killers known as Talon, "Hellraisin' " Frank, and the
Sioux called Black Pot. And they've managed to
escape before Slash and Pecos even show up . . .

It gets worse. The three convicts have turned
Milestown into their own savage slayground.
Drinking, killing, ravaging—and worse—they're
painting the town red with blood and burning it to
the ground. Slash and Pecos manage to stop them
in the nick of time. But getting these three to Denver
is another story—because the trio's leader has offered
a thousand-dollar bounty to anyone who can kill
Slash and Pecos . . . This is going to be one wicked
ride that Slash and Pecos will never forget—
if they live to tell about it . . .

THE WICKED DIE TWICE
A Slash and Pecos Western

On sale now wherever Pinnacle Books are sold.

CHAPTER 1

When Town Marshal Glenn Larsen reined up in front of the jailhouse on Dry Fork's main street very early on a Sunday morning in early July, a cold stone dropped in his belly. He could tell by the look on the dark, craggy face of his deputy, Henry Two Whistles, that trouble was afoot.

As the older man, clad in a three-piece suit that hung a little loosely on his lean frame, stepped out through the jailhouse door, a fateful cast to his molasses-dark eyes was undeniable. Not that Two Whistles was ever all that given to merriment. He was three-quarters Ute from southern Colorado Territory, and he was true to the stoic nature of his people.

As he closed the jailhouse door and turned to face Larsen reining up before him on the marshal's sweat-lathered coyote dun gelding, the old man rested his double-barreled Parker twelve-gauge on his right shoulder.

"Anyone hurt . . . killed?" Larsen asked before Two

Whistles could say anything, the marshal's voice pitched with dread.

Two Whistles frowned curiously, deep lines wrinkling the dark-cherry tone of his forehead and spoking around his eyes.

Larsen canted his head toward his back trail. "I was on my way back to town last night when I met three Milliron Ranch hands. I thought it was a mite odd to see Milliron hands heading back out to their headquarters so early on a Saturday night, and said as much. They told me that Talon Chaney and 'Hell-Raisin'' Frank Beecher had come to town, an' were sort of makin' all the stock hands homesick. They decided to cut out early and avoid gettin' caught in a lead storm."

Two Whistles gave a grim, stony-faced nod. "That damn Cut-Head Sioux is with 'em, too—Black Pot."

"Gabriel Black Pot," Larsen said as he swung down from his saddle. "Yeah, they mentioned him, too. He's an aptly named son of the devil, ain't he? There ain't one thing that ain't black about him, especially his heart."

Henry pursed his lips. "How bad, Henry?"

The old deputy lifted and lowered his left shoulder. "Not bad. This time. They came in late yesterday afternoon. Been holed up at Carlisle's place. All the ranch hands and everyone else in town know 'em well enough by now that they cleared out of Carlisle's as soon as Beecher's bunch bellied up to the bar."

"Not great for business, are they?"

"At least no one's dead. Not yet. They slapped around a couple girls, made 'em dance with 'em while Carlisle played the piano, but they was drunk when they rode into town, so by ten, eleven o'clock, they went upstairs an' passed out with a couple of Carlisle's doxies."

"That was nice of them." Larsen sighed. "When I heard they were here, I expected the worst."

Two Whistles's thick-lipped mouth rose in a grim smile. "That would likely happen today, when they get goin' again. As Carlisle tells it, they're flush. An' it don't look like they're gonna let any of that stage-coach money burn holes in their pockets."

The three killers, along with the rest of their twenty-man bunch, recently ran down a stagecoach hauling treasure from Deadwood to Sundance. They raped the women aboard the stage, killed the men, includ-ing the jehu and the shotgun messenger, stole the gold and the ranch payroll in the strongbox, and ran the stage off a cliff.

The gang split up the gold and separated.

Larsen had been surprised that Chaney, Beecher, and Black Pot had had the gall to show their faces in any town so soon after a holdup, but in a town so close to the scene of their crime most of all. On the other hand, he wasn't all that surprised. Those three killers in particular had reputations for being spitin-your-face brazen about their wicked ways.

Maybe they felt they'd earned the privilege. They were known to have killed three deputy U.S. marshals and a couple of sheriffs who'd tried to run them to ground over the years, and double that many bounty hunters who'd hounded the gang for the bounties on their heads.

They probably hadn't hesitated to head to Dry Fork because they knew an unproven town marshal and his just as unproven, old-man, half-breed deputy were manning the jailhouse these days. Glenn Larsen and Henry Two Whistles had both been working out at the Crosshatch Ranch up until only seven months ago, when the rancher they'd worked for, Melvin Wheelwright, died suddenly from a heart stroke. His family had sold the ranch to an eastern syndicate, and that company's head honcho decided to hire an entire new bunkhouse of hands, despite every one being as seasoned as any other thirty-a-month-and-found cowpuncher anywhere in the territory.

Funny folks, those tailor-dressed syndicate men, most of whom were foreigners, of course. Maybe that was the explanation right there. . . .

Two of those hands given their time, a sack of grub, and one horse each to ride away on were Larsen and Two Whistles. Henry had been the Crosshatch cook since his bronco-busting days had gone the way of the buffalo, leaving him with a rickety left hip and a pronounced limp in cold weather. Larsen and Two Whistles had gotten to be good friends over the four years they'd worked together at the Crosshatch, even though Larsen now being only twenty-seven and Two Whistles somewhere in his fifties (though he'd never said where exactly) were separated by nearly thirty years in age. It just seemed natural that, when the two lone wolves left the headquarters and neither had anyone else in their lives, and nowhere else to go, that they'd ride nowhere together.

The nearest town was Dry Fork, so they'd headed there for a drink or two to drown their sorrows. It just so happened the town had been in need of a new marshal and a deputy and, since no one else had seemed to want the dangerous jobs, here the two former Crosshatch men were now, sporting five-point town marshal's stars.

Not only had a job been awaiting Glenn Larsen, but a pretty girl, as well. The first moment he'd lain eyes on the mercantiler's comely daughter, Tiffanie Bright, he'd tumbled head over heels. To his astonishment, it had turned out that she'd felt the same way about him, so against Tiffanie's family's wishes, they'd been hitched inside of two months. Now they had a neat little frame house, which her father had staked them to, on the corner of Main Street and Third.

Larsen was eager to head home to his pretty wife now, as he'd been away for the past three days, looking for the two men who'd stolen stock from a local feed barn, and he knew Tiffanie was worried about him.

First things first.

"All right," he said now, sliding his Winchester carbine from his saddle sheath. "They're over at Carlisle's, you say?"

"That's where they are, all right. Carlisle's swamper has been keepin' me updated. I wasn't gonna make a move on 'em till you showed up. Not unless they started shootin' up the place anyways. I didn't even show myself, knowin' that would only provoke 'em."

"No, no, I'm glad you didn't. Hell, Bill Tilghman wouldn't make a play on that bunch solo. An' there's no point in provokin' 'em and risking other folks' lives."

"So you're sayin' I ain't just a coward?" Henry gave a rare smile.

"No more than me, anyway." Larsen gave a droll chuckle and slowly, quietly jacked a round into his

Winchester's action, as though the three brigands might hear the metallic rasp from all the way over at Carlisle's Saloon, two blocks away. "I wouldn't go it alone against them three. I sure will be happy to have them under lock and key—I'll tell you that much, Henry. When I took this job, I didn't think I'd be facing the likes of Talon Chaney!"

Again, Larsen chuckled. It was a nervous chuckle. He had the jitters, all right, and no mistake. His knees felt a little spongy, and his hands were sweating inside his buckskin gloves. He hadn't felt this nervy since the night before his wedding.

Tiffanie.

He sure hoped he made it through this morning in one piece, so he could see his lovely bride again. Thinking of her, of walking over to their little house on the corner of Main and Third, and sitting down to breakfast with her, after he had the three killers under lock and key, calmed his nerves a bit.

He kept her image in the back of his mind, and the image of their peaceful, cheerful, sunlit morning kitchen, as well, as he said, "All right, Henry. Let's do this. Me, I'm ready for breakfast."

"Really?" Henry said as they walked east along the main street, keeping to the boardwalks on the north side. "I couldn't eat a thing. In fact, I feel a little off my feed." He winced and pressed a hand to the middle-aged bulge of his belly.

"Truth be told, I was just jawin'." Larsen glanced at the older man walking beside him. "Right now, just the thought of food makes me a little ill."

"Yeah," Henry said.

As the two men walked along, spurs clanging softly,

boot heels scuffing the worn boards of the sidewalk, Larsen saw that the street was deserted. That was strange. It was almost eight o'clock.

Normally, there would be some wagon traffic at this hour. Housewives would be strolling toward Mergen's Grocery Store for fresh eggs and cream. Children would be tramping in small groups toward the school-house on the town's west end, bouncing lunch sacks off their thighs, the little boys triggering tree branch guns at each other or at imaginary Indians, the little girls whispering delicious secrets and giggling.

At the very least, a shopkeeper or two would be out sweeping the boardwalks fronting their stores, or arranging displays of their goods.

There was nothing but soft morning sunshine, a few small birds darting here and there, the light morning breeze kicking up little swirls of dust. Otherwise, the street was deserted.

Larsen didn't even see one of the town's mongrels heading home after a night in the countryside or hunting along the creek, a dead rabbit in its jaws. Occasionally, he saw a face in one of the store windows as he passed—a shopkeeper stealing a cautious glance into the street before letting a curtain drop back into place and scuttling back into the shadows, wary of catching a stray bullet.

Word had gotten around, of course.

Three of the nastiest killers ever to haunt the North Platte country were in town. Folks had learned that the three killers were at Carlisle's, and that the town's two unlikely lawmen, Glenn Larsen and Henry Two Whistles, were going to make a play on them. . . .

Larsen and Two Whistles stopped on the corner of

Main Street and Wyoming Avenue, and turned to face Carlisle's standing on the adjacent corner, on the other side of the main drag. It was a sprawling, white-painted, clapboard, three-story affair with a broad front porch. Larsen had never thought the place had looked particularly menacing. Just another saloon—one of three in the little settlement of Dry Fork, though the largest and the one with the prettiest doxies, as well as the best cook. Magnus Carlisle wasn't known to water down his whiskey, either, so his saloon and "dance hall," which was mostly just a euphemism for "whorehouse," was favored by men who could afford his slightly higher prices.

Now, however, Larsen would be damned if Carlisle's didn't look like a giant powder keg sporting a lit fuse.

He turned to his deputy. "You ready, Henry?"

"No," Two Whistles said, staring without expression at the saloon across the street.

"Yeah," Larsen said. "Me neither."

Squeezing the rifle in his hands, Larsen stepped into the street.

Larsen and Henry approached Carlisle's, whose porch and front door faced the street corner, the front of the building forming a pie-shaped wedge. A large sign over the porch announced simply CARLISLE'S in ornate green letters outlined in red and gold. Larsen felt his heart picking up its pace. The young man who had been sitting tipped back in a chair near the saloon's louvred front doors dropped the chair's front legs to the floor with a quiet thump and rose slowly.

That was Eddie Black, the curly-haired young swamper who had been relaying information about the cutthroats to Two Whistles at the jailhouse.

Eddie moved forward, and as the two lawmen stepped up onto the boardwalk fronting the porch, he came quickly down the broad wooden steps, eyes blazing anxiously. He was of medium height and skinny, and he wore a black wool vest over a white shirt adorned with a red cravat stained with beer and the tobacco juice he emptied from the saloon's brass spittoons.

He was "a little soft in his thinker box," as the saying went, and he sported a bushy thatch of curly red hair. He wasn't really as young as he seemed; Larsen had heard he was somewhere in his thirties. But his simple-mindedness made him seem much younger.

Breathless, he stopped before the two lawmen and said, "You gonna take 'em down, Marshal?" He grinned delightedly but also a little fearfully. He was fairly shaking with excitement.

Larsen and Two Whistles shared a glance, then the marshal said, "Well, we're gonna give it a try, Eddie. You'd best wait out here, all right?"

"Oh, don't you worry! I know who them fellas are!" Eddie scampered off to the left along the boardwalk and crouched down behind a rain barrel at the big building's far front corner. He looked cautiously over the top, as if he were expecting hell to pop at any second.

The young man's anxiety increased Larsen's. He shared another look with Two Whistles, and saw that the swamper's demeanor had had a similar effect on the normally stone-faced Ute. Henry's eyes were a little darker than usual. He was also a little pale, and sweat beaded his forehead, just beneath the brim of his black bullet-crowned hat.

Larsen adjusted the set of his own tan Stetson, then, opening and closing his hands around his rifle, he and Henry started up the porch steps. There were around a dozen steps, but it felt like a long climb. Finally, the lawmen pushed through the batwings and stepped into the saloon's cool shadows.

CHAPTER 2

"*Damn!*" a voice exclaimed.

Jerking his rifle up suddenly, Larsen turned to see Magnus Carlisle standing behind the bar just ahead and on the marshal's left. The man had been rolling a quirley, but apparently the two lawmen's sudden appearance in the front entrance had spooked him. He'd dropped his rolling paper and tobacco onto the polished mahogany bar top.

Larsen gave a soft sigh of relief and lowered the rifle.

Glaring at Larsen and Two Whistles, the portly, bespectacled saloon owner said, "You scared the hell out of me!"

Keeping his voice down, Larsen said, "Didn't you hear us comin' up the steps?"

"No!"

Larsen hadn't realized that he and Henry had been walking almost as quietly as two full-blood Indian braves on the warpath, but apparently they had. He glanced at Henry, who shrugged and gave a wry quirk of his upper lip.

Turning back to the saloon owner, Larsen said, "They still upstairs?"

"Yep," Carlisle said darkly, looking over the tops of his round, steel-rimmed spectacles. "Been there all damn night. You sure took your own sweet time getting here."

Larsen felt his face warm with anger. "I got back to town as quickly as I could, Mr. Carlisle," he crisply replied. And he nearly killed his horse doing it, he did not add. "Which room are they in?"

"Third floor. The big room all the way down on the end, right side of the hall. It overlooks the street. You better hope like hell they didn't see you walking over here." Carlisle narrowed an anxious eye and said, "They could be layin' in there waitin' for you."

"We'll handle it," Larsen said as he and Two Whistles walked along the bar, heading for the broad staircase at the room's rear. The young marshal hoped he'd sounded more confident than he felt.

Carlisle followed them, running a hand along the bar. "Take no chances, Glenn. If they get past you, they'll come down here and tear into *me*. There won't be enough of me left to bury!"

"Keep your voice down, Mr. Carlisle," Larsen said levelly, keeping his own voice just above a whisper.

"Shoot 'em through the door! Just shoot 'em through the door!"

As both lawmen stopped at the bottom of the stairs, Two Whistles turned to the saloon owner and said, "Don't they have a couple girls up there?"

Carlisle stared at him thoughtfully and blinked. He looked a little sheepish. "Yeah, I reckon they do. Claudine and Sally Jane. Still, though, fellas, shoot 'em through the door. Please! Don't take no chances. Claudine an' Sally Jane would understand!"

Larsen and Two Whistles shared a cynical glance and then started up the stairs.

Behind them, leaning forward and pushing his pudgy right hand against the bar top, Carlisle rasped, "Shoot 'em through the door! Don't take no chances! Hell, they'll burn the whole town down! You know how they are!"

Larsen whipped his head back to the frightened man and pressed two fingers to his lips. Carlisle just stared up at him, looking anguished. Turning forward again, Larsen and Two Whistles kept moving slowly up the stairs, keeping their eyes forward. At one point, Larsen's right spur jingled. He stopped, glanced at Henry, and then the two men wordlessly, quietly removed the spurs from their boots and left both pairs on that very step.

Spurless, they resumed their climb, crossing the second-floor landing, then continuing to the third floor.

Slowly, quietly, almost holding their breaths, they made their way down the third-floor hall, which was dingy and sour-smelling and lit by only the one dirty window at the far end. As they walked side by side, Larsen holding his Winchester up high across his chest, Two Whistles holding his Parker the same way, the marshal kept his eyes glued to the last door on the hall's right side.

He pricked his ears, listening.

The building was as silent as a tomb. There were still no sounds on the street. It was as quiet as Sunday morning when the whole town was in either of the two churches—the Lutheran or the Catholic.

A door clicked on the hall's right side. The lawmen stopped suddenly.

Larsen's heart quickened as he turned to see a near door open. A girl, dressed in a thin cotton wrap, stepped into the hall; then seeing the two gun-wielding men before her, she stopped and gasped, her eyes widening.

"What in holy blazes is goin' on?" she said way too loudly. Her words echoed around the previously silent hall.

"*Shhh!*" both Larsen and Two Whistles said at the same time, pressing fingers to their lips.

The girl looked as though she'd been slapped.

Larsen dipped his chin to indicate the door at the end of the hall. The girl turned her head to stare in that direction, then, appearing suddenly horrified, apparently remembering the three killers on the premises, stepped quickly back into her room and quietly closed her door.

Larsen stared at the last door on the hall's right side. He prayed it didn't open. Somehow, he had to get those three killers out of the room without getting the doxies killed. If the killers learned that the law was on the way, they might use the girls as human shields. Or they might just start shooting, and the girls would die in the crossfire.

Larsen couldn't wait for a better time. There might not be a better time. He had to arrest the cutthroats as soon as possible. No citizen was safe as long as the three cold-blooded killers were running free. Now was the best time to take them down, when they were either still asleep or groggy.

The two lawmen shared another fateful look, then resumed their slow, deliberative journey.

Finally, they found themselves standing in front of the door at the end of the hall.

Larsen tipped an ear to the panel. The only sounds issuing from inside the room were deep, sawing snores.

He looked at Henry and arched a brow, silently asking, *Too good to be true?*

The deputy gave a noncommittal shrug.

Holding his rifle in his right hand, aiming it just above the knob, Larsen placed his other hand on the knob and turned it very slowly. He winced when the latching bolt retreated into the door with a click.

A loud click. At least, to Larsen's nervous ears it was loud.

One of the three snoring men inside the room abruptly stopped snoring and groaned.

Larsen's heart thumped.

He shoved the door open and stepped quickly inside and to the left. Henry stepped in behind him to pull up on his right side, aiming the shotgun straight out from his right shoulder. Inadvertently, Two Whistles kicked a bottle that had been lying on the floor in front of the door. The bottle went rolling loudly across the wooden floor to bounce off a leg of one of the four beds before the two lawmen.

The bottle spun, making a whirring sound.

Henry looked down at it, stone-faced.

Larsen sucked a silent breath through his teeth, aiming his Winchester out from his right side.

One of the three men, each occupying three of the four beds in the room, lifted his head from his pillow. He was a shaggy-headed man lying back down on a bed ahead and against the right wall. The man sat partway up, but he didn't open his eyes. He merely groaned, then rolled onto this side, lay his head back down on his pillow, groaned once more, yawned, then resumed snoring softly.

Henry glanced sheepishly at Larsen, who gave him a look of silent scolding.

Returning his gaze to the three killers, Larsen looked them over.

A vacant bed lay to his hard right. The other three beds were filled. The two girls lay in each of the two beds on Larsen's left, each with one of the other two killers. The near girl appeared to be asleep, lying belly down beside a man with long coal-black braids and clad in a pair of threadbare long-handles. He also lay belly down. He and the girl were only partly covered by a twisted sheet.

The man with the black braids would be the Cut-Head Sioux, Black Pot.

The man beyond him, in the bed abutting the wall overlooking the street, was Talon Chaney himself. The second girl lay with Chaney, sort of wrapped in his thick arms. No sheet covered them. They were both naked. The girl was not asleep. Her blue eyes peered out through her tangled, tawny hair. They were bright and wide open, cast with terror and desperation. Silently, she begged Larsen and Two Whistles for help.

Something told Larsen she hadn't slept a wink all night.

He couldn't blame her. Not one bit.

Chaney, who had close-cropped hair and a patchy beard on his blunt-nosed face, lay sort of spooned against the girl from behind, his thick, tattooed arms wrapped around her. His face was snugged up tight to the back of her head, his nose buried in her neck. With each resounding exhalation, the outlaw made the girl's hair billow up around his nose and mouth.

Larsen shifted his eyes to the right, to the third killer lying alone in the bed beside Chaney and the girl's bed. That would be Hell-Raisin' Frank Beecher—shaggy-headed, tall, hawk-nosed, crazy-eyed, and with a silver hoop ring dangling from his right ear.

All three were sleeping like baby lambs.

However, these three lambs had guns close to hand. In fact, the room resembled a small arsenal. At least two pistols apiece were buckled to each of the brass bed frames, within an easy reach of each killer. Sheathed bowie knives also hung from bed frames. Rifles—two Winchesters and a Henry—leaned against the walls, also close to each bed. Boxes of shells littered the room's single dresser cluttered with women's underfrillies.

Three piles of tack were carelessly mounded here and there, including saddlebags likely stuffed with the money these three had taken off the Sundance stage.

The room might have looked like an arsenal, but it reeked of a whore's crib in which three drunken men who hadn't bathed in a month of Sundays had been well entertained.

Larsen chewed his lower lip. How were he and Two Whistles going to get the two girls out of here without arousing the three killers? Maybe he should try to get all of the weapons out of the room first. . . .

He nixed that idea. With so many guns and knives littering the room, it would take too long. Doubtless, one or more of the killers would wake up and begin the foofaraw. Larsen would try to get the girls out first. If the killers woke up in the process—well, then there would be trouble.

One thing at a time.

The marshal leaned close to Two Whistles and whispered very softly into the older man's right ear, "Cover me. If one or more of them wakes up, blast 'em."

The old Ute gave a slow, single nod, keeping his eyes on the room.

Larsen started forward, stopped, and turned back to Two Whistles to whisper in the man's ear again: "But wait till I'm out of the way. And the girls, too."

Two Whistles gave a grim half smile.

Larsen stepped forward. He walked past the girl asleep belly down on the bed with Black Pot. He crouched over the girl lying fully awake, eyes glazed with terror, beside Talon Chaney. He aimed his rifle at Chaney with his right hand and extended his left hand to the girl.

"Come on," he mouthed.

The girl glanced at Chaney curled against her from behind.

She looked at Larsen, beetling her brows, terrified to move.

Larsen crouched lower and said into her left ear, his breath making her blond hair flutter a little, "If he grabs you, I'll shoot 'im." He rose slightly and waggled his fingers at her again.

The girl drew a breath, steeling herself, then, sitting up, slowly lifted her left hand.

Chaney groaned, muttered incoherently.

The girl stopped and whipped her horrified eyes at the man beside her.

"Keep comin'," Larsen whispered.

She turned to the lawman again. She continued to stretch her hand toward him, sitting up. Larsen closed his hand around hers and gently pulled her out of the bed. As she rose away from Chaney, the killer's right arm slid down her side to the bed. He turned his face into his pillow and muttered, "Wh . . . where you . . . goin' . . . sugar . . . ?"

The words were badly garbled. The killer was likely still drunk.

Good.

The girl rose, the long tendrils of her blond hair dancing across her slender, bare shoulders. Larsen stepped aside to let her pass behind him. As she padded on tiptoes out of the room, Larsen looked around at the three killers surrounding him.

All three were still sawing logs.

He glanced at Two Whistles aiming the shotgun into the room, gave an expression of "So far, so good," then moved to the cot on which the other girl slept beside Black Pot.

Larsen dropped to a knee beside the girl. The chubby brunette was snoring softly into her pillow.

Larsen placed his hand on her right arm, which hung down over the side of the bed.

Instantly, she lifted her head and opened her eyes, which were cast with the same terror as the other girl's eyes, and said much too loudly, "Oh, God—please don't hurt—"

Gritting his teeth, Larsen clamped his right hand over her mouth.

She stared over his hand at him, wide-eyed, the light of understanding gradually filling her gaze. Larsen looked over her at Black Pot. The man shifted a little but only grumbled into his pillow, then resumed snoring.

He didn't wake.

Neither did the two other killers. Snores continued rising so loudly that they almost made the marshal's ears ache. The stench in the room nearly made his ears water.

To the brunette before him, Larsen whispered, "Very slowly, get up and leave the room."

She nodded quickly.

Larsen pulled his hand away from her mouth.

Glancing behind her at Black Pot, the girl slid her body, clad in a thin, torn gown, out of the bed. The bed squawked and jounced. Still, Black Pot snored deeply into his pillow.

The girl placed her bare feet on the floor beside Larsen, glanced up at him with a look of extreme gratitude, then shook her hair back from her face and tiptoed past Two Whistles and out of the room.

Larsen looked around at the three killers. He couldn't believe his luck. They were still asleep.

He still couldn't believe his luck when, ten minutes later, he had placed his and his deputy's handcuffs on all three killers, cuffing their hands behind their backs. None so much as stirred through the entire process.

Still, they slept like baby lambs.

Trussed up baby lambs. Only, baby lambs didn't

snore nearly as loudly as these three unconscious killers.

Now all the two lawmen had to do was get them over to the jailhouse and turn the key on them. That shouldn't be hard at all. All three men were defenseless. Chaney and Beecher were naked. Black Pot was clad in only threadbare longhandles.

Larsen stepped back over to Two Whistles, who had been covering him with his Parker, and looked over his handiwork.

The two lawmen smiled at each other in deep relief.

CHAPTER 3

"This soft life you two old cutthroats are living is gonna get you both killed!"

The woman's voice, albeit a familiar one, made Jimmy "Slash" Braddock sit bolt upright in the bed he'd been sound asleep in. "Huh . . . *wha* . . . ?" he said, blinking sleepily, automatically waving a hand toward where he usually kept a pistol within an easy grab.

His vision focused, and his heart warmed. He lowered his hand. A smile played across his lips as he stared into the jadegreen eyes of the woman he'd finally worked up enough gumption to propose to. He'd even done it sober, a fact that still amazed him.

"Huh . . . *what* . . . ?" Jaycee Breckenridge good-naturedly mocked him as she stared into Slash and his partner's sleeping quarters at the rear of their freighting office, one hand on the pine plank door. She smiled that smile that made the whole universe want to dance. In fact, still half-asleep and mildly hungover, as usual, Slash's middle-aged ticker was dancing a jig inside his rib cage.

The ring on a finger of Jay's hand holding open

the door caught the morning light angling through a window behind Slash, and glinted like sunlight off a high mountain lake. That had been Slash's dear mother's wedding ring. Studded with diamonds and rubies, it must have cost his pa a pretty penny. Slash had given the ring to Jay to wear as an engagement ring until their wedding in the fall.

"I'm cooking you boys up a good breakfast for the trail," Jay said as Slash's partner, Melvin Baker, who'd been known as "The Pecos River Kid" in their recent former outlaw days, stirred in his own bed on the other side of the braided rug from Slash.

Slash preferred to be called Jimmy these days, though it was hard for him and his partner to remember to call each other by anything but their old outlaw monikers. They'd put their outlaw days behind them for keeps, and they'd just as soon no one in their adopted hometown of Camp Collins, Colorado, know of their dark history as bank and train robbers of some celebrity and more than a little disrepute.

"Come on, Pecos," Jay said. She also had trouble calling them by their given names, since she'd known them both during their outlaw years, had even been the common law wife of a man, the dearly departed and legendary Pistol Pete Johnson, from their own gang. "You boys are burnin' daylight. Didn't you say you were supposed to be on the trail headed to Dry Fork by eight o'clock? Well, it's pushing toward seven thirty. Myra and I are cooking you up a nice, big breakfast for the trail."

"You are?" Slash said. Sniffing the air, he smelled the savory aroma of bacon and coffee. His empty belly stirred despite the overabundance of tangle-legs he and Pecos had indulged in last night, at the saloon Jay owned right here in Camp Collins—the House of a Thousand Delights.

"We've been cooking and banging pots around for the past forty-five minutes," Jay said, chuckling. "I'm surprised you didn't hear us."

"So am I!" both Slash and Pecos said raspily at the same time, exchanging incriminating glances from either side of the braided rug.

"Like I said," Jay said, "this soft life you two old cut-throats have been living is going to get you killed one of these days, especially if you keep riding for that old reprobate Bledsoe." She wagged her head, not liking their employer, Chief Marshal Luther T. Bledsoe, one bit.

But, then, no one did like that old, pushchair-bound human coyote. . . .

"Hurry up, now," Jay said. "Myra and I will be filling plates in three jangles of a doxie's bell!"

With that, she gave Slash a flirtatious wink, flashed him another one of her million-dollar smiles, and pulled the door closed.

Slash leaned back on his elbows, staring at the door.

Pecos gave a caustic chuckle. It was then that Slash realized his former partner-in-crime and current-partner-in lawdogging—yeah, lawdogging of all things!—was sneering at him from Pecos's bed on the room's other side.

"What?" Slash grunted.

"You two with all your mooncalf eyes."

It was then that Slash realized he'd been smiling at the closed door, though of course it hadn't been the door he was smiling at but at Jay's lovely visage still emblazoned on his retinas.

"You're just jealous," Slash grouched as he tossed away his covers and dropped his stockinged feet to the floor. "You got your drawers in a bunch because you can't have the woman you're pinin' after, because the woman you want is too good for you, not to mention far too good *looking* to give you a second look, ya big, ugly ape. *Not to mention* that she's old Bleed-Em-So's assistant."

"Bleed-Em-So" was the nickname given long ago to their employer, Luther T. Bledsoe, due to his uncompromising and ruthless law-dogging ways that weren't often all that more upstanding than the ways of the outlaws he'd spent most of his adult life bringing to justice. In fact, Bledsoe had pretty much blackmailed Slash and Pecos into working for him—unofficially and off the record, taking on assignments the Chief Marshal deemed too dangerous for his bona fide deputy U.S. marshals. If the two former cutthroats hadn't accepted the job he'd offered, after resigning from the train-robbing business, he'd more or less threatened to hang them.

In exchange for their agreement to work for him, he'd offered them an amnesty—but one that would promptly be revoked if they ever crossed him or decided to stop working for him, which for all intents and purposes would amount to the same thing.

The apple of Pecos's eye was Bleed-Em-So's assistant, Miss Abigail Langdon, a big-boned Viking queen of a gal with long lake-green eyes, like a cat's eyes, and the thickest, goldest hair Slash had ever seen. She was a big gal, but no gal ever wore her size better or in a more beguiling, fairy-tale-like fashion. A fella with a good imagination could picture Miss Langdon with her golden locks in braids tumbling down from an iron helmet, her cheeks painted for war, her supple, shapely body clad in furs and leather, and with a shield in one hand, a war ax in the other.

"If you made a play for that cat-eyed beauty, Bleed-Em-So would throw a necktie party in your honor and play cat's cradle with your ugly head!" Slash laughed.

"That ain't true. You know he treats her like he would a favorite niece. Bleed-Em-So would want her to find a righteous, upstanding man to walk her down the aisle!" Pecos chuckled as he, too, tossed his covers back and dropped his long, longhandle-clad legs over the edge of his bed.

"Hey, what's your boot doing over here on my side of the room?" Slash picked up the boot in question and whipped it at his partner. It bounced with a thump off the big man's right shoulder.

Sitting on the edge of his bed, Pecos jerked his head up and tossed a lock of his long gray-blond hair back over his shoulder. He glared at the smaller-boned, darker of the two cutthroats and said, "Ow, dammit—that hurt!"

"Oh, quit caterwauling, ya Nancy-boy!"

Pecos rose up off the cot to his full six foot six inches and clenched his ham-sized fists at his sides, red-faced and ready to fight. "You do that again, I'm gonna take that boot and shove it up your—"

Someone knocked loudly on their bedroom door, and yet another female voice yelled, "You two stop roughhousing in there and get out here! Didn't Jay tell you we're about to shovel up the grub?"

This voice was a little higher pitched than that of Jaycee Breckenridge.

That would belong to the young former outlaw girl who now pretty much ran the freighting business even when Slash and Pecos weren't out risking life and limb for Chief Marshal Bledsoe—Myra Thompson. Myra was only in her early twenties, but she'd been around the block a time or two, had good business sense, and had a no-nonsense pragmatism to equal that of the most persnickety banker.

Between her and Jaycee Breckenridge, who in her early forties was Slash's junior by roughly ten years, the two women made sure Slash and Pecos remained (relatively) sober during working hours and kept to a solid workaday schedule, whether they were running their new freighting company in northern Colorado or running down bad guys for Bleed-Em-So and Uncle Sam.

"Yes, Myra," both Slash and Pecos replied through the door, sheepish as schoolboys who'd been caught dropping garter snakes through the half-moon in the girls' privy door.

Five minutes later, the two stumbled out of their room and into the living and kitchen area of their shack. The main office was at the very front. Myra had a room off of the front office—a long lean-to addition she didn't spend a whole lot of time in, since she was always filing or cleaning or wrangling the hostlers in charge of the wagons and mule teams in the barn, or going over books or shipping orders, or trying to make sense out of the cash receipts Slash and Pecos brought back from freighting runs.

She was in the kitchen area of the shack now, just

then scooping potatoes out of a cast-iron skillet onto two large stone plates while Jay stood at the range, scrambling eggs in the popping bacon grease.

"There they finally are," Jay quipped. "Drink a little too much last night—did you, boys?"

"It was that card shark from Denver," Slash said, walking up to his betrothed and wrapping an arm around her waist. "He kept buying us good Kentucky bourbon because apparently he didn't think he was fleecing us badly enough without it." He gave a caustic grunt and planted a kiss on Jay's neck.

Jay and Myra chuckled.

"Thank you mighty kindly, ladies," Pecos said, walking over to Myra, crouching down and planting a brotherly—or, given their age difference, a *fatherly*—peck on her cheek. "You sure didn't have to go to all this trouble for me an' Slash." He gave his partner a cold look and added, "Especially for Slash."

Myra blushed and grabbed Pecos's hand before he could pull away from her. She smiled up at the big, blond galoot. At least, he was a galoot in Slash's eyes, though Slash reckoned his partner wasn't nearly as ugly as Slash always told him he was. Melvin Baker was tall and blond—well, gray-blond these days—and broad-shouldered, with pale-blue eyes the ladies found quite alluring.

Slash just liked to get under the bigger man's skin because—well, because they had a relationship similar to that of quarreling and constantly roughhousing beloved brothers, and since Pecos was bigger, Slash thought the bigger man should be able to take the abuse. He just plain liked trying to rile the big man, if the truth be known. He attributed the desire to the ill-behaving boy remaining inside him despite the gray in his own thick dark brown hair, which he wore down over his collar.

Myra didn't seem to think Pecos was at all ugly. In fact, in the year or so they'd been operating the freighting business together—her, Slash, and Pecos—it had become more and more obvious that the young woman was positively smitten by the big, blond galoot. She turned to watch him now as he plucked a strip of bacon piled on a plate on the table. She grinned as she admonished him with: "Pecos, you mind your manners and wait till the rest of us are seated!"

"I'll be hanged if that ain't great bacon, and it sure tastes good after a long night in which I got my pockets turned inside out!"

"Come over here and get your plate," Myra ordered him, lacing her voice with a crispness that was not heartfelt. "I put potatoes on it for you. I know you like a lot of potatoes, so I fried extra . . . with onions and peppers, just the way like them." She blushed as he walked over and crouched down to accept the plate and give her another peck on the cheek.

"Thank you, honey. You're gonna make one of the young men in town a fine wife someday."

"Oh, you!" she said, and turned around to face the counter to hide the look of vague frustration that had tumbled across her eyes. She didn't want any of the young men in town—several of whom had come calling on her here at the freight yard a time or two. She wanted the big man right before her.

"Ain't that right, Slash?" Pecos said, taking his plate

to where Slash stood with Jay, so Jay could shovel eggs onto it from the cast-iron skillet in which she'd scrambled them.

"Ain't what right?" Slash asked.

"Ain't Myra gonna make a right good wife one of these days?"

Slash looked at Myra again. She kept her back to them as she buttered the toasted bread on the counter before her.

"I reckon that's right," Slash said.

Jaycee glanced at Myra then, too, and, sensing the turmoil inside the younger woman, gave her arm an affectionate squeeze. Jaycee shot Slash a conferring look. Slash only shrugged.

"I'm gonna sit outside and eat on the porch," Pecos announced, when he'd piled bacon over his potatoes and eggs, and had accepted a slice of toasted bread from Myra.

"I'll join you," Myra announced, and quickly filled her own plate.

When she and Pecos had stepped out the side door, where there was a short stoop facing the freight yard corrals and barn and blacksmith shop to the west, Slash set his plate down on the table and dragged a chair out with his boot.

As he did, Jay turned to him from the range, with her own filled plate, and said, "That big galoot is going to break that poor girl's heart, Slash. Isn't there something you can do about it?"

CHAPTER 4

"Ah, hell, I don't know what to do about him," Slash said. "Pecos, he don't seem to realize his effect on Myra."

Jay set a piece of toast on her plate, then moved to the table, shaking her copper hair back from her face. She wore a formfitting cambric day frock printed with a wildflower pattern and an apron. The simple dress was a stark contrast to the richly colored velveteen gowns she usually wore at work, managing the Thousand Delights.

This morning, she wore her hair down, and it shone with a recent washing and brushing. She wore no rouge on her face, like she usually wore at night at the popular watering hole, gambling parlor, and whorehouse.

All in all, it was a softer, more domestic look for Jay—one that Slash very much liked on her.

Jay sat down across from him, reached across the table, and squeezed his hand. Gently, she said, "Maybe you should talk to him. Explain it to him—how Myra obviously feels about him."

"Ah, heck, Jay—you know women are always fallin' in love with that big galoot. Big he may be, but he's a charmer with his soft voice and his easy way with women."

"So what are you saying?"

"Maybe we should just let it run its course. How's he supposed to keep the girl from tumbling for him when so many others have in the past?"

"But he's going to break her heart, Slash. She's had a tough time, having such a lousy upbringing, then getting enmeshed in that outlaw gang." In fact, it had been Slash and Pecos's own gang she'd gotten enmeshed in. When Bledsoe had sent the two former cutthroats out to run their old gang to ground, the gang, led by a couple of young firebrands who'd double-crossed Slash and Pecos, had sent the pretty young Myra back to distract them and kill them, though obviously and fortunately for Slash and Pecos, she hadn't managed to pull it off.

In fact, Jay herself had intervened. If not for Jaycee Breckenridge's help, Slash and Pecos would have been crowbait.

"And now . . ." Jay turned to the open side door through which she and Slash could hear Pecos and Myra chatting and chuckling together.

"And now she's got her feelings all wrapped around that big, old cutthroat out there on the porch," Slash finished for her, pausing with a forkful of eggs and potatoes to stare out the open door and into the brightly lit yard. "All right, I'll talk to him on our way to Dry Fork. That's a three-day ride, so we'll have plenty of time to powwow about it. Maybe we can come up with a plan to cushion the blow for her. That big, old reprobate is too damn old for her. I wonder what she's thinkin'."

Jay swallowed a mouthful of the succulent vittles and smiled sweetly across the table at Slash. "At that age, they don't think. They just *feel*. Don't you remember?"

"Um . . . well . . . yeah, of course I do . . ." Slash kept his eyes on his food and kept shoveling it into his mouth, trying to keep the lie from showing on his face. At least, he thought it was a lie. Back when he'd been Myra's age, he'd been so busy stomping with his tail up, chasing women as opposed to falling in love with them, as well as robbing banks, stagecoaches, trains, and anything else that housed or carried money, that he really hadn't taken time to fall in love.

Or maybe he hadn't been capable of falling in love back then.

But he was now . . . wasn't he?

He glanced up at Jay studying him a little too quizzically for his own good comfort. He was in love with her, wasn't he? Wasn't that what he felt for her? Or did he really know what love was even now in his yonder years . . . ?

"Slash," Jay pressed him, "you have been in love before, haven't you?"

"Of course, I have." He chuckled as he shoved more food into his mouth, returning his gaze to his plate. "I mean . . . yeah . . . time or two . . ."

"Slash?"

He felt his shoulders tighten. He didn't like the serious tone of her voice. It meant they were going to have a conversation about something important, and Slash Braddock was a man who preferred to focus on frivolous things.

Steeling himself, holding his freshly loaded fork in front of his mouth, he said, "Yeah, Jay?"

"You do love me . . . right?"

"Of course, I do." Chuckling again, he reached across the table with his free hand and closed it around her own free hand. "Of course, I do, Jay. We're gettin' hitched, ain't we?"

She studied him. Her eyes were painfully serious, probing. They sort of made Slash shrivel up inside and start thinking that it was maybe time for him and Pecos to hit the trail for Dry Fork.

"Slash?"

"Uh-huh."

Jay canted her head a little to one side, narrowing one of her serious eyes. "You aren't getting cold feet, are you?"

"Me? Cold feet? Nah!"

Slash was genuinely astonished by the question. He'd made up his mind to marry this beautiful, copper-haired, hazel-eyed woman. He'd been in love with her—at least, in something very close to love, if he had any idea at all about the nature of love—since she'd been hitched to Pistol Pete Johnson. That had been years ago. He'd loved her beauty, which she still very much maintained even now in her forties. He'd loved her earthiness and practicality . . . the ease with which he found himself being able to talk to her, like no other woman ever before. He liked the way she wore a blouse and a tight-fitting pair of jeans . . . and the way she walked . . . the sound of her voice . . . her husky laugh . . . the fact that she didn't begrudge a man an off-color joke now and then and even told them herself . . . and several other things about her he'd best not think about lest he start blushing.

He really did, deep down, feel that he and Jay were soul mates. If he knew anything else about his often-mysterious self, it was that he could see himself growing old with Jaycee Breckenridge.

"Are you sure?"

"Certain-sure." Slash squeezed her hand a little harder and gave her a direct stare, which was not something that came easy to him, given his shy nature, especially around most women. . . . "I love you, Jay. I am not getting cold feet. Hell, they ain't even chilly!"

They both chuckled at that. Jay seemed convinced.

"All right, then," she said, setting her fork down on her empty plate. "You boys best get moving. It's almost eight thirty. When you get back, I thought we'd go over to that house Old Man Springer put up for sale last week. The one on the south edge of town, by the Poudre River?"

"A house?" Slash said. He'd had to clear his throat to get it out. For some reason, his vocal cords suddenly felt more cumbersome than they had a minute ago.

"Yes, a house." Rising from her chair and picking up their empty plates, Jay laughed as she looked around the cluttered, roughhewn cabin. "You don't think we're going to live here after we're married, do you? With *Pecos*?"

She laughed again.

"You better be talkin' me *up* in there and not *down*!" Pecos yelled from out on the porch.

Slash chuckled, but it sounded wooden to his own ears. "Oh, right, right. You'd get tired of smellin' his socks in no time—like I done twenty years ago." Slash laughed. Pecos cursed them both from the porch.

Then Slash said, "Let's go over and take a look at Old Man Springer's place just as soon as we get back from Dry Fork, darlin'." He winked.

She smiled, then as she dropped the plates in the wreck pan over the dry sink, she frowned over her shoulder at him. "Why is old Bleed-Em-So sending you boys to Dry Fork, anyway? I don't think you told me last night."

"Pickin' up some prisoners, is all. Transportin' 'em via jail wagon to Cheyenne, then via train to the federal building in Denver to stand trial."

"Is it dangerous?" Jay asked.

"Nah, this should be an easy one, for a change." Slash threw back the last of his tepid coffee, then rose from his chair. "In fact, it's so unimportant that the chief marshal only sent a letter this time, giving us the assignment. You know how if it's somethin' bigger and needs more explainin' we meet the old devil himself out somewhere?"

Slash shook his head as he plucked his black hat off a wall peg. "Not this time. The way I figure it, he didn't have some wet-behind-the-ears lacky deputy handy, so he decided to send me an' Pecos. That's all right. As long as the check don't bounce. Me, I'm ready for a nice, peaceful ride in the country, anyways. Maybe do a little fishin' up around the North Platte. Haven't done that in years."

"Yeah, I reckon this is just a little vacation for me an' Slash."

Pecos followed Myra back through the side door and into the cabin. Myra was carrying the empty plates of her and Pecos both. "We'll just have to take that load of dry goods up to Del Porter in Jamestown after we get back next week," Pecos continued, stretching and yawning, the ill effects of last night apparently lingering in the big man's bones.

"Want me to send a telegram to let Porter know about the delay, Pecos?" Myra asked, helpfully.

"Would you mind, darlin'?"

The pretty brown-eyed girl, gifted with a thick head of pretty auburn curls, beamed up at the big, gray-blond ex-outlaw. "I'd love to. Anything I can do to help out. You know that, Pecos."

"Thanks, darlin'." Pecos pecked her cheek again, and Slash thought the girl was going to squirm out of the red calico prairie dress she wore.

The two men said their goodbyes, both ex-outlaws hugging both women, for the four were like a family, after all, then headed out of the cabin through the side door, heading for the barn and their horses. They'd been instructed to ride up to Cheyenne to pick up the federal jail wagon from the barn behind the courthouse.

"Hey," Jay called from the side porch. "I know it's an easy job. Leastways, it sounds like one. But you know how you two manage to get yourselves into trouble no matter what?"

Both men, halfway to the barn, stopped and turned to her, grinning guiltily.

They glanced at each other. Then Slash said, chuckling, "I reckon we do, at that, sweetheart."

Jaycee Breckenridge planted her fists on her shapely hips and canted her head to one side, fixing them both with a pleading scowl. "Please, don't!"

* * *

"So . . . what do you think about that girl?" Slash asked Pecos an hour later as, astride their well-traveled mounts, they followed the Union Pacific rails north toward Cheyenne. The Front Range of the Rocky Mountains lumped boldly up on their left.

"What girl?"

"What girl?" Slash said with a caustic grunt. "Myra! Who the hell you suppose I'm talkin' about?"

"I don't know—I thought maybe you were referring to one of Jay's girls." Jay wrangled a stable of pretty doxies over at the Thousand Delights, and Pecos regularly partook of the lovely ladies' delights, although Slash refrained for obvious reasons—namely, because he was fixing to marry the madam.

"No, I'm not referring to one of Jay's girls. I know what you think of them. It's obvious every time you walk into the saloon and they tumble all over you, and you blush up like an Arizona sunset." Slash chuckled, wagging his head. "No, it's Myra, I'm talkin' about, you fool!"

Pecos scowled at him from beneath his tan Stetson. "Well, what about her?"

"Can't you see she's done tumbled for you?"

"Tumbled?" Pecos frowned, pensive, disbelieving. "For *me*?"

"Yes, for you." Slash stared at him in exasperation. "You mean you really haven't seen it? The way she looks at you and fawns all over you? Not like Jay's girls, but like a girl who has rightly and truly, make-no-mistake *tumbled* for you?"

"Pshaw!" Pecos said. "We're just pals, Myra an' me. Just like Myra an' you!"

Slash shook his head again. "Boy, here I thought I was the stupid one when it came to women." He gave a caustic laugh as he stared straight ahead at the blond prairie rising gradually toward where Cheyenne was laid out amidst haystack buttes to the north.

Pecos continued staring at him skeptically as they rode along the two-track maintenance trail hugging the shiny iron rails. Slash rode a rangy Appaloosa, while Pecos straddled a buckskin big enough, seventeen hands high, to carry his bulk. "Stop insultin' me an' chew it up a little finer for me, will you, Slash—before I haul you out of your saddle and kick the stuffing out of both ends of you!"

Slash sighed. "Myra's gone for you." He spoke more slowly, enunciating each word carefully. "She has fallen head-overheels, bloomers-over-her-head in love with you, you dunderheaded polecat!"

"Nah."

"Yes."

"Really?"

"Yes."

Pecos turned his head forward, staring off to the north, but he wasn't doing much seeing, only thinking.

They rode along in silence for close to ten minutes before Pecos turned to his partner riding beside him again and said, "Well . . . that just purely breaks my heart, Slash."

He looked genuinely pained. In fact, Slash wouldn't have put it past the big, tender-hearted galoot to let out a sob or two. Pecos had been known to bawl and even wail over women in the past, but mostly only over those who, having soured on his outlaw ways, kicked him to the curb.

"It purely breaks my heart, it does," he insisted.

"The point here, Pecos, is what are you gonna do so's you don't break her heart?"

"Well, I don't know," Pecos said. He thought again for a time, then said, "I'm way too old for her. I mean . . . I sorta see her like a younger sister or . . . even a daughter. She wouldn't want nothin' to do with an old man like me. Not *really*."

"You better let her down easy, or you're gonna have Jay on your behind. She feels right protective about Myra."

"Yeah, I know . . . I know," Pecos said, scowling miserably over his buckskin's head at the northern horizon.

"Well, you got some time to think about it." Slash gave a dry chuckle as he put his Appy into a trot. The ugly sprawl of Cheyenne bisected by two sets of railroad lines had begun to show itself on the fawn plain ahead, cradled by tall bluffs. "I gotta hand it to you, partner—you sure have a knack for getting yourself into women trouble!"

Booting his own mount into a faster pace, Pecos yelled ahead at Slash, instructing his dark-haired partner to do something physically impossible to himself.

Slash only laughed.